SHADOWS OF INSURRECTION

THE UNREMEMBERED KING

BOOK ONE

VANESSA MACLAREN-WRAY

Published by Water Dragon Publishing
waterdragonpublishing.com

ISBN 978-1-959804-71-0 (Trade Paperback)

10 9 8 7 6 5 4 3 2

FIRST EDITION

For my dad

ACKNOWLEDGMENTS

My father, William G. MacLaren, Jr.—who served in the U.S. Air Force for over thirty years—demonstrated how a career in the service could have a meaning and a joy all its own. Later in life, I came to understand how well the military can suit a certain kind of personality. When Corren talks about how much he loves his job, his dedication to serving his country, and the importance of respecting the chain of command but also keeping in sight the greater purpose and the need for constant improvement … he is thoroughly channeling my dad. My mother, Lorraine MacLaren, for her part, demonstrated how to deal with the difficulties of being attached to an up-and-coming officer and how to move on with grace when necessary. I think she would have identified whole-heartedly with Eldennian and had a few sharp words to share about Tama's life choices. I wish my parents were around to see this book happen, but like it or not, bits of their lives are unavoidably embedded in this story.

I owe a great deal to the advice and encouragement provided by critique partners representing two different groups. The multi-genre Morgan Hill Writers—Walter Van Tagen III, Geraldine Cynthia Forté, Susan Nicolson, and Chris Harget took on the raw material chapter by chapter, over a two-year period, and gave it critique from multiple angles. Members of the East Bay Science Fiction and Fantasy Writers provided feedback from a larger group who focused on the SFF elements and gave a broader array of commentary. I especially want to thank Mike Verant (*aka* M Verant) for his beta/sensitivity read of the finished work as a whole. While I may not have taken everyone's advice, their honest and constructive responses to the storyline and characters guided my progressive revisions.

At risk of being played off the stage, I need to mention supportive friends. Monica Baltz helped me stay sane on the day job while cheering me on with the writing job. Then there's the Paper Angel Press Gang who recharged my sense of humor and humility regularly: Lisa Jacob, J. Dark, and, of course, the Gathering of Stevens *aka* Steven Radecki, Steven D. Brewer, and Steve Soult.

A monster project like this also relies heavily on a family willing to answer questions like "Does this word look right to you?" while dishes pile up in the sink and nothing's getting vacuumed. My scientist husband, Alan Wray, endured far too many coffee-fueled expositions on the culture and landscape of Jeska while he was trying to analyze his solar simulations during the great transition to work-from-home. My adult sons, who prefer not to see their names in print, dragged me out regularly to play Pokémon and talk politics, economics, and gaming. Thank you, guys.

SHADOWS OF INSURRECTION

I blame Tymon.

I blame him for all of it.

For everything I did.

For everything that followed.

For the shamans' betrayal, the burned city, the woman he put between us.

Of course for the deaths, all the deaths, not least of them his own.

Because then no one would come to me for this.

I could sit on my mountain and chew my soul in peace.

I never wanted to tell this story.

PE⊕PLE ⊕F JESKA

The people in my life, in the order you'll probably hear about them:

Tymon: foster-son of Yutek, my brother, courier with Runners' House Jeskaryan

Me: Corren, son of Orkast, adopted son of Yutek. Member of the King's Guard.

Eldennian: small-holding manager, professional event organizer, keeper of secrets

Orkast: my true-father, armorer, shaman, explorer of thin patches

Yutek of Jeska: twenty-first king of the Unified Districts of Jeska, my foster father

Yutek the Younger: son of Yutek, called Yutek-en. Dead. Not by my hand.

Magaran: senior officer in the Guard, my mentor

The Six, men who stood by me through most of my career:

> **Case:** brewmaster in his spare time, good man to have at your back
>
> **Dramin:** medic, better at politics than you'd expect
>
> **Karthi:** farm-raised, protective—not much of a hunter but ready for a fight
>
> **Andus:** under-aged when he signed up; quick thinker, close-fighter
>
> **Kul:** I call him the bear-man: fast, smart, dangerous, gentle
>
> **Arnim:** upper-class toff. Two-blade fighter. Best interrogator I've ever known

Asdyel: you'll see, you won't mix him up with anybody else

Heyliannin: also called Ta-ma, we'll get to her soon enough

Calestinise: trapper, lady's-maid, spy, rabble-rouser

Fennic: Master Shaman of Jeska, schemer, back-dealer, liar. Typical shaman

Deliasin: my daughter. Most beautiful child you ever saw

Heyliannin's guards:

> **Harad:** dark-minded, sensitive, a voice to listen to when setting strategy

> **Radeo:** practical-minded, good with kids, field cook, inventor

Nandeen: merchant, manager's-husband, border observer, all-around good guy

Velisennin: leading manager of Southeast Township, home of Shamans' House, Lakeside

Stevvin: stableboy, humorist, sports-lover

Racac: Master Shaman of Lakeside. Traitor, conniver, child abuser, profiteer

PART I

THE LIEUTENANT MAKES MISTAKES

1

TYMON KNEW I COULDN'T REFUSE. That's why he came to me first. Not because my true-father Orkast needed help, but because Tymon always did whatever he could to avoid an encounter with the king, our foster-father. If any part of the news he carried had truth to it, he should have gone to the king, but because it would inevitably involve the military, my brother used that excuse to run straight to the junior-officer barracks.

Off-duty at the time, I was busy satisfying the demands of my latest infatuation, Eldennian, a tall, powerful woman with exacting needs and exquisite skill in sharing the experience. At a word from her, to better follow instructions—on where to place what, for the most return on our efforts—I opened my eyes to find Tymon's bemused face gazing over her shoulder.

"Can I play?" Only a runner would ask such a thing.

"No!"

Eldennian pressed a finger across my lips. "Shh, Corren. A moment more."

I glared up at Tymon.

He grinned back.

For a few seconds, I didn't care about Tymon. Eldennian obtained—and shared—what she had come for, and soon enough she was seated beside me and taking the measure of my foster-brother.

"Is your friend in the Guard as well?" She ran her eyes over his torso, shirtless as usual, filthy with grit from the road, with rivulets of sweat twisting by the old scars.

"No," I said, cutting off any invitation Tymon might have come up with. "He's a runner."

"Oh, now that explains it." She pulled her dress on before reaching for her leggings. "You have a message for the lieutenant, then."

"I do." Tymon made a backwards salute, tapping his left shoulder with his right hand. He knew his parodies annoyed me.

As she slipped through the doorway, Eldennian held the drape and glanced back, the disapproval in her eyes clear as they met mine. Eldennian had an inventive style, but she held to a one-for-one arrangement; the communal ways of runners suited her no more than they did me.

Once she'd gone, I pulled my own clothes to order. "What is it?"

"It's your father."

"Ours or just mine?" We'd been foster-brothers together since we were kids; Tymon always seemed to think I could read his mind. I think sometimes he envied that my true-father was still around.

"Just yours. Orkast, I mean, not Yutek."

"So? Orkast wants me to quit the Guard and slink out to the woods for secret shenanigans, pretend I've been to mystical lands, and then sneak around mumbling nonsense like his fellow shamans … and never ever bed a woman again in my life?"

Tymon laughed. "I think your father's past that." He spared a glance to the curtained doorway. "Or he'd better be, now that Yutek's down to one official foster."

I probably scowled at him, which he deserved. Tymon knew I didn't like to be reminded of that. I'd always wanted him to take the king job. Eventually.

His long brown face went still. Almost serious. "This is different. Important."

I shoved my feet into my boots and leaned over to fasten the straps. "How so?"

"He's found trouble, Corren."

Serious, yes. On his own word or my father's? "What kind of trouble?"

"Hard to say." He held up his palm. "Where can we talk? Somewhere with room to sit?" He cast a critical eye around the barely-enclosed space that passed as my private quarters. "I'd hate to see where they put a guardsman who isn't next in line to be king."

I clapped him on the shoulder and led him to the doorway. "Let's use the captain's office. He's in the practice yard haranguing the new guys." As I flicked the curtain into his face, I added, "So, how far have you run today? Do I need to dunk you in the washtub outside before I close myself into a small room with you?"

He followed, chuckling. "Just from the bottom of the hill, today. I had the luxury of a cart-ride from Moress. Though before that, it was either arguing with a pony or going afoot."

"From where?"

"From the Wall."

"Orkast's gone over the mountains? Trying to make friends with the sandblasted folks in the redlands? Has he become a returner? Learned a flying spell?"

Tymon laughed as my questions grew more ridiculous.

Sure enough, Captain Magaran was still out. I dragged a couple of cushions off the shelf and dropped them alongside the low work table. I knew where the captain kept his cider, so I splashed a golden cupful for myself and a double-measure for Tymon.

"Ah, here's where we enjoy your royal privilege." Tymon eased himself down to the cushion and stretched his legs before sitting properly. He took no time to honor the drink, tossing it down as if it were no more than spring water, then leaning back with another long sigh. He'd made light of the run, but judging from the road grime, he was more tired than he'd admit.

I sipped my own drink and watched him over the top of my cup. Tymon smacked his lips and reached for the jug.

Would he ever get around to delivering his message? I slid the jug away. "Well? Jokes aside. What's worth the time of a senior runner all the way from the great barrier range to the city of Jeskaryan?"

He placed his hands flat on the table, flanking his empty cup. His face became still, serious, professional. "You'll not credit it, Corren. Imagine it's another runner, not your misbegotten brother. Take my testimony as true."

"I'll take it as I hear it." I crossed my arms and sat straight, debating with myself whether his seriousness meant anything.

"He asks that you bring a troop of guardsmen to defend a thin patch." Tymon didn't always understand my father's jargon, but that would be the message. At least he didn't play the game of imitating the sender's voice. I hated that.

I probed for comprehension. "He used those words: 'thin patch'? The thing the shamans claim they jump through to get to the other side? And did he mean me, specifically?" I gauged the odds Captain Magaran would let me take off with eight trained soldiers on the word of a shaman.

Not good. But Orkast knew it would be likelier if it were me asking.

Tymon talked while I calculated. "Right, a doorway to the Outer Realm, where they do their magicking. And yes, he asked for you."

Most people believe the shamans' humbug. I thought I'd taught Tymon better. "Shamans say a great deal and prove none of it. What's my father need with a whole troop? One man can look at nothing as well as ten."

"But one man alone cannot stop an invasion." The way he said that, it sounded like Orkast.

I felt like I was arguing with my father. "Invasion? Of what? Magic dust-devils? Clouds of mystical scents? Spell-chanting poets?"

Tymon smacked his hands on the table.

I couldn't help it. The sudden sound made me jump, so I laughed, as cover.

"Corren, it's not a joke."

I took a drink and nearly choked on it. When I was done coughing, I explained. "If there were an invasion, we'd know about it. Plus, you'd need to call up more than a lieutenant and a double handful of men. You'd need an army."

Tymon polished off his drink and cleared his throat. "Hear me. It's not an army of invaders. It's a scouting party, Orkast says, only a few of them." He tipped his head to one side, that coaxing gesture he always used when he wanted something from me. "No soldiers. A good troop could capture 'em, bring 'em for questioning, make sure there's no one comes after them."

Indeed, that would be what I'd do. "Scouts from where? The redlands?"

"I told you. From out of the thin patch, that's what he said."

"He said. Did he show it to you?" I felt my lips curl into a smirk. Tymon looked down at his hands as if they held the answers. I pressed harder. "Did Orkast show you his invaders?"

"They were up the mountain, near the pass." Resentment tinged his voice. "He was coming here to bring the news himself when he crossed my path."

"Yes, and what useful mission did he take you away from?"

"I have seniority. I passed it on to a trusted second." That would be true. Tymon could pick and choose his jobs. "Would you have listened to anyone other than me?"

"Hardly," I agreed. "I'm barely listening to *you*. So where is the great and powerful Orkast now?"

"He went back up the mountain, to keep watch on them."

I waited.

"He gave me a map."

I folded my arms.

He rolled his eyes. "It's in my head, where else? I can't be carrying things while running."

Orkast was a shaman, and therefore a charlatan, but if he'd found a scouting party up from the redlands, it wouldn't do to ignore a chance to rough them up, learn a few things. I stood and lifted the lid on the captain's storage trunk. Sure enough, the boss had a neat stack of map sheets. I had to rummage to the bottom of the box to find a fresh charcoal stick. Setting the tools in front of Tymon, I collected the cider jug for myself, for a bit of comfort as I waited for my brother to show me where I was going.

2

I T TOOK US THREE TRIES to set foot in that place, the spot where my father had reported intruders—whether they arrived by way of a thin patch or not, uninvited guests in Jeskan territory fell under the government's responsibility.

Or so I argued when I showed that map to my commanding officer. Magaran was never one to cut me slack on account of my position with the king; he gave me the bare minimum I'd asked for and made no bones about the fact he considered the mission nothing more than a low-priority training exercise.

The ten of us—Tymon, me, and the eight junior troopers I'd wrested from the captain—made good time on the first leg of the journey north. The more-cantankerous pony we loaded with supplies. I rode the kindlier one, but any time I caught a trooper lagging, I'd make him ride for a while. Magaran used to say I coddled them, but my men ended up knowing more skills than marching and slashing.

I called an early halt, hoping to give my lads an encouraging speech over dinner. Like most of my speeches, it didn't come out as I'd planned, starting from the moment I accidentally kicked my dinner plate into the fire. At least my ineptitude made the guys laugh at me, and that cheered everyone up. They spent the rest of the evening discussing the likelihood of real fighting breaking out in the southernmost district of Jeska, Lakeside. The boys seemed eager to get in on some real action.

All I could think was, *Good thing we got out of Jeskaryan before the call to arms.*

Unlike my fellow under-officers, I'd seen the reports on Lakeside. Extra duties came with the title of Heir-Apparent—my second job since the previous winter, when Yutek's only true-son dropped dead of the shit plague. At any rate, I knew what was going on down there: with a governor treating the district as his personal cash fountain, the place had become a cesspool of instability. Magaran had licensed covert runners to bring intel north on an almost-daily basis. Never any good news.

My gut ached just thinking about it.

Sure enough, halfway through our second day, a runner caught up with us, a sweaty woman with a message for "Prince Corren" to get his ass back immediately; violence had erupted in Lakeside.

"Well, boys," I told my troopers. "Looks like you get your wish."

They whooped and howled into the wind as it blew dust into our faces.

Together, we marched into history.

No, that's not a good thing.

•   •   •

I'm not getting into what happened at Lakeside. Besides, we barely set foot in the district. We met the enemy at NeverSnows, a patch of ground north of the Narrows, flooded with grasses, decorated with summer flowers.

The mercenaries marched north to greet us—the active-duty members of the army of Jeska. There were more of them than we expected. They were more effective than we were prepared for.

We had our archers. They had archers with bows as tall as a man.

We had our practiced formations. They overran us.

Maybe the pay a mercenary earns inspires him to fight harder. More likely, having lost so many to the shit-plague and thinking we were the best soldiers ever left us short-handed and under-trained. The shamans, as usual, roamed the field in their black capes and waved their arms but accomplished absolutely nothing. The mercenaries didn't even bother to run over and kill them.

You can go read the history books and draw your own conclusions.

My troop saved my life more than once, but two men—Keev and Shellon, honor their names—died on the field. When it was all over, we piled up the dead mercenaries for a cleansing bonfire and laid out our own in honor. The condors wheeled overhead, waiting in their solemnity for us to finish.

I'm still not sure I want my body given over to the Great Ones. I think when I feel the end coming, I'll crawl to the nearest crevasse and drop myself into it. I don't have the nerve to set myself on fire, but I can't see as I've earned the right to soar over Jeska when I'm gone.

•   •   •

After NeverSnows, the remaining six and I marched back to Jeskaryan to patch up our relatively minor wounds and restock our kits. I had the added duty to visit the families of the men I'd lost. Shellon's mother chased me out the door, hurling crockery. Eldennian stitched up the gash, so I didn't have to go to a medic. I still have a scar on the back of my head. Keev's father was worse. Eldennian couldn't fix that wound, but she let me talk until her hands took the pain out of my voice.

We itched to be out of the city, away from the shame of our near-defeat. Tymon was on me to get back to helping Orkast. Magaran had no spare men for my troop, and summer was already fading to autumn, so I settled for my six and Tymon. We had two ponies, again, but I walked mostly. The men didn't jibe each other about taking turns at riding. No one whooped and hollered and talked about action.

When we reached Koresh, I rented a whole floor of rooms at the inn, ordered meals from the innkeeper, and told the men to take a day's liberty.

Everyone picked out a bed. Keev's younger brother, Andus, and the retired deer herder, Karthi, picked one bed between them.

I didn't ask anybody any questions.

Below, in the public room, music and boisterous voices blended and rose up the stairs in the evening. We slept, ate, walked down the back stairs to the hot spring, and sat up to our chins until the stars began to come out.

On the second morning, we gathered around a table in the common room and stared at Tymon's map. He talked us through each stage, as Orkast had described them: the long hike up a river valley, the route up the side of a canyon, and the zig-zag course from ridge to ridge, rising to the high pass that was the only known route over the Wall. From time to time, easterners from the redlands beyond pressed as far as that pass, but we only knew by the signs of their visits there. No one had ever seen them beyond that point.

However, if real, a scouting party could be the vanguard of a serious incursion. I saw myself leading my troop to a victory, one we could manage, seven fighters against a party of scouts.

At one point, the barman wandered over and made himself conspicuous. I scowled at him. His wife, the innkeeper, had promised to keep people out of our way.

"Is there a problem?" I put a snarl into my voice.

He shook his head. "You'll not be going up to the pass."

"Why not?"

"Weather's coming in. It'll be winter up there tomorrow, day after." He gestured to the door. Tymon left his map and headed for the exit, so I had to follow. The barman led us out into the street and pointed east, through a gap in the buildings. Where mountains should be, clouds blocked our view—not the bright streamers that always float above the Wall in summer, but a dark, impenetrable curtain covering all but the lower range. One might easily mistake the lower ridges for the Wall itself, we were so close, but I knew better.

I stared at the dark cloud. *Would Orkast have the sense to come down?* "Can a man survive up there?"

"Not likely." He rubbed his hands over his wide belly. "You'd best not go, I say."

"No, I mean, if there's someone up there already, is there hope for him?"

He pressed his lips together and gave his head a shake. "Not unless he's on his way down already. Or unless he's some kind of shaman."

Or even if he is.

I leaned close to Tymon and kept my voice low. "There's no reason to take the men up there. The redlander scouts will have gone home."

"They weren't redlanders," he whispered back, staring at the grim view himself.

"You and I could go up to that first ridge, look for Orkast, or signs of him."

"Best not," our sharp-eared host advised. "No, the weather changes fast up there. You boys come back in the spring, have your adventure then."

I wasn't looking forward to explaining to the troop why we would be marching back to Jeskaryan again.

•　　　•　　　•

Winter in Jeskaryan is nothing but rain. I spent the season putting the troop through rigorous training and enduring endless strategy sessions with the king and my senior officers on how the battle of NeverSnows had gone so badly. The ideas my superiors had for improving things struck me as little more than elaborations of techniques that had failed us in the field.

I said as much.

It didn't go over well.

I was still a lieutenant. I'd fought in one battle. What did I know? Yutek saw merit in my ideas, if only as an exercise for the king-in-training, and ordered Magaran—and me—to follow up on them.

In between jobs, Eldennian and I talked through the ideas I had for reorganizing the troops. I wanted independent units able to act without orders, so we wouldn't have repeats of those awful moments in the field, when leadership chains broke and troopers were left to slash their way out of the riot. Or die trying.

"That's all right for small-scale work, like border patrol," she told me. "But what about big engagements? When I'm putting a festival together, all the town women want to run everything. The families get into conflict. You have matriarchs hurling merchandise across the square. You need to have somebody in charge."

"Someone like you, you mean." I drew her close, watched her eyes, waited for her to tell me what she wanted next. "Maybe I should take leave, the next time you're running some town's event. You could use me to keep people in line."

"Oh? And who'd be keeping you in line, Corren?" She caught my earlobe, twisted it between her fingernails, to make me look up, focus on her eyes.

I smiled through the pain, anticipating her next move. "At your command, ma'am."

•   •   •

Orkast never turned up. Over the years, he'd often gone exploring for thin patches, sometimes vanishing for months, but this felt different. If he thought he'd seen people coming through a thin patch, he would have been hard-pressed to walk away.

With my last shreds of hope, I sent runners up and down the length of the great valley searching for news of him. Cost me all my spending money, but they came back with nothing. I didn't relish the idea of going out to the Wall to identify my father's corpse, but there you have it. It's a son's duty, isn't it?

I laid down the filial duty story to Magaran and the captain took pity on me. Or maybe he was fed up with Tymon hanging around. We got our orders and assembled our gear, claiming three ponies to haul everything. Karthi and Andus tried to raid the armory for materiel, but the quartermaster caught them red-handed and sent them off with a load of spears.

Nobody uses spears for anything but target practice anymore. Even the pony we loaded them onto rolled his eyes in resentment. I tried to inspire my troopers by saying those redlander scouts would be terrified of a band of spear-wielding Jeskan warriors.

Everyone laughed. I hadn't meant to be funny, but that's the way my inspirational speeches seem to go.

We moved fast, arrived at Koresh in late afternoon on the third day. We spent one night at the inn, enough time to get a solid night's sleep and restock our food supplies.

The climb was just another march, up hills, sometimes down, but mostly well-navigated to keep us climbing hour by hour, day by day.

In four days, we reached the pass.

There was nothing there. No shaman. No shaman's corpse.

We fanned out towards the eastern side of the saddle, searching for any sign of people. Nothing, not so much as an abandoned fire pit. Arnim found a historical site, a lumpy grey rock with odd scooped-out shapes in it where our ancestors had paused to grind acorns. So he said. It didn't look like anything to me.

Then we climbed back to the top of the pass and spread our search party along the downslope. Orkast might have tried to get down the mountain that way. He'd have ended up well north of Koresh, far from friendly territory. But if he'd suddenly recognized the danger in the weather, it would have been a quicker route to the flatlands.

Still. Nothing. And more nothing.

Karthi came back from a scouting loop to report a lake not far down, with rocky outcrops that might have sheltering caves.

We came around a boulder the height of the fortress wall at Jeskaryan, and the sun shone bright on the deep blue of that mountain lake, and there he was.

Orkast.

On a wide, flat rock overlooking the lake, he sat like a pillar in the sun, his black shaman's cape hanging from his shoulders and spread out over the granite behind him.

I called out to him and began running down the hill. I don't know what possessed me. It's not like I was a child. He'd sold me off to the royals when I was barely six, after Mother died. But he was my true-father, after all. And he wasn't dead, which was some kind of supernatural event, wasn't it? Maybe there was something to this shaman nonsense after all, something I'd never given him credit for.

When my boots struck the rock, he scrambled to his feet and turned to greet me.

"Father!" I called out, spreading my arms wide.

He made a strange, high-pitched, cry.

My vision blurred. I shook the sweat out of my eyes and stared at him.

It wasn't him.

It wasn't Orkast.

It wasn't even a *him*.

It was a woman, wearing Orkast's cape, staring at me with big round eyes like an orphaned puppy.

They probably heard my shout down in Koresh. "What have you done to Orkast?"

3

IN THAT MOMENT, clouds crowded into my vision. I could see nothing but the stranger who'd killed my father. She was evil personified, the sun reflecting from her pallid skin as if even the light wouldn't touch her. Don't think I was imagining things. People may think capes are the same, but they're not. Each one is an individual, with ripples of browns and greys threaded through the black. A shaman will never relinquish his cape to another.

Not unless you kill him.

And that was Orkast's cape. His *mantle*, as the shamans put it.

Everyone knows women can't be shamans, not even women-looking men. Up north, though, they have weird-women who pretend to some of the same powers as shamans—curing the incurable, talking to the dead, that kind of garbage. What might a weird-woman do with a shaman's cape?

As I approached, she stood her ground and held out one bony hand, fingers twitching eerily. Her other hand pulled the cape closed at her chest. I couldn't tell if the outstretched arm was doing a magical gesture or not, but out of caution, I knocked it aside and grabbed for the cape.

She stepped away, but I managed to snag the edge of the fabric. I tightened my fingers and pulled, hard. If that had been enough to get the cape back, well, it would have been enough for me.

But no, I only managed to stop her retreat. She kept a firm grip on the thing, grabbing tight with both hands, and then she began shrieking nonsense at me. My father had never been one for spell-words, but maybe weird-women had a different way. Maybe her magic wasn't fake. My disbelief wavered as those bizarre syllables splashed into my ears.

I used the edge of the cape to pull her closer and swung my hand—my open hand—across her face. Don't get me wrong. It was just to stop her spellcasting.

"Corren!" That was Tymon, behind me. His feet on the rock whispered, *Stop. Enough.*

Too late. I couldn't listen, not with that weird-woman shouting incomprehensible nonsense, mangled words like the shamans use for their useless spells. She wasn't scared of me, she was angry. Her skin turned bright pink, like a storm cloud at sunset.

Why wouldn't she stop? I swung my hand back the other way. My knuckles came away bleeding from her teeth.

Served me right.

It did knock a little sense into her. She stopped throwing magic words at me, stumbled backwards, and fell down.

The thing is, we were at the edge of that rock.

She tumbled right off, arms and legs flailing. The cape flapped above her, as if it were trying to fly away on its own, but then dropped out of sight as well.

Tymon's hand on my shoulder pulled me backwards and spun me around.

"Corren!" he shouted in my face. "What are you doing?"

I shoved him back and slapped his arm away. "It's not Orkast."

"You think I couldn't see that?"

"It's not Orkast." I rubbed my eyes, even though I knew the shadows wouldn't fade anytime soon.

He pushed me aside and stepped to the edge of the rock. There, he hesitated. Never one for heights, Tymon. He scrunched to his knees and leaned over.

Whatever he saw put him back on his feet again. "My brother is an idiot," he said as he shoved past me.

I watched as he ran to the low side of the rock and stepped off onto the dirt. The blood running down the back of my hand told me he was right. But I was right, too. She would have had to kill Orkast.

I walked directly to the edge and looked down. I can be honest now. At the time, I hoped she was dead.

My father was dead, obviously. I'd never argue with him again.

Still, my hopes didn't need to be true. If I wanted any chance to know what had happened to him, it would be far more useful to have her alive.

As it turned out, the drop wasn't a real cliff. After less than a man's height, the rock stretched a long sloping shoulder to a sandy patch of ground near the lake shore. A lumpy mass of stick-like limbs and furry mantle lay crumpled at the end of the slope.

Tymon rounded the base of the rock and called out to her, but the weird-woman scrambled to her feet and tried to limp away. An unlikely sight, that, a woman trying to avoid my brother.

Tymon overtook her easily and threw her over his shoulder like a sack of grain. She didn't cast any spells on him, not that I could tell. He threw me a gesture of disgust.

Up the hill, the men waited in a tight cluster, watching the fun. I beckoned them down, and we met on the grass beside the granite stone.

As Tymon approached, I hurried to get my words in first.

"Listen up," I said. "Orkast's dead. Everybody needs to understand that this … this woman … isn't some lost puppy we're rescuing here."

Tymon stopped to lower his burden to the grass. The great cape puddled around her, making her look like a child dressing up in grown-up's clothes. She stared at us with her flat sickly face, keeping silent now, despite blood running from the scrapes on her arms and legs. Her clothing was in tatters, as well, but she pulled the cape around her, hiding everything.

"Boss?" Arnim ventured. "You think this little lady killed him?"

"Yes." I kept my tone level and watched Tymon's frown deepening. "That's the only way to take a shaman's cape away from him. And this one is my father's." Tymon had to believe me. I'd given away enough so-called secrets of the shamans to him over the years.

"Well," he said, studying our captive with a skeptical eye, now. "There is that, I remember. Is it any excuse?"

"For what?"

Tymon took in a breath and flicked his gaze from me to my men and back. "We can discuss that later, brother."

4

I DECIDED WE'D MAKE CAMP near the lake and interrogate the weird-woman as soon as possible. However, I didn't need six troopers and my interfering brother hovering around the whole time. I put together two scouting parties: Arnim with Karthi and Andus with Tymon. Karthi didn't mind Arnim's continuous talking, and Andus could nearly keep up with Tymon. I told one pair to circle north and the other south, as far as they could in the rest of the day, to be sure we hadn't missed any other redlanders. Assuming that was what we'd caught here. I wasn't that sure. She didn't match descriptions of redlanders I'd heard before.

The quiet ones, Case and Dramin, I ordered to find shelter, set up camp, and get the ponies settled. Kul, I decided, would be my silent partner in the interrogation. He seemed threatening, in his size and with his broad, serious face, but I could trust him to keep his head.

Before setting out with Andus, Tymon pulled me to one side.

"Just one thing," he said.

"What?"

"Don't be an idiot."

I glared at Tymon's back as he strode away.

My plans could never be what I'd planned, not with Tymon around. "Kul."

"Ya, Boss?"

"Go give Case a hand, would you? And send Dramin over here. Tell him to bring his pack." Maybe treating the foreigner's injuries would soften her attitude.

"Yessir."

I eased myself down to the nearest flattish rock, keeping both eyes on my prisoner. She stared back at me with equal wariness.

"How you killed him, that's what I want to know," I said, not expecting an answer.

I didn't get one, either. As my emotions cooled, my hopes dimmed that I'd get anything useful out of her. The weird words weren't spells. They were foreign. Tymon knew languages. And I'd sent him off scouting.

We watched each other blink until Dramin turned up. I'd drummed him into medic service after NeverSnows, where it came out during the aftermath that he had certain skills, his mother being a midwife. He knew more than any man ought to know about herbs and remedies. Knew good tricks for mending wounds, ones we needed badly after NeverSnows. After that, none of us ever had to ask why midwives always demanded needles and thread. Superstition claimed it was about binding a new spirit to the infant. Dramin spilled the truth. Not that we wanted to think about what midwives actually sewed on. A man doesn't need to know everything.

"So, Boss, Kul says the prisoner's hurt?"

I nodded. He dropped his pack and crouched to rummage through it, pulling out a long coil of bandaging material and a few jars of ointments. I wrinkled my nose. Never met an ointment that didn't stink. He caught my expression and grinned, but didn't comment. Then he paused and patted his pockets until he found the one with the leather pouch he kept his needles in.

Suddenly, I realized I'd taken my attention away from the prisoner and turned in time to see her attempting a getaway. I jumped to my feet, but she fell to the ground after one step. She seemed the sort not to quit just because she couldn't walk, so I shifted my position to block her from crawling in that direction. She immediately began to crawl the other way. I stepped around to block her again, and she bent down nearly to the ground and put her arms over her head. One of the cuts came open again, and fresh blood ran down into her hair.

"Huh, not thinking this'll be an easy job," Dramin said, quietly. Without looking up at me, he went on, "No offense, sir, but seems to me she'd be an easier patient if you'd send Case up here instead of yourself."

He had a point.

I leaned sideways to pick up my pack, and my shadow fell over the weird-woman. She bent even lower and her shoulders shook. I snapped my fingers at Dramin. "Remember, she killed my true-father."

"Yes, sir. Thank you, sir. I'll see she don't go nowhere."

"You do that."

I stalked down the slope and found Case and Kul busy at rolling rocks under an overhang. I threw my pack under the shelter and cracked my knuckles.

Case gestured to show where they'd planned the fire circle. "How's this, sir? If it rains, we're covered, figured best to get the fire under, too."

"Good, good," I said. "Case, go help Dramin. Soon as the prisoner's medicked up, we can start getting answers." Not that I believed myself, but your men need to think you can get things done.

"Yes, sir."

I was tired of searching, tired of waiting, tired of Tymon's words in my head. If I could drop down in a warm patch of sun and take a nap, maybe I'd feel better about everything. But Kul was already back at work on the fire circle. I cracked my knuckles again and set to it alongside him. You can't leave all the work to your men, or they won't respect you.

By the time we'd finished, Case and Dramin were walking the weird-woman across the meadow towards our camp. Dramin had done a wrapping on her ankle, but it didn't seem like she'd be running anytime soon. I pointed them to a piece of log I'd placed under the overhang, and they sat her down there.

"So? Anything I need to know?"

"It's not as bad as it looks." Dramin measured his words. "She wouldn't let me stitch up that arm, so it's bandaged old-style. It'll scar, but maybe she doesn't care. Might have a busted rib or two, but not much anyone can do there. Mostly, it's bruises and scrapes, bad bruises, but not dangerous. Since we were by the water, I did some washing-up where there was dirt, to see for sure, got the right ointment in the right places."

"All right, then."

"One thing …" He hesitated, the color in his cheeks deepening.

"What?"

"That coat of your father's—it's more or less all she's got on. Her clothes aren't much more than rags. That tumble ripped 'em up, and then there I was trying to check injuries. Didn't help matters, anyways."

"So you're telling me …"

"Leave it be, sir, if you can, for the time being, that is. None of us is carrying women's clothes."

"Yes, I know." Trust Dramin to explain the obvious. Still, it irked that retrieving my father's property now would be seen as rude. Does rudeness matter when there's been a murder done?

I studied the weird-woman and she studied me back. Everything about her stank of *wrong*. Her hair hung in matted ropes, all of it a dull, washed-out, unnatural brown. Her skin sagged like an old woman's, but her movements were quick, not old. The overall pallor of her skin made the bruises stand out. Were all redlanders this way? Or was she a freak to her own people as well? I'd always been told they'd be darker brown than Jeskans, the rumor being that the sun baked that country more than ours.

Such questions would have to wait for another day.

I settled myself down cross-legged in front of her and pulled a talking-stick from the kindling pile. I watched her eyes as I stripped the stray leaves and ran a thumbnail down the bark, tearing a white line down the length of the twig.

Then I pointed the stick at her and said, keeping my voice as level as I possibly could, "What happened to Orkast?" I nearly handed her the stick, as one does in an ordinary conference or negotiation. I'm sure she'd have thwacked me with it good. Sensibly,

I lowered the stick, tapped at the bare ground between us, and waited for her to figure out it was her turn.

Her mouth worked. She uttered a few of those mealy redlander words. They didn't sound like spells, but I couldn't be sure.

"Who are you? Where did you come from?" I tried.

Again, nothing but nonsense. She sat stiffly, her fingers white on the edges of Orkast's cape.

I slapped the talking-stick on the ground, enjoying the whistle as it whipped through the air and the soft smack as it struck.

She winced, but said nothing. Did she think I was going to beat her with a talking-stick?

I swore under my breath. All this work, and now I'd have to wait until we got down off the mountains and found someone fluent in redlander talk. Tymon might get us to *hello, how are you*, but I had to be realistic, at least inside my own head.

"Listen," I told her, tapping my ear with one hand and wriggling the stick in what I imagined was a friendly way. Then I swung it again, harder, making the whistle squeal at a higher pitch. The third time, I managed to get the snap to echo from the overhang. It made me feel better. She might have smiled, too.

"Hey, Boss?"

"What, Kul?" I snapped my head up. If it had been anybody other than Kul, I might have barked out some gripe about interfering with an interrogation.

He pointed out to the east. "Tymon's back."

Sure enough, my foster-brother came jogging up the unmarked path. Alone.

I dropped the stick and ran out to meet him.

"What's happened? Where's Andus?"

"I left him."

"What? Is it bad? Did he take a fall?"

"Did ya meet a bear?" Kul chimed in from behind me.

"No, no. A bear? What made you think that? No. Give me a minute." Tymon flopped down on the grass, the meadow flowers flopping their heads around him, and just breathed. "Anyone got water?"

Dramin edged past Kul and handed over a full waterskin. Tymon splashed half of it over his head, then sat up and drank it down.

I held out a hand and he took it and jumped to his feet.

"You get anything out of her?" He seemed distracted, his attention on the campsite, not me.

"No, not yet." What did he expect? He was the only one who knew any other languages.

"Well," he said. "You'd better ask her to stay, then."

The four of us turned as one to see the weird-woman hobbling past the far edge of the sheltering rock. She made pretty good time with that ankle-wrap of Dramin's.

"Case!" I called out. "Take care of that."

"Yessir." Case broke into a run, and Dramin followed. They returned shortly, hoisting her between them as before.

That settled, I turned my attention back to Tymon. "I'm going to ask you this once more. Pay attention. Where's Andus?"

"Oh. I left him to keep watch on what we found." The sun was behind him. I couldn't read his expression, but he sounded anxious. Did they meet redlanders?

"What did you find?"

"Hard to explain." He grabbed my arm by the wrist and pulled, forcing me along a couple of steps. "Come on. We'll need to run."

A runner who won't share news is an odd sight. What had he seen that he couldn't describe? My gut wrenched. Orkast's corpse?

Kul broke in. "Best go fast, Boss. Not much daylight left. Karthi'll be asking after Andus when he gets back. We'll keep the pris'ner safe, don't you worry on that."

He was right. We had a man alone out there. I had to set priorities. "Ya, you do that."

By then, Tymon was already a hundred paces ahead. I jogged to catch up and launched into a lecture. "Tymon, you don't leave your partner behind. You should have taken that year in the guards. Get some sense knocked into you."

"Like you?"

"Yes."

"No, thanks."

Soon enough, I didn't have breath to argue with him.

5

TYMON'S LONG-HAUL LOPING PACE left me with little energy to worry about leaving Kul and Dramin and Case to manage the weird-woman. She hadn't produced any workable spells yet, so maybe she was as ineffectual as a garden-variety shaman.

Then how had she killed Orkast?

It made me sick, not knowing. If there was one thing my father would have enjoyed being surprised by, it would have been a death by magic. He spent his spare time roaming the countryside, hunting down his precious thin patches, then coming home to brag of the absolutely useless things he'd found "on the other side." He put in the bare minimum of duties required of a shaman—comforting the sick, making supportive incantations before a battle, communicating with dead relatives. I had heard other shamans openly refer to Orkast as a slacker.

Orkast had his own views of the meaning and purpose of shamanism, and it had nothing whatever to do with dancing around in front of soldiers or blowing smoke in the faces of sick or grieving people.

"It's mostly a fraud, yes," he told me, on one of his visits, when I was twelve or so and ready to call him one to his face. "Though I wish it wasn't."

"What?" You could have flattened me with a finger-touch.

"You'll have to know." He put his hand on my knee and leaned close in the little closet of a room that I shared with Tymon. "When I'm gone, Corren, you'll take up the mantle. You'll need to know these things."

The stupid cape. The shamans called them *mantles* to make themselves seem important. No one wears capes. They're old-fashioned inconveniences that people used to think of as stylish. Not in a long time. Not since any time that anyone can remember. But shamans continued to strut around in their capes and call them *mantles*.

"No," I told him then. This was long before Yutek the Younger earned the distinction of being the solitary royal taken by the plague. At that point, I was just another foster-son, a purchased playmate and emergency substitute that no one expected to use.

"What? Of course you need to know. You'll be that much further ahead when you go in for initiation. They won't be able to catch you off-guard like they did me."

My father went for a shaman late in life, after he'd had a son. Usually, they're apprenticed in young, like other specialized trades, miners or weavers or smiths. The fees are exorbitant, so shamans tend to draw recruits from the upper classes. I think Orkast joined because he couldn't walk into our house every day and see the empty places where Mother used to be. He must have thought he'd learn that talking-with-the-dead business or find her on the other side of a thin patch and bring her home. Six years later, he only talked about thin patches.

"I'm going to be a guardsman," I told him. "I'm going to go into action and get badges and banners, and be famous."

"No, you're not," he said. "Guardsmen go into action and they get killed and then the condors eat them."

"Not me. Soon as Yutek the Younger gets invested as heir, I'm free and I can do what I want and that's what I want. Soldiers are the best."

"I forbid it."

"You can't forbid it. I already asked Yutek the Elder and he said yes. I can start training with the under-guard next year. They do swords and spears and everything."

He sat back and stared at me and rubbed his wide chin. "The under-guard is for boys they mean to make officers. That means old Yutek wants you to stay nearby. He'll get you trained up properly. Officers have a better chance." He gave that great smith's sigh of his, that could have stood in for a bellows. "I'll see it as a good sign. You can take over from me later. Soldiers retire young, so you'll want something to do by then. I've barely gotten started, Corren. You won't need to follow in my footsteps for a long, long time."

I gave him a happy punch in the shoulder for that. If he had to die for me to become a sneaky fake shaman like him, the longer it took, the better. I loved my true-father. He was my only real family, and I loved him like no boy ever loved his father. So of course I hated him for being a complete fraud.

He never admitted it, though. He never said he was a *complete* fraud. The thin patches were real, and that was the whole point of shamanism, to discover the thin patches and go into them and find … whatever one finds on the other side. I think he imagined treasure, or maybe real magic, spells that worked, or even somebody new to talk to. Mostly, he found interesting scenery to talk about. Seems those other worlds the thin patches lead to are largely empty space. Like our own world, if you think about it. In a city, the world is full of people, but out in the redlands, up on the Wall, you can walk days and days and never see another man. Or woman. Or shaman. Or …

I pulled up and bent over, pressing my hand hard into the stitch tearing into my side. I felt like throwing up.

Tymon somehow noticed I'd stopped running. Maybe the silencing of my thudding steps struck his ears. He paused right before he would have disappeared over the edge of a downslope and walked slowly back.

"Give me a minute." I'd caught my breath, but the stitch needed time to fade.

"Push through it. Pain means you're working hard enough to be training." In the moment, he sounded too much like Magaran.

"I'm as fit as can be. I'm not a runner."

"Well, you could be. Why not? Think of the side-benefits."

"You forget I already have a job with prospects. And one bed partner at a time is good enough for me." I unbent and rubbed the painful spot again, trying to mollify whatever muscle wanted so much attention. "Let's go, we'll lose the daylight."

"We're almost there."

"You've said that a few times, now." I grimaced, recalling the slippery climb down that granite slope and the hand-over-hand scramble up the dry waterfall.

"We need to go quiet from here. We're close to where Andus is waiting."

I followed him silently through the woods, not complaining aloud. Just complaining in my own head.

At the top of a long rise marking a ridge within the forest, he led me along a faint game trail, dodging through a stand of tightly-spaced conifers. The forest floor silenced our footsteps completely, a deep mat of pine needles, a mat as old as the firs towering above us. The trees claimed most of the sunlight, so undergrowth could hardly grow. A scattering of low, green plants dotted the carpet of needles, catching the westering sun like little green candles spread out through the forest.

Tymon halted and gave a fair imitation of a jay's call. Another jay answered. Tymon checked his bearings, then headed down to a spot where the ground rose slightly before a sharp drop-off. We crept along together like boys sneaking out of our room to steal from the kitchens. Andus lay flat on the ground there, near enough to the edge to spy on his quarry, but not so close he could be seen from below.

Had they spotted redlanders?

Why hadn't Tymon said so, then?

The pair of us crawled into position on either side of Andus.

"Are they still there?" Tymon whispered, so low I could barely make out the words.

"Ya, they've been making camp for the night, like you thought."

Tymon leaned over Andus to whisper directly at me. "Mind yourself. When you see this, you're going to want to shout. Maybe even scream."

I fought at NeverSnows. Nothing can make me scream.

6

I F TYMON HADN'T PUT ME ON GUARD, I would have screamed like a goat with its tail on fire.

I pulled my head back and put my mouth next to Andus's ear. "I've gone crazy, trooper. Tell me I've lost my mind."

"No, sir," he said. "You're sane as sane."

I held up my hands in front of my eyes, turned them over and back. They seemed ordinary, real. The long scrape from the weird-woman's teeth made a ragged line across the back of my left hand. So my eyes were working right. I pulled myself back to the edge and forced myself to lie quietly and take it in.

Bears putting up tents in the woods.

I know. Bears don't need tents.

But they weren't bears. They were only *as big as bears.*

Instead of thick furry legs ending in massive paws loaded with dagger-claws, their thick legs were round, bare of fur, ending in fat bulbous feet, like a child had tried to draw a pony. The legs seemed able to bend both directions, maybe every direction. It was difficult to tell, they flexed and straightened so quickly.

They moved like ponies, too, mostly one foot at a time, sometimes bouncing into a weird rendition of a trot. No doubt, with those legs, they'd be insanely fast-moving. My mind clicked into focus. *We'll never catch up to them if they decide to make a run for it.*

Still, their size. Wasn't one of them smaller than a full-grown humpback bear, and most of them were … I could hardly frame it in my mind … bigger.

I could make sense of their size, but the rest made no sense at all. They weren't like anything in this world.

I gave myself an order: *You're an officer, clear your head, observe the field.*

First, I counted them. An even dozen.

I checked for organization. One stood at the center and ordered the others around, so that would be their leader. Two worked at putting up a tent. The tent was like a house. You could have slept my whole troop in there, but clearly it was a tent for one. One of them, that is. Four worked near their firepit—put me in mind of troopers on kitchen duty, sloshing plates in a bucket and flicking water at each other. Three kept ducking in and out of tents. Presumably they were attending to tasks set by the officer-in-charge. One sat undisturbed by the fire, studying a flat object that might have been a book. He kept tapping at it, but never turned a page, as if he had a problem with the text and was determined to solve it. The last one strolled up and down, off to one side, alone.

That one was smaller than most of the rest, but not the smallest of the bunch.

The characteristic that struck most vividly was their coloring. The pacing-around creature was blue, and not the nearly-black blue of a winterberry, but blue like the sky over our heads. The others were colorful, but different—a golden orange, a greenish yellow, even a pale red—except for the book-reader, who might have been deep purple, but in that light became black.

I avoided coping with the arms as long as possible, because it was the arms that made you want to scream. The thing is, instead of a proper pony's neck and head, these things had a lumpy stub of a torso attached at the front, with a head on top like a smoothed-off boulder.

And stuck on the sides, below the head, were limbs, not arms, but snakes that attached at the shoulder. Big snakes with little snakes growing out of their ends, like and yet very unlike fingers. They moved those arms and fingers constantly. The commander, the big rose-colored one in the middle, would fling an arm towards one of the underlings, the snaky bits at the end would wriggle around disgustingly, then the underling would wave arms and finger-snakes around, and be off at whatever the commander wanted done. The blue fellow didn't have anybody to be waving arms at, but he waved them anyway, purposefully, as if he was rehearsing a dance or an incantation like shamans are fond of doing.

Maybe that's it. He's keeping apart like the shamans do.

The worst of it was the clothes, because that meant they couldn't be dismissed as animals. They had shirts, like men wear, but bigger, covering a shape that might have resembled a torso and might not have, and their heads and arms stuck out of holes at the top and sides. The rest of their clothing had complex folds and openings. Not surprising, given the difficulty of fastening fabric around a body with four legs. Because of the clothes, I couldn't tell their sex or even if they had sexes. Maybe they were like snakes, where you can't tell from looking. That would make sense, with the snake arms. I decided they were male, so I wouldn't keep trying to figure it out.

Orkast's original message rolled through my head. *A scouting party*. Tymon never saw them. He'd brought Orkast's message, not an eyewitness report. A scouting party from where? The redlands? When did my father ever care anything about redlanders or Southerners or anything other than thin patches?

My heart stopped right then. Without its incessant pounding, I could hear everything coming together in my head. *This was what my father saw. These were the scouts he wanted to report.*

We need to capture one, find out what they're up to, where they've come from.

I didn't let myself think the obvious. It was too late for that. It had never dawned on my father that if he found a thin patch that led him to people, the people might not be good to him. Did the weird-woman belong with these snake-arm-people, or was she a hapless redlander who came upon my father after these monsters were done with him?

I've got to get back and make her talk.

I scooted away from the edge, my heart pounding away like normal, my head full of insanity. "Let's go," I ordered.

We worked our way back up the little slope and over the ridgetop, keeping as silent as possible. When we reached the spot where Tymon and I had stopped before, I called a halt. First, I leaned over and considered whether I might throw up this time. When I was sure that wasn't happening, I yanked my waterskin off my belt and drained the whole thing.

I checked the angle of the sun.

"Right," I said. "I want the troop here by sunrise. We're going to capture one of those things. I'm thinking the blue one will be a good target. It'll be easy to spot and it strikes me that's the one most likely to be on the fringe of the group."

"Ya," Andus agreed. "You're right. The whole time I was watching them, that one was off on his own. The others would make him do chores, but then he'd go back on his own, wandering up and down. Acts more like a wandering musician than a military scout."

"Might be a child," Tymon guessed.

I rolled my eyes. "Who would bring a child on a scouting expedition?"

"You really think you can take down one of those things?" Tymon had a laugh in his voice that got my back up.

"Not a problem. You haven't seen my men in action," As we set off again, my mind went back to what waited for us at camp. "I'm guessing that weird-woman knows a thing or two. She either came with them and escaped or ran into them when they got here. Has to be an explanation for why she has Orkast's cape and won't talk to us. How many languages do you know?"

"More than you. What makes you think this has to do with Orkast?"

"Thin patches," I said.

"What?"

"The thin patches Orkast was always hunting up. I think he found one. And I think those creatures came through it."

7

B Y THE TIME WE REACHED the meadow again, all those big granite blocks looked alike in the twilight. The three men I'd left behind had a good fire going. That helped us find our camp.

Arnim and Karthi had returned without any redlanders or snake-armed monsters to report. Case had pulled out the rations, and a pot of stew simmered at the edge of the fire.

"Give it a few minutes," he said when we stepped under the ledge. "Should be ready to eat by the time you tell us what's going on."

We sat in a tight circle, close to the weird-woman, and I did my best to describe what we'd seen—those wide, flat faces, the thick-necked torsos that seemed to run right up to hairless heads smooth as river stones.

"Ya, Boss," Andus agreed. "Another weird thing—they got stripes on their faces, colorful, like their skins. And the colors keep changing."

I kept glancing over to our prisoner, trying to gauge if she was following us at all. She listened alertly, seemed to pick up on our general agitation. I thought I detected a sense of relief that it didn't seem to have to do with her. From her wracked appearance, it didn't seem far-fetched that she'd been with Orkast—and had survived whatever had taken him.

Barely. From this angle, with the way the firelight fell on her face, she'd spent a fair amount of that time starving. Surviving alone, that was some feat, if she'd been here through the winter.

I couldn't let myself feel sorry for her. She had information I needed. The cape was proof she'd been there when Orkast died. How much had she seen? What part had she played?

Kul ladled out stew, handing the prisoner a share. She held the plate without taking a bite until the rest of us began to eat. Then she took up the spoon Kul had put on her plate and ate every scrap. I had the impression she might have started licking the plate if Karthi hadn't already gotten to work on cleanup.

I handed off my own empty plate and settled back in the same spot I'd taken that afternoon, before Tymon dragged me off to crazy camp. The weird-woman shivered and pulled my father's cape close around her.

One by one, the men finished up, stowed their gear, and found places for themselves. Case and Dramin covered the entry, blocking any fresh escape attempts. Arnim pulled a blank map sheet out of his bag and settled close to the fire, sketching out what he'd seen that day, and Andus sat close by to add his observations. They kept their voices low, and I let them talk. We'd need those maps. Kul and Karthi finished the kitchen work and then took up position off to one side, silent, watching.

Tymon strolled through the group in a slow looping spiral, making little comments to my men as he passed, but at the same time inspecting our prisoner. She kept her eyes on me. So at least she was smart enough to know who was in charge. Finished with his tour, Tymon eased himself down at my right, setting himself a little distance back, and laid a hand on my shoulder.

"What's your plan, Corren? Obvious she doesn't speak our language."

"You know some outsider greetings. Let's use that to figure out where she's from."

Tymon reached over to the kindling pile and pulled out a fresh talking-stick. "Let me think." He closed his eyes and shredded leaves from the twig.

Clearing his throat, he made a few odd sounds in preparation. "I'll try a couple of greetings we're taught They're mostly from peoples further south of here, but who knows?" He tapped the stick on the ground and said, "Netch-ah-may. Bok Tymon hah-nah-da-wo. Suh-nepah londa?"

Then he pointed the stick at her and we both waited for any signs of recognition.

Nothing.

Tymon shrugged, tapped his stick again. "Shah-yeh-tak. Ma shay Tymon keyishitek." He tapped my shoulder with his free hand. "Corren sishiteh. Nawash illinay?"

I reached for the stick. "I know one." I tapped the dirt and said in my best version of Southern, "Zee-la-kay. Pah-nakka-way alatch Corren." I couldn't remember the other form, so pointed at Tymon then back to her. "Tymon. Tay-zee-ken?"

"Pretty good," Tymon told me. "Didn't think you took any time to listen to those mercenaries while you were killing them."

"They weren't saying hello, Tymon. They were saying die, die, die. So I killed 'em. Isn't that what they wanted?"

He didn't laugh outright, but couldn't stop a low chuckle.

"Corrrn. Tyymin."

I snapped back to attentiveness, away from Tymon's fading grin. The weird-woman snaked one bony arm out from under the cape and pointed her dirt-encrusted finger first at me, then at Tymon.

"Corrrn," she repeated. "Tyymin." She smiled again, just a little, like when I was playing with the sounds I could get out of swinging the stick. But she aimed at Tymon, not me.

I whooped and thumped the dirt with the flat of my hand. She flinched and hid her arm under the cape again. Tymon grabbed the stick back. "Which one worked?" he complained. "She didn't use words, just our names. Start over." He gave her a child's openhand wave and tried, "Netch-ah-may?"

She stared, said nothing.

He tried again with, "Shah-yeh-tak?"

Her lips moved, we both leaned forward, but all she did was repeat back what she'd heard. "Nejammy shattuck?"

"She's imitating us." This was getting us nowhere.

"She's trying." Tymon gave her his warm, friendly, *come play with me* grin. I wondered if redlanders knew about runners.

We discussed what to do next. How were we going to get any useful intel?

She must have gotten bored with waiting. That skinny arm slipped out from under the black and imitated Tymon's baby-wave. "Hai," she said. Then she pointed at herself and said, "Ta-ma." Then at each of us in turn. "Tyymin. Corrrn."

"Hello, Ta-ma," Tymon said. They grinned at each other as if they'd just been introduced at a party.

"Hello isn't good enough. We haven't got all night," I complained. I tried to gesture her a *come on, come on.* "Say more, why don't you, say anything so we can figure out what your language is."

"Well, if *hai* is hello, we're stuck. I don't know any language that fits that."

"Nothing? Not even a 'sounds like'?"

"No."

The weird-woman waved and said "Hai" again, this time with a rising tone, like she was talking to a couple of babies.

"This isn't getting us anywhere." I jumped to my feet. It felt good to move. Annoyingly, the woman acted like I'd scared her, folding in on herself and ducking her head with that "hello" hand held up defensively.

Tymon put on his annoyed tone. "What do you think you're doing, Corren?"

"Something. I'm doing *something*. As opposed to nothing." To the men by the fire, I called out. "Hey, Arnim, how's the map coming? Got anything you can show me yet?"

"Yessir." Andus conferred with Arnim, then rolled up the paper to hand it over. "By the way, sir, I didn't hear any of the snake people say *hai*, either, if that matters."

I froze in the middle of reaching for the map.

"You heard some of their speech."

"Not much," Andus admitted. "Only when the wind came in my direction. They weren't shouting, but, ya, they were talking most of the time."

"The arm-waving, they do that when they're talking or when they're not talking? Could you tell?"

He gave it some thought.

"Can't be exact, sir, but now that you ask, ya, whenever they were talking, they were waving their arms around."

"So what?" Tymon said. "You planning to go chat with them now, instead of kidnapping one of them?"

"No." Where did he get his ideas? "It's intel. Know your enemy." I raised my voice, so everyone would hear. "Listen up. They might have secret hand signals, because they use gestures a lot. If they start waving hands, even if you can't hear words, assume they're talking. Everybody got that?"

A chorus of quiet, assured voices replied "ya" and "yessir." Map in hand, I turned back to the interrogation. At this point, maybe it was more of an *interview*. This feeble little human hardly seemed capable of killing my father. He might have been something of an oddball, in his obsession with thin patches, but he was also a big man, whose first career had involved pounding steel with a hammer ten hours a day. The weird-woman didn't seem to have any authentic magic, so odds were more in favor of her being an accidental bystander. What she was doing bystanding in the middle of nowhere, that was another kind of question.

Maybe seeing the monster camp made for enough contrast to change my point of view. More likely I was tired from running all the way out there and back.

At any rate, instead of sitting back down, I carried Arnim's map straight to the woman, and unrolled it in front of her.

"Tell us where you're from," I ordered.

She slid the map closer and studied it. So, she wasn't an idiot. I've met people who can't read a map. How can a person with a functioning brain be unable to read a map? But there you are. Some can't. That's all there is to it.

She made a little sound in her throat. "Hmm. Hmm." Then, she stood up, sidled away from me, and walked past Tymon to the fire. The edge of the cape floated barely clear of the ground. In the flickering firelight, it swayed and shifted like a live thing. My throat tightened at the memory of Orkast striding down the halls of Jeskaryan, brimming with news of his latest travels, the cape swirling behind him.

8

W HILE I WAS THINKING OF OLD TIMES that I hadn't thought about in years, the weird-woman spread the map out on the ground, near the fire, where the light made it almost readable. She fussed with it, stood to peer over the fire towards the meadow, then crouched and fiddled with the edges of the map. I had to get closer to see what she was up to.

Right. She'd aligned the north edge of the map to the north, and so on. Keeping a wary eye on me, she stretched out her pointy finger and tapped at the farthest edge, right at the toes of my boots. I looked over my shoulder to my brother. "So, east it is. I was right the first time. Redlander."

"Not on my life." Could he ever agree with me on anything?

I bent to touch the place she'd tapped, then ran my finger off the map, into the dirt, about where the redlander country would lie. I made a swirl in the dust, about a half-sheet further. "Here?"

She shook her head. Did that mean yes or no? I repeated the maneuver, a little further. Another head shake. From the frown on her dull bloodless face, that had to be a *no*.

Before I could draw my dirt squiggle any further, she took the map, flipped it over to the blank side, and snagged the piece of charcoal Arnim had left balanced on a rock by the fire.

She proceeded to draw a strange, misshapen beast: a wrinkly, fat lump, like an old dog left to do nothing but sit by the fire and eat until it died, suffocated by its own fat. A thick, leglike protrusion stuck out below the left edge, a puny, atrophied leg dangled off the right side, and a shrunken, misshapen head poked out at the top right. One thing for sure, the weird-woman was no artist.

Finished with the creature's outline, she drew a tight, dark dot in the lower right region of the shape. Was she drawing an imaginary monster or a real animal? Was that its heart? Or an eye? Or was it a religious image, from unknown redlander beliefs?

Then she shifted the charcoal to the left side and carefully drew a second dot about halfway between the top edge and the top of the lumpy leg and not far from the edge.

She sat back to assess her artwork and at last, an entirely familiar, ordinary expression spread across that starved, ugly face. It said plainly, *What a terrible drawing.* She set the charcoal down and rubbed her face with her hand, smearing wet streaks of black across her cheeks. Dodging my stare, she bent her gaze to Tymon.

Pointing at the second dot, she said, "Tyymin," then tapped the same spot again. "Corrrn."

Still with her eyes on Tymon, she reached to her first dot and touched it softly. "Ta-ma. Ta-ma."

I didn't like where this was going. "So you're the monster's heart and we're its ass?"

"No, you're the ass," Tymon said.

"I'm joking, I'm joking," It was obviously a map. An unbelievable one.

Arnim had edged close to watch the drawing progress and now he picked up the charcoal again. "Let's get some detail going." Starting at the Corrrn-Tyymin spot, he sketched in the map-symbols for mountains in a long oval stretching the length of the western edge. He exchanged looks with … with Ta-ma … it was around then that I quit thinking of her as *weird-woman*. Then he scribbled water-wave marks in the blank space at the left. Like I expected, he'd sketched in the Wall, the western ranges, and the ocean. Plus a good portion of the northern and southern lands, at least so far as we knew them.

Ta-ma scrunched her eyes at his ocean, and Arnim added a fanciful fish. She nodded excitedly and made swirly shapes with her fingers at the far side. Arnim added more ocean there. Then he brought the charcoal around the finger-like protrusion to the area near the bottom of the sketch. She smiled, and he marked that as ocean, too. "It's a map, sir."

"It's a fantasy. There's no ocean over there," I objected. "You get down from the Wall and then everything goes on and on."

"Well," Tymon said. "No one really knows. The world is a big place."

While we were bickering, Ta-ma snatched the charcoal back and drew a long, thick line right down the middle of her map. She went over it again, making it wider and wider the closer it got to the southern sea.

Arnim whooped and leaped to his feet, dancing like a fool. "I knew it! It's real! The Great River isn't just a story!"

Startled by his performance, Ta-ma pushed herself to her feet. When she put her weight on the injured ankle, she wobbled. Tymon was up in a flash, his hand on her elbow, keeping her from falling right into the fire. She beamed into his face and that took away the ugliness.

"You should just invite her into the nearest Runners' House and get to it," I said.

"Shut up," Tymon snapped.

Arnim calmed himself. "Sorry. But it's big news, sir."

"Tell me," Tymon said. "what's your favorite story about the Great River?" Everyone ignored me.

"I never heard of any Great River," I complained. "Isn't our own Heart's River big enough for you?".

"Boss," Andus said. "It's the Great River that cuts the world in half. It's in all the stories."

"Oh. Stories." Orkast was never one for telling stories, even when he was around. Mother might have told me stories, but, remember, I was six when she, as they say, departed. When I was younger and people said that, I would hit them. Tymon wasn't always there to stop me. Mother died fighting a terrible sickness.

It took months. I watched it all. It dragged her away kicking and screaming. She did not *depart*.

I watched as Tymon led Ta-ma back to her log, away from the fire. Arnim wrapped up the unbelievable map with the story-time river running through it. Case came up and tapped my elbow.

"Boss? I can take first watch, Dramin says he'll take second."

"Right," I decided. "This interrogation business is over. We have an early start for a big operation tomorrow."

9

I WOKE AT SHIFT CHANGE, like I always do, whether or not I'm on duty. Kul gave me a quick salute as he settled himself at the edge of our shelter, then turned his eyes back to the night. The moon had set, but if anyone could spot anything in that dark, it would be Kul. Our fire still shed a warm red glow that reflected from the overhanging rock, giving the feeling we were safe indoors.

I rolled over, and my hand landed on a mass of thick, hairy warmth: Orkast's cape, where it lay spread on the ground beyond Ta-ma. Our guest snored in a dark heap between me and Tymon. The cape was warm, as if it had stored heat from the fire. I hadn't seen Orkast without his mantle since the day after his initiation. That was the first time he was free to come visit in the almost-year since he'd sold me into fosterage.

"What do you think, son?" he'd said, rubbing his shaved head as if he'd been out drinking, not getting a profession. His eyes were bloodshot, too. I didn't really notice it at the time.

"It's weird, Papa," I'd said. "What's it made of?"

"Well," he said, hesitantly. "I can't say."

"Why not?"

"Just can't." He had on his biggest grin, but I couldn't tell if it was real. "We've got status now, you'll see, everything will be better from here on."

True enough. I got moved from the dorm to a real room, with Tymon. We were first-class playmates for Yutek-en from then on. I never ever told my father about Yutek-en—the things he did to me, the things I stopped him from doing to Tymon, the things Tymon stopped me from doing to Yutek-en.

I ran my fingertips across the cape, remembering.

"What'd you get yourself into this time, Papa?" I murmured, already feeling sleep taking me over again.

"Corrrrynn."

The dry, raspy voice slapped me right out of my doze. I sat up, looked around. No one moved, apart from Kul, who turned to see what I was up to. Nothing had changed, except that Ta-ma had stopped snoring.

It must have been a dream. I lay back down, remembering my father's voice, "When I'm gone, Corren, you'll need to take up the mantle."

I reached over and pushed the cape further from me, to keep the thing out of reach.

Never, I thought. *Never.*

•　　　•　　　•

There was nothing for it. I needed all my men, so Ta-ma had to go with us. Clearly, she wouldn't be fast in the best of circumstances, so I made her ride. I led her pony by the reins, while she clung with both hands to the saddle like she thought soft-hearted Friendly Pony might suddenly run off with her. The troop moved with professional efficiency, and we reached the pausing-point shortly before sunrise. Andus and Karthi scouted ahead while the rest of us unloaded the baggage pony and shared out the spears he'd carried. When the scouts came back to report that the lazy monsters were breaking camp, we gathered close and reviewed the plan.

I needed them alert to danger and prepared to follow through. "We didn't see weapons, but that doesn't mean they're unarmed. So use the spears from a distance, and move on my order. Remember, the goal is to cut the one off from his fellows and capture him. Kul, do you think that throwing-net will hold?"

"Ya, it'd hold a bear." While he talked, he shook the net out and re-coiled it. "If snake-boy has a knife on him, we'll need to be quick, so once I net him, all hands on, got it?"

Everyone nodded.

"Remember the plan," I added. "Avoid hurting his legs. I don't want to waste time cutting poles to drag him out of the mountains on a travois."

Again, nods all around.

"Right! Let's go catch us a monster."

The map portion Andus had drawn the night before proved essential, as once the snake-men finally got moving, they stayed within our map. They kept stopping to inspect rocks or plants or take sightings on distant peaks, which added fuel to the "they are scouts" theory. We kept at a distance and let teams of two move along under cover, reporting back as the snake-men's direction became more definite. A little after noon, Tymon and Andus put their heads together over the map and came up with a prediction of the route the monsters would take. It was a gamble, but it gave me a chance to get us in position for an ambush where we would have a clear attack path down a steep open slope.

The plan went perfectly.

Perfectly badly, that is.

Well, at first it was perfect.

The monsters turned up later than expected, having taken their own sweet time to explore the region Tymon had predicted they'd explore.

They made plenty of noise coming along the hillside below us, so I jumped off my pony to join Arnim at the lookout point. It would be his first time seeing the creatures, and I wanted to enjoy his shock. Sure enough, they were taking advantage of a natural level stretch along the hillside below us. As the first of them—the big pinkish-red one—appeared around the bend, Arnim breathed in sharply and tensed, but kept his remarks to a low "Huh." I gave him a grin, pushed back, and slithered out of sight before I stood and hurried upslope to check everyone was in position.

Something was off.

I counted heads.

All accounted for, with Arnim downslope on watch and Case with Dramin on the far side of the avalanche chute. Tymon sat on the second baggage pony, re-checking the map. The other two ponies had their heads down, eating everything they could reach. They stayed well back from the drop-off, invisible to our quarry.

Wait.

I marched up to Tymon and grabbed the map out of his hands.

"Where's Ta-ma?" I demanded.

He shrugged and pointed.

She crouched behind a tree on the downslope, a little ways above Arnim, and seemed to be keeping hidden. Once again, proving herself not an idiot.

Still. A civilian. In the middle of an op.

One more thing to worry about. But what could I do? They'd arrived; we were in motion.

I slipped to my own vantage point, a thick green shrub right on the edge of the avalanche path. The oversized purple-black fellow trundled along in the middle of the pack, with another of those book-things that he kept tapping on, hardly even glancing at the trail in front of him. I was glad to see him move along and out of reach of our operation. That one might have been trouble.

I chewed on my patience as one by one, the monsters hurried by, then lumbered into the woods.

As anticipated, the little blue guy trailed well behind. He rambled along like a romantic collecting flowers. I bit down a shout when he picked up his pace unexpectedly. Luckily, when he reached the edge of the shade, he unslung his bulky pack and dropped it to the ground, then stepped back into the sunlight.

It was like he'd been in on the plan. I signaled Tymon and he gestured to the men on the other side, out of sight of our target.

Suddenly, Ta-Ma screamed. She hadn't been able to understand any of our discussions, the ones that had prepared everyone else for these monstrosities. Now, what she'd been seeing must have finally hit home. She pushed back from her hideout and shouted again. Then she began to run down the hill, towards Arnim.

"Stop her!" I shouted. "Hey, uh, Ta-ma! Danger!"

Arnim didn't have time to stand before she arrived, still tearing along in a panic, shrieking. He tried to catch her, but instead grabbed an armful of cape. He held tight, which I would have told him was a mistake. She was in the middle of jumping down the short drop-off right in front of him, and her head jerked back as the cape around her neck stopped her flight. Fortunately, she was moving fast enough that the cape tore free, sending her tumbling but not strangling her. Even so, she lay still, and I wondered if she'd managed to break her neck in the fall. I let several seconds go by, time that I should have been shouting orders, as she shoved herself upright again, wobbling on her injured ankle, and continued down the slope without looking back.

No time, no time. Deal with her later. She can't get far.

I jumped back on my pony and kicked him to the edge of the drop-off, ready to direct the action. The blue monster, stupidly curious about the noise, moved further out of cover. That made it easier for Kul and his net to approach under the trees down the far side. Ta-ma's hollering couldn't be missed, not even by our planned captive. The snake-man tipped his bald eggy head in that direction.

Tymon pushed his pony over to mine, but he watched Ta-ma, not our target.

"Leave her," I told him. I gave a loud whoop and shouted, "Case! Dramin!"

Their spears flew towards our target. Dramin's fell right where he wanted it, directly behind the monster, blocking escape, while Case's struck where it would be the obvious threat. It should chase our quarry further out into the open. Ideally, he'd shift down the slope, where he might lose his footing. The snake-man was either genuinely stupid or tougher than he looked. He stood still and watched Ta-ma making her panicked dash down the hill.

At least she's not going towards him.

She was, though. As soon as she hit the level stretch, she turned left, directly into the monster's path.

I wondered how quickly he would kill her with those enormous snake-arms.

When she emerged into the open, Ta-ma began shrieking even louder and waved her arms at the snake-man like she was chasing loose chickens. Did she think she was going to scare him away?

Suddenly, it dawned on me. She was trying to rescue him. From us.

My orders flew out without my needing to think. "Andus! Karthi! Go!"

Their spears hit simultaneously—you could hear the combined chunk of their impact. Karthi's struck barely in front of the monster, while Andus's blocked the way back, should the target try to retreat instead of move forward. The fool should have at least startled, but he held his ground. From the corner of my eye, I detected Kul in motion, still hidden in the shadows, but not far uphill from the quarry.

Distraction time. I kicked my pony into action, heading straight down the hill, tossing up dirt and sticks as we went. Our spear throwers joined in the effort, whooping and waving their swords to draw attention away from Kul. Even Tymon took part— either that, or his pony didn't want to be left behind.

Meanwhile, Ta-ma continued to run at the snake-man until she collided with him. He bent his enormous head and stared at her, completely ignoring us—including Kul, who slipped to the edge of the forest and began to twirl the throw-net, its perfectly-balanced weights ready to carry it precisely to its target.

Still looking at Ta-ma, not at us, the snake-man reached into a pocket in that complicated outfit of his and pulled out a shiny little rod, a nothing thing, not much longer than a man's hand. That lumpy head tipped up and its huge circular eyes swept across us, landing on Kul as he skidded to a stop, his arm cocked to throw. The rod made a little noise, a purplish spark danced in the air, and Kul crashed to the ground, tangled in his own net.

Before any of us could react, the monster did the same to each of my spearmen, then Arnim, who'd run out behind Karthi, then Tymon, who was trying to not fall off the pony charging down the slope next to mine. I had no time to wonder if Tymon would survive the headfirst fall he was taking, before pain blossomed in my skull and the world vanished.

•   •   •

I woke to a hot, wet wind blasting me in the face.

My first thought: I was about to be eaten by a bear.

My eyes flashed open to reveal a huge, brown blob, its long whiskers sweeping over my chest.

My eyes focused on Friendly Pony. *Not a bear.*

I swatted the pony's nose aside. A few feet away, my brother sat pulling twigs out of his hair.

"They're gone," he said.

His voice made my head ring, like I'd spent the past several days drinking. I sat up slowly, so my head wouldn't fall off. Dense shadows spread over the slope, and shades of pink stretched across the sky.

"The weird-woman?" I dared ask. Even my own voice hurt.

"Ta-ma's gone."

"Gone or dead?"

"Hard to be sure. No sign." He sounded sad. True, he'd wanted a chance with her. Wasn't a whole House full of runners enough for him?

"Orkast's cape?"

"Got it, Boss." Arnim squinted under the darkening sky as if even that light pained him. He held up the dark mass of my father's mantle. "It's all yours, now."

I lay back down on the hillside and hoped everything would stay still for a while.

10

W E DRAGGED OURSELVES HOME with nothing of value.
No foreign prisoner.

No captive monster.

Just an old, used shaman's cape.

I dreaded reporting to my captain … and to my foster-father. I was supposed to be a model officer. Magaran had given me a loose rein, supported my expedition, risked his own status with the king. On my return, he detailed my failures loudly enough there wasn't likely anyone from the barracks to the training yard who didn't hear him. I'd dragged a whole troop—well, what was left of one after NeverSnows—on a junket to nowhere, at a time when forces were down and unrest was high. I'd squandered valuable man-hours and resources on a futile attempt to rescue a dead shaman, interrogate a hapless foreigner, and capture an impossible invader. I hadn't even come away with proof the snake-men existed. The commander accused us of inventing those monsters, to cover up a failed attack on a few redlander scouts.

If Magaran couldn't believe the snake-men existed, I wasn't about to bring up the topic of their weaponry. We'd only received a sample of what they could do—a sample delivered by the least of their company. Who knew what devices the others had hidden in their pockets? Whether we'd tackled snake-men or redlanders, it was an operation I'd bungled—taking on a superior force without proper preparation. We could have followed the snake-men (or in Magaran's terms, redlanders) to their base and returned in force, but no, I had to go for the big move.

On the way home, we'd agreed that the weird-woman, Ta-ma, must have been carried off by the snake-men. Case tracked her until her trail merged with theirs. Despite her injury, she'd vanished as completely as they had. Admittedly, we'd snoozed the day away in the dirt and the sticks while the monsters galloped away. It didn't matter, though. I'd known from the way they moved that once they started running it would be a lost cause.

Tymon argued that my true-father must have led those monsters out of one of the thin patches he'd found, and now they'd gone back where they came from. Though we hadn't managed to talk to her about Orkast, that Ta-ma had his cape remained proof of his death. After the debacle with the snake-men, I was more than half convinced he must have died beyond the thin patch.

My brother couldn't have chosen a worse time to lure me away on a pointless quest for my true-father. The battle of NeverSnows had cut a hole in the heart of the Guard. It didn't matter that we won the battle. We lost far too many men. The matriarchs—all the land managers up and down the great valley—screamed outrage at the horrifying expense of it.

Have you any idea what it costs to build and equip an army? To pay off the mothers and daughters of lost soldiers? To placate the farmers who grow the food to feed those unproductive bodies when it's their land you've trampled over in your battles?

And then ... consider ... we needed more than to replace our lost comrades-in-arms. We needed to build a newer, bigger, more effective army. The Southerners would be back, and this time not in the guise of mercenaries in service to a traitor. They would come on their own account, and they would take Lakeside. They might well take Jeska.

If only I'd brought home one of those snake-man weapons. If our smiths could've copied it, we'd have been invincible. Even if they hadn't, Magaran would have believed me.

The king was under pressure from the community and the matriarchy; he didn't need his son gallivanting around the countryside wasting resources and inventing new enemies—or, more likely in his estimation, indulging in intoxicants or hallucinogens. If Yutek had had even one alternate left to choose from, other than Tymon, I'd have been out of the line of succession, possibly even out of the Guard.

I don't know what I'd have done if he'd kicked me out. The Guard was my life.

Yutek needed me disciplined, and it needed to be public.

My ears still ringing with Magaran's assessment, I stood in front of my foster-father, in front of his councilors, in front of my men, in front of everyone, and I offered up my reasons, my explanations, my regrets. Yutek roared right up to me, his face dark with fury, and he tore the badges off my chest and flung them across the room, narrowly missing his chief accountant. My shirt hung in tatters. He held out his hand.

"Give me your sword!" he ordered.

"Uh, sir," I said, fumbling for what to do at that. Had he forgotten his standing order that arms be secured at the door? "Sir, everything I have is at your command."

I had an inspiration then. I can't remember how it happened. Did I think it through, or was I grasping at straws? The image of the weird-woman cowering at my feet flashed through my mind. I remembered how that made me feel, the power it gave me, what I did, and did not do, when she hid her face from me and held her arms over her head.

I dropped to my knees in front of the king and lowered my face to the floor in front of him. His booted feet jerked back, as if he'd thought I was attacking him. My hands pressed into the boards next to my head. That felt too safe, too secure. I lifted my arms, brought my hands up over the top of my head, and spread my fingers. My nose bobbed so close to the floor I nearly sneezed from inhaling the dust.

"My life is yours, sir," I said, trying to balance the loudness of my voice against the fact I was talking into the floor. "My true-father is dead. My life belongs to my foster-father. If he will still have me, I will be the son he demands."

I shut up then, and stared at the grain of the wood in front of my eyes. Under my nose, a beetle scuttled along, waving its antennae, unaware of the drama over its head.

I could hear my men murmuring at the back of the hall. *Shut up*, I thought. I heard a hsst from one of them, Arnim most likely.

One of the boots in front of me lifted.

I drew in a breath and steeled myself for a blow to the head.

But the boot slid back, and the king's knee came down to the floor. The warmth of his broad hand pressed on my head.

"Get up, Corren," Yutek said. "You've been a good foster-son. A good guardsman. You'll make a true-son to me yet." It hadn't struck me until that moment. I'd lost one father to misadventure and the vanity of shamans, but on my investiture as his heir, Yutek would become my true-father. My chest burned with breath I couldn't let go of, realizing what I'd risked.

I lowered my hands and pushed myself back, to sit on my heels, keeping my eyes below the king's, where he knelt on one knee in front of me, in front of everybody.

He looked old. I hadn't thought of him that way before. Orkast, yes, an old man chasing a dream. But Yutek? He had always held power like a radiant lamp in his very person. That day, though, I saw the lines creasing his cheeks, the heaviness in his eyes.

Not weak, not yet. But old. Old enough to need a successor he could trust. A son who would do the right thing.

In that moment, we knew each other's need.

PART II

THE CAPTAIN MAKES HIS MARK

11

I TOOK THE CAPE to the Shamans' House in Jeskaryan, where my father had been initiated. Orkast's old mentor, Master Shaman Fennic, recognized it immediately, I could tell, but he went through the formalities first. How I was feeling, how the weather was affecting his arthritis, how long it had been since he'd seen my father. Finally, he reached out and placed his hands on the cape, where I'd spread it on the table in front of him.

"My condolences, Corren," he said. "Will you be sitting for mourning first?"

"First?"

"It's best not to perform initiation while mourning. It can be disruptive to the process." He kneaded his fingers into the thick fabric of the cape.

My backside ached already from sitting cross-legged on the hard stone floor, barely softened by the ornamental cushion he'd put down for me. That put me in no mood to be anything less than direct. "I've no intention of doing any kind of initiation."

"I understand," he said. "Most people need time to grieve. And of course, there is necessary training."

Orkast had warned me this would come. I hadn't listened. Nor had he listened to me. Had he made promises to the Master Shaman? "I will not be taking my father's place."

"Oh." His face became still, the warmth draining out of it.

"I have other responsibilities." *Especially the responsibility to not be a complete fraud like you.*

"I understand …" It didn't seem to me that he did. I could see his mind working, the thoughts might have been drawn in ink across his face. *Who would turn down a chance to be a shaman?*

Me, that's who. I told him, "I'm sure you'll find somebody."

"Well … But … Later on …"

"There's no later on. I'm fine with being king one of these days. I don't need to be a shaman."

"But—"

"Thanks for your help." I untangled my legs and rocked to my feet.

He stood more slowly and gave me a hesitant bow, like I was a proper royal, not a soldier.

"Thanks," I said again, and walked out.

I never felt more free than the day I got rid of that thing.

•   •   •

Suffice to say I earned my badges back, my rank and position. Once I made captain, our duties were mainly border patrol and law enforcement. I think Yutek directed that, to be sure I'd know the country inside-out. I kept my Six, the men who'd followed me in that first command. We became more than a unit. We were like one creature. Together from the beginning; they were my own true family, the men who stood by me, the men I fought for.

Case, he wasn't much for talking, until you could get some drink into him. It's not that he would get drunk quicker than the average trooper, more the contrary. At the first taste of any brew, he'd light into a critique of the brewer's skill, give you a rundown on the flavors, no matter how bad they were. He'd come to us from a large farm family with a history of their men having too little to do, enough so their matriarchs put them to the task of turning rotten food into profit. Their family dues came in the form of tilling and planting and harvesting when called on. Over the generations, they'd built up skill enough that the brewing business outsold the food business. Soon enough, half the clan was selling its crops to the other half, and the wines and corn fermentations they produced enlivened celebrations—and ruined lives—throughout Jeska District and our neighbors.

When not advising the nearest barkeep of the best approaches to brewing and serving, Case was a solid force to have at your back, not unusually tall, but with the reach of a much taller man and the speed to deliver a killing blow before his opponent knew he was on the attack. I generally had Case behind me when we formed up, unless we had an extra man for some reason, in which case I'd put Case as backup to the newcomer. I could always count on him to know what order was coming before I opened my mouth.

Dramin, I've said before, came from a medical family, his mother and sisters being midwives and doctors and pharmacists. That left their menfolk to cope with the land, a topsy-turvy arrangement that meant Dramin needed strong defenses against insult. A different kind of man would have gone out into the world with a cocked arm, ready to fight anyone, but not Dramin. He had a way of ducking around a slight that flung it back onto the giver. He'd pull out his bag of healing for anyone—a friend, an opponent, a traitor. Human suffering is human suffering, he'd say. If the medical field had been open to men, or if he'd been like Calestinise (I'll get to him, but not now), Dramin would have made a right good midwife. There was a time, much later, when I asked him if he'd ever thought of pretending, making people think he was a girl who only looked like a boy, so he could follow in his mother's footsteps. I expected him to laugh at the idea, seeing as I asked it at a time he had a half-dozen grandchildren, but he looked off into the fading sunset and muttered, "Hmm, never thought of that, Boss."

Despite the healing touch—or maybe because of it—Dramin fought like a wildcat. Fast, fierce, and deadly. He never saw much point to leaving an opponent wounded. If it were a wound he himself couldn't see repairing, he'd make sure the man was dead before he moved on to another target. More than that, in the heat of a fight, Dramin would put himself at risk to deal a death-blow, to keep another from suffering even one moment longer than necessary. In a major engagement, he'd take it on himself to bring up the rear, triaging as he went, killing the doomed swiftly and dropping a marker on any he'd plan to come back to for repairs later. I've seen injured opponents quail at his approach, terrified of his judgment, but I've also heard men shout for him to come to them, no matter the verdict.

Andus, now, Andus is a special case. I think I've mentioned he was Keev's brother, Keev who fell at NeverSnows, that very first year. He was young for a guardsman, and we always assumed he and Keev had both lied about their ages when they mustered in. When we passed through Jeskaryan, after NeverSnows, I left the men at the barracks, with Dramin working alongside the women to patch up the injured, and took myself to their home, a ramshackle house on the edge of town, with a badly-tended garden full of unharvested crops. The place was so dead, there weren't even any flies circling over the compost pile. I found an old, angry man hunched over a table in the kitchen. At my approach, he grabbed empty wine flasks and hurled them at me. *She's gone*, he screamed, *don't be pestering me about the land, it's women's work, farming, and I can't be doing it.* In the light from the half-closed window at the back of the room, I could see tears running down his face. *I've come from up the hill*, I told him. *I came to tell you about your sons.* His face became stone. *I ain't got no sons, and she didn't leave no daughters, neither. It's her fault, she asked for it, she shouldn't ought to have crossed me.* I left him there, in his empty house, a home that had become a battlefield, with the bones of his wife scattered on the land. *Who took her out to the birds?* I wondered. *Keev alone, or did he bring young Andus to help?*

Andus trained hard, and he had a natural talent for close-fighting, the kind of agility that lets a small man slip in under a bigger man's guard, trick him into overreaching, opening up to an unhesitating counter-thrust. For that year after NeverSnows, I never heard him laugh, but Karthi took Andus under his wing, made him his friend, and he came out the other side more clear-eyed than most, ready with a joke when the rest of us were groaning over one thing or another. It took me a while to realize they were more than friends. Like I've said before, I didn't ask questions.

Karthi himself was another one who mustered in young. I always figured Magaran had tossed me youngsters for my futile mission to Koresh because he had no use for them in his preparations for the Lakeside clean-up. Now that I think about it, that could be the thing that made us what we became. Because we came together less than complete, we had to make something of ourselves, as we were.

Karthi, unlike Andus, looked his age until he wasn't a youngster anymore, and then he looked younger than his age. You know the type—a smooth face, thin-featured, with a smallish mouth and a ready grin. Nothing seemed to trouble Karthi. Like Kul, he was farm-bred, an extra son in need of employment who thought the Guard might make a decent enough career, keeping peace in the town, knocking a few heads together when a pub disagreement went overboard. On the other hand, his family farmed meat, not crops, so the whole business of killing came like second nature to him. They ran domesticated venison up in the green hills, and goats, as well as various kinds of poultry, for upper-class folks who wanted the taste of fancy meat. He could kill and dress a deer faster than the average trooper could change his boots. He wasn't that great at hunting, because hunting is its own art, and for that he took a fair amount of friendly abuse. But in battle, there's no need for stealth, and he could kill five men quicker than most soldiers could take down one.

Arnim, now, Arnim didn't belong in the guards. Arnim came from one of those upper-class families who put weird food on the table to impress their neighbors. He could read and write even before that long winter when I locked my men in the guardhouse until they learned the skill. He always had a book at the bottom of his pack, even on treks in the mountains, where every ounce of extra weight sucks the juice right out of your bones. I caught him listening at doors when the king's councilors were having at it over one issue or another. On liberty, in town, he'd sit at the liveliest eatery he could find and listen to people talk. When I pressed him as to why he'd joined up instead of living in the lap of luxury, he would only say that he'd seen what idleness did to a man and he wasn't going to have that happen to him. I thought I understood when I figured out that his older brother was a boy I remembered. He'd roamed the halls with Yutek the Younger, one who enjoyed the same pastimes. I put a mental mark on the man. He'd not be in Jeskaryan long, once I took the kingship.

You wouldn't expect a reader to be much of a fighter, but Arnim was tricky. He had a way of making other men feel small, unimportant, weak. He'd use his tongue as deftly as his sword, whenever there came a chance for a one-on-one. Arnim could read another man's fears, his situation in life, from the way he spoke, the clothes he wore, even the way he handled a sword. At the instant his opponent's muscles tensed, ready for a blow, Arnim would deliver a remark that cut to the bone and follow up with a quick killing slice while the other man was still feeling the verbal strike.

Kul, then. Kul, my right-hand man. He came up from a farm family and it's a wonder they let him go. Then again, once Kul decides on something, there's not much anyone can do to change his mind. Whenever anyone called us a shorthanded troop, we'd point to Kul. Maybe he wasn't as big as three men, but he was easily as big as two, and that was enough. He wasn't especially tall, though admittedly he topped everyone except Karthi. But he was wide as a bear, with arms like a bear's arms. Most big men, they're slow-moving as they don't need to be fast, and they're generally thought of as slow-witted because of that. Those who think that have never seen a bear charge, never had to outwit a bear intent on stealing their food. Kul, to be sure, spoke with that slow northern accent, used the words he'd grown up on, and never bowed to anyone's judgment on that. But he moved through the woods even better than a bear, more like a big cat, so you'd never see him coming, and more than one brigand learned that lesson the hard way.

Kul didn't talk much about his family, but he took off home every liberty and came back filthy from a week's hard labor. Right in the middle of his service time, too, he found himself a wife, a woman who'd seen him working his fingers to the bone for his mother when any self-respecting guardsman would be lounging under the table in the nearest pub. She was a landed woman, too, keeper to a farm even bigger than his own family's. He kept up those hard-working holidays right up to retirement. In the meantime, though, I figure he killed more men than the rest of us put together. I always wondered, and never asked, if he told the family stories of his time in the Guard.

I would guess he didn't. He liked to keep work and home separate.

We each had our reasons for signing up. We were thrown together more or less by accident, but we were as one, Corren and the Six. We went out as ordered, every time, ready for anything.

Or so we thought.

12

FOR MOST OF THE NEXT TWO YEARS, Tymon effectively worked as a personal runner for me. Most people assumed the king had assigned him to the post, that it was official. Those who knew we were foster-brothers assumed I had picked him out of brotherly affection. Others saw him as a money-grubber, one of those runners who picked and chose their assignments in order to pile up a substantial personal treasury.

None of these were accurate, though Runners' House didn't hold back on billing for his services.

It was Tymon's doing. He attached himself to us. He knew where we'd be and when we'd be there, and he made sure to turn up at the most inopportune times.

He was there when Yutek sent me to put down the rebellion in Heart's Bend, at the curve in the river, where somebody had gotten the idea that because the state left them alone, that meant they could do whatever they wanted. Why did it not occur to them they were let alone precisely because they kept to the rules? That didn't entitle them to change the rules.

This time, there were no southern mercenaries to contend with, only an untrained band of self-armed bravos. Their leader, an ignorant fool selected from among his friends by lottery, had collected the taxes, then sliced up the take and shared it out among the local families. Bigger households got more, but smaller ones got their share. A nice idea, but not practical when the district owes those taxes to the king.

Yutek's word to me was, "Make sure this never happens again."

I said, "Yes, sir."

Magaran and I put our heads together and discussed the lay of the land. The commander recommended a full unit, that is, eight troops of eight men each, but I trimmed our force to six troops, such that each of my own six men could command one.

Eldennian came along, for the fun of it, she said, though organizing supplies for a military operation could hardly count as time off for a woman who spent her days planning festivals and suchlike. Though she didn't ask, I signed on her younger brother as a pony-wrangler, to be sure her family'd gain a fair return from her taking time off to follow me around. When we were leaving them at our staging-camp, a shady spot by the river, the boy favored me with such thunderous looks that I had to take action. With those black eyes boring into my back, I swept Eldennian into my arms and we gave him something to look at. The men whooped and hollered behind us.

As we broke off, she caught my ear between her thumb and forefinger and twisted, pulling my face close and smiling into my pain. She whispered, "Come back uninjured, Corren, or I'll not be satisfied with you."

Tymon fell in beside me as I returned to my position. Of course he was there. Have I not told you he was always there?

Our force of forty-three descended on Heart's Bend like a storm front. The rabble fell back quickly, fortunately for them. By doing so, they limited their losses.

But there were casualties.

Some of them thought they could fight, so they made a stand in front of the governor's house.

Tymon pushed himself in front of my troops and shouted. "This is the king's own Guard! Put down your weapons!"

By way of reply, three of the most suicidal defenders dashed forward, slashing at him. Kul gave his troop a sign, and the three lay silent in their own blood. *Finish it. Don't leave them screaming*, that was what I taught. Screamers inspire their followers.

While Kul's men wiped their blades, I dragged Tymon back out of the line of attack.

I took him by the shoulders and leaned close.

"That was your fault," I told him. "Those idiots wouldn't have run out if you hadn't baited them like that."

"I wasn't—"

"Let us do our job, Tymon. Then you can do yours." A firm shove put him behind the last of our ranks.

Then I gave the whistle that was our go-signal, and Arnim lifted his sword. I advanced with the men at the rear, making sure they spread out to cover anyone trying to slip around the edges.

About half the defenders dropped their swords. Dramin's crew, as arranged, surrounded and disarmed them.

The rest had to take their chances with real guardsmen.

Their chances were not good, but a few survived to get bandaged by Dramin afterwards.

Case found their fearless leader cowering in a back room of the modest governor's house. Heart's Bend isn't that big a district; it hadn't needed a formal governor in ages. Like I said, they delivered their taxes on time, and no one really cared how they did it.

I set myself up in the governor's office, a room with soft cushions to sit on and a nice view outwards to the courtyard strewn with bodies.

One of Case's troopers led the rebel leader in and pushed him down to the floor, to fall flat on his face. The position suited him. It seemed to me that face-down on the floor was the right posture for a rebel to assume. When he sat himself up, I felt an urge to jump to my feet and shove him back down again, but I was tired and let him be.

"This is over," I told him.

"What's over?" His watery eyes flicked around the disused room, but there was no way out for him.

"All of this. Keeping the government's revenue. Playing at making up your own rules for your district. It's over. You'll be getting a proper governor, and he'll have a guard unit, and you'll behave yourselves from now on. Or else."

His mouth worked. I had a feeling he had something even more stupid to say, something that might make me want to do more than push him over.

"But, I—"

"Shut up!" I took to my feet again, to stand over him where he knelt on the bare floor, sitting on his heels. I rested my hand on the hilt of my sword and tapped my fingers on the hilt-guard.

He looked up into my eyes and something he saw there made him shut his mouth.

I considered my options. Take him down to Jeskaryan, have him tried for treason? That would get him executed, which would make everyone in the district furious. If I killed him right away, he could be dispersed with the rest of their honored dead out there on the flagstones. He'd be a hero, but not a martyr.

Surely, I could think of a compromise, one that wouldn't put a stain on this floor.

A noise at the door broke my concentration. Tymon stood there, with his big soft eyes, watching.

"Get out of here, Tymon," I said, using my softest voice. Kul, Case, and Karthi stiffened. They knew that voice.

In that moment, the rebel leader leapt to his feet, pulled a dagger from his boot, and sprang for the door, towards the one unarmed man in the room.

I had no choice. My sword flew into my hand.

The new governor bought a nice rug, woven in the north country, to cover the stain.

13

G RADUALLY, TYMON LEARNED not to put himself right in the middle of the action. But he never understood the military. He never understood the need for control. While the borders of Jeska were secure enough to the east, with the Wall rising up between us and the redlands, the rest needed constant management.

To the west, the Inner Range rose dry and inhospitable, reasonable to traverse when necessary, but mostly open country, hard to hide an army in. Not many people wanted to live up in those dry canyons, so it made a useful, if porous, screen between us and the various peoples who traded their way up and down the long thin valleys in between that range and the Green Mountains off by the sea.

I saw the Green Mountains, once, from the top of one of the hills in the Inner Range. A thick grey cloud hung over those distant hills that day. My guide told me those hills were taller than they looked and that the cloud was really sea fog, flowing up and over them. While he was talking, I watched a finger of fog-cloud flow through a gap, like a waterfall on a river.

Why couldn't Tymon make himself one of those runners that went back and forth over to the green-valley people, for trade deals and the occasional out-country marriage arrangement? Why did he have to traipse along with me? It was my job to secure our weak border in the north, protect the citizenry from bandits, and carry out the king's demands, but Tymon treated our patrols like holiday outings.

Eldennian often traveled with us, too, but that was different. Besides the fact we served as informal escorts for her, between festivals in various towns she worked for, I wanted her with me. She reminded me who I was, the smith's son from the lower levels of Jeskaryan. She didn't care about the past. She knew I wasn't that worthless boy any longer. She was equally unimpressed by my future, the plans that Yutek had for me. She saw the guardsman, the man who led his men to protect our country, and she reminded me to stay strong, to never waver, to take a little pain and turn it to action.

In the meantime, I hadn't ignored the potential threat posed by the snake-men. Yutek approved sending scouts up to the pass a few times a year, to keep an eye out for redlanders. That was the story I told. One of my Six would brief the scouts on what they were really watching for. I orchestrated a new guard post at Koresh, a standing squad. The town didn't like it, but the town didn't have a say. The longstanding rumors of redlanders wanting to come down over the pass gave me a good reason, snake-men or no snake-men.

It was getting late into fall, my third year as a captain, when we stopped by Koresh to bring the guard post a few relievers—replacements for men lost to stupidity, fights, and retirement. There hadn't been any incursions of redlanders (or snake-men) to contend with, and the local population was ready to see the troopers gone. I forced a discussion between the town elders and the young captain I'd placed at the head of the post, to settle their issues. I saw no reason these men couldn't live in the town and report to the post on their duty cycles, like men at the garrison in Jeskaryan. That would make them part of ordinary life—and maybe put an end to the fights and other pointless conflict between my men and the people they were supposed to be protecting.

Neither Captain Durek nor the chief elder, Semseh, liked my idea. Durek preferred his men right to hand, no matter how bored they might be. Semseh held that the military had no place in her community. Durek countered that he'd had men turn in retirement requests, due to harassment from townspeople. Arnim showed up at our meeting with proof these retirements were men who'd landed marriage contracts in town. The proofs were attestations from their satisfied wives. I left Semseh and Durek arguing over the scarcity of available housing and the risks to civilians of soldiers carrying weapons when not on duty.

I'd quartered our group in the same inn we'd visited before, to take advantage of their hot springs, but this time we didn't avoid the public room. Eldennian and me, and my Six, we had just settled down to the fine spread the innkeeper and her daughter had laid out, when Tymon appeared in the doorway.

I pretended not to notice him, and listened to my gut. It was not helpful. There was too much food in front of me to distract my inner warning system.

Trouble? Maybe. Or maybe just Tymon.

Arnim stood up, gave Tymon his place right across from me, and moved to a spot closer to the fire. I didn't blame him. It had started to rain that afternoon, and we were not looking forward to moving out in the morning. Best to be warm while we could.

The innkeeper herself leaned over Tymon's shoulder and placed a plate in front of him. He turned to give her that grin of his, then reached for the meat.

"So," he said. "You're still here. I thought you'd be gone by the time I got here."

"What important mission did you drop this time?" I fended off his reach towards the stew and scooped myself a serving.

Eldennian pressed herself close and snagged the spoon from me, then extended it to Tymon. "He means, what brings you here this fine evening, dear brother?"

I started to cut in, then glanced at her face. Her eyes sparkled in the firelight, and she gave me a long, slow wink. I nearly choked, couldn't help it, she had a way of making me laugh.

Tymon ladled himself two helpings and slid the spoon into its place beside the bowl.

He leaned back and shifted enough that he could rest his back against the nearest post.

"You two should get married," he said.

"Shht," Eldennian hissed. "Keep your notions in your head, runner."

I pulled her close.

To a man, the Six stopped eating and stared at Tymon. Kul, sitting next to him, gave Tymon an elbow in the side.

"What? What?" Tymon protested.

"Eat," Eldennian said. "Just eat, will you, the lot of you."

The brightness faded from her eyes, and she laid her head on my shoulder.

Was he really that out of touch with the world? Runners live in their safe little society, with its own relationship rules, but he'd grown up in the king's house, right alongside me. Did he imagine that I had any say whatever in that part of my future? One of these days, Yutek would attach me to the offspring of some high-value personage, maybe not even a woman of our own country, and that would be the end for Eldennian and me.

Tymon fell silent, dodging my gaze as he worked his way into that enormous pile of stew. About halfway through, he paused to reach for a hunk of bread and glanced up. His gaze fell on Eldennian, her fingers working away at a smaller piece of bread, tearing it apart grain by grain. Tymon's face colored, as he looked back and forth between me and my woman.

"Oh," he said.

"Oh, what?" I snarled.

"I'm the idiot today." He stood to lean over the table and lift the tormented fragment of bread from Eldennian's fingers, replacing it with the fresh piece. "I'm sorry."

She closed her hand around the bread and swung her feet over the bench. "I'm tired," she said, giving my ear a pinch. "Wake me when you come up, Corren. Or else."

I didn't turn around, so that I could imagine she was smiling at me. "Yes, ma'am."

When she had gone, I thumped my spoon down on the table and crossed my arms.

"What now?" Tymon wanted to know.

"You never answered our question."

"What question?"

Kul gave him another elbow jab. "Boss and the lady asked what ya came here for."

Tymon dropped his spoon into the nearly-empty bowl. "Oh, that."

"Well?" I prompted.

Still, he hesitated. The listening men wore various expressions of impatience. Except Arnim. He could hide his thoughts better than anyone.

I thumped a fist on the table. "Anything you have for me, my men need to hear it, too."

"Well … there's odd news out of the ghost country." That explained his hesitation. He knew what I thought of ghost stories.

Arnim laughed. "There's no such thing as ghosts."

"Don't be so quick on it," Kul advised. "If Tymon says there's ghosts, I've a mind to listen."

I waved a hand to hush incoming commentary from the rest of the men. "What, exactly, are you talking about, Tymon? Everyone knows 'ghost country' is merely a nickname for the place. Because of the history."

Everyone sat silent for that moment, recalling the true story only the grimmest storytellers will drop into a performance.

It hadn't been that long ago, back in our grandfathers' time, when the chieftain of one of those little northern countries decided to make himself a big man by taking over that upriver valley. Back in the day, it was called the Well, first, because it was a valley that was like a deep hole in the mountains and second, because of the water in it: a big river that overflowed most years, a couple of lakes, and waterfalls all over the place. The people who lived there were soft, complacent. They had it good in the Well: expanses of flat ground for cultivating crops, with a river that dropped silt on the cropland, clean, fresh water year-round, plenty of game. They came down to the lowlands regularly, with furs and salted meat, and other trade goods.

Then this nameless chief—he's been erased from the histories for what he did—got this notion there was more to the Well. He heard rumors of obsidian mines, veins of gold ribboned in the rock, nuggets tumbling in the clear waters of their river. So he marched a little army up into the Well, and demanded the hillmen surrender their lands to him. But the people of the Well raised their empty hands and said, "No, no, we don't have treasure here." He was not buying that answer, and determined to prove his strength, so he threatened to kill a few of them if they wouldn't surrender their mines.

They insisted there was no secret obsidian hoard, so he killed a couple of men.

They offered to teach him how to sift the silt in the river for flecks of gold, so he killed a couple of women. Yes, women. Some tellers will say he murdered elders, but elders are women. Why not be direct?

The Well people took up their farming tools and hunting axes and told him to leave.

Two of the chief's men lowered their weapons and said, "There's nothing here, Boss, let's go home."

And the chief killed them, too, with his own sword, and ordered his army to attack. They obeyed.

All but one. Seeing what had happened to his comrades, one man held his tongue and slipped away, turned his back on the carnage, and raced down the valley. The screams of the dying pursued him.

That's how the story goes, it's always told that way.

The screams of the dying pursued him.

At the time, the route to the Well passed through a narrow defile, a place where the hillmen, had they had any common sense, could have set an impenetrable defensive position. The valley narrowed to leave barely enough room for the river to plunge through. The strip of solid ground that ran alongside it twisted and turned with the river, and wove between giant boulders that narrowed the walkable space even further.

When the deserter emerged to where the valley opened up again, he stopped. He still heard the screams in his mind. Again, that's how the story goes. We're meant to understand that he was overtaken with shame. But no one really knows what the man felt. We only know what he reported in the end.

He decided to wait until his chief came out, then slip back up into the Well and see for himself what had befallen the people there, before he would report the story to others.

We don't know how long he waited. Different storytellers tell it differently.

Eventually, he heard voices approaching. He'd picked out a hiding place behind a growth of sagebrush sprouting from the loose, rocky soil. But as he headed that way, the earth trembled, and he lost his footing and tumbled to the ground. He brushed himself off and stood again, laughing at the earthquake, relieved it was such a small one.

The deserter looked up the valley, towards the narrow canyon, and saw the bright colors of the chief's banner caught in the light of the setting sun. Then the earth heaved, hurling him flat on his back. He knew the hillside above him was unstable, so he scrambled behind the nearest large boulder and held fast.

When the earth stopped moving and the river of gravel stopped flowing past his hiding place, the deserter crept from behind the rock, ready to meet the wrath of his chieftain. A cloud hung over the canyon where he'd seen the chief's banner. Nothing moved. A wind came up, and it blew the cloud of dust away.

Boulders filled the defile completely, obliterating the path, damming the river. Some water trickled through crevices in the rock pile, but the river flow had already fallen to nearly nothing.

The chief and his army lay somewhere under that wall of stone.

None of the people of the valley ever emerged.

The river forced a way through the rocks, during the spring flooding the next year.

In the summer that followed, a few curious men climbed over the dam and made their way to the Well. They searched for signs of villages up and down the valley, but the Well people had favored tents and other movable houses, and those were swept away by the floods. They stumbled across heaps of bones in one corner of the valley, where the river had dropped them. They found no obsidian, no gold, no people.

When they camped at night, they heard strange noises up and down the valley, wails and sighs and sounds like music. When they went home, all they would say was, *At night, you can hear the ghosts calling for you.*

As I sat there with my men, full of good food and cider, warmed by the fire, the story seemed sad and distant. Tymon's spoon scraped at the bottom of his bowl.

I cleared my throat. "So, what, are people hearing ghosts? Do you need me to send Arnim up there to lecture people about the nonexistence of ghosts?"

"It's not that." Tymon studied his empty bowl and twirled the spoon in his fingers. "Not exactly."

"Come on, man," Andus broke in. "We're tired, we have an early start tomorrow, what's your news?"

"Ay," Karthi echoed, a sidelong glance passing between the pair of them. "Some of us need a bit of time in the hot springs before bed." By way of response, Dramin caught up the cider jug and poured everyone refills, to raised voices and laughter.

"I think the snake-men may be up in the Well."

All the joking and jostling stopped. Arnim abandoned his spot by the fire and slid into Eldennian's seat. I held up a hand and cast my eyes over the room to see if any of the townsfolk might have heard. The innkeeper and her daughter had their heads together, strategizing about a group of men in the opposite corner, whose voices were rising over some disagreement. The girl ducked out of the room by the back passageway, the one that ran to the stairs that led to the stables. *Well*, I thought. *You've got seven guardsmen right here. Could have asked us for help, instead of your stable crew.*

Then again, the stableboys might leave their customers alive, to buy another round tomorrow.

To those around me, I said, "Looks like we'll be heading north, not south, in the morning."

We were all of us upstairs, and I was already nudging Eldennian awake, when the fight broke out downstairs.

14

I SAVED DETAILED DISCUSSION to take place well outside town. The last thing I needed was a new rumor running wild in Koresh—*Snake people are coming!*—when I'd barely managed to get the town elders and my post captain talking to each other.

Eldennian took with wry disappointment the news that we were marching north to chase wild rumors rather than south to sit by the warm fires of Jeskaryan. By the time my men were hauling their gear down the stairs, she'd already made an arrangement with the innkeeper.

"You'd best plan your march south to come by here, though," she told me.

"Is it Tymon?" I asked. "You know I'd never leave you behind by choice."

"Ah," she allowed. "That might be part of it, but then again, they're shorthanded here, the fall festival's coming up, and I'd slow your travels."

"I'll talk to him," I said.

"No, no, don't you dare. I can take care of myself, Corren," she insisted. Then she drew me close and reminded me who it was that took care of me.

Truth be told, I'd've rather had Eldennian than Tymon with us on the march north. She kept a six-inch knife strapped to her thigh and was as skilled at throwing and slashing as she was at slicing vegetables. The northern reaches, especially in the foothills, were risky country for a small party to travel in. Runners might pass unscathed, but then again, runners never carried anything worth stealing and weren't worth ransoming. Besides, even brigands need the occasional message delivered.

We made good time, despite Tymon's griping about how slow the rest of us were. The rain let up by late morning, so we were dry enough by the time the shadows began to lengthen. It would be a push to make the outskirts of Tarak by nightfall, but I hadn't any inclination to camp in the mud.

We'd entered a patch of forest tucked between two hills, when the soft snap of a breaking twig caught my ear and made the hair on my neck rise. I gave a quick glance around at my men. No one—apart from Tymon—had missed it. I gave the hand-signal, *Star*, and crooked a thumb at Tymon. Kul caught my eye and nodded. He grabbed Tymon by the arm and shoved him to the center of our formation. Before Tymon could utter a word of complaint, we stood ringing him, swords raised, as if we were his bodyguard. Which we were, I guess.

There were a dozen of them, and a few were big, and a couple were skilled, but none of them were a match for a trained, battle-ready troop. Each of us had two others watching his flank, covering any strike with a flick of a blade. We'd developed a fighting style that I'd heard others describe as odd, but it was nothing more than that we fought in silence. Apart from an involuntary grunt or gasp, our opponents heard nothing from us: no shouted orders, no battle cries, no cursing. To us, it was nothing more than good sense. We had our signals, we had our practiced formations, and we had our close familiarity.

I didn't need to shout "Attack!" when they descended on us. I knew that Andus would take the leaping, yelling bandit coming in to my left while I dealt with the tall, bony idiot who thought he could take me with a frontal charge. Timing is helpful, of course. The scarecrow's death-fall deflected the one coming in a few strides behind him. A short fellow with even shorter legs, that one stumbled over his comrade and by the time he screamed himself to his feet again, I'd already freed my blade and readied it to greet him.

If you had come to me when I was a young boy and asked what I'd most enjoy doing when I grew up, it wouldn't have been killing. I followed my father around the smithy, like any child assuming he'd follow his father's profession, but my heart was never in it. When Orkast went for a shaman, I comforted myself by thinking *at least now I won't have to pound a hammer all my life.* That first year in the king's household, Tymon and I spent many hours spinning dreams, side-by-side on our cots in the fosters' dormitory. We imagined grand futures as councilors to the king—Yutek the Younger it would have been. In later years, before Tymon joined the runners, we imagined all sorts of escape. I built up this complex fantasy of working at an inn at some popular crossroad, where I could see the people going up and down the land and never have to go anywhere myself. I'd make myself so invaluable to the innkeeper that as soon as I married, she'd welcome my wife into the business, and our children would become her grandchildren, and we would stay there forever and ever.

Instead, Yutek the Younger died and I made myself invaluable to his father, and as soon as I married, I'd be invested as his heir, and be parted from Eldennian forever and ever.

Along the way, though, I learned a few things. I learned that our country needed a warrior at the helm, to keep the people safe from criminals, like the determined thieves we fought that day on the road north from Koresh. We needed a strong, well-trained army to protect the nation from organized peril from the south. We needed men who were not afraid to put their lives on the line for one another, for Jeska. And I had found a band of men willing to risk their lives for me, that I was willing to bet my life on. When we snapped into formation and rolled into action, it was like nothing I'd imagined, nothing I would trade away. Those were the best days of my life, the times my band of six and I raised our weapons and dealt death together.

"No! Stop!" Tymon had his hand on my sword-arm, his broad fingers pulling against my swing. Had it been any other man, I might have struck him. The last of the bandits lay at my feet, a gash from the tip of my blade oozing in a dark streak across his chest. I planted my foot on the bandit's sword-hand, feeling the bones crack, and wrenched myself free of my brother. Dramin and Karthi together hauled him backwards, but he shook them off and shouted at me, "He's just a boy, Corren!"

I looked down at the wild-eyed fighter below me. True enough, the bandits recruited them young. Defiance and fear wrestled for dominance in his eyes. Scars from other battles writhed up his outstretched arm, weaving over the tattoo that circled his upper arm: three intertwined ribbons.

"Might be a lad, Tymon," Kul said. "But it's a lad that aimed to kill ya." He pointed to Tymon's calf, where a narrow sliver of a cut dripped a trail of blood down his leg. "That were his blade, I tell ya, I saw him dodge in under Andus's arm. You oughta thank the Boss. Aren't your legs like your most important part?"

Tymon ignored him. "Corren," he repeated. "I'm all right. Don't, Corren."

"My friend doesn't know the law," I said to the fire-eyed youngster, about Andus' age when he'd signed on. "But I expect you do."

He gave me a slow, serious nod, and raised his eyes to meet mine. He tried to say something, but his throat closed over the words. I took my foot off his hand and kicked his sword aside. I flicked my own sword over and extended the hilt to Tymon, giving Arnim a look that said *Make sure he doesn't hurt himself with that.* Tymon sighed in relief and gave me a grateful smile. Then I lowered myself to one knee beside the boy and quietly drew my long knife with my left hand.

"What was it you wanted to say?" I asked.

He coughed, then whispered, "Not the fire, sir, not the fire."

I gave him a nod of my own, and the worst of his fear drained away. "You a Returner?" I slid my eyes to the tattoo and then back to his face. Returners were one of the newer religions; they believed their spirits survived death and that they'd see a new life sometime— not necessarily as a human, though, which made it interesting.

He nodded.

I leaned close and said to him, "Do better next time." Neat and quick, I slid the long knife into his heart. I stayed still until it ended, then stood and took my sword back from where it dangled like a stick in Tymon's hand.

"What are you?" he said, and tears ran down his face.

I didn't know what to say to that. *I'm the man who does the right thing.* That might have done. Instead I shrugged and said, "I'm captain of the best troop in the King's Guard."

"Captain Second-degree!" Andus tossed in.

"Best get the fire started, Boss," said Kul. "It's coming for night, soon."

"Ya," said Karthi. "I'll scout out a good spot to camp."

"Kul." I pointed to the still form at my feet. "This one goes out to the open ground. Let his bones go back to his ancestors." *And let his spirit move on to the next life.*

"Ay, Boss, I'll make sure it's done right."

The others we dragged to a clearing. It took the rest of the daylight to gather enough wood to get eleven corpses taken care of, but we lit the fire by dark. Karthi had hauled our gear well upwind of the fire, to a decently level spot. He had a competing blaze going by the time we had made sure the death-fire wouldn't be burning down the forest around us. Kul came wandering back from his solitary duty and settled down next to me.

"The lad's on his way, sir," he told me. "There was a goodly crowd of vultures come in right away, but a Great One soared over, and they scattered like rabbits."

"Good," I said. I found Tymon standing apart, leaning against a tree in the shadows. "Are you all right?"

"No." He was a dark bundle of warmth, the cooling air catching his breath, turning it to fog.

"I honored his wish, Tymon. He wasn't asking for more than that."

"Small comfort to his family, Corren." His liquid voice caught. I put my hand on his shoulder, and the vibration of his pent-up emotion burned against my skin.

What could I tell him? "Our work is to comfort the families of victims, not those who rob and murder innocent travelers. You know this." *Should I tell him of the old bloodstains on that youngster's jacket, where the spray from his own strikes would have flown? Probably not. No.*

He shrugged. "It reminds me of too much, brother."

As we walked together back to the campfire, I chose not to mention we'd been protecting him, that afternoon. He knew it well enough, as he knew how, all our lives, I'd protected him from worse than bandits in the woods.

15

D AWN CAME LIKE A SKUNK in the night—the wind had shifted, immersing our camp in smoke from the smoldering bandits. We were afoot and on the road in no time, not even breaking our fast. Instead, the men passed around that flask Case always carried, the "special brew" his grandfather fermented out of, it seems to me, rotten potatoes. That morning, I relented and took a swig myself. The rancid bite of the stuff did clear the taste of corpse-ash out of my mouth. Unknowing, Tymon took a long pull when the flask came to him, and we had a good laugh as he choked and staggered, retching into the matted pine needles we marched over.

Case hurried to reclaim the flask before it could get contaminated, but stayed to pat Tymon on the back in his awkward country-boy way. "There, there," he said. "It grows on ya, you'll see."

We had a short climb over a low ridge before the route swept down in easy curves to the little town of Tarak, either the farthest-north town of Jeska or the southernmost city of the northern confusion. The north was scattered over with tiny competing countries, more like agglomerations of disagreeable families than nations. The townsfolk played it both ways, depending on the wind direction and the time of year. Nestled up by the Wall as they were, like Koresh, they didn't fear much from anybody. Their most likely assailants would come up from the lowlands to the west, but who wants to march uphill to take over a town that has worse cropland than you have at home? A town that obviously stands at risk of being overrun by redlanders, any day. Worse, a town that spends a good many months of the year buried in snow.

And one bordered by an unpredictable river.

We reached the river by midday, at which point the Six began a heated disagreement as to whether we'd march upstream, to a ford that Karthi's cousin's wife had told him about, or down, where Andus had heard of a ferry crossing. Tymon let them argue for several minutes before shouldering his way through them and striding down to the river's edge. He crouched, put his hand under the water, and came up with a thick rope. One end proved to be moored fast to a post pounded into the riverbank. The other end disappeared under the ripples.

"Yer not thinking we'll ford here," Andus said. "Looks deep, and the water's running fast."

Tymon gestured up the shoreline. "Have a look yonder," he said. "You're meant to pull the boat well above the waterline, in case of storms or whatnot."

"Oh!" Karthi replied. "They've got a pullboat?"

"What's a pullboat?" Andus asked. "I'm not dragging a boat anywhere."

"You use the rope to pull yourself across the water, sitting in the boat," Arnim explained.

"I dunno," Andus said. "Let's run on up to the ford. I don't mind getting my feet wet. Boats are dangerous."

"Only Arnim and I has heard of pullboats, and none of us knows how to work one," Karthi declared. "A proper ferry would be safer."

"Enough!" I said. "I'm not spending half the day hiking up the river or down. Andus, I can see the boat from here. Go drag it down to Tymon. Now."

The thing hardly qualified as a boat, barely bigger than the reed canoes the fisherfolk of Lakeside use. Once Tymon, Arnim, and Karthi had climbed aboard, the boat bobbed on the surface like a rebellious pony, as if it were thinking of rolling downriver and ditching them in the rapids downstream. Tymon kept a firm grip on the rope, enough so that even from my position on top of the bank I could see the whites of his knuckles showing. "One more!" Tymon called up. "Let's not do this more than three times."

Kul stepped forward, his boots sinking into the soft bank. "Wait, Kul," I said. "You're with me, at the last."

"Ay, Boss."

"Andus!" I ordered. "Get a move on."

"Yessir."

As Tymon hauled on the rope to get them started, and the force of the river became clear, the other three men caught at the line and shared the load. Their going was rough for about the first third of the crossing, but then they seemed to fall into a rhythm. They about doubled their speed on the second two-thirds.

Kul and I, we stayed up on the bank, with Case and Dramin waiting their turn by the water. Tymon climbed back aboard the boat and dragged it back on his own. The two waiting men clambered aboard and caught hold promptly. Despite having only three men this time, their progress was good. I heard Dramin shouting out a count to keep them in rhythm.

This time, though, on arrival there seemed to be a disagreement that took several minutes to be resolved. When the boat arrived back on our shore, it was Arnim hauling at the rope. His face shone with sweat and exultation.

"I'd read about these," he declared as we descended to the water and found our positions. "Never imagined I'd get to try one out."

With Kul aboard, the boat rode low in the water, but we also had the benefit of his over-muscled arms. I think our crew made the fastest time.

Under Tymon's instruction, we hauled the boat out and parked it upside-down on top of the riverbank. Less than an hour later, we were throwing down cool ciders in a tavern at the edge of Tarak. Except Tymon, that is. He left while we were still dragging benches together, saying he would find the one who'd told him about the snake-men up in the Well.

He took long enough. I ordered up a meal. He still hadn't shown by the time everyone had eaten. The portion I'd set aside for Tymon and his mysterious informant cooled at the end of the table. Finally, I sent Andus and Karthi off to scout us lodgings, at least for one night. It wasn't likely we'd be going up into the mountains that day.

Tymon finally dragged his man in when we were loading up packs and paying off the barkeep. At a nod from me, Case edged to the doorway, blocking the exit, and Dramin followed, dropping his pack on the threshold. Tymon let go of the informant, who edged backwards and flicked glances at the tired soldiers who ringed him.

I pulled a bench back from the table and gestured.

"Sit," I told him. "Let's hear your story."

He put his head down and talked to the floor. "I promised not to tell it again. I'm sorry." He had a soft, youthful voice and a body not built for fighting: pudgy overall, heavy in the hips and belly and with lumpy rolls of fat filling out his chest. So Tymon's man with a tale to tell was only a boy, younger by a year or two than the brigand from the day before.

"Promised who?" I pressed. I gave Karthi a sign. He's the one who looks even younger than he is, with not even a little scar on his face. He strolled over, took the trembling boy by the elbow, and led him to the bench. At a gentle push on his shoulder, the lad shuffled his feet and eased down to the bench, holding himself stiff as a frozen tree, one hand gripping the other. I backed away and circled the table, to stand opposite him.

"What's your name, then?" I asked.

"He's called Calestinise," Tymon volunteered. I waved him off with another sign to Karthi, who leaned to whisper in Tymon's ear. *Shut up when the Boss is doing an interrogation,* that would be the message. Tymon colored, but he stood surrounded by my Six, so he moved back to sit at the neighboring table.

"Is that so?" I asked. "What was your mother thinking, then?" Indeed, if this poor kid had lived all his life under a girl's name, he'd carried more burdens than a baggage pony.

"She was thinking I was a girl." His eyes stabbed into mine and his voice strengthened, becoming hot, melodious, and definitely female. A spark of defiance shone in her eyes. "But I'm not."

"What?"

"You heard me."

I could see it now. The shape under that shirt and trousers wasn't soft, it was feminine. "So you're a girl who dresses up like a boy?"

"No. I'm a man who looks like a woman." She glared up at me, dark eyes glowing under her smooth, broad brow, her lashes long enough to brush her cheeks those few times she blinked. I felt my ears growing hot. I'm not a man to stare at a woman I'm not interested in. Let alone a kid. Not like that.

"Never mind all that," I ordered. "What's this story you won't tell? Does it have anything to do with whether a girl or a boy is telling it?"

"Man."

"Boy."

"Anyway, I'm not telling it. The last time, they locked me up for a month, had a shaman dance around me, hollering at me to get rid of demons." She had anger in her eyes, not fear.

I liked her already, a practical northern girl who could see through a shaman's fakery. Maybe her testimony would make sense. "So?"

"So, what?"

"Did he get rid of any demons?"

She unclenched her hands and splayed them flat on the table, then pulled them back, digging in her fingernails. "There aren't any demons."

"I know," I said. I leaned down and rapped on the table, pulling her attention away from the grooves she was making in the wood. "There's no such thing. My true-father's a shaman. He told me so himself."

That caught her interest. "Really? Shamans know this?"

"Yes. The things they do are for show. To make us feel better, my father said."

"Well, it didn't make me feel better."

"I'm not surprised."

"And he charged my mother and sisters a lot." I saw the fury in those eyes: the narrowed lids, the quickened blinking.

"Don't bother," I told her. "You'll never get that money back even if you kill him. And your family must have thought it worked, since, here you are, free and all."

"Huh. Free. Right." She—no, *he* returned to defacing the table.

I dropped to sit on the bench, making sure it made a good, loud clunk, then dragged the bench with my backside, so it grated on the tile floor. That made him look up. "I came a long way to get this story, and I'm having it, or you won't have to worry about anyone asking you questions again." I let my voice go cold and dark, and I kept my eyes fixed on his. He pushed back, and tried to stand up, but Karthi's hand on his shoulder kept him in his seat.

"You best listen, lassie," said Kul.

"Lad," Andus corrected him.

"Shht," Arnim warned them, then promptly added his own, "Talk, if you know what's good for you."

"Just…"

"Just what?" I snapped.

"Just don't be telling anyone I told." He looked over to where the barkeep studiously wiped mugs, keeping his eyes down as if he wasn't listening. Case took my sign and invited the barkeep to step out the back door.

"Conditions met," I said. "Now, talk."

16

"I 'M A TRAPPER, SEE," Calestinise began.

"Ain't a fit job for a girl." There are times Kul cannot keep his mouth shut.

"Ain't a girl," he snapped back at the massive guardsman, and I had to work to keep a smile off my face, seeing Kul drop his eyes and mutter *sorry, sorry*.

I rapped the table again. "I don't think that's the story."

"Well, as I said, I'm a trapper, but it's competitive to find a good spot for a trapline, and there's no one goes up the Well, because of ghosts, you know."

I rolled my eyes at *ghosts*.

"I don't believe in ghosts neither. So, last season, I went up there. It was easy enough, you clamber around the rocks. Earthquakes don't happen that often. I was right, the place was wide open. No one else had any traps out, I found plenty of game trails, so I worked my way along, where there was good cover, setting up my line. I was making good time, until I heard the voices…" His voice trailed off, and the boy sent quick, cautious glances to my face, trying to gauge whether I was believing any of this story.

"Ghosts?" Andus guessed.

I shook my head and summoned words to get the boy talking again. "He already said—" The kid gave me a funny look. What was bugging him now? "There's no ghosts. Right?"

The kid smirked. Scared of nothing, that one. "Like I said. I don't believe in ghosts. It had to be someone else out trapping or hunting. Competition. The noise came and went—it was windy, so sometimes they seemed close, sometimes far off. I sneaked up on them, though. Wasn't going to show myself. Because I was alone, and there was more than one of them, and, because, well, I know I still look like, well …" None of the men said anything, but Kul's lips moved, *a sweet little lassie.*

"Anyway, eventually, I got close enough I thought I should be able to understand them, but I couldn't. The words was all messed-up, half the time sounded like weird chanting, like maybe it was shamans out there telling each other lies. I was going to sneak on back out of there—I'd had enough of shamans. But then again, I had the idea, what if it was redlanders, maybe I ought to make sure, go tell the elders, you know."

"Right," Arnim said. "Smart."

That remark threw him off-kilter. Had no one ever told this kid he was smart? To figure out the best place to go trapping was where everyone else was afraid to go? To stick it out and gather intel where it was needed? He licked his lips. They were dry and patchy with peeling flakes of dead skin. Had Tymon had to chase the boy up into the hills, along some hunting trail?

"What I thought didn't matter though, because then there was this sound."

"What sound?"

"I can't describe it right. It was like a wind cutting through a canyon. It shrieked like an eagle on the hunt. But stopped after a minute or two. Everything else went quiet: the talkers, the mice in the underbrush, the birds in the trees. Even the lizards on the trail froze in place. I could feel the sound. It made the ground tremble."

"Ah, an earthquake," Arnim offered.

"No, nothing like that. It was more like what it feels like in a thunderstorm. The lightning strikes and something runs through the ground. You can feel it, if you're close. I've been close."

"Ya, ya," Kul broke in. "I was out in the open once, with only the one big tree nearby and a bolt came down and turned the tree to tinder and I felt like my feet and legs was on fire, only they wasn't."

I waved him to silence and leaned forward. "I think the important thing is: what did you see when you went to look for the source of that noise? Because you did, didn't you? You wanted to know what it was." I knew he would have. Girl or boy, this kind of person wouldn't be able to resist.

He nodded. "I couldn't help it. I had to know. I never heard anything like that. Not ever."

I waited, already sure of what was coming next.

"But this is the part where you tell me I'm possessed and send for the shaman."

"Not me. Shamans are frauds, and you don't look possessed, if there is such a thing."

He took a deep breath and examined his ragged fingernails, as if surprised to see them so rough and torn. His voice fell very soft, almost inaudible, "They wasn't people, or even redlanders, because those are people too, right, like us, just different. These, these wasn't people at all."

"Go on. If they weren't people, what were they?"

"Boss—" Arnim broke in excitedly. I gave him a look, and he silenced himself.

The boy's face twisted and he reached up to one ear, pulling at it as if he could drag an explanation out of his own head that way. "They was like … like big, big, ponies, with great thick legs. And instead of a head and neck they had like a body on top, like the top of a person's body, stuck-on, but not like something out of a spirit-story, something … something natural, like it was supposed to be that way, and they had rounded-off heads like big river rocks, with flat stripy faces on the front and no hair at all, not anywhere on them. And they was big, bigger than ponies."

"Bigger than a bear?" I prompted.

He nodded. "Yes. Some of them, anyhow."

"And …?"

He squirmed in his seat.

"Go on, I can tell there's more."

"Instead of arms they had …" He looked hesitantly at my team. I held up one hand with the signal for silence, and got back from each the blink or nod of agreement.

"Instead of arms …" I nudged.

The boy folded in on himself again, wrapping his arms around his body as if that would protect him from seven fighting men and one frustrated runner. He spoke rapidly, so fast I might not have followed if I hadn't known the answer already. "They had snakes. Giant snakes growing out their shoulders. And tiny snakes at the end of their arms-snakes, instead of fingers. And they waved them in the air, all the time they was talking, all the time they wasn't talking. And they moved like a swarm of bees, going in and out of this little house they had, a shiny little house set up in the middle of a meadow, where for sure it'd get flooded when the river comes up, like they was idiots, or fools, or just … just …" He ran out of words and simply rocked in his seat.

I let him be for a minute, as glances and nods passed among my men.

"Right, then," I said. "Tomorrow." I rapped on the table a third time, to make him look up. "How long to walk out to that place?" I asked. "Am I clear? You need to take us there, tomorrow."

He shook his head.

"What? Why not?"

"I'm not finished. I didn't tell you the worst part."

"There's something worse than snake—?" Andus started to say, but Karthi shushed him.

"The noise. It came back while I was watching."

"Right away?"

"No, no, I sat there a long time, watching them. It was like I couldn't move. It was like if I watched long enough, it would go away, go clear, that I'd wake up, see nothing but deer in the meadow. Like it should have been. But then, a while after, not very long, maybe a half-hour, I can't be sure, it happened again. The noise wasn't in the shiny house, I'm sure of it. No, it was out front of the house, and … now you have to know why you shouldn't go there."

"Why? Get on with it, my men aren't scared of anything."

"The noise ate them."

"What do you mean?"

"The noise started up, at a place out in front of the shiny house, and then two of the … the …"

"Snake-men." Andus said.

He laughed at that, and the hair flopping over his eyes made him an ordinary kid for a moment. "Ya, snake-men, that's good. Two of the snake-men turned and one took a few steps towards the noise, and then he vanished. And the other one, he did the same thing, he walked straight towards the noise—you could almost see it, like a mirage wavering in the air right where the noise was loudest—and then he vanished, too."

"Did it eat all of them?" I thought of the troop of snake-men we'd followed through the woods. They hadn't seemed like suicidal types. They acted like ordinary scouts. Ordinary scouts with snakes for arms and tree-trunks for legs. It had to be a thin patch. But the noise? Orkast never said anything about a noise, and if there was one thing he liked to talk about, it was thin patches.

"No, just those, then the other ones came out of their house and went back to talking. Or whatever you call it. I didn't stay any longer." He rubbed his nose and studied his fingers again.

"Were they still there the next time you went out?"

"I haven't been back since. I don't want to go back."

"That's not a choice you have." Did everyone in the boondocks think they could defy orders?

"Don't worry," Kul assured him. "We'll keep ya safe."

"You still think it was a waste of time to bring you here, Corren?" That was Tymon, standing behind Case.

I stood. "No. I want to see this with my own eyes. You, Calestinise, you're a brave person. Whether you're a boy or a girl, I don't care. None of us has a choice here. I'm responsible for border safety and you know where a dangerous thing is, so we have to go there, together, as soon as possible. Got it?"

He paled, but nodded. His voice came soft and musical, making it hard to remember he wasn't a girl. "All right. All right."

17

CALESTINISE PROVED A WORTHY GUIDE, as we followed him up the twisting route through the maze of fallen boulders.

Tymon took his usual spot at the front of the party, to walk next to Calestinise and badger him with questions. "So," he said, marching close by, at the head of our party. "You ever consider joining the runners? We've jobs up and down the whole country, could use a person who doesn't get lost."

"No," he said. "I've heard things about runners I don't like the sound of."

Tymon glanced back at me, over his shoulder, and said something else, a little too low for me to pick up.

"I don't care," he snapped.

"So, what's it like?" he asked, after a short silence. "You know, being a, well …"

"A trapper?" His voice rang with derision. "You put out traps, you go back later, when the stupid animals have got themselves stuck, you kill 'em, you skin 'em, you set the traps again. Nothing to it."

"Ah, sounds harder than you make out."

"No, it's like your business, right? You go out, catch somebody doing something stupid, you kill 'em, then you burn 'em, then you do it again." His voice echoed off the solid rock wall we walked under, and the words drilled into my head. *No,* I told myself, *there's more to it than that.*

Tymon tried again. "That's Corren, not me. Anyhow, I meant..."

"I know what you meant. And I'm not having that talk with you." At that, he picked up the pace. Tymon shut up and drifted to the back of the troop, while the rest of us saved our breath for keeping up with our guide.

When the route emerged from the narrows, we began to catch glimpses of the wider valley beyond, and it became a little easier to keep up with Calestinise without having to dodge around the rocks. At one point, the river made a sharp curve and I caught sight of something odd tossed up on the bank. "Hey, what's that down there?" I called out.

Case and Dramin after him jumped down from the pathway and clambered down to the object. It was square, flat, and reflective, more than a man's height in both dimensions. It might have been a carpet, but instead of wrapping itself around the rock it lay on, the thing stayed stiff.

Case caught hold of one edge and tugged. It shifted easily, as one unit.

"Doesn't weigh nothing," he called up. "But I'd swear it's made of metal." He gave it a little shake, and the sheet gave a rattling moan like the wails of a dozen ghosts. Dramin moved further upstream.

"The house," said Calestinise. "That's what the shiny house looked like, made of stuff like that."

At the same time, Dramin shouted out from upriver. "There's another piece here, Boss."

"I told you they shouldn't have put their house there. Flooding was bad this year, not just here in the Well. We had water in the streets of Tarak this spring, when the snow melted."

We've come all this way for nothing, then. If the snake-men's camp had been wiped out, there wouldn't be anything for us to see. My gut was more optimistic—with each step, it tightened, recommending a hasty retreat. I ignored it.

We pressed on. Tymon faded to the back of the party, kicking dirt as he walked alone.

Andus managed to get Calestinise talking. Seems the trick was to ask about anything other than Calestinise himself. We learned a fair amount on the art of placing traps as we followed him in a circuitous route, keeping out of the wide-open meadows, staying under cover. Step by step, we worked our way deep into the Well, the stone cliffs towering high, but seeming to walk away from us as the valley widened. Had that puny river carved this huge place?

"You don't want to get noticed," he said, and I wasn't sure if he was talking about alerting game or the snake-men. Either way, the path he chose largely followed the river, to take advantage of the trees clustered near the water. It made for rough going, because the trees were as likely to be lying down as standing up. "Floods, probably," he suggested, when I caught up and posed the question. My gut didn't like that answer. He seemed to catch something in my expression and added, "Floods happen in the spring. No chance of a flood now. Even if there's a big storm, it'll freeze up on the heights. Won't see anything down here."

"I thought that was your only time up in the Well."

"Stands to reason," he retorted. "Lowlanders know nothing about living in the mountains." That came with a tight sneer that would have fit on the face of any man proud of his place.

"Well, then," I challenged, "you should come back to Jeskaryan with us, give my father and his councilors a few lessons about the mountains."

The sneer faded to a grim line. "Someone like me wouldn't be ..." His face shifted again; I could see the thought crystallizing in his mind. He whipped around, started walking backwards up a relatively clear patch of trail, and ran his eyes over the lot of us. As his mouth twisted to a frown, his jaw tightened and his eyes narrowed. He turned and picked up speed again, but I caught up to him, so that we walked side-by-side.

I tried to push backwards to my invitation. "I was serious. Mountain territory's a place where our plans and strategies are lacking."

He started to respond, but thought better of it. "We're nearly there. Best shut up." His eyes slid to mine, so I gave him my expressionless soldier's face and said nothing.

Imitating that walking-backwards trick, I turned to give the troop our signal for *silence*. Then my heel caught in an outstretched branch lying on the ground and I went flat on my back. I expected Calestinise to hold out a hand to help me up, but he only stood over me with crossed arms until I got myself back to my feet.

As we moved on in silence, I worked through his reactions. So Tymon had let Calestinise know he'd be meeting with a troop of guardsmen out of Jeskaryan, but didn't tell which troop. *The kid doesn't like troopers in general. Fair enough, for someone on the borderlands. Maybe he's got a cousin or uncle who's gone out for banditry. But is it our troop he doesn't like, or is it me?*

Not long after, I signaled a halt. We took drinks, checked our boots and our gear, all without a word. He stood back and watched us and likewise said nothing.

At close to midday, as we moved into a particularly dense patch of undergrowth, he stopped, lowered himself to the ground, and proceeded to crawl under the sheltering bushes. The packs were a problem, but I wasn't leaving anything behind, not with snake-men to deal with, maybe. I gave the signal to spread out, stay in sight, and we each found our own route through the little copse, to the very edge of a wide, sunlit meadow. From where we crouched, we couldn't see above the swaying stalks of grass. I scooted over to behind the nearest tree, eased myself up to my feet, and peered around the trunk.

A breeze swept across the standing grasses, making waves across the field as if it were a golden lake. The waves billowed and flowed away from us, leading our eyes straight to the snake-men.

Yes. They were there. Not many. Two of them—one a sort of greenish-yellow that almost blended in with the grass and the other a bright orange—bent over something on the ground. When their arms came up, I could see tools clutched in their snaky fingers. The third one reminded me of the commander of that company of scouts. It went beyond the pinkish-rose coloring; it was also the way he acted, waving his arms around, wriggling his fingers as he gave orders, and doing absolutely nothing himself. He had one of those books like the studious one, and his was defective, too. Occasionally, he'd look at it, say something, and rap the surface as if punishing the thing. Did they seal their books with locks? I hoped he'd toss it aside so I could slip over there after dark and retrieve it.

At one point, the two workmen set their tools down and began to stretch those weird arms to pick things up from the ground. One loaded himself with small objects that he tucked into pockets on his oddly-hanging clothing, and ended by hefting a large bag that needed both his arms to manage. So that was the end of his arm-waving. The other one lifted two long strips of the same shiny stuff that we'd found at the bend in the river. He held them flat against each other, then rolled them into a tight, shiny tube that he secured under one arm. With his free arm, he stretched down once more and brought up a bag like his buddy's, about as large, but maybe not as heavy, since he seemed to need just the one arm to lift it.

Then they stood there, waiting, shifting their loads slightly, as men do, to keep muscles from cramping under a constant load. Finally, the foreman tapped his broken book once more and barked out an order. The three of them stood very still.

Then the noise came.

Calestinise had described it precisely. The noise came more from the ground than from the sky, but still it sounded like an eagle screaming, like thunder, like a wind at night tearing through a canyon. I wanted to shout, but my men kept silent, and therefore so could I. I clung tight to the tree, to keep myself still. Out in the meadow, the snake-men formed up into a tidy queue, for all the world like a group of little children lining up for the privy. So they were on the march. I glanced up at the surrounding cliffs and wondered where the snake-men thought they were going with such a load of crap to carry.

Then I remembered Calestinise's story, and kept my eyes on the snake-men.

The camouflaged one, the green-and-yellow snake-man with the heavy bag, headed out first. He took three steps, and then I could see it: the thin patch, shimmering in the air like a mirage over a road on a hot day. Green-and-yellow took another step, and then he was grey-and-yellow. Then another step. And he was gone.

Rosy-red gave a melodious shout, waving his arms, and Orange tightened his grip on his roll of shiny stuff and his loaded bag, and followed his partner. First, he was silhouetted against the wavering patch of air, then he was grey-and-orange, then he was gone.

Rosy-red, with no one to give orders to, nevertheless waved his arms as he circled the area quickly. He pushed his book into a large pocket and filled other pockets with small objects as he found them in the grass. Then without further hesitation, he completed his final check and marched into the shimmer.

"Well, that's that," I said.

"Shh," Calestinise said, still watching the snake-men's camp.

A grey silhouette appeared in the shimmer, then turned blue, and a fourth snake-man emerged.

I knew him. I recognized that shade of blue from my nightmares. Those thin orange stripes than ran down his arms, I remembered those, too. I recognized the way he moved, the languorous walk, the slow, appreciative taking-in of the scenery. The idiot who couldn't recognize a spear but could drop ten men in ten seconds with a twig he carried in his pocket.

He pulled one of those books out of a pocket and held it up, like it was a painting he was admiring, and gave it an affectionate tap. Then he turned in a tiny, slow circle, holding the book up exactly the same, the whole time. Some kind of parting ceremony?

The noise only lasts a few minutes, he says. And it doesn't come back for at least a half-hour. And this guy's an idiot.

The instant his back was turned to me, I began to run. I heard my men plunge out of the undergrowth after me. We ran in silence, intent on fulfilling our failed mission of three years back.

He turned faster than I'd anticipated, hurrying for his own reasons, maybe. Blue had nearly turned all the way around, his gaze focused on the book, completely unaware of us, when a long red snake emerged from the shimmer behind him, wrapped its writhing fingers into his jacket and jerked him backwards. He lowered the book as he stumbled back… and he saw us. In the moment that his hindquarters went grey, he raised his other arm and waggled those snake-fingers at me. Then he was gone.

The sound ceased.

The wind waves flowed across the empty meadow.

18

WE ARGUED all the way back to Tarak.

Arnim wanted to stay and go over the multitudinous tracks that ran up and down the valley from the snake-men's abandoned camp. What good was it that he could tell one snake-man's tracks from another? During the half-hour we waited for the thin patch to reappear, Karthi and Andus scoured the area and retrieved an assortment of bits and pieces that might or might not be something. When the thin patch failed to show—confirming my notion that the snake-men were leaving permanently—the two collectors objected to leaving, certain they would find something significant if they had more time.

Kul was convinced if we ranged far enough from the trampled area, we'd find some sign of our lost prisoner, Ta-ma. Footprints, at least. She'd gone off with those creatures, hadn't she? Why not come back with them, too? That notion got Tymon's interest, and the two of them made up several ridiculous theories of how Ta-ma would have told the snake-men about us and talked them into bringing her here.

"Why would she come here?" I argued. "Wouldn't she want to go back where they picked her up?"

"The blue guy was here. We all saw him."

They had a point. But there was no human woman consorting with the snake-men.

Calestinise agreed. "Who would be crazy enough go off with those monsters?" he declared.

Dramin wanted us out of there as fast as possible. He was done with our keeping the snake-men a secret; we should have reported directly to the king the first time, he said. They'd turn up again, somewhere, and it was now clear to us that they had *made* their thin patch.

I didn't want to worry Yutek with any of this business, though I was open to *interviewing* some shamans, about that one real thing: the thin patches. Could shamans really spot them? How? Should we be posting shamans along the borders, watching for snake-men? Dangerous other-world invaders were the last thing my foster-father needed, what with the bad crops in the north driving increased banditry on the border, with the Southerners itching to deploy their battle skills again. Case sided with me, and I set him to persuading Dramin.

Kul then decided that Calestinise needed to go home with him, to be adopted into his family, because obviously the lassie's family didn't understand her and his would welcome her, never mind whether she said she was a girl or not. Calestinise was having none of that. He pushed Kul away—and it was a treat to see that chubby little thing put a hand on his chest and shove him backwards—and marched straight to me.

"You have to make them stop it," he told me.

"Stop what?"

"Calling me a girl. I'm not a girl. I'm a man."

"No, you're not." I could see the argument brewing, but there wasn't any way to head it off.

"I am so."

"Listen." I stopped, and pulled him aside, and waved for the rest to march by. "Let's get this straight. You're coming back with us—"

"I am not—"

"Yes, you are, because I need someone who isn't under my command to tell this story to the right people."

He shut his mouth tight and held his tongue for once.

"Who do you think you're arguing with, here? You're not a man, and you're not going to convince any of my men that you are. Just look at them. They're trained guardsmen, they've fought for their country, they've lost their fellow soldiers—Andus there, little Andus, he saw his own brother skewered, and he went on and killed Southerners, one by one, that whole long day. So all right, you're a boy. That's fine, but you're no man, not to them, not to me."

So then he went and proved my point by bursting into tears.

"I do a man's work," he cried. "I support myself and I don't take any guff from anybody. My mother and my sisters and my aunts didn't know what to do with me, they turned me out when I got my womanhood, because I wouldn't wear the clothes, do women's work, look for a … a boy … to … to … you know. It wasn't that I was being a bad girl, I just was never a girl, not ever. Then I heard it, in the marketplace. They was afraid I'd try to marry a girl and embarrass everybody. I lost my home because they was worried I might ruin someone else."

Ahead of us, Tymon was about to disappear around the next bend. He gave me that sarcastic fake salute of his, and I knew he wouldn't be coming to my rescue.

Calestinise looked up at me with those dark, red, puffy eyes, with his nose dripping and hot, angry tears streaking through the dust on his cheeks.

"Well." I hesitated, wondering if I should, or if I shouldn't, but it came out anyway. "Karthi and Andus are a couple, I'm pretty sure, and nobody gives them any … *guff.*"

"What?" He stopped sobbing.

"You heard me. I'm not saying it twice. It's not any of my business. But you need to know. Your family might care, for their own stupid reasons. But no one else cares, not anyplace south of Tarak. The worst they're going to do is use the wrong words, and then it's on you to be angry or not."

"The wrong words?" Was he himself unaware of what made his eyes blaze every time anyone said *she* or *her*?

"So let's compromise." Did people this age understand the art of compromise? "You're a boy, until such time as you grow up and prove yourself grown up. And I'll make everyone use the right words—he and him and all that—until every time anyone looks at you, that's what they see, and they won't need reminded."

He stared up at me, blinking away the last of the tears.

"All right," he said, finally.

"And you're coming with us."

"No."

I might have groaned. I'd heard adults complain about arguing with kids, but never had tried it myself. I swore I'd never sire a child if I'd have to do this ever again. I took a deep breath, measured the length of the shadows, and said, "Why not?"

"I promised Tymon I'd take him somewhere first."

"What? Where?" It had to be something big, if he'd agreed to go anywhere with Tymon, after the way he kept annoying him.

"There was an herbalist he wanted to meet."

"Tymon wants to meet a healer-woman? Why?"

He shrugged. "Not for me to say. But he's paying me a bundle to take him there, so why should I care?"

He was lying about some part of that. I figured he knew Tymon's reasons but had been paid not to tell. I blew a long breath through my teeth. Then I shrugged my pack tighter on my shoulders and took off at a run, after Tymon. *He'd better have a good reason for this. And he'd better bring the boy back to Jeskaryan with him. Or else.*

19

I DRAGGED AN EXPLANATION out of Tymon over dinner, using a flagon of wine recommended by Case himself. No, what are you thinking? It had nothing to do with recruiting Calestinise to the runners.

It turned out the boy had mentioned that recently, on a trip to a hamlet up north, selling off his furs, he'd met a healer-woman, one of those people who sell useless herbs and such. This herbalist had one of those non-opening books, like the snake-men had. Somehow, someone had stumbled across one of those things out in the wilderness and hauled it back to civilization. Or what passed for civilization up north.

One of us needed to go get that book, and Tymon was right, it needed to be him. First, because I couldn't talk to an herbalist without letting it be known how I felt about the entire profession. Second, because anywhere I went, the Six went, and we'd likely create more resistance by turning up in one of those little towns that bred bandits like open fields bred ground-dogs. I still felt there was something else Tymon was up to, but I wanted that book recovered, and Calestinise's wits were more than a match for my brother's thoughtless curiosity.

We parted in an unusual state of harmony, for those times. I got Calestinise to agree to go south with Tymon after they'd met up with the healer, though the boy insisted it was on trial and I had to write it down on paper that he wouldn't be a prisoner. Not that he could read the paper. I'm not sure how much he believed us, but our boy was willing to take a runner's word, even if it was Tymon. I didn't blame the kid. Regular people generally don't trust the government and are leery of soldiers, and wasn't I both?

The rest of us called a belated end to the year's northern-border cleanup operations, and made our way down to Jeskaryan, arriving in the city barely ahead of the first major rain of the season. I waited for Tymon, but he didn't show. I wouldn't have expected Calestinise to come alone, so with no Tymon, I had no witness to take to the shamans. Or to Yutek, for that matter.

For the first month at home, my foster-father kept me busy. There was new intel from the south, useful intelligence for a change, that spoke of military buildups coupled with some kind of political turmoil at their end. Yutek had a hunch that the southern king—he was called Kor, a similarity in names that gave me the creeps and made Yutek laugh every time he used it—might decide to unify his kingdom by waging war on us. I was glad Case had persuaded Dramin to keep a lid on the whole snake-men business. Surely that was all over, now, anyway. My gut disagreed, reminding me, *If they can build a machine that takes them to the Well, couldn't they build one that takes them to, say, Kor's palace?*

At one point, I hired myself a runner and sent her up to Tarak, regardless of the extra cost, it being a long, muddy road there and back. She returned with no news whatsoever. Neither Tymon nor his "boy guide" had been seen by anybody.

Solstice came and went. I had the Six drilling their on-again off-again troops, the men we'd taken for the cleanup at Heart's Bend. It seemed likely to me we'd be seeing some kind of action soon enough. I conferred with Magaran, who'd risen to commander by then, and we implemented the new organization for the army, the one we'd been working on since NeverSnows. Now, the Guard had autonomous units able to strike out independently but also able to fold into a unified force when called upon. I worked up trainings for likely young officers to lead these strike teams.

It was a grand time, running that school, making those plans. I'd bring in one or another of the Six to talk tactics and skills and how to put together a team that complemented one another, instead of a troop of identical men, each with the same half-developed abilities. I remember Kul standing in front of these young men—half of them from privileged families—instructing them in his north-country brogue, "Ya gots ta build each and every team from scratch, make it so every man knows to cover the other, and knows how without ya having to holler orders. A good troop is a beast, a live thing that runs, and fights, and thinks for itself."

Finally, on a slow morning when I'd decided to go down to the Shamans' House and fish for more intel about thin patches, the Master Shaman came to see me. He turned up in my office—the space that had been Captain Magaran's when I was a mere lieutenant—grunting under the weight of a thick, ornamented trunk, and he dropped the thing on my work table.

I invited him to sit and pulled my own supply of cider from the cupboard where Magaran had used to keep his. We sipped politely for a few minutes, until I ran out of patience.

"What's this?" I asked. "What do you need from me?"

He gestured to the box. "Go ahead. Open it. Won't bite." He grinned at some shaman in-joke.

I scowled and got up to my knees to get the lid open.

Sure enough, inside was my father's cape.

"I told you," I said, slamming the lid down with a crack like a head hitting a wall. "I'm not going for a shaman. Look here, I'm the king's heir, I'm a captain in the guards, I have plenty of work to do. Find someone else."

"That's the thing," he said.

"What is?"

"We can't find someone else. You know full well your father meant this for you. Would you dishonor his memory?"

It was a low blow, that, summoning my loyalty to Orkast. I parried with the shamans' key motivation. "You'll get more profit from someone else. You realize I'm dependent on the state, Master Shaman? I have no funds of my own for your initiation fees. Surely you can find some toff that wants the job whose mother will pay you to take him off her hands." I'd heard plenty of upper-class younglings pining for the easy life of a shaman. *They don't even know how easy it is to run around playing pretend while getting paid so much people toss their kids out on the street to cover your invoices.*

He sighed and downed the last of his cider. For the first time, I noticed the lines on his face, the sag in his cheeks, the way his eyelids seemed stuck at half-open. Like Yutek, the head shaman had gotten old. "It's more complicated than you think. And no. Since you're not a shaman, it's not something you can know the details of." He sighed again, and rubbed his hand over his face. "Why can't you be more like your father? Imagine what you could do with both skills—a soldier's and a shaman's. Have a little faith." His eyes had a glassy, dreamy sheen that gave me the shivers.

"Well." I wanted to shut off the topic, but... *Now's your chance*, my gut said, *get to it.* "There's one thing I *know*. One thing that's not a matter of belief."

"Oh?" He raised one eyebrow, ready for a fresh load of sarcasm from me.

"The thin patches."

"What about them?" I expect he'd heard every joke about thin patches by now. He even tensed a little, waiting for the punch line.

"They're real."

"So you believe that much, then?" His face remained taut, still wired-up for a blow, but his eyes brightened.

"I don't need to believe. I've seen one. I've seen ... people ... go in one. I've seen someone come out of one."

The mug fell out of his fingers. It hit the table, and a fine spray of cider splashed over the table, his sleeve, and his lap. "You've what?"

"I've seen a thin patch in action." I pulled a rag off the bottom shelf and tossed it to him. He patted the spill absently. I went on, "I've been meaning to come talk to you about that. I've been so busy. You understand."

"Yes, yes." His eyes were vague, maybe wary.

I pushed my own drink off to one side and leaned over the table towards him. "So. I'd like to compare notes. Does every thin patch look the same, for instance? Are some bigger than others? Are there any rules about where they can and can't turn up? You can see that this matters to me, right? That people from somewhere else might jump into a thin patch and turn up anywhere, with no warning—that matters to this government, to the Guard, to me."

"I'm not at liberty to discuss such things outside the brotherhood," he said, beginning slowly, then rushing his words so they ran together. He gave the ornamented box a push towards me. "If you've seen a thin patch, then you should do it, you should take the mantle, join us, then I can tell you all." He coughed and gave the box another push. "As a legacy initiate, we'd waive your fees, young Corren." I might have stuck a knife in him, the pain in his face was so clear.

He needed reminded I had another legacy. "Captain."

"What?" He rubbed his chest, almost as if feeling for a knife in his ribs.

"It's *Captain* Corren, heir to the kingship of Jeska. Don't be forgetting who you're talking to." I shoved the box back to his side of the table. "Whatever secrets you're holding, they belong to Jeska. Your Brotherhood exists only to the extent it serves the best interests of this nation."

"But—But—"

I banged my fist on the table, hard enough that I could feel the grain of the wood marking my skin. The shaman's empty mug toppled off the edge of the table and into his lap.

"You'll talk," I told him. "You'll talk here and now, and you'll tell me everything I need to know, about the thin patches and what's behind them. You've not got any secrets you can keep from me. I've seen the snake-men."

"The what men?" His surprise seemed oddly genuine. "You've gone through a thin patch and met men who play with snakes?"

"I haven't gone through a thin patch, and it's men who *look* like snakes."

"Then where did you see them, if not on the Other Side? Only the shamans go through the thin patches, only the shamans can see them, with our ... our ..." His eyes strayed to the rack on the wall beside him, where my swords hung: the one I carried on our forays to the border, the big one for battles, the practice sword with its dull edge. "You have to understand, no one has ever seen anything like you say."

"Like what?"

"Like man-snakes." He took in a sharp breath, seemed to come to some decision of his own. "Those people you saw going in and out of the thin patch, were they … shamans? Were you following shamans around, to learn our secrets? That's wrong, Prince Corren, it goes against our agreements with the government."

"Captain. *Captain* Corren."

"Whatever you say, *Captain*." His lips tightened over his teeth, as if he might have been laughing at me.

"I'm serious," I said. "Don't make me prove to you how serious." I reached down to my leg, drew my long knife, and laid it on the table between us, its dagger-point aimed at his heart.

His eyes fixed on the gleam along the blade. "I'll say it again. No shaman has reported seeing men made of snakes. Or any men, for that matter. We've seen strange enough creatures on the Other Side …" For no good reason, he reached out a hand and laid it on the box. "But we haven't found people. There's never been any worry to the king, the thin patches aren't to other places in the world, the world we know, with people in it, they're to spirit places, where we commune with the greater universe."

"That spirit stuff, that's a load of crap, and you know it."

"It is not."

"Yes, it is. Remember, I know more than your average person. However, my father told me the thin patches are real. And even that I didn't believe until I saw it for myself."

He shrugged. "Believe as much or as little as you want. But this business of snake-men, that's utter nonsense."

"Twice now, I've seen them," I told him. "And my men, my brother, and our guide."

"Your men will say whatever you order them to say. And I say someone has deceived you, there's no such thing as snake-men. Snakes crawl on the ground and slither away at the approach of men. What's to be afraid of? How could snakes be people?"

"Augh," I grunted in disgust, then leaned back and tried to read his expression. *I should get Arnim in here*, I thought. As luck would have it, Karthi stuck his head through the drape right about then.

"Everything all right?" he said. He gathered in the scene, everything from the colorful box to the upended mug. "Anything I can get you, Boss?"

"We're fine here," I told him. "I'm having a chat with my dad's old boss, talking about old times. Say, could you send Arnim up here? It's just I had a question about the cider."

"Ah," he said, and barely hesitated as he translated the code from *a question about the cider* to *catch a liar.*

The shaman picked up his mug and sniffed it. "There's something wrong with the drink?"

"No, no, but this is my ordinary stuff." I gave him my best fake smile, and I could tell he knew it was fake. "Maybe if I give you some of the good stuff, you'll be more … cooperative."

In no time at all, Arnim stepped in, a tall flagon in one hand and a pair of mugs in the other. As the drape fell back, I caught a glimpse of Kul standing at the doorway, his back to us, his hand on the hilt of his sword. The shaman had looked to the doorway when Arnim flicked the drape open, so I knew that he saw as well. *Good.*

Arnim eased himself down next to me and set the new mugs on the table. He topped mine off first, then filled the other two. Setting one cup safely to his left, he reached over the table to hand the other to the shaman. "Pleased to meet you, your honor, sir," he said, all open and honest in his face and voice. "I've always wanted to interview a shaman. You don't mind my sitting in, Boss, do you?"

"Of course not, Arnim."

The shaman's eyes flicked to the doorway. "What's going on here?" he asked.

"I told you," I said. "You're going to answer my questions, and my man Arnim here—" I settled my hand on Arnim's shoulder as I spoke "— is going to listen in. He's a master at listening, this man."

"Thank you, Boss," Arnim said, picking up his mug and sipping slowly, his eyes fixed on the face of our subject.

20

I'D KNOWN FENNIC since I was a kid tagging along with my true-father on my days off, and the Master Shaman had always gone out of his way to be obsequiously kind to me. And to Tymon, too, when Fennic caught me out on the street with my foster brother. Even as a kid, I didn't trust his motives. The sneaky shaman talked my father into abandoning me to the royals, didn't he? Tymon would always push back at my anger, tell me the old man meant well, but my shoulder blades itched in his presence, like they'd used to do when Yutek the Younger stalked the halls of the king's house, looking for victims.

I'll admit I itched to conduct this interrogation in a less... verbal ... way, but I wasn't a raw lieutenant anymore and, besides, an experienced liar like Fennic wouldn't likely yield to physical tactics. My advantage in the situation had to be Arnim, with his sharp eyes and upper-class sensibilities on the alert. I had to face up to being disappointed that for once, the Master Shaman wasn't lying. He'd never heard of any people—snake-men or otherwise—coming out of thin patches. Not here in Jeska or elsewhere. Shamans went into thin patches, on their own and one at a time. He'd hardly ever done the deed himself.

That made sense—he struck me as the kind of man destined for politics, not action. Shamans didn't *make* thin patches, he insisted. They searched them out, using their eyes. It didn't seem to me that he meant what we usually mean by "use your eyes." It sounded like some kind of divination, more of that spirit-world nonsense. I would have guessed that they really found them by accident, but the world is a big place. You don't just stumble across things like that.

Arnim managed to draw out details on the topic. He had a talent for teasing a man's pride into saying something that maybe he shouldn't. Interestingly, the old man's description of thin patches didn't match what we'd seen. Or heard. He kept referring to them as *the silence between worlds*. On the third round of drinks, he rambled into a description of a visit to a "spirit plane" where the land lay under a pall of endless shadow, a shadow belched forth by a distant mountain with endless fire glowing at its peak. Talking it over later, Arnim posed the idea that somehow the thin patch had transported Fennic to the far north, where there are real fire-mountains. Alternatively, he might have made up the story to impress others—and told it so many times he'd come to believe it himself.

Clearly, from the specifics he let drop, shaman journeys went somewhere physical, not to a spiritual plane of existence. So that mirrored what we'd seen. The snake men were weird, but they were people, not ghosts or demons. They made tools, they talked to each other, some of them worked hard, and some gave orders. Some were smart and some were idiots. If only I'd managed to catch that blue one, we'd know so much more. It would have been fun to interrogate one of those creatures, but I'd trade an interview for one of those weapons of theirs.

I ached to know if the snake-men had made a new thin patch somewhere, if they were bringing their strange tools and interesting weapons to some other mountain valley. The lack of reports of anything strange suggested their hiding out in unoccupied places was intentional. If they wanted to interact with people, wouldn't they put their noisy thin patch down the hill? We sent Fennic back to his guildhouse annoyed at being questioned and frustrated that he hadn't persuaded me to shift allegiances. I hoped I wouldn't see that mantle again, but didn't hold out much hope he'd give up on whatever scheme he was brewing.

•   •   •

The rest of the winter went on as before, only more so. We had new recruits to train, officers needing drilled in the new command structure, funds to wheedle out of my foster-father's treasury for weapons, clothing, food. In the middle of everything, Yutek took it into his head to make me governor of Lakeside. He put it to me that I needed to train in governance, not only in military maneuvers. I hated the idea, but I had put myself at his command, his word was my law, so every moment outside my guard duties was spent learning about Lakeside.

The district had been annexed relatively recently, a hundred years back. It had its own rules, its own way of going about some things. The previous governor, he might have managed to keep his criminality hidden better if he'd taken the time to understand the place. For now, Yutek had put some oldster in charge, a man who'd worked for a previous governor, one not quite qualified in and of himself, but a person the people found acceptable enough to put up with for a while. Yutek thought to give him a holiday from duty and put me down there for—I dreaded to think of it—a year.

Worse, I had the sense that should I succeed at that posting, my next assignment would involve an arrangement with some important family that would put an end to my happy little household down in town, me and Eldennian and the baby.

I've left that off, haven't I? We'd headed home from Tarak by way of Koresh, as promised. I could hardly sleep the night through, the day before we got there. Then, on the way from Koresh to Jeskaryan, she told me. Everyone laughed at me when she did, because they already knew. Turns out that was the real reason she'd stayed in Koresh. It was inevitable. Two people couldn't be like we were for too long without procreating. Arnim pulled some strings through a family connection, for a house in town. My men fixed up the place as a baby-gift, and Deliasin arrived in the middle of winter. Not the best time for an infant, what with the cold and the damp, and people coming and going with one illness and another. But she was a strong little creature, reminded me of Calestinise in that.

We were celebrating Deliasin's name-day, right after the spring planting had started, me and the Six and Eldennian and her mother, too, clustered around the table in that little house, when Tymon came in the door. A cheer went up from the men, and Arnim stood, as he always did, to make a place for my brother at the table.

Tymon paused in the doorway and turned, gesturing to someone behind him.

Good, I thought, *he managed to get Calestinise to come with him after all. He'll do better here than up north, even if he doesn't help me get more out of the shamans.*

Sure enough, there was our girl-looking boy, that mass of hair stuffed under a woven cap, as the Tarakmen do, but wearing a Jeskan-style shirt, oversized, that did a better job of smoothing over his curves than his old Tarak-style tunic. Before anyone else could say anything, I stood and said, "There he is! The boy who led us up into the Well. I've told you about him, Eldennian."

"Yes, indeed you have, many a time. Welcome, lad," she said to him.

He put his eyes down and muttered something grateful-sounding at the floor and shuffled his feet. Eldennian's mother jumped up from her seat and offered him a plate loaded with cake.

Meanwhile, Tymon had again turned back to the door.

"Wait," I called. "You're staying, aren't you?"

I couldn't read his expression. "That remains to be seen, brother."

Then he reached through the doorway again, took the hand of someone out there, and drew him—no, her—into the room.

"Wel—" Eldennian began, then fell silent, running her eyes over the strange face of the newcomer.

The Six, to a man, sucked in breath and held it, watching me.

Ta-ma.

He'd found Ta-ma.

21

I T WAS WORSE THAN YOU THINK.

Ta-ma came in, ordinary-looking in northern-style women's clothes, with a plain grey work-dress running halfway to her knees and dark grey trousers hiding her legs. Her washed-out brown hair hung straight and fine, clean and combed, like and yet unlike a regular woman's hair. She still had that weak-tinted skin, but it only showed on her face and hands, and she'd cut her hair to cover her brow and hang close on the sides, so she could hide her face by dropping her head a little.

Now, though, she kept her head up and took stock of the crowd in the room. She recognized me, I could tell by the way her eyes pinched when they passed over my face. She stepped to Tymon's side, and his long arm wrapped over her shoulders. She looked up at him with that expression I'd seen before.

"I think you know my wife," Tymon said. He bent his head towards her and said, very low, "It's all right. Go ahead."

"I, I'm happy to meet you all," Ta-ma said then, her thin voice clear, but tight. Her lips hardly moved as she spoke. At last, her eyes fell on Deliasin and lit up. She said, "Hello, baby," and her voice went high-pitched and sing-songy the way people do when they're talking to infants.

Eldennian didn't speak, as she moved her eyes from me to Ta-ma and back, then pulled Deliasin close. Her mother moved from where she stood by Calestinise, gave Tymon and Ta-ma a warm hospitable bow, and gestured to the table.

She stalked up behind Karthi and Andus and flicked a towel at their heads. "Where are your manners? Look you, Tymon's come all this way and's brought a new wife home. Make a place, you two, go up the stairs there and fetch down a few chairs now."

With Mother Andelian ordering everyone around for the next several minutes, the worst of the moment passed. Once everyone was seated again, I opened my mouth to ask Tymon a few questions, but Andelian stood and raised her cup and launched into the toasts to the day, this day that was meant to be about our Deliasin, and only about her. Well, her and Eldennian.

I had my toast prepared, but every time I looked across the table at Tymon and Ta-ma, the words drained right out of my head. My hand slipped down to rest on my leg, where I could feel the hilt of my favorite long knife, and I thought about whether Ta-ma would be as informative as I needed her to be, now that she could talk properly. When Kul stood to make his toast, I dragged my sight away from the pair of them, sitting there snuggled together like any pair of real newlyweds, arms linked, hands clasped, her head tipped to rest against his shoulder. Instead, I watched Calestinise pick at the heap of sweets in front of him, and fire anxious, embarrassed glances at Tymon and Ta-ma. When the boy caught me spying, he jabbed a thumb towards them, rolled his eyes, and held both hands over his ears as if trying to block out a horrible noise.

That broke their hold on my mood. It was too good of a day to obsess over Tymon's self-deceptions. I burst out laughing in the middle of Kul's *may yer days be as long an' beautiful as yer mother's own hair.*

I stood and clapped Kul on the shoulder and told him "Thank you. I'm sure none of us can top that wish, my friend."

"I meant all them words, Boss," Kul said.

"I know you did, I know." I let my vision fill with the sight of Eldennian and the fuzz-crowned squirming creature in her arms. For this moment, I didn't need to think about interrogating Ta-ma or fighting with Tymon or even interrupting Kul. I snatched up my cup, raised it, and made up new words, better words. "Deliasin, may you be as lucky as I was the day I first met Eldennian and may you be as direct as your mother when you find the man you want, so he can never refuse you, as I can never refuse her."

Eldennian made the strangest of sounds then, a noise I suddenly recognized as a sob, and tears ran down her face. *What did I say wrong?* She swallowed and coughed, then held out her hand for a cup. While Dramin was refilling her mug, she told me, "You never said finer words, my Corren. I'll not forget them." When everyone was ready, she paused before the usual words and said, with a smile for each of us, "May you be as brave as your father, Deliasin, and as clever, and may you bring such people as these close to you."

Then she lifted the baby up, so we could see that scrunched-up horrible little beauty of a face, and said, "This is Deliasin. Let us all here speak her name."

And together we lifted our cups and cried, "Deliasin!"

The rest of the afternoon was nothing but an ordinary party, with the men egging each other into greater and greater feats of drinking, and Eldennian and her mother passing the baby back and forth. I caught Ta-ma watching the women with Deliasin, and her face had an odd, wistful, almost hungry look to it. *Is she pregnant or wishing for it?*

I kept my eyes on my brother the whole while. Finally, Tymon excused himself from Ta-ma to head for the privy out back. On his return, he found me blocking the doorway.

"It's all yours, Corren," he laughed, stepping to one side with a little bow and a broad sweep of his arm.

"I'm fine," I told him. "You and I need to talk."

"Later, later, what's your rush?"

"What's going on here? Is she pregnant?" Tymon was all right with the kids at Runners' House, but it was hard to imagine him as a father.

"What? No! Well, not that I know of..." His voice trailed off and his eyes grew misty.

I caught him by the arm and pulled him around the edge of the house, under the shade of the live oak that spread over the tiny lot, keeping anything else from growing back there.

"I send you to get information from a north country herb-seller, and you come back—months late—with no information but with the woman who knows what happened to my father. Even if she decided she wanted a baby off you—does she know what it means to marry a runner? Were you that flattered? Have you lost your mind, Tymon?"

"There's more to it than that." He edged past me, keeping one eye on the door and the other on the knife at my side. "Let's talk tomorrow, or the day after."

"Let's talk now." My knife was in my hand, then. I'm not sure how it got there. I pressed its point into the front of his shirt, barely piercing the fabric.

"You're drunk," he said.

"I'm not. I'm angry." Why was he being so difficult? What had I ever done to Tymon? "You owe me answers."

Moving faster than I would have expected from Tymon—but then again, maybe he was right, maybe I was slowed by drink—he took my arm by the wrist and wrenched it away, then squeezed with that oversized hand of his until my fingers went numb and the knife fell. My favorite knife, falling tip-first. Any little stone in the ground would dull that tip, grind irregularities into the knife edge. I gasped and dropped to my knees, catching the blade before it could strike.

"I don't owe you anything, Corren," Tymon said, and he stepped over my outstretched hands, the knife cradled between them, blood running down between my fingers. He disappeared into the house.

You owe me. You've forgotten all you owe me, Tymon.

I staggered to my feet, sheathed the knife, and leaned against the wall until Eldennian came for me.

PART III

THE COMMANDER MAKES HIS CHOICES

22

MY NEXT PROMOTION came into effect and ruined my plan to drag Ta-ma in for questioning. Yutek had his own plans, and those generated endless, intense conferences regarding the governorship of Lakeside. Magaran wanted that promotion justified, meaning taking workshops with other new commanders, and then conducting trainings of captains and junior officers in the new protocols. I had hardly any time even for regular workouts with my Six.

It didn't help that Tymon made it complicated, staying by her side at all times. One might have laughed it off as a senior runner playing at being a newlywed, but to me it was clear: he was protecting her.

From me.

I'd walk into a room, and he'd jump to his feet and place himself between us. If they were the ones entering, Tymon would either turn around and leave without comment or shift positions to block my view of her. It was funny for a while, but became tiresome.

Forced to delegate, I commissioned Andus to follow them around, make himself useful, glean what he could from their conversation. He came back with less than I wanted, but more than I'd have guessed.

"Ta-ma changed her name." Andus paused for a reaction, but I was struggling with a page of accounts Yutek wanted me to analyze. "She's taken a more Jeska-style one: Heyliannin."

"Why?" I drew a line between two numbers that matched, but shouldn't have.

"That's not clear, maybe to fit in?"

"Does she expect to fit in, looking like she does?" I stared at the numbers I'd linked. Was one a payoff to the other or were both payoffs to someone else?

"It's not that bad, Boss, when you see her in proper clothes. Most people don't give her a second glance."

Much of what had gone badly in Lakeside involved illicit cashflow. It wasn't that difficult, but it made my eyes glaze over. "What are their children going to look like, can you imagine that?"

Andus rolled his eyes like Tymon might have done. "Do ya ever listen to yourself, Boss? To continue … they were arguing about whether to stay in the Runners' House or move to town."

I put down my pen. Both numbers were bribes. They matched for a reason, but this page wasn't going to give me that. "I'm not surprised that made for an argument."

"No?"

"Runners have their ways."

"Ah." Andus gave the cider jug behind me a wistful look. "I'd always thought those stories of runners and their games were nasty rumors."

"They're not stories, but I wouldn't call them nasty." I watched his face, the way he controlled his expression. I couldn't tell what he was thinking, but I could guess. "Use your brain. Runners have to live different, the way they're constantly coming and going. They're not playing games; it's serious; they're wedded to each other the moment they sign up. It's part of the contract. The kids get whole generations of runners as parents and grandparents. Haven't you ever wondered why they're men and women both?"

"Why anyone would go in for that life, makes no sense to me," he said with a shudder.

"Keep in mind you're talking about my brother."

We let the discussion go, and I poured us drinks.

Maybe it was the cider that set Andus up for another question. Could be he'd been holding that question for a while. "Why'd Tymon go for a runner, sir? If you don't mind my asking, seeing as where you are and where he is, it doesn't match up."

I nearly began to spill out the tale of me and Tymon and the deeds of Yutek the Younger, but closed my lips over that buried history. "He had his reasons, and I respect them." Joining the runners got my brother away from Yutek-en, behind a barrier none could level, the security of Runners' House. It was me led him there, in the dark of night, the day of Yutek-en's investiture.

"Boss? You all right?"

I set down the drink, realizing those dark days had taken hold in my mind again. "Ya, Andus, just thinking. Anything else? About Heyliannin, that is."

"She's not pregnant, if that's your worry, sir."

"Nothing about the snake-men or the thin patches?"

"No, wait, there was one thing …" He tapped his head, as if he could pull the memory out through his own skull. Reminded me of that interview with Calestinise. "Yes, yes, that's it, not sure, but I think she's got one of those books."

"Books?"

"One of those snake-men books, the books that don't open. She put it away fast when I came in. But you don't forget a thing like that, do you?"

"Huh." That proved it, didn't it? That she'd been with the snake-men. What if she had one of those lightning sticks, too?

I tossed back my cider and got up. "Any idea where Arnim is?" I needed to get that woman alone, my questions needed answered.

I found Arnim lazing in the back of the briefing room as Kul ran a session on the necessity of stealth in small-party operations. Arnim pointed out two guys whispering about how unlikely it was that Kul could be stealthy.

"I've got a bigger problem," I told Arnim. "Come on." On the way out, I stopped behind those guys, and gave their heads a smack, so their skulls thwacked together. One soldier leapt up, ready to attack, but his buddy grabbed his arm before he could get himself into trouble.

"That there's what we call a come-from-behind," Kul called out. "Thanks for the demo, Boss."

"Anytime."

•   •   •

Arnim and I put our heads together over a fresh jug of cider. Between us, we assembled a complex scheme involving so many deceptions, mis-leads, and connivances that it was more worthy of being performed as a comedy play for the summer festival than being enacted by a troop of Jeska's finest. The next morning, after an hour of lambasting my newer recruits for their various failings, I retired to my office and reviewed the plan. In the light of day, with a clear head, I could see every flaw. *I'll send Kul down to Runners' House, have him drag her up here. It won't be pretty, but there's nothing pretty about any of this.*

I was about to move on to that revised plan, when the drape whipped open, and she walked in.

Ta-ma. Or Heyliannin. Whatever she called herself now. Was it always going to be like this? The person I wanted to interrogate would simply turn up in my office? Fine by me.

"Where is he, Corren?" she demanded.

"Tymon? How would I know? Runners aren't under my command."

"No, not Tymon, Tymon is at home. It's taken all morning to find a way to get to you alone."

I didn't know what to say to that. *She* wanted *me* alone?

"I agreed to come to Jeskaryan to get back what you took from me on the mountain. As soon as you give it back, we'll be gone to the north and you won't be seeing us again."

I knew she'd mastered our tongue, but it still seemed strange to hear her speaking proper Jeskan, though with a drawling accent that reeked of the rural north. She loomed over me, where I sat at the work table, and I couldn't decide what to make of her, now. She wasn't scrawny and starved-looking like up in the mountains. The healthy flesh under that dull skin made a decent shape, now. It wasn't so surprising Tymon had latched onto this woman. The thoughts behind those too-wide eyes, those interested me. I remembered how she'd broken through our feeble attempts at talk with her map-drawing efforts. She could teach some of our recruits a few lessons in resourcefulness.

From the frown on her face, though, I didn't think she'd come to do me any favors.

"Give it back," she repeated. "Now."

I considered the array of weapons hanging on the rack behind her and wondered if I could draw my knife before she could grab one of those swords and take a swing at me. *Yes. I'd have her flat on the table in five seconds.* I dropped my hands to my lap, for insurance, and shifted back enough to keep my legs free of the table. "I di'n't take a thing offa you," I said, trying to imitate that northern drawl. "You di'n't have nuttin' t' take."

Her face went pink. So she knew what Jeskans thought of the north country. I caught her glancing at the nearest sword, a practice weapon, as it happened. *Good. Pick that one.*

She muttered something incomprehensible under her breath, probably in her own language. Then she took a step towards me, away from the weapons rack. Oddly disappointing.

I thought of standing, but decided against it. *Don't want her running off.*

She held up both hands in a conciliatory gesture. "Maybe," she suggested, "you thought what you took was nothing. It was … what was that word, again? … what I had wrapped around me, it was big, black—"

"Orkast's cape."

"*Cape*, yes, yes, that's the word. *Orkasts*, that's a word I don't know. Is that a kind of cape?" She stopped meandering through the word maze and fired her gaze straight at me. "You understood me the first time, didn't you? You took my cape. Give it back."

"It's not yours." I drew my knife and pretended to study it, while watching her from the corner of my eye. "It's mine."

"It is not, it's mine, and I'm here to get it."

"Well, you're not getting it."

"Why not?"

"I don't need to answer your questions. You need to answer mine." I stood up then, smooth and fast, and walked past her to the doorway, leaving her to turn awkwardly in the little space between the table and the wall. "How did you kill him?"

Her face went even more pale. I hadn't thought it possible. "Who?" she asked.

"My father. Orkast."

"I haven't killed anybody. I swear."

"Then how did you get his mantle?" Figured I'd try her out on the word the shamans use.

"His what?"

"You're worse than a spy; you're a fool. Do you not even know what you stole from his corpse?" I used the hand with the knife in it to gesture at her. The moves were meaningless, but I timed them, so on the words, *spy, fool, stole, corpse,* the dagger tip pointed at her heart.

"I haven't stolen anything, either." It was working. I could see little tremors running up and down her body.

"You expect me to believe that? There's nobody hasn't stolen *something.*" I made the blade point to her left eye, the side of deceit, they say.

"I—well, I stole food, when I first came down out of the mountains. And some clothing. Well, I tried to, but the lady caught me, and … and …" Her stammers faded as I lowered the blade and used it to scrape imaginary dirt from under my nails.

"When was that?"

"When was what?"

"When did you come down out of the mountains?"

"Um, um, nearly two years ago, now." Finally, some solid information.

"And when did you meet up with Tymon?" *Back off, go for the easy questions, make her talk about something she likes.* I leaned against the doorframe, and slipped the long knife back into its sheath.

"Last summer. Well, it was fall. It was starting to get rainy."

"Huh. And?" Talking about the weather is always an easy in.

"And the weather was bad, so they stayed."

"They?"

"Tymon and Calestinise."

While she spoke, soft footsteps slipped up beyond the doorway, and the steps stopped when she paused. "So what did you think they were?" The man outside moved right up to the wall behind me; I caught the hint of a creak as he leaned on the partition, out of sight.

"What do you mean?"

"Let me put it this way," I said, rambling while listening. "You're wherever you were, doing whatever you've been up to. A man and a boy appear at your door, asking questions, some of them questions you don't want to answer. You think you maybe recognize one of them, the tall one with the big grinning teeth, but who's the kid? Is it his son? His daughter? His wife? His servant? How did you take them? What made you let these strangers in?" Around about *maybe recognize*, three taps came in the particular rhythm that told me it was Arnim out there, listening. *Good.*

She hesitated. Did she hear the signal?

Did it matter?

"I suppose I took them as they showed themselves. Tymon the runner, with a message for me, about a book, he said. And Calestinise, yes, at first, I thought she was his sister, or maybe a younger runner. Runners can be girls, even down here in Jeska, right?"

"Runners have to be both," I agreed. "It's necessary. Tymon must have explained that to you." Did he explain that runners don't wed one-to-one, that everyone beds everyone else, regardless of who is landed and who is not, that they raise the children that come like wild ponies raise their young, in a galloping herd? I wanted to hit her with those words, to see how they'd rebound from whatever promises Tymon had made. Instead, I walked straight past her to the shelves, pulled down the thickest of the cushions there, and dropped it into the empty place behind the table. "Sit. Talk to me, sister-in-law."

She took a step towards the doorway, but stopped as if it were Kul standing in front of her, not a loose, hanging drapery. She looked over her shoulder to me, and her eyes narrowed. *Go on*, I thought. *Try it. Remember the first time we met. Wasn't so bad. A few scrapes, a broken rib or two.* The thought of getting my hands on her made my palms itch.

"I just want what's mine," she said. "I don't want any trouble."

"To be sure," I said. "You'll get what's yours."

It seemed we'd reached another frozen patch. "I don't want any trouble," she repeated.

"Then talk to me," I repeated. I strolled past her again, and pulled the cider jug out from its hiding spot. "We'll share a drink, like civilized people."

She held her position, there by the door, until I'd poured two cups and reclaimed my place, on the second-best cushion. Only then, with a skeptical, longing flutter of her eyes towards the seemingly unsecured exit, did she move to the opposite side of the table and take her assigned place. *All right, following orders, that's a start.*

"Tymon knows I'm here," she announced.

"No, he doesn't," I replied. *Time to break that confidence a little more.* "Tymon would never send you here alone."

"Why not?"

I shrugged, then changed the subject. "So, which is your real name, the one you gave us up on the mountain or the one you gave my brother when you seduced him?"

"I didn't—"

"Focus," I ordered. "How shall I address you? I can't be calling you *Tymon's Wife.* People in the south do that, you know—when a woman weds, she loses her name entirely, she's a wife only, and her property becomes her husband's." I could see her thinking about that, as if she was making a study of us, of our ways in the world. I could tell it was news to her, that our neighboring country was so different. Odd, that she seemed *interested*, not disturbed.

"We used to … Where I came from … It used to be that way."

"But you're not from the south. You told us you came from the east. From a long way to the east. Was that a lie, to trick us, or the truth, because it's so unbelievable you didn't need to lie? And you still haven't told me your name, Tymon's Wife."

"It's Heyliannin," she said. "The name was a gift, from a friend." Her eyes were clear and sharp. Even without Arnim beside me, I could tell that there was more truth in that statement than it seemed.

"Kind of a nonsense name. What's it mean?"

"Stranger," she said, with no trace of irony.

23

HEYLIANNIN. STRANGER. Weirdly appropriate. "Some friend," I said.

"The best."

I lifted my cup in a toast to her "best friend," then took a sip, and another, let the flavor roll over my tongue. I've always preferred cider to the stronger drinks and to wine. Liquor muddles the mind, and wine tastes too much of fermented fruit. Hesitantly, she reached for the cup I'd set at her place, and seemed to drink. I couldn't be sure. It's easy to pretend. I held my tongue and watched as she tapped her fingers on the outside of the cup. I shifted in my place as if uncomfortable, pulled my knife out again and laid it on the table, crosswise, not pointed at her, but, still, making my point. I put my finger to the hilt and gave the knife a nudge, making it twirl around. It stopped pointed at the door. I gave it another flick. It made a sweet skittery noise as it spun.

She took a breath, and I looked up at her, as if I'd forgotten she was there. I made a smile, probably not a particularly friendly one, but it was enough. She smiled back. *That trick always works.*

"I just want—" she began.

"Ya, ya, you want, you want. What about what I want?"

"I just—"

I cut her off again. Best to keep her off balance, but not too far off. "Not yet, not yet. Talk to me, I said. I want you to talk to me about Tymon, about my father."

"I don't know anything about your father."

"Then tell me about Tymon."

"We're, we're married."

"Sort of," I allowed. "He's still a runner, yes? And you're not?"

"Um?" Did she really not know? *It's not my job to educate her.*

I pushed in another direction, more towards my own purpose. "But why? Why would he marry you? He was hunting for information I wanted. Was that the only way he could make you come to Jeskaryan?"

She crinkled her eyes and tilted her head.

"This isn't the south," I said impatiently. "Or your country, for that matter. Marrying someone doesn't make you their servant. It didn't obligate you to come south to answer for your crime. You could have stayed safe up north, beyond the border. Did my brother trick you somehow?" As if Tymon would do such a thing. Even I could tell he was infatuated with this woman.

"No," she said. "I've come for my—"

I waved a hand, "There's nothing here."

Her eyes focused on the trunk in the corner.

I laughed. "There's nothing in there but old maps and plans."

"I don't believe you."

"Very well." I shoved myself to my feet, hefted the trunk out of the corner, tipped it on its back on the tabletop—ignoring the way the wood planks groaned—and flipped the lid down, right in front of her. A couple of maps slid out. I shoved them back as I tipped it onto its base. The trunk may have been empty, but it was well-made and its weight proved it. I grunted as I dropped it back to its usual place and resumed my seat.

"You proved your point," she said, grudgingly.

"I aim to please," I replied. "Now, your turn. About my father ..."

"I told you, I don't know your father, and I certainly didn't kill him."

"You had his cape."

"So you say."

"I'd recognize it anywhere."

"So?"

I smacked my hand on the table, as Tymon had done the day he dragged me out to the mountains where we met this woman. It made her jump, as I had done that day. "A shaman doesn't give up his cape unless someone kills him."

She ran a finger around the rim of her cup. Maybe she was thinking up a lie. I slid my knife back in front of me and gave it another twirl, enjoying the way her shoulders twitched when the table vibrated to the knife's motion.

"What if..." she said, "what if... what if a shaman simply... dies?"

"What do you mean?"

"What if a shaman catches the plague or falls off a cliff or gets old and doesn't wake up in the morning? Just... just *dies*?"

"That wouldn't happen to Orkast."

"Why not? Tymon says you don't think shamans are really magic. So couldn't he get hurt or sick or something?"

The idea shook something deep inside me. "That's ridiculous. Orkast traveled all over. He was healthy, and smart, and not that old. He wouldn't just *die*."

She slid her cup across the table, watching the trail of moisture it made on the wood. With one finger, she traced a design in the wetness. "Tell me about your father. What did he look like?"

"Like me, but older," I snapped.

"No, really. Tell me. Maybe I met him somewhere. Maybe this is nothing but a misunderstanding." She leaned across the table towards me, with an earnest expression that reminded me so much of Tymon, despite everything.

"Like I said," I told her. "He was taller than me, though not by much, thicker, more obviously muscular. He was a smith before he was a shaman. He had wrinkles, from being outside so much, but not so bad you'd think he was an old man. He had the same big sharp nose I have, so Tymon is fond of telling me. He used to say Orkast and I could smell each other coming." I gave her a real smile then, not intentionally, but there it was. The smile she made seemed real too—until it disappeared. It was like the sun had been out and then dropped behind a cloud.

"I think, I think maybe I saw him once. When I first saw you, you seemed familiar." She pressed her lips together and avoided my eyes. So there was more she could say, but not that she wanted to say.

"Tell me." I wanted to say more, but controlled myself. *Don't force it, let her talk, let her bury herself.*

"It was years ago. I was … working … for my sister's … friend … No, that's not right. What can I say? My sister died, and there was this man, she was going to marry him, but they didn't, because she …" She took a drink and tapped a finger on the table, like that would gather her thoughts. "The thing is, I took a job. It wasn't in my field, but I needed work, and they needed a … *goah-fur.* Can't translate … it means a person who runs and gets things." She waved her hands vaguely.

"The word is servant." I told her. "So, what?"

"Well, something bad happened to me …"

"What happened?"

Frowning, she shook her head. Her eyes squinched tight. Maybe she had history of her own she didn't want to talk about. "It doesn't matter, but I was hurt, and a man helped me." She stopped and studied my face. "I'm not sure. You sort of remind me of him, I think. Maybe more the way you talk. He didn't speak our language, but his voice sounded like yours." Then she shook her head again and set down her cup. Her hand quivered, and some of the drink sloshed out onto the table. Judging from how little spilled, I'd say she'd actually drunk a fair amount of that strong cider. She rubbed at her eyes. "I don't want to talk about this here. Let's go find Tymon."

We were getting close. I could sense it. "No."

"But—"

I pulled the warmth out of my voice. "No. You're here now, and you're going to talk to me, now. Right now."

She started to stand up.

"Arnim," I said, loudly enough to reach him.

"What?" Heyliannin said.

"Ya, Boss," came Arnim's voice from the hallway. I kept my eyes on Heyliannin, watching her fears being realized.

"Is Karthi around?"

"He's right here, Boss."

"Let's send him to give Tymon a hand, at his place, all right?"

"Sure thing. Can he take Andus, or do you need him here?"

"No, good idea. Better if they're together."

"Anything else?"

"You can let Kul take over out there. Want a drink?"

"Sure, Boss."

I leaned to the shelf and snagged an extra mug for Arnim, as he ducked past the drape and nodded to Heyliannin.

"Afternoon, ma'am," Arnim said, grabbing a cushion from the shelf above her head. She shrank away from him, the most easy-going man in my troop. But then, she was face-to-face with his right-side knife sheath, and Arnim carries not one, but two long-knives. Like I've said, he enjoys the close-fighting. When he sat, he drew both knives and laid them neatly on the table, side-by-side, to the right of his cup, well out of her reach. He took a deep swig and said to Heyliannin, "So I didn't quite catch all of that, ma'am, but sounds like Orkast helped you out. Where was that?"

"It's hard to explain." She clutched her cup like she was thinking about throwing it at one of us.

"On the other side of one of those thin patches, I'm guessing," Arnim said.

Her eyes narrowed. "What do you mean? What's a thin patch?" It felt like an honest response.

Arnim is good at ignoring answers that seem truthful. He pushed the discussion closer to what we suspected. "You know, like what the snake-men use to jump from here to there. Wherever there is," and he laughed at that. "We ran clear across the meadow to catch that little blue guy, and—poof—he was gone. Now, that's a *real* shaman, if you ask me."

She stared from Arnim to me and back again, her eyes wide, now. "What are you saying?"

I could have sworn she reacted more to 'blue guy' than to 'snake-men.' Did she *know* him?

"What the boss is wondering, what I'm thinking," Arnim said, "is this: Did Tymon's Wife jump through a thin patch, kill Orkast, take his cape, and then, somehow forget her escape route?"

"No, that's not what happened!" Heyliannin smacked her hand on the table, exactly as I'd done before. Then she shook her finger at Arnim. "The old man, he came to us, he came out of the night, alone, with nothing but his big black coat, right out of a snowstorm. And then … and then the … thing happened, and I was hurt and crying and sitting by myself, and the old man, he came over to me and pulled off his coat and wrapped it around me. And then … and then …"

Her face crumpled, as if she'd let herself get talking too close to that hidden history. Grabbing her cup, she took a long drink. For courage? Or to hide something? "Then I had a really bad reaction—to the thing that happened—and it made me throw up and gave me the worst headache ever. He stayed with me, made sure I was safe, until I could walk."

I had to admit, though I didn't say so, that this sounded exactly like Orkast. He'd never leave a person in difficulty.

She wiped her eyes again and went on. "It turned out he'd been faking. The old man *could* speak our language after all. He said he knew a safe place, with a warm fire. We went a little way down a trail I hadn't noticed before, and he was right, there was an overhang, and a sort of cave underneath. He had the fire built up in no time, and he talked to me, listened to me." Her voice trailed off again, and her eyes went vague, and I wondered if she was going to fall into a drunken sleep.

"… and then?" Arnim prompted, his voice low and gentle.

"He told me to go to some place I never heard of, and I told him I'd never remember that, couldn't he write it down, and he said his friend would remind me, that I wouldn't have to remember it."

"What friend?" I broke in. "You didn't say anything about a friend."

Arnim held up his hand. "It's all right, the friend doesn't matter. Tell us what Orkast did next."

"He died." She flicked a glance at me, or rather, at the knife on the table in front of me.

"You mean that's when you killed him," Arnim said slowly.

"I didn't."

"Maybe you didn't mean to. Something bad happened to you. People do bad things when bad things happen." Arnim could make an accusation of murder sound like a description of an incorrect place setting.

She was weeping outright by then, I figured to cover up her guilt, but, maybe not, maybe not. Her eyes got red and her cheeks went pink. "I didn't, I didn't," she cried. "I di'n't do anything." She took a deep breath, and wiped her face with both hands, then dried them off on her dress, the same nice country-girl work dress she'd worn at the party.

She leaned towards Arnim, as if I wasn't there at all. "He finally stopped talking, and sat down next to the fire, and then he lay down, and then it got so quiet. Then his friend said I'd better move him away from the fire, it wouldn't be right to let him burn." She sobbed again at the memory, and more tears washed down her face. "It was so weird. I don't know why, but I did what he said, what his friend wanted."

"What did his friend want?" Arnim asked, casting a glance at me to be sure I was playing the game. Tag-off is the best game, but I've never found it easy to be the one who has to sit back and listen. Especially not then, listening to my father sit down and fall over dead.

"He wanted me to drag the old man's body right out into the open, like it was trash, and leave it there. And I did what he said, because I thought I had to, but then I ran away. I ran straight back to where we'd come from, and everyone was gone, there was nobody there. My sister's almost-husband, the *truks* they had, the *masheenerry* they had set up, the tents, all the people. There was no one there, no one, only me, on the mountain, me and … and …"

"And?" Arnim prompted, so softly I almost couldn't hear him. He wasn't puzzling over the strange words she'd thrown in there, like I was. "Go ahead, tell us about his friend, now."

"I can't, I can't."

"Why not?"

"Because when I turned around, there was nobody there. There was only a voice in my head, and that meant I was crazy." Her eyes stretched wide, like a person struck by fever madness.

"So what did you do?" Arnim coaxed.

She breathed for a minute, calming herself. "I screamed at the voice to shut up. I kept on screaming until it stopped talking at me.

Then I wrapped myself up in that big blanket of a coat, and I sat down by the fire, and then I lay down by the fire—not where he'd been, not there—and I went to sleep. I convinced myself it was a bad dream, that when I woke up, everything would be normal again."

Whatever normal meant, in the land of *masheenery* and *truks*.

"But it wasn't. I was stuck there. Here, I mean. And we walked so long, trying to find a way down the mountain. When I first saw you, I thought you'd come to rescue me, that you'd take me home. And he said I should trust you, but you were so … mean. So angry. So not—"

At that, she collapsed forward, dropping her head to the tabletop and folding her arms over her head. Her breathing echoed thick and ragged from under that shelter. I could see the ideas flickering through Arnim's eyes like birds flocking in the trees. I gave him the sign, *go ahead.* The old anger still wrenched at my gut, but my training told me to tamp it down, be patient, let the game play out. There's many a time I've seen an accused criminal claim insanity, only to be proven later to have been shamming.

Arnim chose to open that gate. "It's not your fault." He paused as she sat unmoving, then went on, "An act done by an unbalanced mind, that's different from a crime. You know that, don't you?" He used her name carefully, choosing the old one, the name that went with the deed. "Ta-ma, a killing done in such circumstances, it's an accident, not a crime."

She stirred, dropped her hands to the table and lifted her head. That thin, weak hair stuck to the wetness on her face like a mask, turning her into a ghost out of a story. She stared across the table, directly at me, even though it was Arnim doing the questioning. "But I di'n't," she said, stranded in that ignorant-sounding north-country accent. "I di'n't kill him. He just … just …"

"Anyone would understand," Arnim said. "A bad thing happened to you. And a voice in your head told you to do things. Things you wouldn't ordinarily do."

She shook her head, ignoring the rivulets of tears and snot running down her face. "I di'n't."

"A person in such a state, Ta-ma, such a person may do things and not remember what they've done."

"But it wasn't an imaginary voice," she protested. "That's what I didn't understand."

"What didn't you understand, Ta-ma?"

"That … that it was … a real person." Her eyes remained fixed on the long knife rocking gently on the table in front of me. She bit her lip and sniffed hard, then pushed the hair out of her face and wiped her cheeks clean again. I kept my face still, though the sight was disgusting, the snot and tears that she smeared onto her dress, leaving bright, slimy streaks. "I could prove it to you, I could, but you took … and I promised … I can't … can't …"

"Promised who, Ta-ma?" Arnim asked, making a *hold on* sign to me. He had an idea. Arnim was always one for an idea. "Remember? You were alone when we found you. Do you mean something we did made the voices stop?"

"No, no, that's not right, that's not it," she replied. Her voice was calm, but her face roiled with conflict. She turned back to me, sucked in a breath like a dying man gasping for air, and said, "I want to say more, but I can't. I just can't." Then she folded her arms on the table in front of her and rested her head on them, turning her face away from the both of us. She murmured something to the wall, something that might have been, "I'm sorry." And then, even more softly, barely a whisper, she said a word that dragged me back to my childhood, "Asdyel."

24

I REMEMBER VERY LITTLE of the week of my eighth birthday, the one that should have been my last. What I do remember is clouded with heat and the smell of my own sickness, but clear as anything, I remember it as the day I learned adults can be afraid. That evening, the one that came back to me so many years later, I remember the room shimmering with the light of a dozen candles set up on the shelf. Shivering in my little bed, I hunched against the wall and cried for Tymon while my father knelt on the floor, cleaning up vomit. His mantle lay stretched over the back of the chair he'd dragged in to stand on, to reach the high shelf. The mantle's colors flowed and shifted under the flickering light.

Finished, for the moment, my father pushed the soiled rags into the bucket in the corner and came to feel the heat on my face. The fever sent tremors over my whole body, and every slight movement of air across my skin felt like a blast of icy wind.

"I want my blanket!" I complained. "I want my brother!"

"The blanket will make you hotter, Corren. And you don't want Tymon to get sick, now do you?"

"Do the magic, Papa," I begged him. "Magic me better. Magic the ghosts away."

"Ghosts?"

Why could he not see them? The floating images swirled closer, wove towards me, incoherent globs of color and light with indistinct markings that might have been faces, that became faces as soon as I looked at them. They came at me, swooping through the candlelight. I flailed at them helplessly. "There! And there! And there! Get them, Papa!"

That was when I saw it for the first time, that bright, hot spark I couldn't then, but now know too well: fear. He made a low noise in his throat, and his gaze drifted from me to his mantle. In my fevered mind, the cape seemed to reach towards him. Hope rose in my heart, that I'd finally see the magic he'd abandoned me to claim—that before I died, I'd see a shaman at work. Maybe he saw that hope in my eyes; more likely, he was desperate to do something, anything. He snatched up the mantle, then as gentle as a nursemaid, settled it around my shoulders.

"He's not a coat or a blanket, Corren," Orkast said to me. "Asdyel's here to be your friend, for a little while, to help with your fever, to help you be strong and get better."

There came a soft, hissing whisper in my ear, like an echo of my father's voice, "Corrrryn."

At that my father said, "No, no, not yet, draw the heat, my friend, take it up, what you can, soft, soft, he's only a child." And he reached a hand to stroke my shoulder, his fingers sliding over the thick mantle.

That other voice, the one so close it seemed to be inside my head, whispered, "Ay, Orkassst."

"Who's there?" I whimpered, paralyzed, certain a ghost sat on my shoulder.

My father settled down close to me and rubbed his hand down my back. "It's all right, Corren. It's only our friend, Asdyel."

Even as he spoke, the ghosts in the air began to quiver and fade. My shivering eased, and I curled up, my head on my father's lap. His broad, rough hand smoothed my sweat-soaked hair until I fell into a sleep full of dreams. So many dreams flowed through my head that this one time, the night I wore my father's mantle, became a dream in my memory—until I heard that name again.

•   •   •

"Asdyel," I barked at Heyliannin, ignoring Arnim's upraised hand. "Where did you hear that name?" I couldn't believe it. If he'd told her its name, that changed everything.

She started up, nearly jumping to her feet. Her eyes fell on Arnim, on the guarded doorway, on me with my knife at my hand, and she sat down, though she pushed herself backwards, as far from the table as she could move. "What name?"

"Asdyel. Where did you hear it?"

"I didn't say … I di'n't … I … *can't* say." She was quoting one of the rules I wasn't supposed to know.

"He put the cape on you," I pressed on the point where Orkast gave the thing to her, left the question of names aside. "Orkast *gave* you the cape, because …"

"I was … was hurt. And it was cold, and I'd lost my coat, because …"

I pressed my hands onto the table and leaned forward. What other shaman secrets had he shared? "Listen. I don't care about your coat. Did Orkast say anything, anything at all when he did that?"

"Boss?" Arnim interrupted.

"Not now," I told him.

"Well, he said something like, *There's no time to wait, we need to cross back over, to the cave.* But I hadn't asked him anything, and I didn't know his camp was in a cave. Is that—"

"Boss, a moment," Arnim said.

"What?" I whipped my head around to find Arnim pointing to the doorway, where Dramin stood, his eyes darkly serious.

"Dramin's here," Arnim said.

"I can see that."

"It's Yutek. The king's asking for you," Dramin said.

"Asking?"

"Demanding."

"Of course." I heaved myself to my feet and stared down at Tama. Heyliannin. My father's heir. To Arnim, I said, "Take Tymon's Wife down to the Shamans' House."

"What?" Arnim jumped to his feet, stepped close to me, flashed a few quick signs: *true? now? joke?*

"Tell the Master Shaman you've found Orkast's chosen successor. He'll know what you mean. Now. No joke." I did give him a quick response in sign at the same time: *not tell brother.* Tymon would not like this, not one bit. Too bad, he should have known better.

"We need to hurry," Dramin said.

"Right, it's always a hurry." With both hands, I slicked my hair into some sort of order and hurried after Dramin, leaving my knife gleaming on the table, its point leveled at Heyliannin's heart.

25

D RAMIN FELL BEHIND as I charged up the steps towards the audience hall, my mind full of that interview with Ta-ma, the shamans' Big Secret. *The capes aren't capes, they're creatures, creatures that talk, that do something to people, something … dangerous, maybe … permanent, probably. That's what initiates learn, when it's too late to back out. What was Orkast thinking? Was he saving Ta-ma or protecting his … asdyel? Is that the word for the creatures in general or the name for his in particular?*

I'd taken three long strides into the great hall before I realized it was empty, apart from a pair of workmen repairing a window shutter. The past winter had been extraordinarily wet, and there were patches of mold and rot cropping up everywhere. "Hey!" I called out to them. "Where is everybody?"

A scruffy young man holding a hammer stretched and pointed the tool first to the door I'd come in by and then to the back, where stairs led down to the king's apartment. "All the toffs went that-away, and the king went that-away, with all them doctors following him."

Doctors? I started towards the private stairs, then caught myself. If Yutek was in a demanding mood, best not try his patience by presuming on my position. I backtracked and found Dramin halfway up the stairs. He seemed more anxious than he ought to have been if it were nothing more than me ignoring his directions.

"What is it, man?" I asked him, but he shook his head and waved me ahead. My gut twisted, and suddenly I realized I'd had a cramp working the whole time, even before Ta-ma had turned up, since morning. I'd let myself be distracted by my private little feud. The warning ache had started over breakfast, in the same apartment I was heading for, over cold meat and fresh bread, as I listened to Yutek extol the virtues of my serving as interim governor of Lakeside.

Yutek's chief bodyguard stood at the door to the king's apartment, the position normally kept by a matched pair of troopers. He opened the door before I could ask him a single question, leaving me to walk straight through, unprepared.

With talk of doctors, I'd half-expected to find Yutek confined to his bed, surrounded by yammering women. Half of what I can't stand about doctors is that when you're at your worst, bleeding all over or spewing your breakfast on the floor, it's always women telling you what to do. Because only women can be mothers, we think only women can take care of the sick and injured? How inane is that? As foolish as saying only men can be shamans.

True, he was surrounded by doctors, if two young women and one old one, uniformly drab in their shapeless brown smocks and black leggings, could be said to surround a cantankerous tree of a man. He sat at his worktable, the same one he always used when instructing me on the finer points of Ruling Jeska the Yutek Way, sorting and stacking papers as if he'd developed a new calling as an accountant or a scribe. As I approached, the old doctor urged him to go and rest, but he waved her off with an imperious hand that narrowly missed hitting her. She dodged backwards.

"I'm here, Father," I announced, and I slipped to my accustomed spot, pausing long enough for the nearest servant to drop a cushion under me. Yutek had lectured me no end about doing for myself a task belonging to a servant. Good thing he never set foot in my office.

The moment I'd folded my legs properly and faced him across the table, Yutek ceased his paper-shuffling.

"Get out!" he ordered the rest of the room. "All of you!"

The doctors milled around while the bodyguards stepped out, one through each of the two doors to that room, and the servants vanished as if into thin air.

"I mean it," Yutek said, favoring the youngest doctor with a frown that spoke louder than his words. She caught her young colleague by the elbow and hurried to the exit, with the chief doctor following them reluctantly. She turned at the door and began to speak, but Yutek shouted, "Out!" and she left without a word.

Once we were alone, Yutek sagged and put a hand to his belly, pressing with his palm as if working out a cramp.

I waited, my own intestines clenching in sympathy.

Still with his hand on his gut, Yutek jabbed at me with his free hand, saying, "We need to move up our schedule."

"How so, sir?" I asked, trying to guess which schedule he was speaking of. Next week's meetings with the elders of Jeskaryan? My dreaded tenure in Lakeside?

"I've been made aware of certain developments. We need to get you invested right away."

"What developments? If I may ask, sir?"

"You may not." He looked down at the fingers mashing his stomach and dragged that hand to the tabletop. "Never mind."

My own gut wrenched with fresh vigor.

"The point is," he said, "you need to get married. Right away. No time for political finagling. Doesn't matter. Marry the one you've been habiting with."

"Eldennian? You want me to marry Eldennian?" The contrast between the pounding of my heart and the twisting in my innards must have made for a puzzling facial expression.

"Don't look so horrified, son. Hasn't she already proved fertile? Foster a couple of boys and get an heir off her as soon as you can, that's all."

I didn't dare say a word. I hadn't even hoped for such a chance.

"Well?" Yutek glared at me over his mess of paperwork, his dark eyes like gleaming stones in that long face of his. It may have been a trick of the light, with candles at one end of the room and a stream of daylight flowing in from the window, but his cheekbones stood high and cast deep shadows, with the wrinkles around his mouth and eyes making harsh dark lines, so that he seemed more like a badly-drawn image of the king than the living man himself.

"Yes, Father," I said. "Whatever you wish, sir. Of course. I'll bring her the news this very day." I must have been grinning like a fool, like Tymon and Ta-ma, because Yutek's frown shattered for an instant into that startling grin of his, the one he used to charm any diplomats that ventured as far as Jeskaryan.

"Ah, that's more like it." Then he winced, and the brilliance faded. "Next, we'll have your investiture. That will take time we can't avoid. It has to be done properly or the matriarchs won't approve it." He sighed, and his hand went back to pressing his stomach, as if nothing would stop it, not even the king's own will. He forced his lips to curve back upwards, daring me to ask a question he wouldn't answer. "You'll need to go to the head of the Council, to request the event be planned. Here—" He yanked a signed, stamped document from the middle of one stack and thrust it across the table at me.

It was a formal order, from Yutek to the Council, to prepare the investiture of his adopted true-son, Corren, as heir-in-deed. As he'd taught me, I said nothing until I had read the order through, from top to bottom, right to left. "Yes, Father, this goes to Barris, correct? As director of the order of ceremony?"

"Right. Good. Next—" Again, he rummaged into papers and withdrew a command order. "Once you are invested, there will be certain complications, some things will be awkward, you understand. Here."

I read through the second order, one that directed Eldrim, the chief of his bodyguards, the man who'd just admitted me to his presence, to refuse me such admittance unless the king were attended by a minimum of six of his own bodyguards. "Sir?" I asked, not quite sure what this signified.

"That order goes to Eldrim the moment you are invested. You understand son, that at that moment, if I die, for any reason, even at your own hand, you become king."

"Oh." *How have we survived so long with such a rule?* Then another thought chased that one. *I'll change that rule before I invest a successor.* I extended the order to him. "Then this needs must stay in your hand, sir."

"Correct. Next, your own guard."

"What?"

"You'll need your own house guard."

"Right."

"Easier for you. I didn't come up from the military. I expect you can hand-pick your men."

"I'd say I've already done that, sir." *I won't need anyone other than the Six.*

"I see. Now, about your practicum in Lakeside."

"I understand, sir. You'll be canceling that." I couldn't have been happier.

"What? Far from it. It is the most important training task you've yet to complete."

"Oh, but—" He wasn't making sense, now.

"But what?"

"How am I to go to Lakeside, and get married, and get invested, and all that at the same time?"

"Don't get in a lather, boy. Lakeside's not far, two days' march, less if you ride. You'll start at Lakeside as soon as you're married. The people down there will like that. They're big on marriage. Not so keen on unmarried men fooling around with their women."

"Um, well, I see." One of the problems the previous governor had introduced: mercenaries roaming the streets of Lakeside, making themselves unpopular.

"And soon as the planners have the investiture ceremonials arranged, we'll call you back for a couple of days, get it taken care of, then back to work for you, laddie."

"Yes, sir." Not what I wanted to say, but if Yutek wanted it done, I'd do it.

"I knew I was right. Pick the one with a military background."

But people hate the military. "No, sir," I said, without thinking.

"What?" Yutek was so surprised, he even quit massaging his abdomen.

"Ah, sorry sir," I stammered. "I mean, I always thought you'd choose Tymon. Because he's good with people. Everyone likes him. He'd have been a more popular king than me, sir."

He stabbed the air with his free hand again. "Listen up, Corren. This is not a time for a popular king. This is a time for a king who can hold things together, make the difficult decisions, who will take the right action even when it makes people unhappy. I need someone I can trust to keep this country together, not let it fall apart into squabbling sub-countries or get overrun by organized invaders from the south. You know that."

"Yes, sir," I said. "Well, I guessed. I've done my best to serve you in that way so far."

"So you have, son, so you have. There's but this one last thing you need to learn: governance. Harder than it looks, let me tell you. Best to practice on a little place before you take the reins here."

"I understand."

"Do you?" His gaze was both skeptical and distracted. Suddenly, he moaned and bent sharply forwards, until his forehead touched the table. I couldn't see his face, but I could see how his jaw tightened, like he'd bitten into a stone but refused to unclench his teeth.

I caught up to the doctors before they were even halfway to the stairs.

"He needs help," I said. "You need to get back in there."

They wheeled around like a troop executing a formation. I caught the arm of the youngest woman, and held her back as the others hurried to where Eldrim stood at the door, waiting for them.

"What is it?" I demanded.

"I can't say," she said.

I clamped down hard on her arm. "I'm done with people saying 'I can't say' today. What's wrong with Yutek? He's my foster-father, my adoptive true-father. I have a *right* to know."

"You're hurting my arm."

I pulled her closer and grabbed hold of her other arm as well. That way, I could glare straight into her eyes and ignore her incompetent struggles to get free of me. "Listen. You're telling me what I need to know. And you're telling me right now. I have orders from the king and I need to fulfill those orders. I'm not going to put up with any delays from you."

"Um, I'm not supposed—"

I gave her a little shake, barely a joggle. She was a doctor, even if a junior one. Doctors are important. I leaned close and my voice hissed over my teeth. "You're supposed to follow the king's orders. I have an order from the king that I can't fulfill unless you answer my question. So that's an order to you as well, an order from the king."

Tiny, bright tears leaked from the corners of her eyes as she blurted out, "He's dying. He has the wild growth in him. It's in his gut. It's probably everywhere."

"When will he die?" I couldn't help it, I felt tears of my own leaking out. Yutek wasn't Orkast, but he'd been a true-father to me, far more than his son had been a brother, and he'd taken me as his own when Orkast was out playing at shaman. Yutek had made me the man I'd become, the man who would do anything for Jeska.

"Sooner than we hoped. A few months, maybe. It's hard to tell."

My hands were cramping. I released my hold, giving her a shove in the direction of Yutek's apartment. "Go," I said, my voice rough and wetter than I liked. "Do what you can for him. Do everything you can."

I watched until she disappeared into the king's rooms. Then I turned and ran for home.

26

I FOUND ELDENNIAN in a rare peaceful moment.
Perfect.

Her mother had gone off on some errand.

Eldennian sat on our bed, gently rocking and humming as
Deliasin nursed. That baby drank like Case emptying a flask—
happily, intently, vigorously. I settled myself at the opposite end
of the bed, so as not to disturb them too much, and waited. It
doesn't take long for even the fattest baby to fill itself up, it's just
that they need refilled so often. When our ball of fat had subsided
into a milk-drenched stupor, Eldennian carefully eased herself to
her feet, without shifting her upper body in the slightest, and
transferred Deliasin to her little hammock, letting the wrappings
hold her as if she still had her mother's arms around her.

I followed Eldennian to the kitchen, where she immediately
began rummaging through the larder for something to eat. I
touched her shoulder.

"I have good news," I said. I was about to melt into a puddle
at her feet, I was so hot with the news.

"Well, that's a change," she said, tearing into a pan of cornbread. That smell filled the kitchen, the aroma of fresh bread that everyone says tells you you've come home, a smell I hadn't known since Mother died and Orkast sold me off as a foster-son. *I'm home*, I thought. *Really home, like regular people, and I don't have to leave it. It's mine.*

"We're getting married," I announced. Then I saw her face. *I said that wrong.*

"Oh?" She used the tone that meant, *Oh, really, what makes you think that?*

"I mean, what I mean is, Yutek has given his permission. We can get married."

"How can that be?" The creases beside her eyes conveyed annoyance, not happiness.

"It's true, I've come from a meeting with him. He practically ordered me to hurry up and get married." *Should I tell her he in fact ordered it? No, no, she wouldn't like that.* I rushed on, because it did seem outlandish. "He's decided he wants me invested right away. He's gotten worried something might happen to him." *Like dying this summer, maybe sooner.* "And I can't be invested unless I'm married. It's the law. And he doesn't want to mess around with a political marriage. Things are too unsettled."

"Oh."

"So we're free."

"So you say." She tore off another hunk of bread and filled her mouth, like she had more to say and had decided not to say it.

"But we are, it's true. Do you not believe me?"

"Hmm," she rumbled, working her way through the bread at full speed.

"Just think, by tomorrow, maybe the next day, we can be husband and wife, like we've imagined we could be. You can talk to your mother, your brother, your friends. I can throw my weight around for a good place, you can plan a real celebration, and I'll round up my Six and Tymon."

"No," Eldennian said, scraping the last of the bannock out of the pan.

"I know it's awkward with Tymon right now, what with the Ta-ma business, but he's my brother, still."

"No," she repeated.

"Come on, Eldennian. You know I can't cut him off."

She held up her hand, saw the spoon still in it, licked the spoon and set it in the pan. She took a deep breath. "Listen, Corren. Listen carefully. *No.* I'm telling you no to all of it, to a celebration, to rounding up people, to this whole marriage idea."

"But…"

"No buts. Just no." The thunk of her spoon on the table sounded like a blade on bone.

What was her problem? "I'll be king, Eldennian. Maybe sooner than we thought, but it's not like it'll be tomorrow. We'll have time enough for ourselves. You'll see."

"I'm not putting Deliasin into that."

"Into what?"

"The whole princess thing."

Where was she going with this? Did she not want status for our child? Or did she dislike the word, like I disliked *prince*? "That's not an issue. You don't have to call her that if you don't want to."

"You'll be king. She'll be your legal daughter. That's what a princess is, Corren. Just because you won't let people call you a prince doesn't mean you aren't one."

"Well, ya, I know that. I just don't like it."

"And I liked that about you, my dear."

"*Liked*?" My body was throwing a whole new set of warnings at me. I couldn't tell if my heart was still in there, because it didn't seem to be beating. My lungs wouldn't take in air. Spots floated in front of my eyes.

"You may have not wanted to be called a prince, but it was real. It still is. It's why we couldn't get married, all this time, even when we knew we had a baby coming."

Barely able to exhale, I breathed out nonsense. "That reminds me, is Ta-ma pregnant? Is that why Tymon told her they're married?"

"Her name's *Heyliannin*. And no. And also no. What does it matter? It's not a valid marriage."

But we're different, Eldennian. "Ya, ya. But ours would be. Valid that is."

"That's the problem."

I slumped into the nearest chair. My feet were tired of standing. My heart was tired of breaking. My gut was tired of clenching. I wanted to pound something. The table, the wall, that woman *Heyliannin* who sat by and watched my father fall over and die and did nothing but lie down and take a nap.

We sat silently for a while, Eldennian watching me with that face I had thought meant affection, but now I wondered. What did she really feel for me? Was I no more than a tool for her to get a baby, to make her mother happy? Women were all about keeping the lineage going, ensuring inheritances flowed in the right direction. Wasn't there some value to inheriting a kingdom?

It was me that had to yield. That was the way we were, always. "What's the problem?"

"I'm not putting Deliasin into a situation like you've had. I don't want her forced to marry or not marry, based on some political scheme. I don't want her married off to make a deal." I opened my mouth, ready with arguments, but she held up her hand, and not to pinch my ear. "I don't care if it's a deal that stops a war or makes for good trade that benefits people in general. Let someone else carry that burden. Not my little girl. No. I saw how it hurt you, Corren. I'm not going to make you hurt your baby like you were hurt."

What was I going to say to that? What could I say? I did have one idea to offer. "I'll be king, Eldennian. I can change the rules. We can change things, you and me, for her. See?"

She shook her head. "No, Corren."

"Why not?"

"Because I know you. I know what you care about. If marrying off your daughter to some black-hearted Southerner would stop a war that would leave a thousand soldiers dead, you'd do it. You'll do anything for this country, no matter the cost to you. You'd cut off both your arms and walk the country barefoot if it would save Jeska. You know it."

"Well, ya, I'd hurt myself. I wouldn't hurt Deliasin. I wouldn't."

"You would. Only if you had to, only if there were no other way, but you would. Worse, you'd raise her up to thank you for it, to see it as you did." How could she be angry and sad at the same time? Tears rolled down her face.

I stared at her across the table. Was she right? Could she be right? I was sure she was wrong, but … was she?

She came and wrapped her arms around me. Her breath warmed my cheek as she bent over my shoulder. "I know you too well, my Corren. Let me protect you from this one thing. I can help you not hurt your child."

Somehow, then, we were tight-tangled so close you couldn't have passed a feather between us. My arms locked around her, and I wasn't sure if the wetness on my face was her tears or mine. I'd lost nearly all my words. "Don't say no, don't say no, don't."

"I've already done it. I won't say it again. You don't have to hear it again."

At that moment, Arnim barged into the house, with that Heyliannin woman right behind him.

"I told you to take her to the Shamans' House." I couldn't shout, not with the baby sleeping.

Arnim stopped in his tracks, his gaze leaping from my face to Eldennian's.

"What's happened?" he said. The color drained from his face. "The baby—?"

"The baby's fine," I snapped my fingers at him. "Why is *she* here and not happily playing with her peers?" I wished I had a knife I could throw at Heyliannin right then.

"It's gone," Arnim said.

Heyliannin burst into tears.

I half-expected Arnim to start weeping as well, if only to fit in with the crowd.

He shrugged. "The cape, it's gone, they sent it off to find a— whatever they call it—person to wear it?"

"A candidate," I told him. "A man who might 'take on the mantle' as they say."

"Right. That. They didn't have any candidates, so they sent it to another Shamans' House."

"Where?"

"Lakeside."

Where I had to be in a few days.

"No," I said. "I will *not* take that woman to Lakeside."

"I know," Eldennian said. "Why don't you *marry* her? That'll satisfy the king and make her legal besides." Then she turned on her heel and disappeared into the bedroom.

"What?" said Arnim. "You're getting married? Is that why Eldennian's upset? Who to?"

"Not me," Heyliannin announced. "I'm already married."

I sighed.

"No, you're not."

She stood in the doorway, as snotty and tear-streaked as I'd left her in my office.

"Tymon's a runner," I reminded her.

"I know."

"Talk to him," I told her. "I've got bigger problems than some half-baked shaman thinking she can marry a runner."

"What do you mean?" She turned to Arnim. "What does he mean?"

Arnim took her arm. "I'll walk you down to Runners' House, ma'am. Tymon will be there."

They left me standing alone in the house that wasn't mine anymore.

27

I WALKED UP TO THE FORTRESS, to my empty office. *I have to marry somebody in the next few days. What am I going to do?*

I stared at the walls. No time to enter negotiations for a political marriage with a non-Jeskan family. Yutek-en's wife had hated him more than I did, but she seemed to think well of me. Would the alliance transfer or had she found a better opportunity already? If not, would she be willing to set foot in Jeskaryan after that first experience? If all else failed, the Council of Elders would happily pick out a woman who'd serve the matriarchy's purposes.

Did I want that? Did Yutek? He hadn't involved the elders, so the answer to that was clear.

After I'd drunk more cider than I should have, I was beginning to imagine opening negotiations with the snake-men.

A thump at the doorway interrupted my mental wanderings. Heyliannin held the drapery in one hand, and from the expression on her face, she appeared ready to tear the drape free of its hangers. "So we're not married."

"Na," I admitted.

"He lied to me." She took a step in and flung the fabric loose. One of the hanger loops tore free, leaving a gap in the entry, but no one was out there. We were alone. People knew to leave me be when I was in a dark mood.

"He didn't see it as a lie," I said. "Tymon's good at convincing himself what he wants is what's real."

I couldn't bring her shape into focus. It was like she was on fire, throwing off heat into the air, spitting sparks. Was it the drink?

"Give me some of that," she ordered.

I snagged an extra cup and filled it. Without even sitting down, she grabbed the cup, sucked it dry, and held it out for a refill.

"Sit, sister-not-in-law. Let's have us a chat."

She wavered on her feet, but the heat-halo around her seemed to be cooling. "Not like last time."

"No."

"All right, then." She fetched her own cushion, put it where Arnim had sat before, so she could reach the jug easier. She'd washed the disgusting fluids off her face, but her eyes were bloodshot and the cup vibrated in her hand. Was this sadness or anger? She'd seemed sad and confused before. This was different. I wished Arnim was there.

I waited until she'd drained her second drink. "You're angrier than a woman who's found out some legal technicality changed her status."

She smacked her lips and grabbed the jug. With all that tension in her, no surprise she sloshed half a dose onto the table. "Nothing you need to hear about. Explain this marriage thing."

"He's already married. To the runners. They're all spouses."

"That makes no sense." She stared down at her drink, possibly confused why the cup wasn't full, with the splash having stolen half.

"Signing with Runners' House is a polyfidelitous marriage contract. Do you know that word? It means they're all pledged to the others, all at once. He probably expected you to sign, once you came down to Jeskaryan."

She took a deep breath. "He asked, 'Don't you want to be a runner, too?' But I'm an accountant. A numbers girl. I *hate* running." With that, suddenly her face lit in that expression I recognized from our first encounter, up on the Wall. The wry smile of a clever, educated person. One with self-reflective sarcasm to it. Like Arnim's.

Not like Tymon's. My brother took the world at face value. "What about my brother? Were you using him to get the cape back?"

A different kind of warmth washed across her face, and her eyes softened. "No, no, nothing like that." She sighed and rolled her shoulders. The way her body moved sent me back to my drink. "He's so good in bed."

I didn't need to hear that.

"I didn't mind that he'd done it with others—it made him experienced. He listened to me, he did what I needed. And I needed it so much. I went without for so long. You know?"

I didn't need to hear that, either. All I could think of, right then, was Eldennian, her whisper in my ear, *yes, Corren, like that.* Good thing there was a table in between us. Had no one told her women don't tell men this stuff?

She ran her finger through the spilled cider. "So. Lakeside."

I stared at her. "No one's going to let a woman walk into the Shamans' House down there and take a mantle."

"But you sent me to the one here."

"I sent you to the one *guy* there. Fennic. We have a … relationship. He wanted me to have it."

"Would the guy down south give it to you?"

I thought it over. Technically, the guilds were under the government's hand. But there were all those unwritten rules. "Maybe. It'd take time. Leverage."

She shut up then, busy emptying and refilling her cup. I followed her lead.

What were we doing?

"About what Eldennian said …" She left the words hanging in the air, like a mist.

I floated some words of my own. "She won't have me, for the baby's sake. But I promised Yutek. And there's no one else."

About the time I was shaking the last few drops out of the jug … maybe into her cup, maybe mine, I can't remember, she put her hand on my arm. Her skin was warm, her fingers sticky. I would have flinched away, but it didn't seem worth the effort. Her face was flushed, her eyes bright. She didn't look angry or sad right then.

"Let's do it," she said. "Eldi's idea. The marriage thing."

I blinked at her. Each time my eyelids dropped, she vanished along with the rest of my problems. When my eyes met hers, I felt like I was seeing my one way out of everything. "But why would you do that?"

She ran her hand down my arm and licked the dregs of cider from her fingers. "Leverage. You'll get me my mantle back. Eldennian likes you, so you must be *oh-kay*." Blinking slowly, rhythmically, she rolled her gaze over whatever I couldn't hide behind the table. "Ya. *Oh-kay?*"

I'd have to get her to explain that word.

With my head full of cider, it all seemed so reasonable. Tymon would be happy, because he could still see Heyliannin whenever he wanted. I could do that for my brother. And Eldennian would be happy, since she'd know I was unhappy. A great solution all-round.

Nobody questioned us, reeking of cider in the records department at mid-afternoon, filling in forms, requesting contracts be drawn up. There might have been someone there who knew Eldennian, but no one was talking, no one told the king his one remaining son was taking up with a foreigner. After, we retired to my office with another jug, but didn't drink much. Somehow, it tasted bitter.

•   •   •

I remember very little of the wedding preparations, though I can attest I was fully sober at the right moments. The story is that the groom readied himself, once the paperwork was verified as in order, by drinking himself into a stupor. His friends spent the twelve hours before the scheduled ceremony hiding alcohol and dragging him back to his rooms. That can't have been accurate. I never drink to excess.

Yutek couldn't know what he'd driven me to. We used the ritual of the masks, because—I told him—it's traditional and people like anything that makes a ceremony more colorful. So he never saw Heyliannin's face, and we'd be off to Lakeside the next morning.

The staff ran around all that day-and-a-half, putting together as dramatic a public show as one might assemble in such a short time. No quiet family gathering in the back of a pub for the heir-apparent, the soon-to-be-invested one, no, it had to be out in the public square, surrounded by the people, or at least as many of the people who cared to take a day off for merriment at the expense of the government.

By dawn, I'll have to give them credit, the cobbled-together scene captured the air of a perfect spring celebration: a colorful canopy floated silken ribbons atop a platform raised high enough to give everyone a view of the proceedings, flowers hung from the doorposts, little braziers sat high on posts, ready to send scented smokes up to the heavens. I would rather have had a proper fire, but there were too many people, too many close-in buildings for that. Besides, who was I to care or not care what decorated the wedding, when the woman beside me would not be Eldennian?

The bride prepared for the ceremony by chasing some hapless runner around town, screaming at him. Again, this is second-hand knowledge. Remember, I was drunk out of my mind. Or so they tell me. It felt backwards, given what I remembered from before my unlikely binge. Tymon and Heyliannin sat at my kitchen table and talked through the points in the marriage contract while I packed my things. She'd seemed strangely triumphant. It had been my brother who looked ready to start screaming at any moment.

While the groom was being forcefully sobered up, half of his bodyguard dragged Heyliannin back to the Runners' House, where the women consoled themselves for her abandoning them by making her up like they imagined a northern bride might paint herself for a wedding. I'm told there was a spirited debate as to whether to let the bride get drunk for the wedding.

I presume there were invitations to join in some of the regular Runners' House shenanigans, but I never asked if she took part in any of that. What she did before the wedding would be no more my business than whatever my Six did in their free time. I did learn how the intoxication debate ended, as Heyliannin's speech, although clear, had the slow cadence I remembered from our last meeting in my office. We arranged the wedding party so that Tymon could whisper her the correct responses . . . and prop her up if she lost her balance. Attendees were moved by the way she kept slipping a hand under her mask to brush away the tears of joy.

We stood up in front of the people.

We said all the words.

Yutek wrapped the yellow string around our wrists, binding us together, and I shut my eyes and imagined it was someone else's as I raised her arm with mine to the cheers of the crowd

Music rose up, first the rumble of drums, then the screeching of the flutes, then the voices, in-tune and out-of-tune flowing together like merging streams.

Tymon stepped back, giving Heyliannin a push so that she slumped against me instead of him, and from the edge of my mask I saw him drop to his knees and cover his face. Someone stepped in between us, but all I could see was the blur of a bright-colored robe. Then I felt the Six form up around the two of us, dark solid shapes in their formal uniforms. I was trying to remember if there were anything unlucky about tearing off that binding string—with our arms tied together, if Heyliannin stumbled, there was no way I could catch her—when the Six shouted out a cheer in unison and she stood straight, startled into alertness.

They must have rehearsed, because they moved straight into the next stage of their drill. Two of them—one on either side of us— dropped with a thud to their knees and bent over, their hands on the deck. Another pair stepped right behind them and bowed low. I could hear the last two right behind us, their breathing quick with suppressed laughter.

"Hah!" came the order, in Arnim's voice, and they took hold of us. The men at our feet grabbed our ankles. The bowing ones grabbed us round our waists—Kul had me nearly crushed with one arm. The ones behind merely rested hands on our shoulders.

"Hey!" Arnim shouted, and they lifted us as smoothly as a gang of carpenters hoisting a rafter-beam. It was Karthi holding my shoulders up, one hand steadying my head, the other flat on my back. I could see that grinning face edge-on, and I guessed that Andus did the same for Heyliannin.

"Ho!" At that, they marched us off, right down the stairs that had seemed so rickety when we mounted up them not an hour previous. I might have heard a board crack when Kul's foot struck it.

Cheers echoed around us. People surged close, stretching out their hands to touch us, or to catch an edge of those rainbow robes as we plowed through the mass. It was like being assaulted by a mob of puppies, or like being landed upon by a flock of birds. I surrendered myself to it, to the feeling of soaring through the air above the plaza. I stretched out my left arm, the unbound one, and felt the warm touch of hands on mine, little hands, sticky hands, rough ones, smooth ones. A chant started up as we passed: "Corren! Corren! Corren!"

A little of that joy of theirs seeped into the dark space in my heart, the empty place that Eldennian had owned.

28

WHEN THE DOORS SLAMMED CLOSED against the crowd, the Six set us neatly on our feet. Arnim tackled the tangle of string, freeing us to walk more or less normally. I put a hand to my mask, but felt someone's fingers on my wrist, so I listened instead.

"Well done, my son," Yutek's voice rumbled from my left. Half-blinded by the mask, I could hear the hesitations, the way he paused after *well done* and sucked in a breath with a hint of a whine, before going on to *my son*.

I'd been anticipating this moment after the ceremony, when we'd doff those masks and face Yutek's dismay that he'd married off his heir to some diseased-looking northerner, instead of a hale and fertile Jeskan woman. "Thank you, Father," I said, tilting my head to see his face through the slits in the mask. He seemed pleased, proud even, and my heart sank at the deception we'd done. "Father, I—" I began, but then his head dropped suddenly and the doctors flowed around him and drew him away. I tore my mask off and watched them go. Yutek walked half-bent, his arm low and curled over his belly. *Should I not go to Lakeside? Is he going to last the month?*

Before the king had disappeared around the corner, Kerrin, the head of the Council, that prat, bustled right up into my face. He wore a sneer I looked forward to wiping off his face someday soon. "Well, now, youngsters, first we feast and then there's that last bit of ceremony to attend."

Beside me, Heyliannin turned to stone.

•   •   •

The wedding feast provided a delay from the inevitable. With Yutek not in attendance, the festivities became less formal. At least there was plenty of food. The Council, the invited town dignitaries, the staff coming and going in shifts, everyone ate like there was no tomorrow. Heyliannin ate practically nothing. I forced down the bare minimum to avoid insulting the cook, and my men took it by turns to stand at my shoulder and take away any drink that was set near my hand. There were speeches to endure. Lots of speeches about the number of children we'd have, the many years we'd serve at the king's side, on and on.

Finally, that was over, and the officials took us away, leaving the celebration to those more likely to be enjoying themselves.

They took us to Kerrin's apartment, the Council head's own rooms, and the smarmy bastard slunk along beside us the whole way, extolling the virtues of his bedchamber.

I'd rather have had my own corner of the barracks, or the unheated closet Tymon and I had once shared. But neither suited the wedding night of the king-to-be, nor did either provide convenient accommodations for the witnesses. I swear, the entire council had crowded into Kerrin's sitting-in room.

"Out!" I ordered. Unmasked, my eyes stabbed each of them in turn.

"But, sir ..." ventured the smallest, skinniest councilor, Caldrim, who managed accounts.

Arnim sidled close to me and murmured, "Pick three, it's the minimum by law."

I tipped my head close to his and whispered, "Should have talked this part through."

He grimaced. "Sorry, Boss. Kind of forgot. It's not ... usual ... not for regular people ... you know ... not anymore."

I lowered my voice even further, "Tell me they don't have to watch."

He shook his head and a half-dozen invisible rocks fell off my shoulders. I pointed to the three councilors I hated the least: Caldrim, Arrestal, and Dineen. "You three, stay. Over there." I indicated the side of the room furthest from the bedchamber.

The Six moved to herd the rest of the busybodies out the door, with Kerrin protesting the loudest, "But this is my apartment! You can't kick me out!"

Kul loomed over him like a bear considering his next meal.

The coward quailed and retreated.

Arnim saw the selected three seated against the far wall, then rummaged in the nearest cupboard until he found Kerrin's stash. Wine, of course. The expensive kind. "Sirs," he said, in his most servantish tones. "You may as well take your ease." It worked, I'll give you that. The color came back to their faces, and Dineen gathered three cups and worked the stopper on the wine.

"All right, then, sir, ma'am," Arnim said to us, and he gestured to the bedchamber doorway, ornamented with a fine-woven fabric in a distinctly southern design.

"You'll stay, keep an eye on these bureaucrats," I told him.

He nodded. "Sure, Boss. Some of us will be keeping tabs on the others."

"All right." I knew I could trust Arnim with arrangements and persuasions. I grabbed Heyliannin by the arm, the same arm she'd been bound to me by, and drew her behind me, straight through that drapery, before she had a chance to make any comments.

•   •   •

Kerrin had not been exaggerating. His bedchamber boasted thick layers of imported carpets, making walking across the room like squishing across a muddy field. Wall hangings of ostentatious imported fabrics hid the walls, some of them featuring designs that in a better light might have been obscene. Thankfully, only a few candles lit the room.

The bed, however, that thing was truly an obscenity: tall, wide, bearing a thick mattress that must have taken the lives of a thousand fowl for its stuffing. I made a mental note to have Caldrim audit Kerrin's accounts.

Heyliannin stopped inside the room, not taking a step further once I let go of her arm and the drape whispered at her back.

"Best get this over quickly," I sighed, unlacing the long overrobe that I'd been stuck in all day and peeling it off. In the candlelight, its colors glowed dimly, a faint reminder of the day's celebrations. I wanted a chair, a table, anything to drape the expensive thing over. But there was nothing; the bed filled the space. "Well, so much for that idea." I dropped the robe to the floor, turning it into a pile of ordinary laundry. Had I been in my own chamber, I'd've stripped off the rest of my clothes as well, and rummaged in my trunk for something fresh. I knew I stank of sweat and annoyance and an unsettled stomach.

Instead, I turned to my wife and set to unknotting the tangled laces of her even-more-complicated overrobe. She stood still as a post for a moment, then jerked aside and slapped my hand away. I tried again, freeing one lace before she dodged away.

This time, she backed into a corner, a gaudy purplish hanging billowing around her. I leaned my face close to hers and spoke while I fought those idiotic laces. "In the old days there would have been servants to help with these things." I freed the second strand and shifted my gaze from the work to her eyes. Wide, angry eyes. What was I doing wrong? It felt strange, undressing a woman shorter than me. Only one more knot to go, to clear the last two laces. I went on with my history lesson. "Then again, in those days the witnesses would be standing right here, ordering the servants to hurry up, taking notes, making remarks, giving pointless advice."

"But they're not here." Her breath, washing across my cheek, smelled of sour wine.

"No, they're not. I think some intended to be, though." I may have smiled then, thinking of the day I'd throw Kerrin out on his ass, but then the tight knot finally yielded, and I tugged at the freed laces, letting the pair of narrow ribbons slip through their holes like snakes flicking through the grass. "There. That should do it." I tapped the shoulder flaps. "Pull here … and there … and it should come right off."

She didn't move. "Why?"

"What do you mean? You want to stay in that ridiculous costume?"

"No, no." Her shoulders slumped. She wouldn't be familiar with these costumes, would she?

"All right. Let me help." I caught hold of the flaps, but she suddenly flailed out with both arms. Surprised, I let go, but a little too late. As I pulled my right hand away, that side of the robe fell free, leaving the whole weight of the thing dangling from her right shoulder. She moved to catch it, but her change of position sent the massive robe into motion, and the bright fabric slid to the floor, folding back and forth over itself to make a tidier heap than mine.

Underneath, she wore the same plain grey dress—or did she have several of those things? At least someone had talked her out of the leggings this time. She'd have died of the heat.

Still, like me, she was drenched in sweat and shivered in the chill air that flowed through the room.

"That's not what I meant," she hissed through her teeth.

What could she be angry about? "No? What did you mean?"

"Nobody said there'd be people watching. Why?" Her voice rose, and broke on the *why*.

"Keep your voice down." I stepped right up close again, keeping my own voice to a whisper only she could have heard. "They're not watching, but they're listening."

"So all we need to do is make the right noises."

The ache in my gut reminded me it was there. "What? This isn't a time for joking around."

"I'm not joking. If no one can see, then it doesn't make any difference." She flushed crimson and shoved me, hard, but I held my position. "I'm not putting on a show for those … those …"

How could she turn everything upside-down and inside-out like that? "A show?" I grabbed her wrists and pulled them around me, wrapping my arms around her body the moment I released her wrists. "Whether or not someone's watching, we do the right thing. Arnim's out there getting them drunk enough that we don't have to think about them listening, either."

Heyliannin twisted in my arms, pressing against my embrace even as she raked her fingernails across my back, to make me twist in turn, allowing memories of long nights with Eldennian to overtake me. I leaned into her, rubbed my hands down the nubby woven cloth of that little dress of hers, letting sensation and memory summon what I needed.

She kept talking, talking, talking!

"What right thing? There's nothing *right* here. Hey! What are you *doing*?" She snapped her head up, cracking it into my jaw, making me bite my lip. That hurt, and not in a good way. She shoved me again, and I stumbled back and put my hand to my mouth. It came away bloody.

The scar on the back of my hand reminded me of the cut she had made, that first day we met, when her teeth sliced through my skin as I struck her. I shouldn't have done it then; I wouldn't do it now. I didn't need Tymon to tell me that. Her eyes flashed in the candlelight.

"This was your idea, Ta-ma. Nobody hid anything. I showed you the contract. Eldennian broke down the details for you—I think she wanted you to get it *right* because she knows I didn't want this. Tymon told you—I sat in the next room and listened to him explain every little bit of it. Were you too angry about the sham marriage to listen?"

As I spoke, I advanced on her, keeping my eyes fixed on hers and my hands low, ready to defend myself. She retreated, sidling up the far wall, further and further from the doorway. "I wanted Tymon," she said. "Not you. Why did he do this to me?"

"That bird has flown. You can't waste time blaming Tymon for being himself. It's exactly his kind of mistake, the kind of fantasy he'd make up, that he could keep you for himself and share you with the other runners, at the same time." I kept my voice low, soothing, trying to imitate Arnim's conversational, persuasive tone, the one he uses in interrogations. I had her nearly cornered again, and stopped, so she wouldn't get rattled and stop listening "Tymon's the past. Eldennian's the past. Now is just you, and me, and we're *wedded*, Heyliannin, you and me, at the hand of my father, the king, before all my people … *your* people, now. And this that we do here is our sworn duty to our country, to our king, to the future of Jeska."

She stood silent.

"I'm doing the right thing, Heyliannin. And you agreed—"

"I was drunk. I didn't agree."

"You did, you signed that contract, yesterday, clear-eyed and sober. And it was you demanding the drink, don't imagine any bit of information doesn't come to me."

"I didn't understand."

"Yes, you did."

She crossed her arms and glared at the floor. "I didn't think he'd let it happen."

"What you think, what either of us thought before, none of that matters. Where we are now is what matters. You're my wife. I'm your husband. We have a duty to fulfill, and I'm not going to soil your honor by faking any bit of it. We'll do as we've promised. The both of us."

She might have been any woman, her face in shadow, watching me with eyes that flashed when the candles flickered. I took a step back and peeled off my shirt, hoping the scars weren't too obvious. The trousers were a little more awkward, but I got my feet free and kicked the clothing off to the side. Pretending not to keep an eye on her, I settled down on the edge of that expensive bed, sinking into its softness. Swiftly then, I reached out and caught her by the hand, pulling her close so suddenly she didn't have time to resist the motion. She took a good hard swing at me with her free hand, but I was ready for that. I used her movement and a push-off with my feet to sling the two of us up onto the bed, tangled together. Her feather-soft hair brushed my shoulders, as her dress, a sweat-smoothed sheet of roughness, rubbed across my abdomen.

"Let's finish this," I said. "Any way you like, you tell me. I like following orders."

Her mouth set in a line, but then the corners of her lips tipped up slightly. She said, "So Eldennian told me true."

It wasn't particularly pleasant, it wasn't pretty, but no one was watching. We made good on our vows.

29

L ET ME TELL YOU ABOUT my Jeskaryan, my home, the city I remember, the heart of Jeska, the city on the hill.

True enough, I can hear you saying it, what town isn't built on a hill, when the good farmland is in the valley, not to mention the rivers overflowing when the snowmelt comes down from the Wall. Bear with me, listen, see the place as it was, not the Jeskaryan of today, but the place we set out from, that warm spring morning, me and my Six and my wife and our various retainers.

Whereas most towns find a flattish area somewhat upslope, lay out streets around a nice open market square, Jeskaryan's built around a fortress, a defensive bulwark set up before the Great Quake closed the westward pass, cutting us off from the coastal people for a few generations, while they worked out their own differences. Before that time, they'd come over the range, raiding parties of ten and twenty and a hundred, to *gather*, as they might have put it, from the bounty of our inland harvest. Back then, even inland, we weren't a country, we were a rabble of competing extended families, each with their own version of our language, each with their own favorite foods, music, and styles of dress. Hard to believe now, but it's true, it's in the written histories that Tymon and I had to read, hour after hour, with that tutor ready to rap us a good one if we started to nod off.

Our ancestors, the original Jeskans, their mothers and grandmothers managed the lands where the raiders were most likely to arrive, from the eastern hills, about halfway across the valley towards the Wall and about as far north from there. Over time, naturally, the raiders became adventurous, and even selective. They would peel off search parties to fare south to the Lakeside region and others to troll straight through Jeskan lands to our neighbors to the north and east.

Nobody was happy about this.

Well, no, the raiders were highly satisfied. They came again and again. They came armed and ready to fight for the goods they sought.

Finally, the women of Jeska and Lakeside and Heart's Bend and Moress and Koresh and the others kicked their men in their respective asses and told them to do something about it. At first, they tried simply forming up a ready militia in each town, like our Guard, though less well-trained and hardly armed at all. But once they set foot in the wide-open valley, the raiding parties could seemingly vanish—until they struck a granary or a smokehouse. So the defenders decided to take a stand in the gateway, to put the militiamen in one place, at the entry point, and plug that leak in the hills by sheer force of numbers.

You couldn't have hundreds of men camping in the fields forever, so when they weren't out chasing down raiders, they got to work and built the original fortress. I doubt it was much more than a barracks. But the more the men worked together, the more they became a unit, a common force, and they needed a permanent place to work, to train, to live through the rains of winter. So the towns pitched in funds, and the leaders of Jeska brought in proper workmen and built a real fort, on the last hill of the range, affording a clear view up the pass for the watchman. Once there was a fortress, and a standing army, a new town formed around the fortifications, a town with winding narrow streets twisting around the hillside, taking odd jigs and jogs to follow the landscape underneath.

In Jeskaryan, the market wasn't a wide-open space with people milling about, it was a maze of short, narrow streets running together, separating, and curving around the hill, through the northeast section of town, right up against the fortress wall. If Tymon and I managed to slip the clutches of the tutor for an afternoon, there would be no safer place for us than the market of Jeskaryan, an endless array of booths and tables and little shops with their goods spilling out into the walkway. The makers—the smiths and the armorers and the woodworkers—all had their workshops on the northwest sector, close enough to the market to be convenient for anyone needing work done and also needing to shop. Houses spilled out from the market side along the wall and down the slope to the edge of the farmland.

Jeskaryan was my place, my heart's home, and here I was leaving it to live like a Lakesider in their flat-country towns and houses where half the walls were windows, to get some air in during the endless heat of summer. I'd be back, but you can't leave a place for a year and not have it change on you. You can't go away that long and come back the same man. It hurt almost as much as leaving Eldennian.

• • •

Lakeside is normally less than two days' walk from Jeskaryan, but we weren't visitors, we were to be residents. That meant we traveled with two fully-laden carts, one drawn by two ponies, the other small enough for a single draft animal. I'd stolen my two favorite packing ponies from the stablemaster. Good old Spear Carrier huffed along under bags packed solid with my men's supplies. I'd urged each of them to make sure they had clean garments, including something fit to be seen by regular civilians, as opposed to border bandits. We were a household on the march now, not a merry band of warriors.

Just as I had my Six, protocol demanded Heyliannin be accompanied by her own circle. Magaran selected two of his best swordsmen and assigned them as her personal bodyguard. I'd begun to raise an objection, but abruptly realized the wife of the designated heir needed real protection, so I demanded four more

177

men. Magaran gave me two, but they were good, experienced soldiers—I remembered them from the long trek north after NeverSnows. Harad had a wry sense of humor that could break through anyone's dark mood, and Radeo—besides his skill at arms—was an excellent cook. We made full use of his secondary talents, both nights of our journey. The dutiful father-in-law, Yutek, dispatched a midwife, Ganderrison. Heyliannin had a heap of objections. As a responsible husband, I overruled her order to send the woman back. Did she think midwives limited themselves to that one thing? Even as a bogus herbalist, surely she'd picked up a few basic facts about authentic medical practitioners.

The Runners' House had scrounged up funds to hire Heyliannin a personal servant—who might have been useful had she been on hand for that awkward first night—but as of our departure time, no one had taken the job. At the last minute, Calestinise turned up, carrying nothing but a one-strap shoulder bag and the contract Tymon's friends had offered.

"Isn't this a job for a girl?" I asked him.

"A man can serve a lady just fine," he responded. "And you're crazy if you think I'm staying in that place."

"What's wrong with Jeskaryan?" How could anyone not love my city?

"The only place willing to take me in was the Runners' House, and they are every bit of what I was told, and I'm not having it."

"Not having what?"

He glowered up at me, one narrow eyebrow lifted so high it nearly disappeared under his hair. "You know ... it," he said. "They are all of them, all the time, at it, and every one of them wondering, you know, what it would be like if ... you know."

"Ah." I remembered Tymon and his unwelcome curiosity, on the way up into the Well. "I should have known. I've seen a few things in that house, my own brother being a runner and all."

His face went so dark, you might have thought all his blood was crammed into his head.

I glanced around at the troopers readying our gear, and pulled Calestinise off to one side. "Listen," I said. "I don't know what's troubling you, but you have choices, boy. I know you hate me, but you'll be stuck with me if you're working for my wife. You could go to

Eldennian. She's done with me, but she's got nothing against you. She's been growing her business, could use a real apprentice. She's never liked runners, and Tymon especially she dislikes, always has."

"No," he said.

"No, what?"

"No, sir?" I couldn't read his expression at that point. Maybe what he needed was some sense smacked into him, but then again, the boy still looked like a girl.

"Listen." I felt like one of those exasperated mothers I'd seen in the marketplace, arguing with toddlers. "What are you saying 'no' to? Staying with Eldennian or coming with us?"

He grunted a non-answer and scuffed his bare foot into the dirt, as if measuring how dry it was getting. Then he scratched his head with both hands, like a dog trying to chase a flea out. "I meant … what I meant was …"

I wanted to shake the words out of him. Unfortunately, I didn't have my hands on the boy, so all I could do was glare down at the top of that disheveled head.

"I meant … no, I don't hate you." He tipped his head to one side, peering up at me with just his left eye, ready to hide his face again. I almost smiled at him. He went on, "You're a bad guy, Corren—"

"Commander Corren," I snapped, before I even heard what came before that. Did he say what I thought I heard?

"Commander. You're bad, sure enough, but you ain't evil. I can get along with that." Then he shrugged his little grey bag over his shoulder and ducked past me, to stand by the pony-cart, where Heyliannin still stood arguing with the midwife.

•　　•　　•

We had more than the usual departure delays. At the last minute, Yutek dispatched a few extra retainers. Now we had a couple of stableboys, which seemed excessive with five ponies on the march; then again, there's always a need for someone willing to do scut-work. And, riding up on a bony old pony more ancient-seeming than himself, came a wizened oldster who pronounced himself our accountant. At that, Heyliannin stepped up and put her foot down.

"Go on home and stay alive," she told him. "I'm an *embeeyay*. We've got that covered."

Flustered, the old man waved a big fat book around and declared that he had been dispatched to take an official audit at Lakeside.

Heyliannin deftly snagged the volume right out of his grasp. "I can manage a ledger just fine. Thank you. Trust me, sir, I got *ays* in accounting."

Whatever that meant.

"It's not fit work for a lady." He dropped the reins and shifted his weight, readying himself to clamber down and reclaim his job.

"I'm no lady." Picking up the rein ends, Heyliannin turned the pony around, and gave it a mild slap on the rump. The beast flicked its ears happily and trundled towards the stables, disregarding the old man's rein-pulling. She walked past me without so much as a glance and stowed the book in her own baggage.

Because we'd set out late, I pushed the pace as much as I could, but we had a mixed bag of travelers. I wanted to talk to Heyliannin, to pump her for information on the snake-men. Instead, I kept finding myself paced by Calestinise, who pumped *me* for information. I was expected to explain everything from why the soldiers wore boots even though the road was smooth and flat to how Jeskaryan had grown to be such an oversized jumble of fortress, houses, markets, and manufactories. Giving him a short, concise answer meant I'd be tasked with yet another question. I was about to throttle him, when Arnim fell into step with us and took over the job of answering those endless questions.

I was never so glad of Arnim's company as I was that day.

The first night, we camped at HandOverHand. We shared a quiet meal at the edge of the old mustering-ground. I remembered Keev and Shellon, their shouts rolling over the field as they sparred, their wooden practice swords thunking together like logs being thrown on the fire. Silence ruled, as others focused on times past. Andus picked at his food until Karthi came and pulled him to his feet and led him off somewhere in the dark.

Calestinise, parked between Heyliannin and me, watched them go. "What's that about?" he demanded. "Why's everyone so down?"

"Enough," I told him, and I flung my plate in the fire and stalked off into the dark. Behind me came Case's quick footsteps, with Dramin's right after. Neither said a word as they caught up and took position, Case a few steps ahead of me, Dramin as much behind. They didn't need to speak. I knew I'd never be free to wander alone again. Even so, I walked as I would have done on my own, circling the camp out of reach of the firelight, where I could watch, and listen, but remain unseen.

Arnim's voice floated from the warm-lit patch around the fire, gathering in the four new men and sorting out the night watches. Calestinise finally got to being useful, hauling bedrolls out of the pony-cart and distributing them. I watched as he brought two out to Heyliannin, layering one under the other, to make for a more comfortable bed. *Where'd he find a spare*? I wondered, until I noticed that he carried a blanket like a cloak, draped over his thin shoulders. It was his own bedroll he'd given her. When he returned to the spot with a third bundle, Heyliannin began arguing with him. I paused to watch as the little drama played itself out: Calestinise marching over to Arnim, then back to Heyliannin, who gestured to him to take the thing away.

We were close enough at that point, having returned roughly to where I'd walked away from the fire, that I could hear part of the exchange, at least Calestinise's half, delivered at theatrical volume.

"The captain says it goes here," he shouted.

My wife faced him with arms crossed and shook her head.

"The captain says there's nothing you need to worry about."

Heyliannin said either "I'm worried," or "I'm not worried."

Calestinise threw the bundle down next to her, saying, "It's all right, ma'am. They're arranging guards and stuff. No one's doing anything but sleeping tonight. Except the guards."

Oh.

A broad shadow loomed in front of us.

"We got the first shift, sir," said Kul's voice. "Me and you. Hope that's good for you."

"Yes," I said. "I'm thinking it's good for my cranky wife as well."

Kul's laugh made me feel better. "You better go get some rest," he told Case and Dramin. "You're down on the list for next shift."

"That so?" said Case. "Good night, then, Boss." He rested his hand on my shoulder for a moment, then was gone into the night.

"Right," Dramin agreed. "I'm off, then, too. Make sure he stays awake now, Kul."

They were barely gone when Kul brought me back to the task at hand. "I'm thinking it best we post right where we're at, Boss. We're up a bit here, can see the whole camp circle. And your lady's close, figure that's something, too."

"Fair enough," I said.

We settled down then, sitting back-to-back, each of us scanning half the view, talking in low voices when the mood took us, keeping silent when we felt like it. A normal watch, like old times.

30

AT SHIFT CHANGE, I let Kul go round to wake Case and Dramin and walked down to unfold my own bedroll next to Heyliannin. As I slipped under the covers and began to relax, she started up with a gasp. Her eyes glimmered like coals in the glow from the banked fire.

I groaned and shrugged myself deeper into my blankets. The night had gone chill. "Go back to sleep. What Calestinise said is true. Nobody's doing any of that tonight, least of all me."

"Not nobody," she said, her voice a tight, low, hiss.

"What?" I puzzled. Then I remembered Andus and Karthi. I groaned again. "You don't understand."

"What don't I understand?"

My eyes kept dragging themselves closed. Why couldn't she let me sleep?

"We walk through NeverSnows tomorrow."

"Sure. Like it ever snows around here. So what?"

I rolled over on my side, to face her, so she could see my anger. "You're as ignorant as any natural-born northerner," I spat out. "If you knew anything about anything, you'd know about the Battle of NeverSnows. We lost a lot of friends on that field. Andus's brother, for one."

Her voice went small. "Oh. I'm sorry."

"I don't want your *sorry*," I growled at her. "You think I want you to *comfort* me? You think you *could*?"

"Sorry," she said again.

I flopped to my back and stared up at those useless stars. Suddenly, the thing I wanted most was comfort. I remembered Eldennian's touch, those long dark nights, the things she did to help me not think about Shellon's heart-blood in my eyes, about Keev's eyes staring at the sky from his shattered face. Warmth flushed over me, my eyes itched. I wrenched myself over, to lie with my back to Heyliannin's questions and empty apologies. I tried to breathe easily as if I was asleep. Closing my eyes tight, I went through the names of the kings of Jeska. I made it back about twelve generations before exhaustion overtook me at last.

•   •   •

I woke at shift change, like always.

Heyliannin was still sitting there. Or was sitting up again.

"Volunteering for target practice?" I said.

She jumped a little, her face moving in and out of the light as she searched the darkness for danger. "Target practice?"

"It's what we tell new recruits. To get them to get their rest. If there's bandits out there, and you're sitting up, that makes you a target."

"I never figured on joining the army." It seemed like she might have been smiling then, but all I had to go on was the lightness in her voice.

"Well, you're married to a soldier, so get used to it."

"I was just thinking."

"What, again? I explained all I want to explain."

"No, not that. I was thinking about how I got myself into this. I was angry."

"At Tymon?" I shouldn't have spoken. She'd be wanting to talk and talk, wouldn't she? "Well, we've been through that."

"No. I mean, it was more than the non-marriage. I caught him."

My turn to be confused. "Did someone trick him into overcharging on a commission or cheating at dice?" That could happen, if Tymon thought a fellow runner needed his help.

"No, he was … was …" Couldn't she just say it?

Across the dim campsite, two of the new guys dragged themselves out of their slumbers, to take their turn on watch. "Spit it out," I told Heyliannin. "I'm going back to sleep in a minute."

She took a breath, and blew it out slowly. I watched a cloud pass over, making the stars vanish as it approached, then reappear at its trailing side. I was fading to sleep when she started up again. "It was after I came back from meeting that know-it-all creep at the Shamans' House."

"The Master Shaman? Fennic?" I silenced a laugh, imagining my father's old boss hearing her introduced as Orkast's successor.

"I suppose. Yes. We went to your place, and Eldennian was shouting at you, and your guy took me down to the Runners' House to find Tymon. Calestinise was there, in the kitchen, eating. Does she ever stop eating, by the way?"

"He," I interrupted.

"What?"

"If Calestinise is going to work for you, and you don't want him to hate you, you better start calling him he. You keep saying she."

"Oh," she said. "I didn't even realize I was doing that. Do I really?"

"Yes. Fix it. Go on with your dramatic story, so I can get back to sleep."

"Hmm, yes, you're right. I'm sorry. Calestinise was in the kitchen and I asked, 'Where's Tymon?', and he pointed to the back room, where we'd been sleeping, and said 'Better you than me.' So I thanked him, and I went in there, and found Tymon in bed—with two women." Her voice caught, but she forged on, with breaks and sobs between words. "They were all over each other, and another man was sitting off to the side, eating a piece of fruit. Just watching, like it was a play or a *teeveesho*. And Tymon. Tymon … he …" Her voice shuddered.

"Tymon invited you to join them."

"How did you…? But he couldn't make me. I wouldn't. I couldn't. How do they…?"

I stretched and tried to rearrange my blanket again. "I told you. You weren't listening. They're all married to each other. They don't keep ordinary families because they're never in one place long enough. Wherever they are, any runner they meet is family. People marry into Runners' House knowing this. Some embrace it. Other runners hover at the fringe, because they love the work, or prefer to be raising the children. Some outsiders despise runners because of it. But everyone knows."

The silence between us condensed like fog. "And that's why Tymon didn't tell me. Because everyone knows. Everyone except me."

"Eh, he should have explained. You're not from here, and he knew that." That explained her fury, then, when she came to see me and drank all my cider.

"*Sheeayyitt.*" She had interesting curse words. "I jumped into this arranged marriage thing because I wanted to hurt him as much as I could. And here it doesn't matter to him at all."

I thought of Tymon, down on his knees on the wedding platform, his shoulders shaking, his face in his hands. "Oh, it matters," I said. Tymon hadn't even come to see us off. I wondered if I'd ever see my brother again. "But, hey, I was completely drunk when we came up with this plan. So you're not the only one sitting out here in the dark thinking they're an idiot."

"Mm." She sounded almost sleepy.

I shrugged myself back down into my bedroll. "But if we're asleep, we don't have to think about it." I turned my back on her again, and went back to counting kings, starting with the ninth generation back. Those guys are so boring, I barely made it back five more generations before the dark overtook me again.

31

I'M NOT GOING TO TALK about the walk through NeverSnows. It's always the same, walking through an old battlefield. You'll think you're in the clear, and then you'll step on something that cracks, and you'll look down, and it's someone's calf-bone. Your heart stops, and your memory breaks into a run.

We'd taken barely twenty strides onto the field when Heyliannin drew to a halt. She turned in a circle, holding a hand up to shade her eyes. "Where's the … thing … sorry, I don't know the right word."

"What are you talking about?"

"The thing you put up on a battlefield, to remember it, to remind you of the people who died."

I knew what she meant. I'm an educated man, remember. I did know, even then, that elsewhere people put their honored dead under the ground, as if they were farmers, and then build towers or sculptures on top of them. That way, people make themselves feel better, as they tell themselves they're honoring the men who died, and they won't have to be reminded what it means to be dead. They contemplate their green, green battlefields and see a beautiful object to record for all time what great people the builders are, how respectful they are, how much they love their lost men. I thought about what to say, as the wind-brushed grasses brought back memories of that long, long, day.

"Look down," I said, choosing the simplest reply.

"What—"

"Look, really see what's here, where you're standing."

She frowned at me, and her brow wrinkled with thought. When she finally cast her eyes downward, I quickly brushed the fleck of moisture from the corner of my eye.

"What am I looking for?"

"Ask with your eyes, not your mouth."

She crouched and peered close at the ground in front of her, the grass bent and flattened by others that had gone before. I spotted the smooth curve of a rib, a pale arch cresting over the grass, and an irregular series of disconnected vertebrae, scattered like gambling stones rolled off the edge of a table. She reached a hand towards the rib, and I dropped to my knees and grabbed her wrist before she could touch it.

"Did I say *touch*?" I squeezed, feeling all the little bones where her hand met her arm. "Do you *see*?"

"Is that … what I think it is?"

"What do you think it is?"

"A bone. A human bone? Maybe. I can't tell, I was checking, to see for sure." She sounded so analytical. Maybe there were doctors in her family. What did I know about this woman I'd married?

What did she know about me?

This, though, she had to learn. "Don't fool yourself. It is what you see. You don't see with your hands, you see with your eyes. You think about it, you know what happened here. And you don't forget what you've seen for yourself."

"But—"

"Listen. This man here, he died fighting for Jeska, for us. You think you're ever going to forget walking through this field, seeing this man's bones right in front of you?"

"Um, no." Her eyes flicked further ahead and side to side, searching for more signs of death. Suddenly, I realized I was still gripping her arm, and let go. The mark on her wrist made a red band, like a thick bracelet, but as I watched, the red began to fade. I couldn't tell if the hard knot in my stomach meant I should have crushed harder or that I hadn't needed to hold her that tightly.

"Well then," I said, standing and shaking out my fingers. "It's a long walk across NeverSnows. You're bound to step on a few by mistake. By mistake. But you're not to take hold of anything here, understood?"

"Yes," she said, and stood beside me again. "I'm sorry. I didn't know."

"Don't be sorry," I told her. "Be careful." I brushed by her and strode ahead, stepping lightly, keeping my eyes focused on the ground. To either side, men and women bobbed and wove their way across the field, each doing as I did. There was plenty of time; I'd sent the pony carts around the long way, by the road. I paused at one point, to check on Heyliannin. Though she'd fallen behind, she was making her way properly enough. I didn't look back again until I'd jogged up the rise at the south edge of the field. I sat down in the early-summer grass, listening to the wind and watching Heyliannin's slow progress. I thought on Shellon, and Keev, and all our lost comrades, and I knew that Eldennian had been right. I'd've married off her daughter, our one and now forever only child, to my worst enemy—to a snake-man even—if it would prevent losses such as those.

And yes, I did say I'd say nothing about the walk through NeverSnows.

•　　　•　　　•

After the long, slow walk across the battlefield, we made good time.

We camped the second night a couple of hours short of Lakeside, the city that is. We'd crossed the district boundary when we first set foot on the field at NeverSnows. Yes, we'd come that close to losing Lakeside to the Southerners that day, and who would have stood between them and Jeskaryan if we'd fallen short?

At any rate, with the crossing behind us and the plunge into Lakeside society ahead of us, we all felt a need to stretch the night out well past the rising of the waning moon. Radeo cooked us up a feast, making the most of the rations we'd hauled from Jeskaryan. The man was sorely misplaced as a guardsman, to be sure. We took advantage and stuffed ourselves. The troopers put on their usual campfire entertainments: a song from Karthi, a skit from Case and Dramin making light of the trials of a new recruit, and a recitation from Arnim that involved too many puns for me but that drew outright laughter from Heyliannin.

When he'd finished, Arnim went straight to Heyliannin and handed off the talking stick he'd been waving in the air the whole time he'd been reciting. I think he does that to keep everyone's eyes turned his way. Or to keep people from falling asleep.

"What's this?" Heyliannin said.

"Your turn," I told her.

"My what?" She turned the stick over in her hands, asking the question with her eyes.

"Your turn to do something," Arnim explained. "Doesn't matter what. Anything. It's just us."

She stood slowly, and those gathered around the fire smacked their hands on their knees encouragingly, making a sound like fat raindrops falling around the circle. Arnim settled in the nearest open spot and joined in the applause.

"I don't sing … or tell stories … or … well …" She seemed to think I'd rescue her from this.

I snapped my fingers to tell her to get on with it. "Doesn't matter. Count backwards from ten in your own language. They'll think it's poetry."

"Poetry?" She tapped her head with the stick, lightly, the wood creaked as it swayed in her hand. "I had a friend who was a poet. I could try to translate one of his poems."

"Fine."

"Give me a minute." She bent her head and muttered softly to herself, sounding out foreign words, their possible translations. Then she lifted the stick, imitating Arnim at first, but soon shifting into moves more like a painter or a calligrapher at work.

"The fire falls, and the colors rise

"Rivers … flow?" she stopped herself. "Oh, right, cascade, that's it." She lifted the twig and started over:

The fire falls, and the colors rise
Rivers of amber, gold, and rose
Cascade their way around the sky
Pushing back the dark from the east
Holding the light for one last hour
Giving us time, time to remember
All of the days we have had together,
The glorious days beneath the sun.

Silence fell around the campfire, so you could hear the fire's crackling again. Heyliannin lowered the stick, and said, "It's better in the original, has sounds that match up, what do you call those?"

"Rhymes," Arnim said. She held out the stick to him.

Across the circle, Kul's low voice started up in a familiar melody, that old ballad everyone knows, about a pair of brothers who are parted as children but find each other again in old age. By the second chorus, everyone around the circle was singing along. Nearly everyone. I kept thinking of Tymon and Orkast, and Eldennian and Yutek, and I couldn't find my way to that happy ending. Heyliannin hummed along during the chorus; clearly, she didn't know the song. When Kul launched into the fourth verse, she tilted her head in my direction and said, "I can't tell if this is a happy song or not."

I murmured back to her, "Much like your poem."

"Oh, that, well, he liked sunsets a lot."

"Who?"

"My friend."

"Oh. Was he sad?"

"Sometimes, sometimes. Not more than most people. But he was a poet. So, well…" She shrugged. I had to wonder what degree of *friend* this man had been, that she memorized his poetry. The final chorus rolled up, and she managed most of the words that time.

PART IV

THE GOVERNOR TAKES PRACTICE

32

F OR OUR ENTRY INTO LAKESIDE, I had imagined arriving in disguise, dressed like ordinary farmers or merchants heading into town. We'd walk alongside regular citizens and listen to their thoughts on the incoming governor, on the crimes of the previous one. My Six and I, we'd turn up at the welcoming banquet and be refused entry, until we finally revealed ourselves in a dramatic moment.

That daydream hardly suited our caravan of nearly twenty. Instead, once we'd packed up the camp, my troopers and I pulled our best uniforms out of our baggage. Heyliannin's Four, as I'd begun to think of the new guardsmen, hadn't had the benefit of my lectures, but they each made themselves reasonably presentable. Meanwhile, Calestinise and Ganderrison dragged Heyliannin behind the larger wagon and there conducted an argument on proper attire for the Governor's Lady.

She emerged from that altercation bound up in a too-long dress, one hanging well past her knees, but the colors—flamelike shapes in gold and red flowing upwards and fading to a pale yellow at the top—suited her. The outfit had flash enough for a runner, suggesting it had come out of the hefty trunk those ladies from the Runners' House had dragged out to the cart the morning we left.

Calestinise pulled on a coat and trousers clearly borrowed from one of Yutek's house staff. When did he have time to get hold of a uniform between snagging the contract and meeting the travel party? My estimation of the boy's capabilities went up another notch.

We made good time until we reached the east-west road, where we encountered a crowded parade of caravans not unlike our own, and heading east like us. I'd've thought the people were fleeing an invasion if the marchers hadn't been so cheerful— people laughed and sang as they went, with ribbons fluttering from wagons and everyone in their brightest clothes.

I dispatched Dramin to ask questions. Meanwhile, our group had to bunch up tightly to fit ourselves into the queue. *Is this to do with me?* I wondered. *Did the interim governor call a festival in my honor? Who's going to pay for that?*

I untied Friendly Pony from the back of the wagon and mounted up, to assess the situation. The view wasn't much better, but I could see ahead, over an endless line of heads.

Kul grabbed at the reins, complaining, "Boss! Don't be makin' yerself a target, sir!"

"It's all right, Kul. We're the only fighters out here."

"You can't know that sir," he insisted.

Did I tell you there's no arguing with Kul? Probably. True then. True now. I hopped down again and handed the reins to Karthi.

"Ride up along the road. See how far ahead it's this crowded." I congratulated myself again on making sure my men could ride.

"Sure, Boss. Maybe a wagon's tipped over or something." He clambered aboard and threaded his way out towards the uneven grassland alongside the earthen road.

Not long after, Dramin returned with his report.

"Turtles, sir."

"Ya, I know. They're moving as fast as turtles. Tell me something new."

"No, sir. I mean, that's it, sir. It's the turtle festival in Lakeside."

"The what?"

"Turtle festival. There's a huge harvest of turtles from the lake, everyone celebrates, it's a few days of nonstop parties, they tell me. Food, music, all that."

"For turtles."

"Good eatin', turtles," Kul contributed.

There was nothing for it. We became one more party of dressed-up travelers, inching our way along the road to Lakeside City. Karthi came back eventually, having ridden miles up the road. As best he could tell, there was a backup at the great bridge that crossed Heart River just outside the city. The bridge had been one of the Great Works of the last generation, but it didn't need to be wide, ordinarily.

"We couldn't have chosen a worse day to arrive," I reported to Heyliannin, who'd put up with sitting on the bench at the front of the big wagon, scrunched between the midwife and her servant. I waved Calestinise and the medic to get down and took my place next to my wife. For show, I pretended to drive the ponies, who needed no driving at the pace we were going.

"We are become turtles," Heyliannin sighed.

"At least we're well-dressed. You are, at any rate."

"What, this old thing?" she said, with a wry twist to her smile. "If I'd known I'd have to wear clothes like this, I would have run back north faster than any runner."

I bit my tongue. That was a line of discussion I wanted to avoid. Yutek would tell me, in a difficult diplomatic moment, focus on the most-trivial topic you can think of.

"All right," I said. "I'll hire you a tailor. Get you a whole new wardrobe. Whatever you like."

"I do not need a new wardrobe. I have perfectly good clothes."

"No, you don't."

She rolled her eyes and groaned. "The first time I ran away from home, it was to get away from the stupid clothes."

Now there's a story I'd like to hear, I thought. "Easier for me, I can put on a uniform, and I'm done."

"You shouldn't, though."

"What?"

"You're not a guardsman any more, Corren. You know that don't you?"

Not what I wanted to hear. *Focus on the trivial.* "So I need a tailor, too?"

We talked about clothes for the better part of an hour. For a person who hated the idea of new clothes, she had a lot of ideas about them.

Maybe I wasn't the only one who'd been taught diplomacy.

•   •   •

By the time we reached the bridge, I'd memorized the words to the most popular Turtle Festival song, unavoidable with the groups in front and behind competing to see who could raise their drunken voices the loudest. At least we'd have a place to stay when we arrived. The group behind us spent half the time arguing about who had failed to make arrangements.

In the end, instead of two hours, it took six to drive from our campsite to the governor's house. Ternak, the old fellow who'd been managing things in the meantime, dispatched a cadre of servants to wait for us at the city gate. They directed us to the house, helped haul baggage off the pony carts, and instructed everyone to be prepared for a formal dinner that evening. Evidently, Ternak planned to take advantage of the festival to introduce us to the council heads and matriarchs of a half-dozen of the nearest townships. It was a brutal introduction to our way of life for the foreseeable future: unwanted meals with difficult people conducted while exhausted and crammed into uncomfortable clothes.

We had the luxury of a couple of hours to prepare for this first event. After being lectured by Heyliannin on the negative impression I'd give if I showed up to a social event in battle dress, I did my best to assemble something less threatening-looking. Arnim, who had only to dust off his reasonably-clean uniform, helped, but laughed at me the whole time. Calestinise had the first major challenge of his position as lady's maid, with Heyliannin objecting to every single one of his suggestions, her voice rising with each new proposal.

Finally, wearing a pair of non-uniform trousers borrowed from Arnim and with a bundle of completely unsuitable shirts in my arms, I marched in on them. Heyliannin had on one of her boring grey dress-things. Calestinise looked like his head was about to explode.

"Ma'am," he was saying. "If you were a landed lady, no one would care. But you have to do whatever you can to impress them, don't you see, so they'll respect you in your own right."

"Landed lady?" Heyliannin said. "I'm landed. I've got my acre up north with a house on it and everything."

"What he means," I tried to explain, "is that usually a governor, or here in Lakeside, any township director, will be married to a woman from a family that manages big property, someone whose mother's important in the matriarchy. That would mean a major farm up in Jeska, maybe down here a fishery. It's a way of forming alliances. For someone who's supposed to be king, it's worse, usually they want to see a connection from outside Jeska."

"Oh, really?"

"Yes, really. Now let Calestinise do his job, why don't you?"

She frowned at me, but this time it was a thoughtful frown. I wasn't sure I liked that kind any better.

33

T HE DINNER INVOLVED ... food ... drink ... the usual. I had to be talking so much, it was essentially impossible to eat anything. Fortunately, most of the menu involved eating turtles, so I was content to go hungry. As instructed, my Six made sure I kept away from the drink. I noticed the Four did the same for Heyliannin, without being told.

There were speeches. Turns out I was supposed to make one. I managed to put together enough words in a row that it sounded like I had planned for it. The trick, Yutek taught, is to say a few complimentary things, say some grateful-sounding things, and then give more compliments. He was right, that works every time.

After the meal, a crew of energetic servants appeared. They removed most of the chairs and pushed the tables to the side of the room. Attendees milled around, forming into clusters and little groups, mostly separating themselves by gender and occupation. Servants strolled through, distributing drinks and little plates with cut-up fruits. My stomach rumbled at the thought of edible food, but it was not to be. The interim governor looped his arm in mine and walked the room with me, forcing me to greet and make small talk with the little clique-masters and power holders of Lakeside. He'd roped in the directors of the seven northernmost townships of Lakeside, as well as the husband of one of the biggest fishery managers, who'd made the long journey from South Point. The directors each sought to impress me with the critical needs their managers wanted attended to: fishing rights, water rights, worker shortages, and damages from the southern incursion. Some of those needs might be genuine; their desires to secure promises from me certainly had the ring of truth. I resolved to send Arnim around, with friendly-faced Karthi at his back, to make inquiries into the facts, in his own way.

The night had almost become unbearable when Ternak paused at an animated circle surrounding a far-traveling fellow, a merchant type by the name of Nandeen. He'd been enlivening the party with stories of festival days on the border with Alcala, our nearest neighbor and sometimes our ally. I'd patrolled that border once, before NeverSnows, as a junior trooper. My Six and I had never been sent that far south. From the talk I was hearing now, the border there had become fluid, with people passing north and south more or less unchallenged. Was this a part of Yutek's strategy for peace, to maintain friendship with Alcala in exchange for acting as a buffer against incursions from further south?

The moment he noticed us on the periphery of his group, Nandeen approached with great interest. "It's glad I am to make your acquaintance." He bobbed his head awkwardly, his round face split by a wide, affable grin. "Is it true you're the king's own son? It's a bit of a comedown, isn't it, to be sent off to Lakeside to watch over us fishermen and farmers?" He thrust his hand towards me, in the greeting so common in those parts.

The courtier types around him all but gasped aloud. I swept my gaze over them, catching their frozen disdain at this countryman's vulgar approach to their prince. *If only it were in my power to cut them off at the ankles.*

I threw my head back and laughed, then reached out and clasped his hand firmly. He had a good, strong grip, and it was eminently satisfying to feel his calluses against my own. "On the contrary, I'd say it's a nice step up for an armorer's son to hobnob with these fine people." I snagged a plate of fruit and nuts from a passing servant. "But, yes, it's true, I'm Yutek's now, to do with as he wishes, and it seems he wishes for me to step into those enormous boots of his one day." *On a day far too soon, I think.*

I kept an eye on the shocked crowd, picking out one or two whose reactions tended more to anger than confusion or embarrassment. That tall, thin fellow with his over-thick hair pulled back too tightly seemed ready to stick a knife into somebody, possibly me. *Definitely put the Six onto that one.*

"Oh, my, well, won't my wife be disappointed now, that she couldn't come represent South Point Fishery at the festival this year." He bent forward slightly, as though sharing a state secret with me. "Normally, now, I can get her to delegate the management to her sister, but this year, don't you know, she's expecting something enormous." He arched both arms over his belly and puffed his cheeks out.

I half-expected Tight Mane to pull out a knife right then and there.

Myself, I rattled off the usual pleasantries, the congratulations-are-in-order, laying it on thicker than I ordinarily would, until the angry courtier whirled around and removed himself from the scene. I watched him go. *Don't think that'll take you off my watch list.* Inside, though, I reeled from an abrupt realization of my own, under the heading of Duties of Royalty. I cast around the room until I spotted Heyliannin, stuck in a circle of women in long, colorful outfits, finely tailored even to my eye. Shorter than any of them, stiff in that flame-decorated monstrosity, she might have been more ready to kill someone than the man who had fled my presence.

Yutek's advice rang in my ears, *Adopt a couple of boys until you can get a son off her.* Granted, he'd been thinking of Eldennian. But that's what was expected of me.

Of us.

It's me she's going to kill.

•   •   •

Given the circumstances, it took time to maneuver myself into the same corner of the banquet room as my dutiful wife. The circle around her had shifted, with one set of sneering female faces replaced by a new set. As Ternak tried to steer me into another engagement with a township supervisor, Heyliannin caught my eye and gestured to me.

"Duty calls," I told Ternak, and snagged a fresh plate of fruit from a passing server as I joined the ladies' torture session.

Shifting her wine glass to her other hand, Heyliannin looped her arm through mine. The smile she directed my way might have killed a weaker man. Then she turned that elegant grimace on her opponents, and not one of them batted an eye.

"May I introduce my husband, Corren, son of Yutek."

I gave them a proper smile. "Ladies."

"Governor." The thick-set woman at the center of the group lifted her glass, and the other women followed suit.

I proffered the plate of fruit. "Berries, anyone?" A cascade of murmured refusals spared me from sharing my dinner. "My tenure here will not be overlong, I think. How shall I advise my father on the selection of my inevitable replacement?"

My salvo was met by a round of silence, broken by the ringleader. "I am sure that the managers of the Eight Townships will be more than happy to form a selection committee." Her fringe-edged dress, that barely reached to the tops of her well-filled-out calves, had been cut from fabric featuring stripes of blue and yellow, with a distinctive design that I recognized, but from where? Probably one of the men I'd met this evening wore that design. Which meant, most likely, I was being baited by one of the senior managers of Lakeside.

"So be it." I drilled into her cold, businesslike gaze with my own and tightened my smile. "Would you chair that committee, Madame … ?"

Little crows-feet fanned out from the corners of her eyes as her lips imitated benevolence. "Velisennin. Of South Bank."

Indeed. South Bank. The largest fishery on the Lake, its territory straddling Southeast and South Point townships. "A pleasure, Ma'am." I toasted her with a plump purple berry.

"And your Lady, here, Governor, she has most politely listened to our talk of Lakeside, yet we yearn to hear news of Jeskaryan, the grand city of Jeska."

"Indeed." What had she told them? Did they see a highborn landed lady of Jeska or a country herbalist from the north country? I wondered what they would think if she told them she was a shaman from beyond our world.

One of the younger ladies, perhaps a representative of her mother's clan, spoke up. "Tell us, Governor ..." I turned my eyes on her and she stopped short, sipped at her drink. Her thin pink tongue flashed between her teeth, catching the drops of wine on her lips. "You are newly married, we hear. Tell us, how did you find your bride? There was no word of a search, merely an announcement of marriage."

"Highly irregular." Velisennin's expression betrayed nothing, but she chose her words for maximum effect. "Who is your mother, Heyliannin? Do your family holdings lie distant from Jeskaryan or close by?"

We had a story planned, worked out in detail on the long drive south. It involved a blend of truth and fiction, so that the inquisitive could be steered to verifiable facts. I felt Heyliannin grow still at my side, and glanced down at her. "Shall I?" I suggested. She might not have taken in the seriousness of Velisennin's challenge.

"No. It's my place to speak of my family." She lifted her chin, standing as tall as she could manage, and swept a regal gaze from one to the other of her inquisitors. "My mother? My mother is Jeen Lohrayne Roe'ee." She spread out the syllables, as if giving them time to recognize the name. "Manager of *jee'orjee-ah'atlantik coreporeayshun*." The first word might have been several, but she ran through them so fast, it was hard to tell.

Dark lines formed across Velisennin's brow. "What is your crop?"

My wife sneered at her. If she'd been taller, it might have been more effective. "The Roe'ees are not farm people. Or fishers. We manage timber."

"Timber?" That was the younger woman. "You mean, wood-cutters?" She had the audacity to snicker.

Heyliannin leveled her with a sharp scoff. "We are the number-one leaseholder in Region Nine, processing over two million board feet of lumber per year. Of course, we operate well beyond Region Nine. We are *the* supplier of lumber to all the premium builders in the Southeast." She sipped her wine and glanced up at me over the rim of her glass, daring me to interrupt.

I kept my lips clamped shut over the questions. Region nine? Of how many? The Southeast of where?

"The South East, you say?" Velisennin pursed her lips and narrowed her eyes. "Are you a Southerner, then?"

Heyliannin's fake smile widened. I hadn't noticed before: her teeth were perfectly straight, as if installed by a master-crafter. "Why, Velisennin, *blayess yore hahrt.*" It did not sound like a compliment. She lifted her glass. "In my own country, I'm considered a Southerner, but, do not let that confuse you, my dear. My country is far, far to the east of Jeska." I dropped my eyes at a tug from her hand on my arm. "Isn't that so, Corren?"

Shaken off-kilter by this impossible-to-verify story, I could do no more than support it. "Indeed, Madame Velisennin." I fixed my gaze on that imposing figure and her glare of consternation. "Yutek seeks alliances when they come to us. Heyliannin traveled here from far beyond the mountains of the Great Wall. These Easterners have much to offer, despite their remoteness from Jeska."

The Chief Inquisitor narrowed her eyes, focusing on Heyliannin with new interest. "Oh, really?"

This seemed a good moment to leave them wondering, before my gut-ache became more than a mere annoyance. "If you ladies will excuse us, we really must circulate." I pressed my arm close to my side, that arm Heyliannin had in her grasp, and drew her along with me, towards the next clot of nosy Lakesiders.

34

T HE BED WE SHARED in Lakeside may not have matched our marriage bed in opulence—I judged it wider but shorter—but it was a proper bed. It had a nice, firm, wadded-reed mattress and smelled freshly stuffed. So, somebody in this household wanted us comfortable. *I bet our Calestinise could find out who. Best to know our allies here, from basement to attic.*

Heyliannin shed the yellow-and-orange abomination and dragged a shapeless sack of a nightdress over her head. She caught me watching and rewarded me with a scowl.

"Like what you see?"

"Not like I haven't seen it before." No denying it, either, how much better she looked compared with that day we met in the mountains. Dramin had told me he figured she'd been starving to death out there.

I realized I was still looking her way, so I strolled to the long window that filled the wall opposite the door. The room faced the mansion's inner courtyard, and I tugged the shutter open at one end, to watch two … make that three … lanterns floating through the dark—people making their various ways along the paths that led between the residential, service, and public areas of the building.

Before I turned back, I snugged the shutter closed, but teased the slats open enough to let the cool night air flow in. I missed the hills of Jeskaryan already.

I expected to find her curled up, pretending to be asleep.

Not sure why I thought that.

All that talking on the road ran through my head.

She sat in the middle of the bed, her legs curled under her, feet out of sight under the tent of that ugly nightdress.

"Your turn," she said.

"For what?"

"You're not coming to bed in that mess, are you?"

I looked down at Arnim's dress shirt and trousers. Three short streaks of purple followed one another from the shirt to the upper thigh of the pants. Berry juice. At least it wasn't red—people would have thought I'd been out killing people on the way to the banquet. "Arnim's not going to like this. He hates doing laundry."

"I have a suspicion there will be people here to do your laundry."

"Arnim's fussy."

"Which one's Arnim again?"

"How can you travel with people for days and not know who's who?" I was one to talk. I still hadn't sorted out the names of half her guard.

"That's the thing. You know each other. You never use names. It's all hey and ya and Boss. How come Boss and not Commander? Calestinise calls you Commander, but your guys don't."

I unlaced the shirt and peeled it off. "So. Arnim's the toff, the book-reader, the wordy guy with the smooth face. He carries two knives." Surely she recalled that day in my office.

"Ohhh, at the campfire, the other night, he did the thing with all the puns in it."

"Right."

She had an odd expression on her face when I turned back from rummaging in my bag for clean clothes. Was it all the little scars from years of skirmishes and border patrols, or the long one slashed from my right shoulder blade down to my hipbone? Yutek the Younger hadn't liked blunted swords at practice.

Had she talked with Tymon, about his scars? The rippled stripes, the soft translucencies, nothing you'd get in battle. At the time, I'd tried any ointments I could cadge, until I learned the best thing was to sneak him down to the barracks for a dunk in the cold pool. The inner scars? Well, here we were.

I dropped the clean stuff on the bed and wriggled out of the borrowed trousers. Arnim was my height—short—but skinnier. The waistband left a deep red mark circling above my hips.

Ya, first thing tomorrow, get her to send Calestinise down to town to scare up a tailor.

A phantom smile danced at the edges of those thin lips of hers. Her gaze never wavered, but it wandered.

The heat in the room became unbearable. "Listen," I said. "It's our first night here. We spent a full day on the road and then had that banquet to deal with."

I reached for my clothes, but she grabbed them and pulled them out of reach. "So where are you going?"

"Going?"

"You're getting dressed."

"What? Like it or not, I'm not going anywhere."

She held the shirt out of my reach and lifted it to the light. Then her eyebrows did that thing where one scrunched and the other tilted upwards. Even from where I stood, you could see the candle-light glowing through the worn places. "Wait … this thing is trash."

I had to lean halfway across the bed to snatch my favorite old shirt out of her hands. "It's not trash. It's a little worn. It's comfortable."

She was about to grab my pants for another fabric inspection, but I beat her to it.

Eldennian had never cared how I dressed. "Listen, don't worry, I won't get confused and wear these things to a banquet and embarrass you."

She crossed her arms and tipped her head to one side, watching as I pulled on the shirt and tied it closed, but loose. Not quite as old as the shirt, the trousers lacked see-through patches, but years of laundering had rendered them light on the skin.

"You're really going to sleep in that trash."

When someone criticizes your stuff, it's like they're criticizing you, personally. "I told you. Not trash."

"Tymon sleeps naked."

Did she have to bring him into this? "That's just like my brother. What if something happens, you have to get up suddenly?"

For example, what if your brother wakes you up in the middle of the night because Yutek the Younger has gotten himself invested, and now there'll be no stopping him, and your brother needs your help to get out of the house. Now, not tomorrow. He needs a safe place out of reach of the royal hands, and there's two possibilities—the shamans and the runners. You've laid out a course before you even reach the back door to the kitchen, to the panel that opens onto the long gutter where they throw the waste water, the gutter that's a snap to slide down, but is never guarded because who would try to climb up a drain?

It works, because you didn't have to waste time putting on clothes. But I wasn't about to let her trap me into talking about Tymon.

I gestured at her silly costume. "You have sleeping clothes. I'm not mocking you."

She spread her hands and patted the air between us. "All right, all right. I was surprised, that's all, because, you know, before …"

I pulled on my trousers quickly, before the memory of our wedding night could have too much of an effect. "Like I said, it's been a long day—"

"I heard you." Her eyes were definitely not focused on mine.

I tugged my shirt down, but it was a work shirt, not a dress shirt, wasn't meant to fall too low. "I meant—"

"I know what you meant."

"All right, then." So long as she didn't sit up all night waiting again. Kul had been—what's the word for politely not commenting? But Andus and Karthi had had a few laughs at my expense, during watch changes, while Arnim had done those other things, like making her talk at the campfire, trying to make her part of it. Other companies, you don't laugh at the boss or approach his wife, but, like I've said, me and my Six, we were our own family. Still, it meant everyone noticed.

She pursed her lips and avoided my eyes. "No, it's not all right. I'm not up on your politics, but you're even more under a *mykroskope* here. It's obvious from the way people watched you tonight, the things they said when they thought I wasn't listening. Whatever we do—or don't do—people will know."

So, both allies and enemies in the house? Calestinise has his work cut out for him.

"Besides," she went on. "It wasn't … too bad."

I had to laugh. "'Not too bad.' That's what they'll put in the histories when I die. 'Corren, son of Yutek. Not too bad.' Then again, Calestinise might have other words."

She laughed in turn and patted the bedcover with one hand. "With a little work, I think we can get to 'not bad.'"

With caution, I decided that gesture was meant as an invitation. I sat on the edge of the bed and slid back until I could turn and sit cross-legged next to her. Not exactly typical newlyweds. "Work, you say? You think I need work?"

"You think it's a skill you're born with?"

"And you don't think so?"

She shook her head. It was kind of pretty, the way her fine hair floated around when she did that.

"I suppose back home you're a great teacher of the art."

"Well, I wouldn't say that. But there's things I know you probably don't."

"You're joking."

"I'm not." She tipped her head to one side again, studying me. "Remember, I talked to Eldennian. Or, I should say, she talked to me."

My first night with Eldennian ran through my head like a herd of wild ponies. The arch of her lips, how her scent drew me in. The way she ran one finger down my face, tracing the broken and rebroken bones in my nose, and said, "Don't worry. I'll tell you what to do." I was a guardsman, and Yutek's foster-son, and more than once had a girl taken me to her bed, but never more than once the same girl. Eldennian changed that.

The candle on the low table behind me guttered in the breeze from the window and went dark, and Heyliannin's face fell into shadow. The lamp in the corner, behind her, made a blurry golden glow around the edges of her silhouette. She'd gone quiet, and the blank formless shape in front of me became a ghost staring into my soul.

I've told you though, I don't believe in ghosts.

"You can stop staring at me," I told her.

"I'm sorry." She turned away from me and pushed herself to the edge of the bed, where she dropped to her feet with a dull thump. "I wasn't thinking. I'm sorry."

"But you're right, though." I had to bring it up, I wasn't the kind to leave things be.

"I'm right?"

"Ya. People are watching. And there's another thing. Someone reminded me, tonight, right before you told those lies to the ladies of Lakeside."

"They weren't lies. What other thing?"

"Sounded like lies. Did you see Velisennin's face?" She might have shrugged; it was hard to tell. "About the other thing. It's important, but Tymon might not have thought of it, for all that the reason we're here is because the king's one true-son did that single good thing for the world."

My ghostly wife's hair floated in the candlelight as she rummaged in her own bags. She stood up with an armful of blankets. "All right. Tell me. What great thing did he do?"

"He dropped dead. Blankets? Are you cold?"

"Yes." She shook one blanket out to cover her side of the bed and tossed me the other. "Am I to think you killed your brother so you could be king?" Her voice had a catch to it, as if she thought that might be true.

"Foster brother. And, no, I never wanted the job. I was supposed to be guard commander. Come to think of it, probably the elders would have had me kill him, eventually, for the sake of the country. But I'd've given Tymon the king job. People like Tymon." Couldn't I have stopped before mentioning him? Probably not.

She turned to the lamp and snuffed the candles. The bed creaked as she climbed back up. Under the soft whistling of the breeze flowing through the window slats, I could hear the blanket rustling against the fabric of her nightdress. She made a faint sound, like a sneeze held back.

Or a sob.

I couldn't tell.

I flicked the lightweight blanket and lay down, letting it settle over me like a sigh. It smelled of wood ash and earth.

"I can't leave this be," I said to her back.

She neither moved nor spoke.

"I'll scout for foster sons, it's budgeted for. But we have to produce an heir of our own, first. We need a child, as soon as we can, within the year if possible."

Her voice came muffled, so I knew she'd buried her head in the blanket.

"Forget it. I'm not having a baby."

I blinked hard and saw little Deliasin's red face, her wide eyes staring, gathering in the whole world in every blink. I could almost smell the sweet memory of the milk on her breath, feel the tightness of her fist wrapped around my little finger.

Heyliannin may have had more *experience* than me, but she hadn't had a baby before.

So there was something I could maybe teach my wife.

"You'll see," I told her. "It's not too bad."

35

T HE ONE THING I'D BEEN DREADING was Heyliannin figuring out where she'd got things wrong in her plan to get Orkast's mantle back. Sure, we were in the district the Jeskaryan shamans had sent the mantle to, but like as not she was figuring Lakeside was Lakeside. Every morning, I waited for it, the demand to go to the Shamans' House and fetch her property. Once in a while, I thought of bringing it up myself, but I didn't like to think of her reaction.

Thing is, the Shamans' House in Lakeside District isn't in North Township, where we were. It's in Southeast Township, practically at South Point. It wasn't like running down the hill at Jeskaryan, a ten-minute walk from the fortress gate to the Shamans' House.

Lucky for me, she was busy with a project of her own. One thing I was beginning to learn about my wife: she tended to jump into things with both feet. Not necessarily looking first at what she was leaping into.

Early example: running to warn the snake-man we were planning to capture him.

More-recent example: marrying me to get to Lakeside and get even with Tymon.

New example: auditing Lakeside's accounts. That big fat book she'd taken from my father's chosen accountant? Heyliannin laid out the ledger on the biggest table she could get, in a room with no windows and a door that locked. She demanded all the keys, and sent her meanest-looking retainer, Harad, around the sub-offices in the place to make it known what would happen to anyone who dared intrude on her domain. Then she hauled in the accounts reports from two years before NeverSnows and piled them on one side of the table. She did the same on the other side, for accounts since Ternak took over the governorship.

Every morning, straight after breakfast, Heyliannin disappeared behind that door. And locked it.

I came to look forward to hearing the grind and clank of the lock. At first, I was thinking, *I don't have to be worrying about her bothering me*, while I was wading through the morass of politics that kept getting in the way of the practical needs of the district. Later, the sound of that lock engaging became more about safety than annoyance.

My conversation with the South Point manager's husband, the one overeager to describe how pregnant his wife was, had raised suspicions in my mind. I wished I could make a grand tour of all the townships, circle the lake, and investigate what was going on under the surface in our largest district. That was impossible, for a lot of reasons, not least of which being that any day I'd get called back to Jeskaryan for my investing, and any other day we might get word of Yutek's death.

Arnim and I put our heads together on that problem, and the Six took it in turns to make their off-hours into work hours, crawling the pubs and gambling dens of the northerly townships. Karthi and Andus made for a hilarious team, as Karthi would get himself thoroughly soused—or apparently so—and then Andus would play the role of friend-needing-help-to-get-drunk-home. Any volunteers would be drained dry of intel by the time they parted ways at the rooming house we'd commissioned. Wasn't long before they'd walk into a pub and the barkeep would start lining up the glasses for Karthi. The others had their own schemes.

Arnim played the world-weary aristocrat from up the valley, attracting managers' daughters eager to soothe his tortured soul. And his beautiful body, no doubt.

Day by day, the reports Arnim brought me—from his own and the others' gatherings—became more and more disturbing. We'd thought sending the mercenaries home and routing the corrupt governor would put an end to treasonous behavior in Lakeside.

We'd only shaved the hair off the bear.

Everyone grumbled about high taxes, low income, crummy roads, poor fishing (as if that was the governor's job, to make fish swim into nets), and the military-service requirement. Everything had been better in Lakeside before the annexation with Jeska, that was the story. They'd voluntarily annexed . . . no, they'd begged to join the Unified Districts of Jeska three generations ago. None of the whiners remembered the Jeskan doctors who came down to treat the plague, the fact that there were no roads before the annexation, that every year before then raiders regularly emptied storerooms all around the lake. What was wrong with asking the district to send a reasonable number of likely lads up north to test out for the Guard?

My mission had been to tidy up the income stream, normalize government structure, and make nice with everybody. It was going to take more than a year of making nice to clean up this district. Worse, the people in Lakeside had a general mistrust— make that dislike—of anybody from "up north" as they called it, and anybody from "way up north" was nothing more than a savage. The dialect that Heyliannin knew, the northern accent, marked her indelibly. She worked on it, but you can never really get rid of an accent. When she locked her door to do her *furrensick* accounting, as she called it, I breathed a sigh of relief, but put a guard on the door anyway.

Nights, we did what we could to keep the gossips satisfied. Heyliannin's midwife made her a chart of what she— Ganderrison—called "likely days" and my wife made good and sure to be indisposed when those days came around on the calendar. Outside of those times, I had to put up with a lot of lessons on what I was doing wrong. It wasn't so bad. I thought of it like the first month of guard training—the real thing, not the fun and games we had in the under-guard.

In between instructions on positions, acceptable and unacceptable techniques, and mental—yes, mental!—exercises she wanted me schooled on, I got previews on her accounting results.

"It's a horrible mess," she declared one horrendous midsummer night, flopping back down beside me, the sweat running over her like she'd just climbed out of a bath.

"What'd I do wrong this time?" I sighed. Not that any of it felt wrong. I felt . . . though I'd've died rather than admit it, then . . . good. I put an extra edge into my voice, to keep that feeling hidden. "I did everything you said." Every rotten gut-ache I'd built up all day was gone, my muscles were like braised meat, hot and relaxed, and I could have fallen asleep right then if she hadn't answered me.

"Not that. The accounts. They are totally *scrood*." I was beginning to enjoy her foreign profanity.

I pulled up from my doze, enough to pay attention. "Explain. Scrood is bad, right?"

"Right. Bad. Intentionally bad. Like they've been *haaked*." Not all of those curses made sense.

"What's haaked? Is that another sex word, like scrood?"

"I'm not teaching you dirty talk tonight. But haaked means messed with by an outsider."

I stared up at shadows on the ceiling. "Outsider?"

"There's an unknown agent acting on the cash flow in this district . . . I'd call it a hidden hand . . . And it's not to the benefit of Lakeside or Jeska as a whole." She pulled the blanket up and wiped sweat from her face with one corner. "I'm out of my depth, Corren. I can't figure out the source of it, not with paper records. I need a *sordabledaydabays*."

"I'd get you one if I had any idea what it was."

"Never mind."

"But I have an idea who it is."

"Who?"

"Outsiders, you said. The Southerners had people embedded with the old governor, the one who was skimming funds. I'm guessing it was more than mercenary soldiers. I met Gorton, when they dragged him up in front of my father afterwards, before they executed him. He wasn't smart enough, I think, to do what he did, not without direction. I'm thinking now, Father should've kept him alive."

"Why? You getting soft on the death penalty now?" She sounded bitter. She didn't like the idea of killing criminals. What were we supposed to do with them? Build houses that lock from the outside, to store them in until the shamans figure out how to magic them into good people?

"No, being practical. We could go and ask him, then."

"Ask." She snorted. After all, hadn't I interrogated her, what, three times?

"You know what I mean."

She sighed and rolled over, away from me. "You're always talking about Southerners. Isn't everyone here a southerner? Who are you so worried about? That guy with the pregnant wife who runs a fishery?"

"No, no, the people of Lakeside are Jeskans." *Whether they like it or not.* "Then south of here, it's Alcala. They're allies. Not very strong, themselves, but they're a buffer against the real Southerners, the Hashteks and *their* allies. Those people are dangerous."

"You mean Aztecs? Like, *pirramids* and human, uhh, don't know the word, where you kill somebody to satisfy the, what's the word? Big, powerful beings?" She rolled back over, a strange kind of interest in her eyes.

"Murderers, that's what I call people like that. And you're saying it wrong. Hashteks. You're always doing that, Ta-ma, hearing a word and filling in what you think you heard, not what was really said."

"Whatever. But what's the word for it? When they cut out somebody's heart. Shed blood for the *gawds*." Her curiosity didn't stop at anything, did it?

I recalled how our tutor would tell us stories from the old oral histories, to remind us how much worse off we'd be anywhere other than Jeska. She must have had crazier tutors than mine. "Are you talking about religion? What's the point in killing people over spirit stuff? I've studied more history than you can imagine, and I've never heard of anyone doing that. Do they murder people over religion in your Atlantis?"

"Atlanta. And no, we don't do that. We just have regular murder. And hate crime."

"What's that"

"When some idiot doesn't like your skin color or your ancestors or the way you say potato."

"Your Atlanta seems to me like a very scrood country."

She was silent for a while. I figured I'd insulted her. Fair, after her remarks on my deficiencies as a husband. I had almost managed to start going to sleep, when she started up again, on a brand-new topic.

"Listen." She poked me in the shoulder, hard, as if her voice wasn't enough to wake me up. "I'm thinking I'm more wrong than you think I am. Where did your people come from?"

"Where did *people* come from?" I yawned and stretched. "People came from animals. Everyone knows that."

"Oh." I wished I could see her face. Was she surprised to learn this or surprised I knew it? "I…" *thought you backward Jeskans didn't know that.* For once, she decided to refrain from insulting me and my culture. "That's interesting. But what I meant to ask was, how did your people get to Jeska?"

"Ah." We had been talking history, not biology. "A few thousand years ago, we traveled up from the south. History wasn't being written down then, so the stories vary. Seems there was a drought, and disagreements with the predecessors of the Hashteks. Anyhow, our people—and the coastal peoples, and probably the redlanders, too, come to think of it—we hiked across the desert, kept going until we found what we liked."

"You didn't come down from the north."

"No."

"Then how did people get to where the Hashteks are, down south?"

She wanted the truly ancient stories, then. How had she missed them? The tales of the boat people wove themselves into songs and stories. Some of the most-venerable landkeeper names, like Velisennin, claimed their origins in the great crossing. "If you're hearing this for the first time, best do it right." I shrugged off the bedlinens and lit a lamp, I sat us facing one another, the lamp between us, so she could see the gestures that go with the story and I could see the dawn of learning in her eyes.

I'm no storyteller, but the tale suited that little hotbox of a room, with barely a breath of air, hot and humid like the islands of our most-distant ancestors. She did keep interrupting, but that proved her interest. Evidently, on her side of the thin patch, people thought it was easier to walk the long way around than build boats and take a direct route.

"So where are your boat-builders, now?" She had a good question. I didn't have a good answer.

"Exploring other places?" The distances weren't as great as Heyliannin seemed to think, but, still, it didn't seem to support trade. A shame. Imagine if you had trading partners halfway across the great ocean—likely you'd see goods from even farther off, from their other contacts. "Maybe when I'm king, we'll get together with some coastal family and build a few boats of our own. Go find out."

"When you're king." She snuffed out the lantern. First light turned the window slats to bands of black rimed with silver. "Why not now? Wouldn't Yutek let you?"

"Yutek's not one to look much beyond our borders. I wonder what he's missed besides the graft down here in Lakeside?" My gut snagged on the thought, clenched itself in a way that wasn't hunger. What had I missed? "Well, at least we're not in Atlantis, where hate is a crime."

Heyliannin scooted out of bed and started throwing on clothes. "You're right," she said. "I'll go back there, eventually, when I get Asdyel back. But I won't be staying. There's a whole other lot of worlds out there, and that one is scrood-up, big time."

So she hadn't forgotten about my father's mantle.

36

I BARELY HAD TIME to put Arnim on the task of snooping around the governor's offices. Heyliannin could tell me who had signed off on what, but just because a functionary signs a document doesn't mean he or she knows what's in it. I needed to work out which office-holders belonged in their positions and which ones were either rattlesnakes in dogskins or had been bought off by Southern spies. From what my wife told me, there was a lot more money circulating in Lakeside than there ought to be.

Why no time? Because a runner came tearing into town with the news I had to go to Jeskaryan immediately. At least the runner wasn't Tymon.

The scrawny young woman trembled with exhaustion, as if she'd run without a break. I had a horrible feeling that Yutek had up and died already. "Why?" I demanded. "What's wrong?"

"Your investing ceremony. It's in two days. You're supposed to have gone up to Jeska three days ago."

"I never heard anything about that."

She leaned over and panted for a minute. When she stood, more in control, she seemed worried in a different way. "Your brother set out for Lakeside nearly a week ago. He didn't make it?"

"Tymon probably stuck his foot in a ground-dog hole," I told her. "I'll send out a patrol with a medic."

"No time, sir, you need to leave right away, sir," she said.

We were standing in the governor's office. My office. Case had brought in Arnim's latest report on tensions in Lakeside. He nudged my elbow. "I'll round up the Six, Boss." He led the woman to the door, saying "Runners' House is right on Water Street. You can't miss it. Tell them to put the fee on the governor's tab."

I stared at Arnim's report but couldn't see any of the words. I had to make plans. Couldn't take everyone with me. Someone had to stay and mind the forge, as Orkast would have said.

I was already late. We needed to ride, and ride hard. Case, me, and Dramin would be enough, on the off-chance we ran into problems. I leaned out the door and hollered for the major-domo.

Heyliannin came into our bedchamber as I was stuffing clothing into a bag. I had half of my uniform. That wasn't going to look good in front of the king and his council.

"What's going on?"

"I'm supposed to be in Jeskaryan three days ago."

"What do you mean?"

"Where's my uniform shirt?" I cast about the room, certain I was missing something else I'd need. "The first runner—" I didn't want to mention Tymon. "—got lost or laid up. The word didn't make it. Ceremony's in two days. We're riding out soon as the boys get the ponies ready."

She had crouched to rummage through a trunk and turned with the missing shirt in her hand. She also turned pink. "We're supposed to ride? I can do a lot of things, Corren, but I don't know how to ride!"

"Doesn't matter. You're not coming."

"Why not?" She wanted to attend that boring investment ceremony? Was she really insulted or teasing me?

"Like you said, you don't ride, and we need to move fast. I'm leaving Arnim in charge of our little project. You'll have your Four and Calestinise, and Kul will be here. Andus and Karthi, they're on assignment in town, so you won't see them much." I cinched up the bag. If something was missing, well, too bad. "Stay close."

"What do you mean, 'stay close'?"

"I haven't got time, talk to Arnim." I stopped at the door. *I'm not being clear.* "I mean, stay safe. We've put a kettle of rotten fish on the fire, and the stink is going to get worse before it gets better."

She wrinkled her nose. One more thing Eldennian never did. It was … I don't know. Anyhow, it made me feel strange. She laughed. "You have a way with words, Corren."

"See you in four days. Five at most."

Case and Andus met me at the back door, the one that led down to the stable. Case handed me my sword belt. Strapping my weapon on again put me back in the mood to ride.

My fingers brushed the empty sheath strapped to my leg.

That was what I'd left. My knife was on top of the little table in the bedchamber. Where I'd looked at it a half-dozen times while packing.

"What is it, Boss?" Trust Case to catch my backwards glance.

"Nothing. I've turned into a bureaucrat, is all. Let's go."

37

I WAS GONE NEARLY SIX DAYS. The ceremony—make that ceremonies—took up the better part of a day. And the night after required a banquet, one that ran until nearly dawn the next day.

I remembered the night of Yutek the Younger's investiture, how I crept back into the fortress alone in the predawn light. Tymon had cried like a child when I left him at the Runners' House. Not because he didn't like them. I knew he'd like the runners. They're all about taking care of everybody. But we hadn't been apart from each other since the day my father took me by the hand and walked me into that place and took the money to the Shamans' House to pay his induction fees.

Another thing I hadn't thought about in a long, long time.

My father sold me off in order to become a shaman. No wonder I hated them so much.

Would Orkast have felt proud that day, the day I became Yutek's true-son, his heir-in-fact? Or would he have regretted what he'd done?

I didn't waste much time wondering about what we'd never know.

Yutek held up in fair strength through the day. Either he was feeling well or the medics had dosed him up with pain-killers. He stood through the adoption ceremony, the one that made me his true-son, and his embrace when that was finished felt almost like the old Yutek, the vigorous king of my childhood.

For the approval of the heir, Yutek could rest. The king is expected to sit silent in his high seat, out of the way. Approving the heir isn't in the purview of the king; it's under control of the matriarchs of Jeska proper. There'd been a move, back in the day, to have representation from the other districts, but travel is a burden for the aged. Besides, Jeska District gave up more than any of the others, as host to the military government that protected the unified districts. These women had no desire to share the power they wielded.

Good thing I hadn't brought Heyliannin with me. All the elders could get out of anybody was that I'd married a nice young lady from up north, an independent woman with her own small holding. They weren't impressed, but they couldn't find fault, and the reason for being expedient was so obvious. There's no way they didn't know Yutek was dying. The medics report to the matriarchs first. Everybody knows that.

My military record should have spoken for itself. They needed to see my scars to give credence to my claims.

I confess, that was the worst part of it. Another reason to be glad my wife wasn't in attendance.

She would have fallen down laughing.

The Council of Elders must approve what the medics call the 'body entire.' That is, the king's true-son strips naked in front of a gang of snoopy old ladies. And not in private, either. It's a grand public event.

That ceremony was shortened a little because I could prove my fertility. Eldennian had to show up, make an attestation, and pass Deliasin around the circle of judges. They cooed and made baby-talk at my little girl. I did not get a turn to hold her—Eldennian didn't even look me in the eye.

Once I'd won the approval of the true powers of Jeska, they brought out fresh garments, including an overrobe even more gaudy than the one I'd been married in.

Then it was off to the investiture ceremony itself. That one involved a lot of droning speeches, some of them mine, following forms I'd been required to memorize years ago. I stayed on my feet under my ridiculous robe and sweated rivers, but when Yutek stood and lifted the sigil from the brazier smoking beside him, I was ready. He beamed with pride as he pressed the hot iron into my hand, branding me forever with the sign of the king.

Yes, it was worth it.

I'd made my father proud.

38

N OUR WAY BACK SOUTH, we met the runner on her way back to Jeskaryan. Like us, she was taking a reasonable pace now. Yes, Tymon had turned up. No, she didn't hear what had happened to him, but he seemed all right.

We let her pass on and continued our slow pony-ride along the now-familiar road. None of us felt like talking much. Most of us had hangovers to recover from. The extra men were more clear-headed. They hadn't had to stay at the feast until all hours.

Yutek retired early, so I sought him out the next morning. He seemed well, or he did a good job of faking it. The awkwardness of cramming six of his guard and my two into that little room with the pair of us made for enough distraction.

True to form, he went straight to business. "How fares the work in Lakeside?"

"There's much to be done," I told him. "We're looking into accounts as best we can without ruffling the feathers of the local powers."

"What are you finding?"

"It's inconclusive. Sorry. We've found irregularities, but there's no telling yet if we'll be able to recover the losses or track down the culprits."

"Ah. That's my fault, son. I let the situation down there go on too long. Didn't listen hard enough to the complainers."

By then we were talking across his work table, like old times. I could almost ignore the heavy breathing of eight guardsmen in the room. I didn't want to put more worries in his mind, but this might be my last chance to get Yutek's counsel. "We've got signs that the South still has people operating in Lakeside, putting cash in the hands of the weak-minded and the greedy. Not clear what their close-in plans could be. Long-term … well, they won't be giving up lightly."

"Ehh," he sighed. "I wish I could've got you and your boys down there quicker. Ternak's not one to think anyone on his staff might be cheating him. At least we got Gorton out of there. Trace the money, that's your best course of action."

"Yes, Father, we're doing that. That river of cash should lead us to them."

"Good, good. Send word back with one you can trust, like our Tymon." He reached to clasp my arm. "Married life treating you well, son? Will we have news on that account soon?"

There was a tricky question. "Well enough, Father. I've been busy. She puts up with me, more or less."

He laughed. "Can't hardly ask for more. Surprised me, though. Thought you'd be taking the one that mothered your child."

That hurt. Not as much as it might have a month previous. "Ah, well, it was not to be. One can't be forcing a woman to marry, sir."

"No, no, that one can't," he agreed. He still had a questioning eye.

"She turned me down, sir."

"Hmm, good you had a backup plan, then. None of this could have waited any longer. Well." He patted the top of his desk with both hands. "Travel safe, then, son."

"We will, Father. I've two of my best men with me."

"Take a few more. This is not a time to take risks lightly."

"No, sir. I will, sir."

He seemed tired, but I didn't feel right asking, not with all those people in the room, even though they were his own men and mine. As we left, I caught sight of Yutek's flock of doctors hovering in the adjacent hallway. They weren't too happy about me questioning them, but the mark on my palm left them unable to refuse.

No, he wasn't miraculously getting better. Yes, he seemed stable. No, the prognosis was still bad. Yes, they had medicines that helped him.

They still couldn't tell me how long he had. Or refused to guess.

As we rode south, my aching brain mulled on the possibility I might never see Yutek alive again. When we hit the mustering ground, even though sunset was well off, I called a halt.

"I've got to get some sleep," I told the men. "Sort out watches, Case. Just don't put me on first." I barely had energy to drag a bedroll off the back of my pony and curl up in it.

They parceled out the watches without me. I think Yutek's men took the first two shifts. It was Case and Dramin who woke me at dawn.

"Through the battlefield or around it, Boss?" Trust Case to be direct.

"I don't think I can make that walk today," I said. "There's not much hurry. Let's take the road."

Yutek's men seemed relieved by my decision. Maybe they lost friends at NeverSnows, too.

The longer route meant we had to camp again. It was cold rations and short ones, too. None of us minded it, not after downing the equivalent of several meals at the feast. I woke at shift change, like normal, but now no one would let me take a watch. The king's men were especially against the idea. "Go back to sleep, Highness," the oldest one said, the soldier with grey at the edges of his hair. He had that commanding tone you get from battlefield experience. I thought it best to obey his orders.

39

W E RODE INTO LAKESIDE AROUND NOON, eager for a solid meal and plenty to drink. None of us had packed enough water and it was one of those scorching south-district days where the sun becomes unbearable a few hours after dawn. Once we'd handed the ponies off to the stable crew, it was all I could do not to dunk my head right in the nearest water-trough.

The major-domo'd had word of our arrival, and there was a decent spread laid out in the dining room. My father's guardsmen held back at first, but seeing Case and Dramin sit by my side and start on the meal, they pulled up chairs and joined in. Arnim and Kul turned up not long after, and we rearranged ourselves so Arnim could brief me on the latest news. He'd had a few good leads, thanks to names Heyliannin had ferreted out of her locked-away accounts records.

The news on Tymon was confusing to say the least. He'd turned up drunk in a pub, a place run by one of the people on what we were now calling The List. In my mind, that name moved up that List. Had they been trying to get information out of my brother?

"

Were they scheming to sabotage my investiture? Or had an unrelated event made my ordinarily health-obsessed brother want to get drunk?

Possibly all three.

No one knew where he was now. Runners' House, most likely.

Heyliannin was most likely locked in her private room, wrestling with her numbers. She'd gotten after Arnim to take her to the Shamans' House while I was gone.

He'd told her where it was.

"You shoulda heard that woman yell," Kul remarked. "Coulda heard her up in J-City. 'Southeast? That's nearly in South Point!'" He scraped his plate clean and reached to refill it. "She's got the map down, Boss. She di'n't have any misunderstandin' on how far off that is. Clever woman, that wife o' yours."

I focused on finishing my meal without overdoing. I'd be in for an intense conversation with my wife soon. Before I pushed back my chair, I gave a few orders, urged Arnim to explore further on the follow-the-money course, and thanked Yutek's men for their service. Arnim said the major-domo was already setting up rooms for them. It wasn't clear to me yet if they were staying longer than overnight. Their orders had come from Yutek, not me.

"I'm for a bath and a change of clothes," I announced. "And then I'm thinking I have a stack of governor jobs waiting in my office."

"Ya, Boss," Kul agreed, around a mouthful of meat. I hoped it wasn't turtle meat.

Our bedchamber was up a flight of stairs and down a hallway. Fortified by good food, I took the steps as if I hadn't been riding for two days. Halfway up, I remembered my knife, my favorite knife, that I'd taken out to give a good cleaning, the night before the runner arrived. My step lightened. I hoped Heyliannin hadn't put it away somewhere, like she'd done with my uniform shirt.

The room was dark, with the shutters closed and the slats tight.

Sounds came from the bed: a low moan and soft, indistinct words.

Heyliannin's voice.

Had she taken ill? It would be just like her to not tell the staff.

The shadowy shape on the bed struck me as wrong, too bulky.

More muttered words.

Not Heyliannin's voice.

The shape moved in a rhythmic, recognizable way, and Heyliannin cried out again.

I reached towards the table along the wall, and my knife came to my hand.

I didn't want to risk striking my wife by mistake, so I grabbed the nearest shutter and flung it wide …

My guess was right, the shape on top was a man. I leapt from beside the window, swinging the blade as I moved. I made no sound, but the light bursting into the room was enough. He jumped up and back and tumbled to the floor.

I was on top of him before he could make another move, and my arm was already twitching into a fresh strike when the shouting made it into my ears.

"It's me, Corren! It's me!" in that voice I'd known forever.

"No, no, stop!" in that off-kilter rendition of northern Jeskan.

I could no more halt my strike than I could stop a wildfire, but I broke my own aim by leaning back. It was mostly a startle in response to the screaming, but enough was by intent that my blade only cut a long arc across my brother's chest instead of slicing his throat.

•   •   •

It was a surface wound, but a long one, and it sprayed a lot of blood. Not to mention my knife, on the follow-through, flung droplets across the room—across the bed—into Heyliannin's face. I'm not sure she noticed it herself, but the sight brought me out of my fighting mind, back to the mundane world.

"What's going on here?" I said. As if I didn't know. As if it wasn't obvious. I wanted to make her say it, though. I wanted her to admit it.

"We … I … Tymon." She was dressed for an instructional session. That is, in nothing.

Likewise, Tymon.

Tymon sleeps naked. Why those words hit me out of memory, who can say?

My brother squirmed under my weight. I shifted to apply more pressure, grinding road dust into his over-used equipment, still wet from my wife. He shouted at me to get off, and I wiped my knife clean on his stomach. He went quiet then. He had a look on his face that reminded me of the rebel up at Heart's Bend, the one who'd tried to kill Tymon that day, the one I'd killed for him.

For once, he didn't say anything.

The blood oozed steadily, slipping between the curves of his ribs, flowing down to stain my floor.

"Get the midwife," I told Heyliannin.

"What?" she said. "Why?"

"Do as I say."

She scooted across the bed and leaned over the edge, then froze, staring at the blood. She wasn't seeing Tymon, or me, or even my knife. All she saw was blood.

This woman had walked through a winter on a mountain, starving. She'd been captured by snake-men and escaped. She'd set up a business in a strange country and tracked down a piece of stolen property she hadn't seen in years. But she saw a little blood and whomp, she fainted.

There was nothing for it. I'd have to get the medic myself. Dramin might have done the job, but Tymon didn't deserve Dramin.

He kept his mouth shut, only whimpered a little as I was getting up. I pointed at his testicles with my knife.

"If it was any other man, I'd cut those off. You know that, don't you?"

He blinked back tears.

By the time I got back with the horrified midwife, and swore her to secrecy, Heyliannin had gotten herself dressed. She stayed on the other side of the room, where she couldn't see the blood. It hits some people that way. Ganderrison didn't say anything as she cleaned Tymon's wound and sewed it up neater than Dramin would have done. It took a long time, and Tymon cried the whole time.

She cried too. Heyliannin, that is.

"Go," I told her, when the midwife was about halfway done. "Go wash, and change, and go back to work. You can see he's not going to die, right?"

She nodded.

"Then go. We'll talk later. When he's gone."

She went without a word.

While the midwife finished up, I sat on the floor and cleaned my knife. That made me feel better. I slipped it back in its sheath, where it belonged.

Ganderrison had wound care instructions. Neither Tymon nor I listened to them. I dismissed her.

"If I hadn't left my knife on the table," I told Tymon, "you'd be dead right now."

"I know." He had no voice, that was his lips moving.

"I'm glad I didn't kill you, Tymon," I said.

"I'm sorry."

"But I wish you were dead."

"Me, too."

"I want you gone before she comes out of that office of hers, you understand me?"

"Yes."

"And I never want to see you again."

"No." I could see an idea forming in his head. A bad idea.

"And you're not allowed to kill yourself. If you do, I'll have your corpse burned. You got that?"

"Yes."

"Yes, what?"

His face went confused. I held up my hand, palm out, showing the mark that Yutek put on me.

"Yes, Highness."

"Be glad I'm not Yutek the Younger." I walked out then, and didn't look back. I don't know how he went or where. His clothes were gone later.

The midwife did good work. Tymon left no blood trail in the hallway or on the stairs. The bedding was soiled, with more than blood. I wanted to have it burned, but that would have raised questions. Instead, I ranted at the chambermaid that the fabric quality was unacceptable to the newly-invested heir, and I'd better not see those particular items ever again.

The servant who tried to clean the blood from the floor scrubbed with all his might, like he thought I might kill him for his failure. I sent him to fetch a rug from one of the other rooms and we put it down together.

Heyliannin never saw the stain.

40

WE NEVER HAD THAT TALK.

Heyliannin hid in her number fortress all day and into the night. I assume she sneaked out and back in a few times. The servants said she got meals, but I never saw her. Long after nightfall, light leaked from under the door, and you could hear her thumping around in there.

When I woke at dawn, after a night full of the worst kind of dreams, the far side of the bed was undisturbed.

We met briefly, on the stairs. She looked to be heading for some sleep, knowing I'd have to be at the usual morning meetings. She wouldn't meet my eyes, so I couldn't tell if it was shame or anger.

It was me who said, "Are you all right?"

"I'm working on it," was all I got out of her.

She brushed past me. I didn't have time to follow her, have it out. There would be gossip, but what could we do?

I was glad I'd gotten that rug down. Maybe she'd sleep without dreams.

Arnim headed me off before I could take the long hallway to the meeting rooms, where the major-domo would have sorted the day's applicants and complainers and officials into groups to howl at me in turn.

"I've cancelled your meetings for today," he said.

"You can do that?" I studied his expression, but he had his soldier face on, betraying nothing. "Well then, why?"

"Officially, you've declared a holiday to celebrate your investiture." He shifted the thick folder he had tucked under one arm.

I kept my eye on that folder as I replied, "And unofficially?"

"Unofficially? You're taking the day to enjoy the water. I have a pleasure boat reserved. Case says he knows how to work it."

"I hate boats." The last time anybody'd had me in a boat was our second crossing of the river near Tarak. I could still feel the gut-ache from waiting for the current to tear our fingers free of the pull-rope and drown us in the rapids.

"You'll like this boat … Highness." His eyes went past me to a pair of servants scurrying down the hallway. They bobbed in my direction, and kept glancing at me anxiously. As they passed, Arnim bowed at me instead of saluting. "The lake is beautiful this time of year."

He strode ahead, and I followed him, puzzled and strangely pleased.

A holiday? Me, declaring a holiday? I hadn't even realized I had the authority to do that.

I congratulated myself again on the men I'd surrounded myself with.

·　　　·　　　·

The lake wasn't a river. It wasn't even much of a lake, to my eye. Reeds, reeds, and more reeds, with paths among them barely wide enough for our flat-bottomed boat. Birds screamed at us from the forests of dull green stems as we floated by, Case and Kul pushing the boat forward with long poles.

Arnim kept scanning our surroundings as if he expected a horde of Southerners to attack.

"Get us out to the open water," he told Case.

"Sure, sure."

Not long after, they had to abandon the poles in favor of paddles. Eventually, we emerged from the reeds to the vast expanse of the lake.

The water spread out as far as you could see, beyond the horizon. It felt like the world had come to its end, that you could float and float and never come to land again. The tunnel in the reeds beckoned as it dwindled behind us. I wondered if we'd ever find it again.

Not a breath of wind stirred the water, and it reflected the summer sky like a smooth-beaten blade. I put my hand on the low rail that circled the boat's platform and hoped no one noticed how tightly I clung to it.

Arnim had no mercy for my longing to get off that platter of still blue. He sat next to me, in the shade of the canopy that covered the center of the boat, and tugged open the laces binding the folder he'd been carrying since he stopped me in the hallway.

"No picnic first?" I joked, having no desire to find out what would happen if I tried to eat out there, bobbing and swerving as Kul swept his paddle on one side and Case counter-paddled on the other.

"Sorry sir," he said. "In my estimation, there's no safe place to discuss any of this in Lakeside."

"Not even in my office?"

"Rats roam in the walls, sir." One of his favorite proverbs, and one of my least. Then again, Arnim came from the upper reaches; he hadn't ever had to pull his feet up and listen to the rats scurry under his bed.

"What have you got, then? And what's so different between now and a week ago?"

"Heyliannin came to me last night—" Arnim said.

"— to you?" I barked, my voice rising higher than might have made sense.

"Ya, Boss," Karthi said. "Me and Andus had just come in with news, too."

"Arnim said you'd gone to your bed, sir," Andus chimed in. "Should we have waked you?"

I waved away all that. "No, no, you're right. But what was my wife up to?"

"What she's been up to the whole time," Arnim said.

What she's been up to? I thought. *Down to, more like.*

He gave me a sharp look, like he was reading my mind. "She'd a question about something she'd found in the accounts."

Andus dropped to sit beside Arnim and ruffled through the papers, until he found one of those reports he'd been writing. "Here, she saw this …" He handed the report to me.

Seemed a pretty typical Andus/Karthi spy report. Notes on gripes and whines voiced over drinks in the pub, followed by a long tale of woe from a volunteer helping Andus haul Karthi "home." Andus had made an extra note about how much the guy liked Karthi. "Is there something I'm not seeing here? Apart from Karthi having a not-very-secret admirer?"

Andus ran a finger down the lines of his report, a smile coming and going on his lips. "Not that, sir. We're making notes on people we can get more out of later. No, see here. He kept referring to someone who's been working hard on behalf of Lakeside, who's going to make everything right for Lakesiders, someone rich, powerful. At one point, he said, 'It's all thanks to the manavee.' And later on, see, he tried to recruit Karthi—we let him think we were both willing, but it was Karthi he wanted—"

"I get it, go on. Get to the point."

"Yessir. What he said was, he'd introduce Karthi to the manavee. So we have an entry, if we find that same drunkard again, when he's more sober."

"What's a manavee?"

Arnim jumped in at that point. "My theory was that it's the title they've given the man who's directing the insurgency. He seems to have plenty of funding, access to people at every level of society. Heyliannin came in when we were talking through that theory, and she put us right."

"She what?"

"She took the paper, shushed us all, and then wrote on it—look, it's on the back."

I turned the paper over. In Heyliannin's scribbly scrawl was *Manavee = Manager Vee = Manager Velisennin.*

"She uses those paired lines to mean 'is the same as,'" Arnim volunteered.

"I know," I claimed. I'd had no idea. It would have to involve numbers, knowing my wife.

"But you see why we're out here, now?"

In the distance, other boats floated on the still water. Some glided steadily, others stayed more or less stationary, like ours. They were far off enough that nothing more than garbled shouts carried across the water. I lowered my voice anyway. "You don't want to be making accusations about a manager where anyone might have a chance of hearing it." I read Heyliannin's inscription over three or four times. "Is Velisennin the only Lakeside manager whose name begins with V?"

"Yes." So Arnim had thought of that, too. "And there aren't any others significant in the families that have names like hers. It's evidently a hereditary special name."

I remembered the woman's cool, predatory gaze. Anything she owned, she wouldn't be interested in sharing. So the powers of Lakeside were supporting this rebellion? Unlikely it was Southeast alone. I wondered aloud if any of the townships remained loyal.

"We'll need to expand our investigation," Arnim said, anxious, for a change. This was not the kind of problem that could be solved with a pair of knives in a fair fight. "But there aren't enough of us. Can we spare any of Heyliannin's bodyguard? Could we bring on the men Yutek sent with you?"

I didn't like the idea of reducing my wife's protection. That could get her kidnapped for ransom, or worse. Yutek's men? Two of them I knew from well-back, one—the oldster—struck me as trustworthy. The fourth, a new recruit, I'd not want to bring into a secret. "I need to think about it." An unformed idea nagged at me for more information. "You said Heyliannin approached you. It wasn't that she already knew about Velisennin, was it?"

"No, no, she had a list of names, wanted to know who they were. But I didn't recognize them. I was going to ask the staff later today. Probably people who've moved on or died."

It didn't seem to me that Heyliannin would have been that worked up about outdated records signed by people who weren't around anymore. It would have been names attached to the suspicious cash flows she was tracking. "I don't think so," I said.

"What? Sorry, sir, but, why not?" Arnim was already putting away his folder. He didn't look happy about being contradicted. Too bad for him.

"Let me see that list of names."

Arnim rummaged through the folder for a few seconds, then handed over a scrap with three names on it: Fennic, Aldern, and Racac. My blood froze in my veins, on a blazing-hot summer day, with the sun reflecting off the water, determined we couldn't escape it.

"What is it, Boss? Ya look like ya seen a ghost," Kul commented.

"What have I missed?" Arnim asked.

"Nothing," I told him. "You wouldn't have recognized these names, and I'm glad you didn't talk to staff. Fennic—that's the Master Shaman of Jeska. I've known him since I was a boy. Aldern … I'm less sure, but … Orkast dragged me to a gathering once, to introduce me. The shamans all treated him like someone important." I looked around the circle of skeptical faces. "Listen, the shamans always expected me to follow my father into the business. Racac … I don't recognize that name, but I'd be willing to bet if you stop by the Shamans' House here in Lakeside, you'll find him there, high up in the organization, maybe even the Master Shaman."

"But those names, she said they were people likely involved in moving around the hidden money."

"I expect so. That's who she's looking for."

"But if these men are shamans …"

"Then the shamans are working against Jeska, either in league with the managers or on their own. Either way … you're right, Arnim, we need more resources." My head ached, trying to think of help beyond our small cadre of guardsmen. An alternate idea came to mind. My Six wouldn't like it. "There's more to our resources than we've been thinking."

The faces around me seemed ready to be impressed by my great wisdom.

"We've got two stable lads, a midwife, and Calestinise."

"Don't be joking on us, Boss," Kul grunted. Water plunked into the lake as he lifted his paddle for another long stroke.

"I'm not joking. They're true Jeskans. Calestinise is northern, but he's worth the rest of them together." A sudden thought hit me. *Calestinise didn't report on that business with Tymon. Why would he help them? He hates Tymon more than me.* "Where has that boy been? He didn't show for lunch yesterday, haven't heard his voice ranting at all."

"Probably shopping," Case said. "He's been sweating his way down to the town every day on Heyliannin's orders. There's plenty complaining goin' on about that, when the lady isn't listening, trust me."

"What's he buying for her?" I was thinking I hadn't left much in the way of cash. Was I now in debt all up and down the shopping sector of Lakeside City?

"Fancy dresses and suchlike," Kul said. "She don't wear none of them. She dresses like a proper north country girl, your wife."

That gave me pause. "She's been sending her handmaid to town to buy her *dresses*?"

"Ya, Boss," from Case on the opposite paddle, shoving our boat in one direction while my stomach continued to float in the opposite. "Every day at lunch, Tymon would come around and tell him she weren't pleased with yesterday's and Calestinise had to go trade it in."

"Tymon?" I must have turned purple. I thought my head might explode. I needed something to kill, right there, right then.

"You all right, Boss?" Arnim asked. "You got the seasickness?"

At the word, my stomach decided that was definitely the case. Moments later, I was leaning over the rail, getting rid of everything my stomach thought was a problem.

•   •   •

As if he'd been listening to us, Calestinise turned up at the dock when we returned from our excursion.

I must have seemed eager to see him, given I was first off that floating death-trap.

He launched right in. "Can I get help from you on this, Commander?"

"What? And they've given me a new title, if you didn't know."

"Oh? You lose your commander job, sir?"

I grimaced. "In a way. Doesn't matter here, but back up at the house, call me Highness."

"What? You don't look no taller, sir." He put on a vague, childlike expression, but I caught the grin he was hiding.

This one time, I'd let it go. I wanted a different kind of answer out of him. "What have you been up to while I was away, boy?"

"Man. Sir. Highness." He grinned again, still running his joke through his head. "That was what I wanted help on. Sir, I've been down to the tailor's every day, and nothing he sends up will do. When I walked in with yesterday's return, the tailor said he'd cut my throat for me. He waved this blade that will cut fabric right in the air it's so sharp. Can't you lend her an extra guard or two, so it's safe for her to go down to the shops herself? She's got me round the bend, sir. If she sends me down there again today, I'll cut my own throat, I will. Highness."

I waved my hand in a potentially royal fashion. "As your future king—and my wife's husband—your wish is granted. Not that she needs extra guards. The Four would be plenty."

"Tymon says not."

"Tymon's full of shit."

He stood flapping his mouth silently.

"And Tymon's gone, so you don't have to listen to him anymore."

I hadn't thought Calestinise could be happy. I'd been wrong about that. He looked like I'd handed him a bag of gold.

"And here's an order for you."

"Yes, sir."

"Don't take orders from anybody other than me and Heyliannin. Directly. Don't be letting anyone say 'she told me to tell you …'"

His delight faded, with that realization I meant for him to have. "Oh. Uh. No, sir."

"That said, Arnim's going to have work for you. That's my order, and you're getting it now."

"Yes, sir." The idea of more work wouldn't be likely to make him happy.

"Interesting work. No shopping for dresses."

That cheered him up. I gave him a pat on the shoulder and led the way back up the maze of streets to the governor's house and the stack of ordinary business that waited for me there. Every time we passed a group of Lakesiders, I watched for the narrowed eyes, the frowns, the general air of *fuck off, Northerner*. At least a quarter of them had it, maybe more.

My gut ached like crazy.

41

TOO MUCH HAD BEEN LET SLIDE. Too much remained hidden. We had to investigate. That meant we needed to split up.

My father the king needed to know the depths Lakeside had sunk to. Were the managers of Jeska District in on this, or were the managers of Lakeside targeting their seniors in the home district, aiming to take control of the country? That was my suspicion. If the Lakeside elders could wrest control of the land from ours, there's no telling what they might do.

At the top of the list, they'd replace the government: remove the king, his councilors, and the upper ranks of the guard. If I'd still been a captain, I might've escaped notice. Not anymore. If it was nothing more than a power play among the women, it'd be a bloodbath in name only. I might even keep my job in the guard. For the landkeepers, though, it would be disaster. We hadn't had a takeover like that in a very long time, but everyone knew if the authority changed, they could redraw the boundaries in a district. Farms, fisheries, even small landholdings could be overwritten.

Eldennian could lose our house.

Arnim, we agreed, should go to Jeskaryan, because he could talk to the upper echelons in their language. Dramin took the second spot. The way a medical family works, he could ferret out news from the matriarchal system easier than any one of us. Doctors are everywhere, they know everyone, and they're not too full of themselves to speak truths to their sons.

We had to tread lightly on that snake den. You don't rile up the managers without having demonstrable facts.

"I need proof," Arnim told Heyliannin, the four of us locked in her secret hideout with Dramin hovering awkwardly at the corner of the table and me lazing in the one comfortable chair.

Dramin waved an arm over the neatly-stacked papers. "We can't take all this with us, can we?"

"No, you can't," she growled, and I could tell she didn't mean what he was thinking.

Arnim took over. He knew she was touchy about her domain. "So what should we take? What's the most damaging document you've got?"

"You're not taking any of this," she said. "It's chain of *evvydense*"—her word for proof—"and I'm not risking any of it getting lost, stolen, or doctored."

"What do doctors have to do with documents?" Dramin should've known better than to pick on my wife's choice of words. She spent a good ten minutes explaining why doctoring meant making a good document into a bad one.

Arnim had to shut them up. "Lady Heyliannin—"
She snorted.

"Sorry, ma'am?" He made an apologetic gesture. "Should I be calling you Highness, ma'am?"

That made her laugh, which let me breathe. "No, no," she said, flapping her hands like a pair of flags. "Use my name, like you never do with Corren."

"Ya, Boss," Dramin piped up. "How come her ladyship doesn't have a nickname yet?"

"Can we stay on the subject, for once?" I complained. "Wife of mine, if Arnim presents information to the king, he has to bring proof. You can't hide this here. Arnim will bring it back. I promise."

"Not good enough." She crossed her arms and put on a fierce look—but a sneaky smile kept trying to break out on her mouth. I wondered if anyone else noticed it.

Arnim flung his hands up in surrender and dropped into the nearest chair with such force that the chair slid back, grating on the tile floor. Dramin put his hands over his ears until the noise stopped, then leaned on the table. He seemed to be trying to figure a way to scoop an armload of paper into his arms and make a run for it.

"There's a better way," Heyliannin said. She lifted one side of her ledger, the enormous book that lay open on the table, and retrieved a tight-wrapped packet from underneath it. With delicate motions, she unwrapped the package, leaving the object inside resting like a jewel on the thick, expensive fabric.

It looked like a book: flat, rectangular, about as thick as two fingers. The cover had a grey-green sheen to it, like it was made of metal. She opened the cover and ran her finger over the front page, except it wasn't a page but another layer of dull greyish stuff.

"*Dayyam*, needs *chaarjed*," she said under her breath. With the cover closed again, she flipped the thing over. The back side had deep bluish rectangles on it, circles embossed in the rectangles, with delicate copper outlines.

I recognized that pattern.

That design marked the snake-man's book—the one he'd held up, as he turned in a circle, right before he dissolved into the thin patch. Maybe he wanted us to see how pretty the back of his book was.

All that effort to retrieve the rumored object, and here it had been, this whole time, in Ta-ma's hands.

Still.

"How can a snake-man book prove anything about the goings-on in Lakeside?" I demanded.

"It's not a book." She rewrapped it and handed the bundle to Arnim. "This is the greatest treasure in this world." I studied her expression. She seemed more serious than I'd ever seen her. "If you lose it or damage it, I'll kill you and eat your heart."

Arnim's mouth tried to smile, but he fought it to a frown. It was his own favorite fighting words she was throwing at him. "I won't," he agreed.

"Take it outside, set it in the sun with the blue side up, for … oh, an hour. Guard it with your life."

It took me waving him out the door to get him moving. "What's she up to, Boss?" he muttered at me as he passed. I shrugged, ignorant as a turtle at a Lakeside barbecue.

•　　　•　　　•

There were no hours to be wasted.

While Arnim stood in a courtyard garden, pretending to admire the flowers, I sent Dramin to get them both packed for travel. My father's guardsmen, I barely caught them as they headed out for their planned return to Jeskaryan.

I pulled the older man aside.

"Wait, Captain, I've got two more men to send with you, and I'd ask if you could lend me your more-seasoned men to stand in for them while they're away."

"Of course, Highness." He had a respectful smile, but a warm one, recognizing our common background. "My orders are we're at your disposal, but didn't seem we were needed."

"I've news for Commander Magaran. Chain of command, Captain."

"Yes, sir." That assured me he'd not be sharing any of that with the new recruit, the one I didn't trust.

I needed Magaran informed there were likely insurgents hidden somewhere in Lakeside. Probably many somewheres. It's a big district, plenty of rugged territory that's less farmed than it might be elsewhere, what with the community so focused on fishing. We'd be searching them out, but our commander needed to be ready. I'd leave it to Yutek to share more from the top, once Arnim made his report to the king. In the meantime, Magaran could be calling up reserves for "training." That would put us ahead of the game.

Unless it was more than Lakeside.

The Hashtek Empire down south is rich, and what we'd found in Lakeside was a river of money flowing northward through the district. Unless South Point had a secret gold mine, the worst was yet to come.

•　　　•　　　•

When Arnim brought the book—or whatever it was—back to Heyliannin, I dragged Kul and Case along for the great unveiling. Karthi and Andus missed out, already back on pub-crawling duty.

Heyliannin called the thing a *tayablett*. This time, when she flipped open the cover and ran her finger over the surface underneath, a soft yellowish glow spread across that steel-like page. Seconds later, the simple candleglow was replaced by a luminous image, a picture in light and dark, as if someone had taken a pen and scratched black lines across the glowing surface. She held up the thing and turned it so everyone could see that awful sight— a book afire, without being consumed, with a vision of horror inscribed on it. While the drawing might have been meant as an abstract thing, to us it screamed *snake-men!* with a long snake-like design coiled around the page, ending with an impression of a snake-man hand, its serpent fingers splayed below a strange sigil.

"How does it do that?" Arnim shed the chills quicker than the rest of us, in favor of his unflinching curiosity.

"If we ever have a month to spare, I can try to explain it to you." She laughed, but the edge in her voice made it clear it wasn't a joke. "All you need to know is how to work it." She slid her finger across the thing, and the gut-twisting snake picture disappeared, replaced by an array of twisty shapes too small to distinguish as anything in particular. Tapping one of those shapes, she lifted the book and held it above her open ledger. A second later, she shifted it to one side and gestured to us to come closer.

Kul, I noticed, held back. That the thing wasn't magic likely seemed implausible to him. He's courageous, but cautious about what he doesn't understand. I wasn't about to show any of my fears. They weren't reasonable. The thing was an object, one the snake-men played with as easily as any of us played with knives. Then again, knives can be dangerous in the wrong hands.

The twisty snake-arm drawing didn't reappear. Instead, the surface of the tayablett was now covered with numbers, digits laid out in neat rows and columns, with lines across the page to keep them in their places.

I recognized it. Everyone did. You couldn't miss it, given Heyliannin held the tayablett next to the ledger. What was on the thing matched exactly what was on the ledger.

"I've been doing this all along," she said. "I have copies of everything that matters. Arnim, if you can show this to your king guy without *freeking* him, you'll have everything I have here in one package."

"What's freeking? Is it harmful?" That came from Dramin, and he sounded inordinately concerned. The thought crossed my mind that maybe he knew about Yutek's illness. He might have recognized the sickness on his own, or heard something from one of the medics.

"No, no, sorry. It means scared or surprised."

"Yutek's not afraid of anything," I bragged.

"Oh, come on," she said. "I saw your face when I turned on the *skreen*."

Arnim lifted the tayablett from her hands. "Boss, I'll need to get skilled at this before we go."

I wished we could all stay and learn more about this snake-man tool, but I'd have to hope it survived the journey. "Right, you and Dramin both. Just in case. Kul, Case, let's get on to the tour planning."

"Tour?" Heyliannin had a sharp ear, I'll give you that.

"Tell you later."

She nodded, but I could see her brain working behind those too-clever eyes.

·　　　·　　　·

No sooner had Heyliannin locked the door behind us, than the major-domo panted up with an urgent need for me to meet with an important local official.

"Can't it wait?"

"No, Governor. Sorry ... Highness."

"Governor's fine, man." I waved Case and Kul off towards the stables. "Take care of that recruitment job for me," I ordered. I figured bringing our stableboys would go better without the monstrous Prince Corren glaring at them. We needed runners, loyal ones. My most-trusted runner had already betrayed me.

What I didn't guess was the identity of the important official. I was hoping it was the Master Shaman, so I could squeeze him for information. I hoped it wasn't one of the managers. I might not have been able to keep my hands off her throat.

I didn't recognize the official rising to greet me. She was as tall as Eldennian, but built like Tymon, not an ounce of her devoted to anything but muscle. It gave me pause. Too old to be a runner, not an active one, but more fit than half the recruits who came up for guard duty.

She saw my hesitation. I didn't like that, but there you have it.

"Tanasialis," she announced. "Of Runners' House Lakeside. Apologies for disturbing your household, Highness."

Trust a runner to be up on the latest news.

"No disturbance, Master Runner," I replied. "Do I need to get after my accountant to settle monies owed? Whether under my administration or any previous, we'll have you made whole." I made a vague hand-waving gesture. "Though we're still sorting out matters from Gorton's tenure here."

"No, no, all is well on that score. I've come about your brother."

Had he whined to his superiors that I'd threatened him? Even a runner isn't entitled to jump into bed with another man's wife. I held my tongue on guesses. "Tymon? Yes, we fostered together."

"He's one of our foremost runners, sir, as I'm sure you know."

I didn't. "Yes." Did it matter whether I knew?

"Then have you any knowledge of why he retired so suddenly?"

"Retired?"

"Yes, he withdrew all his funds—and, sir, to that end I might have to place an appeal for temporary financial assistance while the order conducts certain transfers—" My confused stare stopped that digression. "He said he was ready to retire, took what he was owed. He gave no reason. He didn't seem ill or injured. It's most extraordinary."

I took in one breath, then another, while I decided what to say. It needed to be asked, because of that dangerous thought I'd seen in his eyes. "He didn't make threats of harming himself, did he? Or anyone else?"

She might have been about to ask me why, but held herself to, "No, sir."

"Where is he now? If he's retired, I suppose he won't be staying at your House now?"

"Correct, sir. But I have no idea where he went. At first, I presumed he'd taken a position here. I'd come to persuade him to return. You understand, sir, there are certain … attitudes … people hold against runners. It can make retiring early difficult."

"He hasn't come here." I looked her in the eye. Something in her stance, perhaps the way she reminded me of Eldennian, made me speak. "My brother and I argued recently. He wouldn't come here."

"Has he other family? Here or in Jeska District?"

"None." I had no ideas. He wouldn't have taken his money if he meant to kill himself, would he? I tried to make light of it. "Any minute now, someone will come in yelling that a madman is handing out wads of cash in the marketplace."

The joke withered in my mind. That would be exactly like Tymon, to give away his possessions first. Before going off and killing himself out in the wilds, where I couldn't find his body and carry out my threat.

As if I would do that.

He was my brother. He was weird. He broke my trust. But he was still my family.

I haven't got time for this. It's Jeska that's at risk of burning.

Tanasialis recognized my distraction. "I see I've run out my time, sir. I'll let you know if news comes to me."

"Thank you, Master Runner." She turned to give me a bow before leaving the room.

I wanted a meal, a nap, a long evening by myself with nothing but a full jug of cider for company.

What now?

Oh, right, recruit the midwife.

I dodged out of the office wing before the major-domo could catch me again.

PART V

THE FAMILY TOURS
THE LAKE DISTRICT

42

W E CREATED A TYPICAL FAMILY for our journey. Heyliannin made a convincingly officious lower-level manager. We couldn't very well spy our way through the district under our own names, so she called herself Tamakinroy, supposedly something like her original name. I played the role of her bossed-around husband, Castor. Not much different than real life, that. Calestinise had to choose between acting like a girl or taking a boy's name, so he chose a hero's name, Callas. We'd brought along the younger of the two stableboys, Stevvin, who was supposed to take care of the pony and run errands, while posing as the little brother.

Calestinise chafed at having to shorten his name, but he enjoyed the freedom to tell everyone he hated his father. That is, me. No one bats an eye at a young man complaining about his parents.

Kul played the role of my wife's thick-bodied, and thicker-headed cousin, who came along to give me something to gripe about at the inns we stopped at. He was good for hauling bags in and out of our pony-cart, but not for much else. I'd say these things right in front of him, and Kul would stare blankly at the men around us, and sip his beer, then listen long and hard after I'd strolled away.

Naturally, to annoy my wife, I'd invited along a couple of my own "cousins," Harad and Radeo—her two seniormost guards. Harad played the serious family watchman—picking over every fault in an innkeeper's provisions. Radeo managed meals and the kids. Calestinise didn't rankle at everything his "uncles" told him, like he did with my advice. Stevvin had a fascination with toss-up, that game where kids use long sticks to hurl bits of leather and wood around. Turns out Radeo was something of a master of the sport, and so became Stevvin's mentor. Much to Radeo's amusement.

I learned to be alert for the distinctive sound of a mis-thrown toss-up whirring towards my head.

We made our way south in a circuitous way, along the east side of the lake. We'd roll into each town from a northeasterly direction and head out in a southeasterly one, each time making up a new story about where we'd come from and where we were going. There were always functionaries bustling up and down the main roads on both sides of the lake; this way we avoided them. It also gave us more opportunities to scout out what might be going on out of sight.

In between dodging stray toss-ups, I missed having Case at my back. I'd dispatched him on his own tour of investigation down the west side of the lake. The midwife, Ganderrison, made a plausible manager-wife for Case to be traipsing along after. For one thing, she was a Lakesider herself; though she hadn't been out of Jeska District in a decade, her accent was perfect. Their company had Andus and Karthi for pub-spying, the other stableboy for a runner if needed and for a fake son to deflect questions. And the other two of Heyliannin's guard, for general labor and the occasional killing.

On both sides, yes, we left a few bodies in our wake.

There are criminals everywhere. I wasn't going to let things slide because we had a primary mission. The government is responsible for dealing with such things, and we represented the government of both Lakeside District and Jeska as a whole. Besides, if a few vermin turn up ready for the bonfire, isn't that to the good?

My knife-hand itched to find a few insurgents to take care of. Not that we'd be in any position to tackle a force of any scale, but I'd grown weary of driving a pony-cart and making up new reasons to whine about my fake family.

We'd crossed the vague boundary into Southeast Township before we struck any trail worth following. It came to us on a dusty afternoon, with me and Calestinise at the latest inn.

"Hey, Dad." Calestinise had taken quickly to the Lakeside jargon. "My new friends invited me to go camp out in the foothills."

I glanced around him to the gathering of young men at the far corner of the inn's public room.

"No." I said.

He pulled back his foot and kicked the table-leg hard, sending my dinner plate into the air, spattering my shirt with sloppy red sauce. "I'm a grown man. You can't tell me what to do."

I lifted my voice and ground gravel into it. "And I'm your mother's husband, and she's not having you traipsing around with riff-raff."

"They're not riff-raff!" he declared. Facing me, he mouthed, *they are the worst kind of trash.*

"You tell him, Callas!" shouted one of the boys across the room.

I made a show of wiping at the smears of sauce. It still made me uncomfortable, sending Calestinise off with the likes of these. If it gave my objections an authentically paternal sound, that served the game. I worried every time though, that they'd see through his masks and punish him for deceiving them, as they'd see it. "Absolutely not." I added a thump of my fist to the table, which served to spatter more sauce, giving me the excuse to jump to my feet, cursing, and pound up the stairs to our tiny little rooms. I far preferred camping, but it was a town day on our tour.

Harad sat on the edge of his bed, sharpening blades. His knives lay side-by-side on the blanket beside him, as he worked on his sword. The scrape of smooth stone on a polished edge set my mind at ease, put me back at home, in Jeskaryan, evenings in the barracks with nothing to do but tend to our edges and gripe about the bruises we'd earned that day.

"Boss," he acknowledged.

"Castor, to you, Cousin," I said. "Listen, our boy is off with another gang of ruffians. Grab Radeo and be out after them."

"Yes, of course, anything you say, my dear Cousin Castor." Harad had a sly, secretive air that reminded me of Calestinise, as if we were all related in fact. He wasn't much for talking, but I'd come to rely on his subtle sense of humor to keep the long days from getting too dull.

He and Radeo were shadows on the stairs before I turned the corner to the room I'd crammed with my wife and "sons." I pulled off the freshly-stained shirt and dragged on a cleaner one. I'd gotten used to servants to do my laundry, back at the governor's house.

Heyliannin had gone off to attempt woman-talk in the shops along the market, with Kul at her back. It made me nervous. I checked my knife and headed out after them. Calestinise and his "new friends" had left, and likely would never know a pair of king's guards tailed them.

Stevvin caught up with me as I wandered up and down the streets searching for my wife.

"Hey, Dad." He made a plausible sibling for Calestinise, with a similar rounded face and sharp tongue. The boy was wasted shoveling manure.

I cut him off before he could take more liberties. "Report."

"There's a rumor the governor's dead."

"We've heard that one."

"And one he's gone mad."

"Sometimes feels that way." We'd left the two Jeskan soldiers on guard, turn and about, protecting Heyliannin's secret room. The servants were supposed to be telling people the governor and his wife had gone into seclusion, trying to get a baby started. A nice story is never any fun for the rumor-mongers.

"And one that he's sent out shadow assassins to murder anyone who says anything bad about him."

"Don't I wish."

"That's a bad rumor, sir."

"Dad."

"Awww, Dad!" The little monster wrapped his arms around my waist, and hugged me. I held my hands up, in case I accidentally seemed to hug him back. He whispered to me, "Sorry, sir. People watching. That rumor's spreading fast. Can you stop?"

"Stop what?"

He pulled back, walked beside me, scuffed at the dust in the road. The flecks glittered in the sunlight, reminding me of something I couldn't connect to in the moment. I felt oddly paternal. "Na, kid, I get it." Not doing enforcement would save us time, but I would miss it. "What else?"

"The usual. Jeska is bad. Lakeside is great. Jeska is rich. Lakeside is poor. Lakeside elders have your back. The governor is anti-shaman." He pulled a bundle of pegs and leather out of his pocket and made a show of knotting a toss-up together.

Naturally, half his materials fell to the ground, so we had to stop and crouch together, gathering pieces. "Explain. I haven't heard the anti-shaman one."

"It's old. More popular here. Lotta shamans in this township, if you look for them. Not all of 'em have the cape." He dangled one completed toss-up. "Want a game later?"

I snapped my fingers. "On the job. You're talking about apprentices. Lakeside's Shamans' House is down here somewhere."

"Ya. Next town on the main road. Frogtown. They have their own festival where everyone eats frogs." He stuffed the extra materials back into a pocket and hurled the toss-up straight overhead—two pegs rotating around the straps binding them together.

I had to catch the tumbling mess, or it would have hit me in the face. "Like Lakeside City and the turtles?" I gave the toss-up a half-hearted throw, and he retrieved it with a lightning-fast jump.

"Not so big, but, yeah." Luckily for me, Stevvin decided he needed to make some adjustments to the toy, so I didn't have to defend myself again.

I glanced up and down the crowded street. No sign of Kul's wide shape. "Don't be telling her—your mother—about this shaman business."

"Why not?"

There were people around. People with ears. "She's afraid of shamans, that's all."

Next stop: Frogtown. I wanted a little chat with their Master Shaman.

43

CALESTINISE AND HIS GUARDS caught up to us at our next out-of-town camp. Harad and Radeo demanded water and cleaning-cloths and settled by the fire. Calestinise ran to Heyliannin, threw his arms around her, and burst into tears.

I gathered the campout hadn't been fun.

"What was it?" I asked Harad, watching him swab away dried blood trapped in the grooves of his sword-blade. "Did they find out he's a girl-looking boy, or what?"

He shook his head. "That wasn't it, Highness." His lips twisted and his eyes narrowed. He tilted the blade, to get more firelight on the joint between blade and hilt. "Give us a minute." A bead of moisture formed at the corner of his eye and slid down his cheek. Sweat. I'm sure it was sweat.

Radeo sat with his blades still sheathed, a wet rag in one hand. He stared into the fire, blinking slowly, as if there were answers in the flames.

I took the cloth from him. "Here, Cousin," I said. "This's a job for an armorer's kid. How about you do up some food for the rest of us?"

He tipped his head towards me. "Yes, sir, I can do that, sir."

While he banged around with pots and pans, Harad and I took care of the blades. Radeo's sword had a nick in the edge, about two-thirds of the way along. There were fragments of bone embedded in it. I didn't ask. Calestinise left off blubbering and disappeared behind the cart. When he came back, he had on my old uniform. The pants were about the right length, but he'd had to roll up the sleeves on the shirt. He put a bundle of black cloth in front of me, then went to the fire-bucket and washed his hands as if the black cloth had been drenched in poison.

The heap stank of blood and vomit.

I hoped I wasn't supposed to unwrap it.

The wind shifted, and the smell got worse. I moved closer to the fire and used my boot to shove the heap further back.

The food wasn't up to Radeo's standard, but no one complained. Calestinise at first refused to eat, but once started, he put away a full day's worth. Finished, he went to the stinking pile of cloth and gave it a kick.

"Wanted to burn it straight away, sir," he said. "But it's proof. There's too much ya won't believe."

Kul lumbered to his feet and went around collecting plates. "Whatever ya tell us, kid, we believe ya." He looked like he wanted to pat Calestinise on the head, but instead rubbed his own belly and set to the washing-up. Radeo handed him cooking gear to clean.

Harad sat as far from me as possible, on the opposite side of the fire. The fading flames sent strange shadows across his face. He kept his eyes down, turning his freshly-cleaned knife over and over in his hands. The reflection flashed in my eyes like sunlight off waves on that summer day on the lake.

Heyliannin did something very strange, then. She started singing. It was that old saw about the lost brothers. She only knew the chorus, but she had the sound of it right. Soon enough, Kul took over the song, with the splash and slosh of his work adding a wet rhythm to the verses. By the time we got to the old men finding one another, everyone had joined in. Me, I couldn't put my full voice into it. That song used to make me feel close to Tymon, now it made me feel as though he'd died and no one but the condors would be meeting him now.

As the silence settled over the campsite, Calestinise's voice drifted from his soft-lit shape on the broken log he'd dragged over to the circle.

"The first thing they did was, they took my clothes."

He let that statement fall into the fire like a fresh log. I jumped up as if a flame had flashed in my face.

Something about my reaction made him nearly smile. "No, they didn't care I'm a woman-looking man."

I didn't correct the boy.

"They got girls in their army, anyway. They don't care what you are. They care what you'll do for them."

I wanted to start questioning him, but the thoughts that came to mind were all wrong: worries about him, about Calestinise. Plus a gut-level reaction to the idea of girl soldiers that had nothing to do with how well Eldennian could handle a knife.

It was Kul who kept the focus. "Army, ya said. What army?"

"Shamans." He pointed at the stinky black cloth. "That's why the uniforms are black."

"It's a uniform?" I walked over to the pile and kicked at it until the pieces unfolded. Ink-black pants, smoke-black shirt, with a gold-colored insignia on the chest, like one of the badges on my uniform, the one Calestinise had on.

I wanted to do what he'd said, toss it in the fire, but he was right. It was *evvydense*.

Once they'd made their new recruits strip and put on these uniforms, they'd burned the kids' clothes, the ones they'd come in.

Some of them thought it was a game, and they sang and danced around the fire like burning clothes was normal. A few kids complained, and the others laughed as they roughed them up. One wouldn't stop complaining, and a couple of them grabbed her and threatened to throw her into the fire.

I'll say that again. Before the organizers even started on them, some of these kids were ready for murder.

"They seemed serious about it," Calestinise insisted. "I thought they might really do it, but a man came out of the house—"

"Ya say they'd a house?" Again, Kul was ahead of me on the details.

"There were several buildings, Boss," Radeo volunteered. He spoke to me, as if I'd been the one to ask. "A cookhouse, two larger buildings, and a small cabin set back from the rest. The adults were in the cabin."

So there was more than one adult.

The one who'd come out made the potential killers stop. Not that he didn't want them to be murderers. He still hoped the victim could be turned into one, too. He made them line up and marched up and down in front of them. Radeo and Harad couldn't hear the rant; they were up a slope, under a mess of chaparral. They had the scorpion bites to prove it, too.

Calestinise got to hear the lecture. They were to be a part of the glorious army of light. They would save Lakeside from the horrors of the evil northern governor. "They didn't convince me, Commander," he told me. "I never thought you was evil."

One of the complainers announced he didn't want to join the army. His family needed him. His mother would kill him if he didn't show up to harvest.

"If your mother doesn't support the cause, she's a traitor," the fake commander told him. "If she finds out you've become one of us, I promise you, she'll call up the governor's assassins, and you'll be dead."

"But I'm not ... she's not ..."

"You put on the uniform, soldier. You're one of us. And you've told me she's a traitor. We'll protect you from her."

In the middle of that exchange, one of the more quick-witted recruits took off at a dead run. He didn't make any announcements. He just ran—directly towards my hidden men, as it happened.

A half-dozen older kids—boys and girls who'd been there when they'd arrived—chased him out of the firelight and into the shadows. There was a horrible shriek, and the seniors came back without him. One of them had a knife. Calestinise saw him wiping the blade on his sleeve, leaving a smear of darker black.

"That's the due of a traitor," the adult announced. "Well done, well done," he told the gang of six.

Harad spoke from the far side of the fire. "They'd not done it proper. The boy wasn't dead, and he wouldn't survive, either." The knife in his hand flashed as he turned it. "I had to break protocol, sir. It weren't right."

"They didn't see," Radeo said. "Harad was only down there long enough to fix it."

"Fix it, ya," Harad slid the knife into the sheath on his calf. "Lied to him, sir, said I wouldn't let them burn him."

"That's a good lie, Harad," I said. "You did the right thing." If he'd moved the body, that would have alerted them. Couldn't be helped.

Calestinise went on with his side of the story. "They made us do it in the morning, when it was light, so none of us could think about sneaking off in the dark."

I guessed it was more about using the night to get them more compliant.

I was right.

44

THE NEWEST RECRUITS to the glorious army of light had a special role at the grand dinner served up that evening: to sit and watch, not eat. Instead of camp songs, they were treated to more lecturing from the leader, about the thievery of the north, the crimes of the king. Every time he paused for breath, the seniors applauded and cheered. Then he moved on to the worse crimes of the king's minion, the governor, who wasn't even his real son, but a jealous peon who'd tried to become a shaman and been rejected as unworthy. Soon enough, a few of the new recruits started cheering. The smart ones followed along with the game. Those who didn't pick up on the new rule got knocked to the ground and told, "Pay respect! Honor Truth!" Each time, the rest would chant it out, "Honor Truth!"

By the end of the meal, the call echoed up and down the canyon, young voices in unison, like a song but very little like music.

"Made me sick," Radeo remarked.

The recruits were marched into one of the larger buildings, each one with an older kid, an "officer," marching alongside. Inside, the place was one big room, with sleeping mats laid out. The hungry, exhausted kids spread out, each finding a spot, ready to sleep away the weird nightmare this had become.

"We weren't there to sleep," Calestinise said. "We were there to practice our lessons."

"What lessons?" Heyliannin must not have been paying attention.

"All that garbage they'd yelled at us. One of the officers—that's what the army kids called themselves—would jump to his feet and shout out something like, 'The governor—' and we were supposed to jump up and holler out one of their lies."

All the officers held sticks, long, flexible willow wands, and anyone who failed to jump up in time or who said anything 'wrong' got a lash from one of those twigs. If a kid put up their arms to fend it off—or, worse, fought back—they'd get a pummeling. The one thing that protected those kids was that the officers were kids too, and they got tired. Gradually, the beatings eased off, because the officers began to take naps. Calestinise told us his beater would wake from his naps in a panic, looking to the door first, as if watching for someone to come after *him*. Then he'd lay into Calestinise a few times, because 'I know you failed tests, I was just giving you a little rest.'

"We didn't see any of that, Boss," Harad said. "Once they went indoors, we took our chance to go spy on the bosses."

"The traitors," I snapped.

"Right, sir. Where Callas went in, you could hear voices all the time—guess that was the 'lessons' he was talking about. In the other big building, there wasn't any noise, figured those ones got to sleep. The cabin had two adults in it, both men. They talked for a while before bed, useless stuff, predicting the weather, complaining about insects." Harad sounded disappointed. The heads weren't conspiring about their evil plans?

Radeo leaned forward. "Highness. That boss-man, he's a Southerner. I wouldn't ever mistake that accent. Not since NeverSnows." He shifted again, and his face returned to the shadows.

Harad took the talk back. "The crazy thing is, Boss, this whole operation, it was mostly run by the kids they'd already trained."

Heyliannin held up her hand. "You all keep saying kids, boys, girls. How young were they?"

"From smallish—younger than Stevvin—to our spy-boy's age, best I could tell."

"I got disciplined for not bringing my brother," Calestinise said. "I had to promise to recruit him once we finished training." *Disciplined*, my foot. He got *beaten*.

"Thanks, big brother," Stevvin said, from right next to me. It made me jump. I hadn't noticed him creeping up to sit by me. He had another of those toss-ups in his hands, but he wasn't playing, just tying and re-tying the knots in the cords. The pegs clacked together softly, like small stones tumbling in the distance.

In the morning, the exhausted officer-kids were rewarded with a hearty breakfast and sent off to rest in the barracks building.

The senior officers took over.

The new recruits would have a lot of objections to burning the runaway's body. For one thing, farmers and fishers bury their dead. Fishers take it a step further: once a corpse is down to bones, they dig it up and put it in the lake. Don't ask. People have their traditions. For another, everyone knows that burning is for criminals. And besides, the returner religion had its pockets of believers even in Lakeside. They think burning breaks the connection with whatever mystical thing it is that sends them into a new body after they die. Like I said, traditions.

The dead kid had the twisted-ribbons tattoo on his arm. All the kids, apart from our boy, were Lakesider fishers and farmers.

"Who else here is a traitor?" the biggest of the seniors screamed at the recruits. "Who else here needs to be cleansed from the soil of Lakeside?" He had a sword, not a little knife, and he waved it around with a certain amount of skill. It would be plausible to believe he could kill any one of them.

Nobody wanted him to name them a traitor.

"Returners deny shamanism!" That was the next lesson. "They believe the lies of demons who tell them they have a life force that goes beyond life! They spread that poison into other people's heads! Do you want that? Do you?" I remembered the young raider, up in the north country, how he'd accepted his sentence from me with that one request, to let his soul fly free. What did it hurt to let him have his belief? Who could call hope a poison?

They had to shout that lesson back: *Poison! Poison! Poison!* Some of them shouted and cried at the same time. Probably returners themselves, Calestinise guessed. "They kept tugging their sleeve ends down."

To warm them up to the deed, the seniors got the recruits gathering wood. They spread out—each still with an officer watching them—and collected sticks until the boss-senior decided the pyre was big enough for that little guy's corpse. By that time, the kids were so used to following orders, they picked him up like another bundle of sticks and dropped him on the pile. The boss-kid lit the thing before any of them knew what was happening, and the flames surged high.

The adult came out again, with his praise for the seniors. "Well done! Well done!" They made the recruits line up in ranks again.

This time, the big boss walked up and down the ranks and said kindly words to each of the dazed, ravenous kids. "Good job!" "Nice uniform!" "Ah, so proud, standing tall!"

After their terrible night, a lot of the kids soaked up the praise, but Calestinise wasn't the lone nonbeliever. He could tell by glancing around the group that the level of faith was low enough they'd be in for more "training." When his turn came with the boss, he put on his sweet, sincere, I-never-did-nuthin' face and smiled up in rapturous adoration to receive the compliments on his "fine military bearing." How had 'Callas' come by it?

"I told him I'd always wanted to be a soldier but my mean, cruel papa wouldn't let me join up."

"Nice touch," I told him.

"Lies are best with truth inside them, sir," he reminded me.

The boy learned well.

He was right, too. The kids—regardless of how well they'd fawned on the boss—had a tough afternoon of marching training. Yeah, marching. Up and down. Back and forth. Carrying sticks "for the next bonfire." Keep in mind these uniforms did not come with boots. They did this barefoot—and farm and fishing kids, by and large, despite what people think, don't work barefoot. There's a lot of bad stuff in dirt, and you don't want to stand all day in muddy dirt during planting. Same for frog and turtle fishing, which is mostly wading in water you can't see the bottom of.

There were a lot of tears. Calestinise, our barefoot trapper, still had his calluses. He came out of that session at the top of the list.

They did get fed, though, at the end of it. Top-listers like Calestinise were sent to the front of the line. They didn't get more food, but they got it quicker. Some ate fast and stole extra rations from latecomers.

"Calestinise looked to be doing well, sir," Radeo assured me. "We knew you wanted the most information you could get. The shaman kept himself hidden until the sun went down."

At that spookiest time of day, twilight, the shaman emerged from the forest edge, as though he'd popped through a thin patch right there. The boss-man gave him a huge welcome and a dramatic introduction, which meant the recruits had to get back on their torn and blistered feet and look military again.

The shaman danced around, flapping his cape, waving his hands in those dumb-ass gestures the shamans use. Then he announced that the new batch of recruits were good, loyal Lakesiders … all but one. Together, the boss-man and the shaman marched up and down the rows. There's no doubt each and every kid in the bunch believed they were about to be singled out for execution. The fourth or fifth one decided to speak up.

"Honor Truth!" she shouted with all her might.

The next one missed the cue, nearly falling over with exhaustion, but the shaman simply blew dust in the boy's face and made an incantation against evil.

The one after that took up the chant, and each one after cried out "Honor Truth!" as best they could.

Calestinise didn't miss a beat. "Respect, sir!" he shouted. "Honor Truth!"

"I'm sorry I did that." Fresh tears chased themselves along the side of his nose. "That meant the ones after me had to say that whole thing. Plus, I think it gave me away. We were supposed to be brainless by then." He sniffed and bent his head to wipe his face dry.

The shaman and the Southerner ended their tour without anyone being called out. But the shaman still insisted the group harbored a traitor. He went into one of those shaman dance rituals, mumbling nonsense, turning round and round so the huge cape would swirl around him, exaggerating his size and warping his shape as the light dimmed.

When he stopped his routine, he spread his arms wide, holding the cape in his fingers to make himself a tremendous figure embraced in black. He cried out random shamanistic syllables, dropped his arms, and pointed at our Calestinise.

That's when Harad and Radeo started running. Trained, fit guardsmen, armed, experienced, they fell on that mob like eagles on a fishery.

Not one of the recruits stood for Calestinise. By the time my men reached the campsite, our boy was being dragged towards the smoldering remains of the morning's pyre. My men cut their way through them—boys, girls, recruits, seniors. The recruits fell back quickest, some screaming at the sight of their comrades' blood. A few made for the hills as fast as their legs would carry them.

The seniors became demons, piling in hard, though none of them had more than a simple knife, not even the one who'd waved a sword around that morning.

The moment they'd beaten off enough of them that Calestinise could run free, Harad took up a rear-guard stance and ordered Radeo to flee with our boy.

"I told them," Harad said, the smoke from our fire disguising his expression. "I told them we'd been in the war, they shouldn't take us on, but they kept coming, shouting 'Traitor! Traitor!' and 'Honor Truth!' I wanted their bosses. I wanted that Southerner's head. I wanted that shaman's heart. But I couldn't get to them, sir. They ran to their safe house, and the kids kept coming at me. Soon as Radeo was out of sight, I made my run for it." The smoke shifted, and his gaze struck mine, direct and clear, dark with his own deeds. "I didn't kill any more of them than I had to." He put his head in his hands. Even from where I sat, I could see how his fingers trembled.

Radeo's whisper echoed him. "They was just kids, sir, nothing more than kids."

"And there's lots more of them, too," Calestinise said.

45

T HE ROOFS OF FROGTOWN appeared on the horizon. I flicked
my switch at the pony pulling our cart, but it ignored me and
kept its slow, steady pace.

The face of a shaman floated in front of me—a mishmash of
all the smug, self-important shamans I'd met in my life—and the
lash of the switch cut welts across it, and kept cutting, peeling
away the flesh strip by strip.

"Not what the switch is for, sir." I lifted my hand for another
try, but the whip was gone. "Commander Corren." Stevvin's voice
became Tymon's, his constant interference: *stop, Corren, enough,
Corren.* I turned my head, almost expecting to see my brother, but
it was just the kid, the stableboy posing as my son. "I'll drive, sir.
You're not looking well, sir."

"I'm fine. I can drive."

"Sir. It's my job. You'll not take my job from me, will you?" The
calm reproof didn't sound much like a boy begging to keep his
position, but it just so happened I was suddenly tired. I hadn't had
any sleep last night. I kept stumbling into a dream where Calestinise

screamed at me from a blazing fire and my hands melted away when I tried to reach through the flames. Or if I missed that dream, I'd be staggering through NeverSnows, cutting down Southern mercenaries, and I'd look at them, and they'd be children, mad children with crazed eyes, an unending flood of them.

Calestinise had said there were dozens of such camps, most of them further along in training their underaged troops. They were pushing further north, week by week. They might already have a thousand to deploy, another thousand in the pipeline, true believers in thrall to a pack of lies. They'd have forgotten they wanted to escape, knew nothing more than that anyone who ran was a traitor, anyone who opposed them should die. And the rumor-grinders of Lakeside thought it was bad that Jeska asked for Guard volunteers?

I threw the reins at Stevvin. I wanted to crawl over the rail and find a way to nap on top of the bundles and supplies in the back of the cart. My knees buckled as I jumped to the ground. I nearly fell, but for Kul's arm turning up, a thick post to grab onto.

"First step's a big 'un, Boss," was all he had to say about that.

We walked together for a while, me and Kul, with Heyliannin and Calestinise far enough behind I could hear the murmur of their voices, but nothing of what they said. Harad patrolled ahead of us, while Radeo watched our rear for any sign they'd been followed. I wished we had the time and the men to make a real effort on that camp. Like Harad, I wanted the two adults dead at my feet, but first I wanted every piece of knowledge in their heads.

I peeled off the gloves I'd been wearing since we set out from Lakeside City and ran my fingers over the scar that marked me Yutek's son and heir. Maybe it was time to drop the fake names and come at them as ourselves. There'd been no news. Had Arnim convinced Yutek? Was Magaran mustering forces? Did Dramin find out if the Jeska matriarchs knew about the insurrectionist Lakesiders?

"Let me see." Heyliannin had sneaked up on me. She had hold of my marked hand. "What happened?"

"What—?" Sometimes I forgot what she was. "It's the sigil of the king. It's proof of my position. And yours, wife of mine."

"I'm not having a baby." I'm sure that's what she said. It's what she always said when I brought up our status.

"Not important right now. Listen, we'll foster in Calestinise and the two boys. That'll be a good enough start. Their families will like the payoff."

"You're not listening."

I was supposed to listen to her with my head hurting the way it was? "It's not the time. We're dealing with an insurrection. There might be a war on. You've got nothing to worry about."

"I said—" She caught at my elbow, pulled, made me stop walking. "I said, I'm having a baby."

What was going on? Was I not walking with my wife, but having weird dreams in the back of the pony cart? It couldn't be possible. This wasn't Eldennian, who'd drag me under a blanket anywhere, anytime she felt like it. Heyliannin was all about privacy. She couldn't stand the idea of doing anything while camping, sometimes not even in a proper bed at an inn. She didn't know—or didn't care—that it meant more chatter behind our backs, not less, but you can't argue with a woman about sex.

"Are you paying attention?"

She'd been yammering, and I hadn't followed it all, but I wasn't about to say so. "Ya."

"What did I just say?" Her muddy brown eyes had that angry intensity I'd seen a few times, now. What was she mad about?

"You said you'd have a baby. Which is a good thing." I felt like I was the one being interrogated. Was she listening to me? "And I said, even though it's me saying it for once, not now. Let me kill a few shamans, first. And Southerners." Just thinking about that made me feel better.

Her voice went up, like a hawk yelling about her territory. "All you talk about is killing, when I've told you I'm pregnant." If she'd had a knife in her hand, she might have stuck me with it.

If she'd stuck me with three knives, I wouldn't have felt it. "You're what?"

"Mom's preggers, Dad," Calestinise said, coming up on my other side and looping his arm in mine. "Your lady's gonna have a bay-bee."

I had nothing to say. I was doing arithmetic in my head. I didn't like the answers, but allowed myself one question. "Am I the last to hear this?"

"Calestinise seemed so depressed, I thought the news might cheer him up."

Didn't make any sense to me, but it had done that. Young people. Too easily distracted. Harad and Radeo still had ghosts dancing in front of their eyes. My head was full of ideas for killing shamans. But Calestinise shed his horror of being burned alive on hearing the news his boss carried a child.

Go figure.

Kids don't really believe they'll die. Maybe that's the true dividing line between children and adults. It came to me, then, where the power of the "army of light" came from. Their soldiers had no idea their lives could end. Other people die. Traitors die, and it's your job to "honor truth" by killing them. But a true soldier? No, a true soldier doesn't fear death, because, in his mind (or hers, in the case of this army), she or he cannot die.

There's no negotiating with an army of immortals.

46

H EYLIANNIN'S CHEERFUL NEWS didn't cheer me up. The dates in my head wouldn't align. Or rather, they did. Too well. It wasn't my baby. It was Tymon's.

For a couple of hours, I was consumed by a familiar cloud of anger, the kind that might make me do something Tymon would have stopped me from. I strode ahead, to Harad's position. He wouldn't let me relieve him, but two in the vanguard is better than one. As I've said, Harad wasn't much for idle talk, and that suited my wild mood.

When my blood temperature fell off to a low simmer, the solution came clear. Practical, and wouldn't rile up Heyliannin like shipping the kid off to be fostered elsewhere.

No, we'd foster the child ourselves. That would answer both our needs. I was short on backups, and there'd be people who'd think the child mine. It might feel strange, fostering my own brother's kid, but if it turned out to be a boy, that put us ahead, and wouldn't cost the government anything. Fosters are expensive, rightfully so.

Another good reason to walk with Harad—he didn't bat an eye as I laid out my plan to march into the Lakeside Shamans' House, slash our way through that vile company, then set the place on fire and burn it to the ground with the dead traitors conveniently inside. I made passes in the air at imaginary bodies, turned them into imaginary corpses, and he nodded appreciatively at my good form without interrupting his regular scans of the horizon.

The sun beat down, and our sweat failed to cool us. I was still tired, though, from lack of sleep.

"We should camp outside Frogtown, get a good night's rest first," I declared.

"First?"

"You know." Without bothering to draw any blades again, I sketched out a few imaginary strokes.

"Ah."

We strolled on. I began to work out the numbers. How many shamans might be there—masters, journeymen, apprentices? There'd be staff as well, functionaries. Possibly townsfolk, people being suckered into handing over good money for fake magical help. We'd have to pull them out of there. I hoped there'd be a few Southerners cowering in a back office.

"You have an alternative, Highness." The title seemed to come naturally from Harad, senior to me if you counted years instead of promotions. He'd spent a lot of those years listening in on my foster-father's councils.

Still. "What could be better than killing them all? Come on, Harad, you know you want to."

"Respectfully, sir, you won't find all of them in that one building. But here you are, Tamakinroy's-husband Castor, an aggrieved father, with your son battered and abused and nearly burned alive, saved by luck, because his uncles came to tell him the family had to move on."

"So?" Wasn't that enough to burn them all? Might be more work than I'd thought at first.

"You've a suit, sir. A right of complaint. Strike the shamans where it hurts them most."

"And where's that, if not their guts?" My imaginary sword slashed a new opponent.

"Their purse, sir. You know they've a dire love of money, shamans." He pulled out his own purse and jangled it in front of me. It made me feel like a kid, but had the effect he wanted.

I sheathed the invisible sword. "Go on."

"Consider what they charge for their services—let alone what it costs to enter an apprenticeship. You've a valid claim of abuse. Demand compensation. Make a lot of noise about it. Demand records, information. Make a racket in the town. Better yet, let your pregnant wife make that noise, put it about that Southerners are stealing children."

"Seems roundabout to me." Then again, it was money that had got us started on this trail in the first place. Those records might show funds flowing from the south. There might be Southerners there, right now, with big bags of cash that we could confiscate. The Master Shaman's name was at the top of the list Heyliannin had extracted from the records up in Lakeside City.

Harad interpreted my thoughtful moment for resistance. "Sir, we're deep in enemy territory, and there's only the four of us. Though Calestinise is decent with a knife and Stevvin could distract them with a hail of toss-ups. But then, your lady's with child. Isn't that fifty-fifty putting your own son and heir at risk?"

I didn't share my calculations. In the end, maybe we'd let everyone think the child was mine. There's nothing magical in royal blood, no more than in shamanism. It was just another tradition. Besides, why was he back to arguing against an attack? "Shamans aren't fighters, and we've four of the best."

"With a legal incursion, sir, not a military one, we could scout out the situation, take more information back to Jeskaryan. They're planning a war. And the king doesn't know the half of it. I'm worried."

He left unspoken, *as you should be, Highness.*

I still wanted to kill them, but we could do that later. Case and Arnim would want in on it, wouldn't they? I told Harad I'd consider his idea.

47

HEYLIANNIN OVERRODE MY PLAN to camp outside town. She'd had enough of the hard ground, she said. And the rest had gone soft on our lady's needs, now she'd revealed her condition. As we settled the group at the new inn, I watched and re-thought my take on that.

They hadn't gone soft; the command structure had changed. She wasn't the north-country weird-woman their future king had married in a hurry. Heyliannin was our matriarch.

Even I felt it, that pressure to conform, despite growing up the way we did, me and Tymon. Even in the king's household, you always knew the government was the instrument of the matriarchy, not the other way around.

The system worked for Harad's approach to our attack on the shamans. He talked to my wife. She talked to me. She had one demand, over and above our information-gathering. She wanted that cape.

How was I supposed to make good on that? If they had it, they wouldn't be handing it off to a stray manager's-husband. They might not even surrender it to the king's heir, and I'd just agreed not to put the nation at risk by revealing myself inside the enemy stronghold.

At any rate, the scheme we came up with made good use of my fury. It transferred well to Harad's script. To bring the cloud of anger down, all I had to do was think about what they'd done to Calestinise.

Callas, rather. My son, Callas.

I dragged him by the arm up the steps to the Shamans' House. My cousin Harad followed. He'd left his sword at the inn. That's not to say he wasn't armed. Like Arnim, he was a two-knife fighter and carried spares, just in case. No one would spot them. Harad had come up from the ranks, like me, spent tours of duty embedded in town-based forces, and knew how to keep a low profile.

I had my sword at my side, though. I was a manager's husband, and a veteran, and it was my right.

"You'll have to put that aside, sir," the gatekeeper wanted me to know.

"No!" I put my hand on the hilt and my shoulders tensed.

"Castor," Harad said over my shoulder. "It's all right." To the gatekeeper, he added, "My cousin's upset, you understand. We're here to see the Master Shaman."

The little man at the entry frowned, his eyes on my weapon. "Do you have an appointment?"

"I don't need an appointment," I snarled.

Harad gave the better answer. "He'll want to see us. There's news spreading through town he needs to hear. Today."

"I'll go talk to his aide. But I'll need that thing put aside, first." The coward cringed away from me when I moved, even though I was only unfastening the belt.

I held it out. "You better not damage it. I got this when I was in the service, and it's mine, and it's valuable. If it's not perfect when I get back, I'll use it on you."

He took it by the belt, letting the loaded scabbard swing, nearly striking the floor.

"Watch it!" I cried. "You're doing it all wrong!"

"Come on, Cousin." Harad nudged my shoulder as he passed by. We were past the gatekeeper before he figured out we'd skipped his plan to keep us waiting while he talked to that "aide." Since when did shamans have military-style assistants?

Calestinise dragged his feet behind me, whining in a convincing way. "Daaad, no, I don't want to!" He even managed to grind in a scared-sounding tone. The boy was a wonder.

The Master Shaman was in a meeting. He wasn't in his office. We'd have to wait.

All that came from the aide. He sat behind a desk, a table, really, blocking the walkway in front of the office entry. Calestinise squeaked with more than fake alarm, and sidled behind me, out of the aide's sight. I noticed the uniform, then. Ash-black shirt. A row of military-like insignia. Above the shirt, a too-young, expressionless face, with cold, staring eyes.

"Where's the meeting hall, then?" Harad asked, in mild, uncle-ish tones.

The youth's eyes flicked to the left, briefly, then fixed on us again. "That's not your right to know."

We pivoted left, as a unit. I kicked the table as we turned, enough to distract him as Calestinise followed Harad. It was an unintentional bonus that a protrusion on the table's underside caught the aide's knee. We left him howling.

The place was laid out not unlike the Shamans' House in Jeskaryan. Other youngsters in black-and-black patrolled the long hallway that split the building. I kept a steady, confident pace, straight to the double-wide door that should open to the general meeting room. We flung the door open and marched in. Their hall outmatched Jeskaryan's, reminding me more of the king's council chambers. Such a wide space inside a common building made me nervous. I glanced up at the rafters. Orkast's lectures about the responsibilities of a maker had instilled caution in my bones. Builders in Jeska planned for earthquakes—these beams were under-sized and over-spaced.

We'd walked into a lecture. Apprentices sat in rows on the floor—upwards of thirty of them, each fully attending to the mystical nonsense delivered by the man in the cape. He'd been pacing like the fake commander Harad had described, but froze in mid-turn, his cape swirling out like a cloud of poison, when we three invaded his territory. I had no doubt that was Racac, Master Shaman of Lakeside.

"What's the meaning of this?" he demanded.

I launched into my rant. I doubted anyone could follow everything I was saying, but I stayed on-script and I talked fast and loud. I had lines about my son being abused by shamans, about children being held prisoner in the hills, about fires being set in the dry season.

Calestinise was supposed to be backing me up, by showing off his bruises. He'd dressed Lakeside-style for the purpose, in a sleeveless shirt and trousers that didn't even reach his knees. Those bruises had made Heyliannin choke and turn and run from our room at the inn. Counter to plan, though, he'd frozen in place behind me, like a block of stone. His breathing sounded rough and shallow, as if he'd fallen ill.

"It's all right," Harad was saying. "You're all right, boy."

"It's the same, it's like it was." Calestinise's bold voice had become a feather brushing air. "Don't let them take me. Don't."

In a flash, I saw the room the way he did. The neat rows of humble supplicants, the man in the cape marching up and down in front of them—and now, standing from a chair positioned in the far corner, the one I hadn't seen before. That was no shaman, in his dead-black uniform. I'd've bet the compensation I was shouting about that he was a Southerner.

He didn't betray himself by speaking out loud. He strolled to the shaman-in-charge and bent his head to offer advice in private.

The apprentices, not as compliant as the tortured kids, sneaked peeks at the uncouth intruders. A low buzz of whispered discussions swelled among them. One in the front row didn't take part in the guessing games. I wouldn't have noticed him if he'd stayed still, but he started to stand up, and one of his fellow students grabbed his arm and pulled him back down.

Tymon.

With his hair shorn off like that, he looked so much younger, like a kid. The shapeless sack-like clothes concealed that runner's body of his, made him seem as weak and helpless as the rest of them. He kept his eyes on me. There's no doubt he'd recognized us. I flicked my fingers in an old, old hand-sign we'd used as kids, the one that meant *stay quiet.* After seeing the military presence inside the Shamans' House, I knew Harad's plan had been the right one. With one call-out of my name from my brother, the game would be over.

What exactly did shaman initiation rites involve? I'd always thought it was mostly study, learning incantations (not that they did anything, but, still, there'd be a formula), practicing those useless gestures. Were these young men and boys as trapped in some way as those kids out in the hills? They'd paid dearly for the privilege, too. *So we know where Tymon's retirement money went. But why? Is he here under duress? How do we know he's not a prisoner, like the kids in the camp?*

Distracted by Tymon's presence, I'd eased up on my performance. Harad nudged my shoulder.

"You've got his attention, Cousin."

The shaman approached us with an oily, wheedling smile that reminded me of no one so much as Kerrin, that asshole I was going to eject from the council the minute I took the king job. "What seems to be the problem? Let's take this to my office, gentlemen. As you see, we're conducting a program here. You can't interrupt."

I watched Tymon out of the corner of my eye, waiting for a sign back from him. I expected to see *help*. I might have edged in that direction. I might have put my hand to the sleeve where I had a knife ready. He signaled *no*. And *all right*.

No one could have been forcing him to give me secret signs that no one else in the world ever used for anything.

It was all I could do to leave that blade in its hiding place. That bastard shaman had his sweaty hand on my arm, pulling me around. I threw one last glance over the assembly and stopped short. In front of each apprentice lay a squarish dark object, each a bit different from the next, but all of them thick, furry, black in their essence, as if they consumed the light in the room. Capes. No, *mantles*.

I was too far away to be sure, but my gut insisted the one in front of Tymon was Orkast's.

I took a step back into the room. Training takes a year, my father made that clear. In part because taking on the mantle can be dangerous. My skin crawled with the memory of the words my father had used. "There's a process," he'd explained, "to be sure an initiate will survive induction." Tymon had been here a month, maybe. What was he doing with a mantle? My feet wanted to march straight to my brother. My arms wanted to grab him and Orkast's cape and haul them both out of that place.

My brain took in the Southern soldier, with his massive sword, standing not two feet from Tymon. "Oh, my goodness," I exclaimed, in the most idiotic tones. "Are all these guys about to become shamans? Can we watch?"

The shaman tugged at my arm. "No. They are but prentices, fool." Almost reassured, I yielded to his pull.

In the hallway, with the door shut on whatever lies that Southerner was reciting for the apprentices, we were herded—not politely, to the offices—but forcefully, to the front door. A troop of those dead-eyed youngsters formed a barrier that I knew Harad was not ready to cut through, not that day. He seemed to struggle to shake himself out of a daze, then produced the wordy document we'd struggled over the night before. "We've serious complaints that must go directly to the Master Shaman."

"That would be me," the teacher-shaman rumbled, reaching for the paper.

While the shaman read the thing over, Calestinise edged his way around to put both me and Harad between him and those dead-eyed kids.

When I saw that Racac had reached the boring pieces at the bottom of the paper, I launched in. "My wife is out for your head, shaman. Callas here is our oldest, and we've no daughters. He's almost ready to marry—"

"Am not!" Calestinise blurted out.

"Your mother will be the judge of that, nephew," Harad said.

"So?" the Master Shaman said.

"You'll pay compensation, that's so." My voice was getting hoarse after the shouting. It made my growling more serious-sounding. "Or we'll be hiring runners to send up complaints to the governor and to the king, and then you'll be paying for that expense, too."

He held up both hands and made his smarmiest smile. "Rest assured, good sir, we'll be taking these allegations seriously. I will launch an investigation this very day. We will find out the miscreant who's been misusing his station as a shaman, and he will be stripped of his position." He pressed one hand to his chest and met my angry eyes with his lying ones. "You have my word, sir."

He shifted his gaze to Harad. "Sir, my apologies on behalf of the order. We will take this compensation request under due advisement, but please allow us time to complete our enforcement efforts first. That must be of the utmost urgency."

His smile became sickly-sweet and he bent his head towards Calestinise. "Young man, I am heartily sorry to hear of your sad experience. I'll not let this happen to another. Thank you for reporting these terrible events."

He stepped back, through the phalanx of the soldier-kids, who closed in, all but pushing us out the door. I had to kick up another fuss to get that weasel-faced functionary to fetch my sword from wherever he'd stored it. My checking it over as we made our way back down the stairs was not any kind of play-acting. I'd never seen a man so incompetent with a weapon.

We'd hardly made it halfway back to the inn before the conviction fell on me that I'd made a terrible mistake.

Since when had Tymon been clever enough to know when he'd put himself in a bad situation?

Why had I let him stop me from rescuing him? It would have been dangerous, but me and Harad against a few lumpy apprentices, an old shaman, and one grim-looking Southerner: no contest. I had to put it down to habit, to Tymon's voice in my head, triggered by that old hand-sign, *Stop, Corren.*

My first impulse was to turn back right then. I stopped in the street, people flowing around us like we were rocks in a stream.

"What's wrong, Cousin?" Harad asked.

"Nothing. Everything." I moved into a run. To pull Tymon out of there—and collect Heyliannin's mantle—we'd need Kul and Radeo. We needed Harad's sword, my favorite knife, and maybe a few of the other useful tools stowed away in our gear. For the next hour or so, we knew exactly where Tymon was, what he was doing, who surrounded him. It could be done.

Plus, Heyliannin would get her precious cape back.

48

I NTENT ON MY NEW PLAN, I nearly ran past Kul. That bear-paw hand of his flicked out and caught my arm, holding me upright even as it yanked me off my feet for an instant. I grinned up at him, feeling like a freshly-minted captain again. "Just the man I'm looking for. Come on, we need a few of our special tools."

"Castor, brother-of-mine," he said, always sharp, never missing a beat in our cover story, his eyes on the passers-by with their alert, gossip-ready ears. "My *sister*, your *wife*, has had news. Would you come back to the inn, talk with this runner?"

"Your sister?" I had to pull my head out of my battle plans. "A runner? Who? Stevvin's little friend from the west side?" By now, Case might have run into one of these army of light camps on the far side of the lake. According to Calestinise, there were plenty.

"No, but she's plannin' on sending Stevvin to him with this news."

"What news?" My voice was going up. People around us stared.

"Best come back with me. Listen to your wife."

I had a feeling it wasn't anything I wanted to hear.

We went at a good pace, but my rescue plan was already in tatters. Any news that could distract Heyliannin from getting her cape back had to be something bad.

There was no one in the inn's public rooms. Kul led us straight through and up to the chambers we'd picked, the ones furthest back, out of the traffic. He rapped on the doorway to mine—the room where I got to *sleep* with my wife, with our fake sons snoring in the same room. Stevvin's skinny arm pulled the drape back, and we stepped through, all of us crowding in. A wiry little man with wide eyes, his hair pulled back tight in the Lakeside style, sat cross-legged on our bed, with my wife sitting at the further end, by the window that faced the back alley.

Heyliannin pointed to us, or more exactly, to me, using one of my knives as a pointer. "Tell him," she ordered.

"The king's dead." The runner cringed, as if he thought he'd be next on the death-list. He rocked back too far, and his head hit the wall with a thump.

His words went in my ears, rattled around in my skull, failed to turn into sense. "What? Say that again."

"The king's dead." This time, he did that thing some of them do, that usually I hate: imitating the voice of the sender. Magaran's voice. I'd have bet that knife Heyliannin held, my favorite knife, the one I'd marked Tymon with.

"When did Magaran send you?" I demanded.

His eyes went wider. You could see the white around the brown. It made him look like a ghost.

Heyliannin seemed to suddenly realize she was waving a knife around and shoved it back into its sheath on the table under the window. "Sorry," she told the runner, but it didn't seem to ease his fears. He'd gone from being held at knifepoint by a vicious kid and a strange woman to facing our gang of armed ruffians.

I peeled my gloves off and held up my marked palm. His eyes were still darting around, from the knives, to my sword, to those horrific marks up and down Calestinise's arms and legs. I snapped my fingers and presented my mark again. "Runner! Look here!"

He leapt to his feet.

I figured he was about to shout, *Highness!* or, even worse, *Your Majesty!* Before he could open his lips, I hissed, "Shh, don't even think it too loud. We're under the covers, here."

Heyliannin snickered. "Under cover." Her Atlantan jargon had several useful phrases, but they didn't always translate right. "Sit down, Runner. Tell him your story." She gave us her new matriarchal glare. "Everybody. Sit down. Before he has an attack heart. I mean, heart attack." See? Like I said, good phrase, bad translation.

Trusting to blind luck, Magaran had spent a fortune on a flock of runners to find, not me, but Heyliannin. Her appearance was odd enough, even wrapped up in clothes, to be recognizable. I wondered, and should have thought of it sooner, if her snake-man book could draw pictures of more than words and numbers. If you pointed it at a person … or a wide meadow up in the Well … what would you get? *Aha*, my slow-moving brain told me, *that's what the blue monster was doing: making himself a good-bye picture of the world on our side of the thin patch.*

While I was reminiscing, the runner rambled through the setup part of his story, his mission to hurry straight to this township, leaving his fellow runners to stop, one by one, at others along the way. Each was directed to inquire after a northern manager suffering from a chronic illness, whose family needed her to return home for a newly-discovered cure. He'd arrived while Heyliannin and Kul were down at the market, testing out responses to our story of shamans kidnapping kids into forced labor. The little guy had begged the innkeeper to let him wait for them, to deliver this "deeply personal" news in private, then to find himself a prisoner the moment he'd delivered Magaran's message.

The commander's voice had a few more words for me. "Get yourself safely back to Jeskaryan, at greatest speed, at any cost."

I turned on Stevvin. "Kid, you need to move out now. Find Case and the others. Tell them to head for Jeskaryan. Take the short road, south and back up the west shore. I expect you'll find them in South Point by now."

"Yes, sir. I mean—" His voice cracked.

I didn't like to think it myself. King of Jeska? People calling me *Majesty*? "No, not here. Go. Now."

"Yessir." Seconds later, his feet hit the stairs. Like a real runner, he hadn't even paused to grab anything to carry.

I turned back to my fake family and Magaran's messenger. "Let's not get ahead of ourselves. It's happened. I was expecting this. What's important is: how fast can we get back to Jeskaryan?"

49

T HREE DAYS. ME, HARAD, AND RADEO on hired ponies. We traded
for fresh ones before Lakeside, to avoid stopping there and
raising questions.

Our cart-pony wasn't inclined to move fast, and, besides,
Heyliannin and Kul needed it to haul our goods back home. Calestinise
would have to stand as both trainee bodyguard and lady's-maid for the
time being. Yes, I worried about them, but I couldn't put them first, none
of them. Without Kul at my side, I felt half-naked. Radeo and Harad
were experienced, senior captains, but they weren't part of my Six.

Tymon would have to fend for himself for the time being. It
was what he'd asked for, so I couldn't feel too bad about it.

It was Heyliannin it bothered. Not so much because Tymon
was stuck in the depths of shaman territory; she was worried
about something other than the conspiracy. Was it more her need
to get the cape for herself?

She followed me down to the livery stable, talking the whole
time. "It can't be safe for Tymon in there. If he's got the cape, why
doesn't he leave?"

"That won't happen until he's made a shaman."

"When will that be?"

"Takes a year, normally." I'd already told her, though, that nothing in the Shamans' House had felt normal, least of all that those beginner apprentices had been issued mantles. That normally came late in the training process.

"What if I go visit him? Find out more?"

At the risk of delaying our departure, I came to a stop and took her hand. "Listen, wife of mine. Don't be causing trouble. It's a tricky time right now. Tymon told me he's all right, and he has your precious cape, so can't you be patient? If you can't make it to Jeskaryan, find yourself a safe place and stay there." I let my eyes drift down to her belly. "Hadn't you better think about taking care of his baby?"

Before she could rise to that, I whipped back around and jogged to catch Harad and Radeo. The news of the king's death wouldn't be a private message for long. Given the circumstances, the council would be trying to keep it a secret, but in that large a household, the secret would be public knowledge soon. Most likely it already was. We raced for Jeskaryan ahead of a storm. I could feel it at my back, rumors spreading like thunder in the distance, the gathering mass of the army of light.

I'd given Kul instructions to keep Heyliannin out of the way of any troop movements. As if we knew where the troops were and what routes they'd take.

•   •   •

It had been a while since I'd been on a pony. By the end of the first day, I was so stiff I could barely walk. By the third, I had my riding legs back. Outriders from Jeskaryan were waiting for us with fresh animals a few hours out of the city. Familiar faces, at last; however, these men I'd known since our under-guard days—when we were boys with wooden swords—hung back, saluting instead of clasping arms with me. I wished Arnim had come to meet us, to remind me how I was supposed to behave, now. If I'd found a pony big enough to run with Kul, he would have thrown an arm over my shoulder, shown them I was still Captain Corren, despite the other title that had just dropped on me like a falling tree.

Looking like an ordinary party of soldiers, we didn't draw any special attention in the ride through town. Magaran met us at the fortress gate. I wanted a council meeting and a conference of the commanders as soon as possible. He took one look at us—or one breath of us—and led us straight to the barracks for a dunking and fresh uniforms. I scrubbed off the road grime as fast as I could, wishing we had time to take a soak in the cold-pool, which had eased worse pains than saddle soreness over the years.

"We haven't got royal finery for you down here, Corren." Magaran held out an odd-looking uniform for me. "This here's old-style, so it'll stand out. From what Arnim and Dramin brought, seems we'll be at war."

"We already are, sir." I pulled the thing on, rolling the sleeve ends under. At least the pants weren't too long.

"Don't be doing that in front of the rest of them."

"Don't do what? There's no time to have this tailored." I held out my arms. Even rolled up, the sleeves were too long

"We'll get people in for that, *sir.*" He put a hard emphasis on that last, in the voice he used for orders. The voice he couldn't be using to me. Not anymore.

"Right. Master Commander. Thank you."

He beamed at me. You'd have thought I was his son, a son he was proud of. "You've done well, sir."

"Due credit to you, Magaran. And I'll thank you to call me by my name, when it won't burn the ears off some protocol officer, or I'll get my head full of sirs and turn into another Yutek-en."

He teared up. No lie. The officer who'd burned my ears off in drills, set me to scrubbing privies for insubordination, told me straight out I'd better train harder than anybody on account of my size—he let his eyes fill up with wetness and didn't even bother to wipe the overflow off his cheeks.

He'd been in the training yard that morning, the day Yutek-en ran his blade down my back. Magaran had a scar across his arm, from the next blow the king's son had planned for me. I'd've bled myself dry fighting back, too, if Magaran hadn't held me flat on the ground until the doctor came to stitch me up with her flaming-hot needles.

"You'll never be like him, Corren," he told me. "Don't be afraid of that. Listen to your brother, listen to your men. You'll be fine."

Listen to Tymon? Those days were over, but he wouldn't know that. I grabbed his arm, pulled him close and embraced my teacher, thumping his back hard.

Feet shuffled in the doorway. Radeo and Harad stood waiting. Their uniforms even fit.

"Let's go," I ordered.

"Council first, or commanders?" Magaran had already sent orders for staff to arrange those meetings.

"Eh, let your under-commanders start without me, tell them to put together two or three workable plans. I'd better meet with the council first, or they'll get mad, and then there's no telling what treason they'll think is reasonable."

We moved out in tight formation, Magaran leading, talking over his shoulder, and the other two a step behind me. I remembered old Yutek walking the corridors like that, his favorite retainer in the lead, two men at his heels, armed, their eyes alert for anything they didn't like. A shiver rolled through me. I put it down to wet hair and damp skin, but my gut knew better.

PART VI

THE HEIR MAKES PLANS FOR WAR

50

OUR ANCESTORS CREATED the union of Jeska to stop the incursions of raiders from the west. At the time, we were a loose confederation of landkeepers managing cultivated and wild lands up and down the great valley. Our adversaries were equally disorganized sporadic adventurers hoping to gain from the hard work and meticulous husbandry of our people. Over the generations, we've made peace with the westerners, who've advanced enough to learn the difference between trade and theft. They've remained an agglomeration of family-states, protected by mountains and a great inland sea.

Jeska went the other way, found value in our unity and protection from aggressors in the north, plus security from whatever lay over the mountains to the east. The king of Jeska's responsible for keeping that peace, maintaining border security, hunting down criminals, and settling disputes—even between landkeepers. Anyone who thinks women never get angry enough to come to blows never met a woman with power, or one who wanted it.

Becoming one nation served us well. Gradually, everyone came to speak the language the same way, so runners couriering up and down the valley bring news and never worry about being misunderstood. Or murdered. People got used to differences in traditions from north to south, so there aren't those feuds sparked by confusion about which party proposes a marriage and who brings what to the arrangement. There are places parents don't even have a say at all, if you can believe that.

The net result is, everybody in Jeska is richer than anybody outside Jeska. The westerners don't care—they're all about being "free," even if that means starving during a drought year. The redlanders beyond the Wall seem uninterested in bothering Jeska. Maybe we're too puny for them, or maybe they're too lazy to climb over the pass. The northerners are still trying to figure themselves out, while their raiders still cross the border regularly. If the gang isn't big enough to pillage a storehouse, they can waylay travelers. Because, remember, Jeskans are rich. Even poor Jeskans are rich, by northern standards.

Both safety and prosperity brought Lakeside into the fold. Our own raider-days were long over, but they'd been having issues with forays from various peoples along their western and southern borders. As soon as they annexed, we put a stop to those raids. It cost us. Lakeside had been a buffer against those southern coyotes for years.

We should have pursued them, burned 'em out at the source.

That's what we in the government call hindsight.

The common people of Lakeside saw in annexation the prospect of getting rich. Trade with the other districts surged, once we dropped patrols on Lakeside's northern border. Cash flowed to their farms and fisheries. People in the central and northern districts developed a taste for turtle meat and rice grown in the water-rich lands of the south. Lakesiders were happy until they learned about taxes.

Nobody ever gets used to taxes, though complaining about taxes brings people together.

You can't have a government without funding. If you're a tiny family-state, a couple of the uncles go around and make everyone put in a share. Maybe they beat up a new brother-in-law a couple of times until he understands he's joined an organization that needs to pay its bills.

Then again, maybe he doesn't get the point. Maybe he wants to be a freeloader, enjoy the benefits of the resources his wife's family has taken care of since people first walked out of the hills and learned to farm.

Maybe he's a Lakesider, ready to listen to lies about what Jeska does with that paltry percentage of his income. He's got no idea of the costs of supporting the soldiers who keep raiders out of his house, keep him safe on the roads, keep his wife from killing her second cousin, whose mother wants to kill *her* mother.

Lakeside was full of such people, primed and ready to listen to lies. We—well, Yutek—failed to pay attention through years of Gorton as governor, manipulating those lies to his own advantage, being manipulated in turn by men he'd hired to protect himself. Men who weren't true mercenaries, but agents of the south.

When we marched onto the field at NeverSnows, at the first major battle that I fought in, it wasn't a party of soldiers-for-hire that we met. We confronted a skilled, well-commanded army from the south.

For us, it was a disaster: a battle we won by the skin of our teeth.

For them, it was an exercise: a skirmish to gather intel on our forces, at the cost of a few bodies. I'd heard the tales, that Southerners treated their soldiers like carrion, to be used and discarded. They must have had a lot of spare bodies to spend, given how many we burned that day.

This time, they were coming to conquer. I had no illusions that any of this was about Lakeside. They could have taken Lakeside the last time, if that's all they wanted.

They were coming for Jeska. They wanted my country. I wasn't about to let them have it.

51

MAGARAN DID HIS BEST to fill us in on the way from the barracks to the king's house. Arnim took over at the door to the council chambers. I can't tell you how it felt to clasp arms and thump each other's backs ... because we couldn't do that. I can say that my gut-ache eased itself, and his "Afternoon, Highness," had a hint of Arnim's old sarcasm, that said a title wasn't what mattered, it was the man behind it.

Harad and Radeo stayed beside me, prepared to mount a defense against our company of councilors. We'd had enough time for conversation over the past few weeks. They knew the council's weaknesses.

All the councilors, suspect and loyal alike, scrambled to their feet, murmuring a blend of *Highness*, *Your Majesty*, *Prince Corren*, and one *Captain-sorry-Highness*.

I let the errors slide and jumped to the key point. "Gentlemen, we're at war."

With Arnim at my elbow and my former fake cousins keeping the path clear, we waded through the commotion until I reached the gilt-edged chair that Yutek had used to survive council meetings. Having everyone else standing at least set a time limit for those events. I put one hand on the back of the chair and thought. It's hard to calm down—and easy to do something stupid—when you're on your feet.

Time to change one thing. "Have them sit down," I told Arnim.

He blinked at me, and I could see the thoughts behind his eyes. He raised his voice and gestured. "Please, gentlemen, sit."

There weren't any chairs or cushions. No one ever sat in front of Yutek.

While the confused toffs figured out how to fold their knees and put their butts on the floor, I let my eyes drift to the bank of windows on the east side of the hall, to the sunlight playing over the rooftops of Jeskaryan. Did anyone else here care about this place as much as I did?

Once they'd finally settled, with not a little grumbling going on between them in voices they must have thought I couldn't hear, I gave Arnim a nudge and gestured to the edge of the dais. When he sat on that step, it placed him that much above the councilors.

Yutek's old chair had a soft cushion on it, and I was still hurting from the ride.

I dropped the cushion to the floor, in front of and a little to one side of the chair, and made that my place.

There were more murmurs, less grumbly than before.

I cast my eyes over those familiar faces, making sure at least a few names had stayed stuck in my mind.

"Councilor Kerrin!" I called the name, but pretended I had trouble spotting him among the rest.

"Uh, yes, Prince Corren. Here, uh, sir." So, that was him, still calling me by the title I hated most, after he'd stood through my investiture ceremonies.

I let him stew a few more seconds, let him wonder if he was supposed to stand, now. "You're excused, Kerrin." I waved my hand lazily to the back of the hall, where Harad and Radeo each took one side of the double door and pulled it open.

"What?" Now, that was just *rude.*

"You'll need to be clearing out that apartment my father assigned you. Off you go." I waved again.

"But—"

"My wife will be arriving shortly, with my three foster sons, and you're not to be here when she arrives." I did not want Heyliannin to have to see or hear that *creep*, as she called him, ever again. "You are excused from this council as of today."

Harad stepped forward and extended a hand to Kerrin. "Sir? Do you require assistance?"

Kerrin stared wide-eyed at the sheathed sword swinging so close. Harad didn't wait for a reply, but bent to grasp the fool by his upper arm and pull him to his feet. When Kerrin tried to break free, Harad gave Radeo a nod. It took until they were dragging him to the door for the ex-councilor to figure out what was happening and start screaming objections. They passed him off to the outer guards and closed the door on his protests.

The moment he'd gone, the rest of them began sorting out who would take over Kerrin's responsibilities. It was like they'd been planning his exit themselves, they settled it so quickly.

I looked out on a roomful of satisfied faces.

So that was good.

Then Dramin turned up. Not through the door, not even showing his face. His voice whispered from the stairs behind me, the ones that led down to Yutek's—make that my own— apartment. "Boss—important news."

I didn't need to ask Arnim to get back there, find out what was up. He returned almost instantly, crouching to put that important news into my ear and no one else's. "The elders are coming. They have a problem with the succession." He was back in his place before too many of my councilors noticed.

"Ah, well," I said to no one in particular. "If Heyliannin needs another day to travel safely, that's all for the best, what with the baby and all."

That got the councilors going on congratulations, as if it was something I did on my own. When, in fact, I hadn't been involved. Not that I was going to share that detail.

Meanwhile, the ache in my innards kept me focused on guessing what the elders could possibly be objecting to.

A ruckus broke out beyond the door, and I gestured for Harad and Radeo to let them in.

No sense putting off bad news. It'll come get you in your sleep if you try.

52

T HANKS TO STUDYING THE OLD LADIES as they'd each in turn made their inspection of my person, during my investiture, I knew the five elders on sight. The women flowed through the council room like wolves on the hunt, and my remaining councilors scooted out of the way as best they could. One or two weren't fast enough and took blows from elders' staffs.

Me, I stood up. I knew better than to lounge around in front of a matriarch, let alone a senior one. Arnim followed my lead, but he was slow and earned himself a smack from one of those hardened-oak sticks. He shuffled back, more out of range.

The one in their vanguard, Adestinian, held sway over half of Jeska District. With four daughters under her, there was no doubt her lineage would retain management of all that territory.

Unless the Lakesiders took over.

Did our senior Jeskan matriarchs know about the colluders in Lakeside? Were they part of it, complicit in those camping trips that left young bodies on fire in the hills?

"You won't take your father's seat," Adestinian said. Tall as she was, the woman didn't have to tip her head up to meet my eyes. So they weren't contesting my adoption, but the investiture? Hadn't they seen enough that day?

I chose to misunderstand her. "There are protocols, ma'am. I haven't had time to go up to the field, to say my farewell." Likely I wouldn't get a chance to walk the hill where Yutek's bones were being picked over, not until after whatever this war would become. If I survived it.

The stout matriarch at the far right, Maledestine, didn't wait for her senior to react to my reply. "We've had a complaint against you, Corren. You'll not sit over the government while the charges stand."

Not a complaint then, but charges? "What charges?"

Arnim spoke up. "Shall I remove the councilmen, Elders?"

Adestinian glanced over her shoulder, as if the cowering officials had passed beneath her notice. "No," she declared. "The law applies to all."

So much for that. Whatever they'd come about, it would be well-shared news by day's end.

Still playing at major-domo, Arnim asked, "Shall I call for chairs, Elders?"

She glanced over her other shoulder, noticed those high-and-mighty councilors on the floor, and this time when she turned back, a smile lingered on her lips. "No. We'll not be long." She turned her head to the women on her right. They nodded and tapped their sticks on the floor. She repeated the routine with the two on her left, then rapped with her own staff. "Corren, son of Yutek, you stand accused of slander against the worthy brothers of the House of Shamans, manipulation of funds in your purview as governor of Lakeside, excessive taxation of our sisters to the south, dereliction of duty, and murder by assassination. You'll not take one action as king unless and until all these charges are cleared."

I cleared my throat before Arnim could jump in. "These are lies, spread by agents of the South, our known enemies." How could they not recognize that?

"Those enemies are gone from our land. This is a fact attested to by all the elders of Jeska, from Lakeside to the north."

Arnim earned himself another thwack by saying, "They are deceived, Elders."

I held up my hand. "If you must be striking at someone, strike me." I met Adestinian's eyes. She didn't seem to be shamming, but what did I know? "We have *evvydense*—that is, proof—to strike down most of what you've said. But how am I to make proofs of things that never happened at all? Assassinations? Slander?"

"You deny that you call shamans frauds?"

"Is it slander to speak the truth?" I'll admit, I spoke too loudly. Arnim dodged a staff-strike and reached my side. I thought he might jab an elbow into my ribs to shut me up. I lifted my hand again and ducked my head. "I apologize. My emotions are high. My father's just died, my country's at war, and I'm cut off because soldiers joke among themselves about shamans? Shamans joke equally about soldiers. I've heard them myself—my first father was a shaman, as well you know."

The rumors Stevvin had brought to me every day from the marketplaces, the ones Kul heard in the public rooms, the secret revelations that drunken men shared with Karthi and Andus day after day in Lakeside City … Hearing them now, in my own council chamber, as if they were real, made me dizzy with anger. If Tymon had been there, he'd have been saying, *not now, Corren, not now.* I made myself imagine him saying it, as I looked into Adestinian's eyes, sunken into their sockets and surrounded by wrinkles like desiccation cracks in a dry lakebed.

She had an answer to my objection. "Not all the charges need to hold, Corren. Any one of them would require your removal."

Arnim caught my eye. I couldn't tell what he meant to signal. If it were up to him, I think, he'd have politely set aside the time, arranged for an orderly finding of facts, until all was laid clear and everyone made content. But he had no idea of the imminent danger. No one did, except me and my fake cousins, who'd had to fight children to free Calestinise. Should we tell the elders I'd sent my men to the hills to kill kids?

No.

"Elders, respectfully, we're at war. Who would you have direct the government now? Can you not—" My hand made a vague go-away gesture, a wave less regal and more plaintive. "Can you not conduct your trials and leave me to conduct this war?"

She turned to the window, to the peaceful light flowing over our town. "I see no war."

"The past three days, I've ridden full-tilt from the vanguard of a force that may well overmatch us."

Her lips quirked derisively at what would have seemed to her nothing more than a desperate lie. If only we had a dozen of those snake-men books, to make pictures of what we'd seen, to carry them as proof.

Harad's quiet voice fell into that silence. "It's true, Elders. I've fought them and barely escaped with my life."

She didn't even look at him. "You inspire loyalty, Corren. I'll grant you that."

"Then let me spend that loyalty, in defense of Jeska. The commanders are with me, and the men will listen. We can win this if you allow me to lead them." I wondered if I should drop to my knees, like I'd done with Yutek that time. I wavered, and the chance passed.

"You must answer the charges."

I offered the one thing I could. "Then I'll agree to them, if you'll let me conduct this war first."

"You say they're all true?" She seemed genuinely shocked. Perhaps she hadn't believed all the lies, only some of them.

"No! No! None of them are true." I took a step backwards, and my legs struck Yutek's chair. My knees bent, and I fell, landing awkwardly in the old king's seat. It took time to right myself. I meant to stand, to get out of that chair I didn't own, but from there I was below her—differently than if I'd been kneeling, but also somehow the same. I put my hands on my knees and leaned forward, bending my neck to look into her face, begging her to understand what I was offering. "I'm saying I'll *say* they're true, and walk away from the kingship afterwards, if that will make you go away, *now*, and let me do the job that Yutek raised me for."

The elders formed a circle and argued among themselves. Being old people, they were each hard of hearing to one degree or another, so their conference was by no means secret. It wasn't that they didn't know we were there, listening. They didn't care. We were beneath them, the mistresses of the land, the stewards of the future.

One wanted me hauled off and thrown on a pyre that afternoon. One very loud, querulous voice wanted me installed in the position right now—they were a bunch of old fools, and didn't they see what was going on here? Two of them would have followed Arnim's approach—whatever could be wrong with stopping this fighting nonsense for a while to sort out fact and fiction? Adestinian may have been contributing, but she had such a mild, even voice and she didn't raise it as much as the others did.

When they reset to their line formation, I had no guess what they'd decided. I desperately hoped I wouldn't burn that day. I doubted I'd have everyone calling me Your Majesty anytime soon.

Adestinian didn't mince words. She took my offer.

That one who'd called me out at the start, Maledestine, seemed grim and dissatisfied. I guessed she was the one who thought the claims were true and I should pay the full price. Adestinian took the practical view. "If you're lying about this war, we'll know soon enough. If you're not, the nation can't risk disaster while we fritter away time in legal proceedings." That's when I decided the women of Jeska weren't in on the scheme. I must have betrayed how pleased I was by that realization, because she tipped her head and added, "I never thought I see a man so happy to resign the kingship."

"No, ma'am," I told her. "I'm happy to serve Jeska." I untangled myself and stood, so I could bow to her. "If you'll pardon me, Elders, councilors, my commanders are gathered. I'm keeping them waiting." I threw an arm over Arnim's shoulders and drew him with me, straight through that phalanx of puzzled, angry women. Harad and Radeo formed up behind us. We paused as we exited, so I could tell the outer guard to find Dramin in my apartment, and send him to the commanders' conference.

The sound of the council-room door booming shut was like music.

53

TRADITIONAL WAR IS A MATTER of hurling one set of bodies against another, whether or not the damage is complicated by each side also hurling arrows into the opposing mass of flesh. One thing new in the upcoming conflict: the bodies the Southerners were prepared to spend belonged to us.

They were children of Lakeside, which made them Jeskans, not Southerners.

That was the toughest message to deliver to my commanders. I put Harad and Radeo on circuits of duty where they spoke to small groups of officers and soldiers, telling the story of their one encounter with that single training camp.

The commanders and I ran in circles, trying to find a way that wouldn't lay the bones of Lakeside's progeny down in the grass. We had to talk through the worst arguments, such as: after a battle, assuming we win, do we let them lie? Do we burn them? Do we send the bodies home to families for whatever rituals? If so, how? Could it be done quickly enough to not layer decay on top of death? I had to walk out of one such meeting, where Dramin had brought in his aunt to explain exactly what happens to a body after death. Never listen to doctors talk if you've eaten in the previous hour.

I stayed out long enough to get rid of my lunch, then returned. We had no time. Yutek had authorized a mustering-out, but the process had been interrupted by his death. Magaran got everything back on track, but we'd lost ground. We had household staff working to quarter late-arriving reserves, while the regular support squads hustled to HandOverHand to establish the base camp for Jeska District. I wanted a posting at the north edge of Lakeside, but we knew the enemy would be coming from both directions there; we couldn't be caught in a squeeze, and we didn't have time to form up enough men to march down both sides of the lake at once. The river channel made a sort of a funnel an hour's march south of NeverSnows. We hoped to begin there.

I had no hope it would end there.

The histories show I was right. You can read the public record for yourself, the troop actions, the casualties. You'd have to dig through command records to sort out the hows and whys, what we proposed, argued over, and settled for, the day-to-day toil of planning for war.

·   ·   ·

While I was setting out to explore Lakeside with my fake family, Arnim and Dramin made it north with our preliminary report and the snake-man book full of proof. Yutek called in smiths—as well as an entertainer skilled in tricks of light and shadow—to assess the device. They couldn't tell him much beyond there wasn't any detectable trickery; that was enough, combined with Arnim's attestations, for the king to accept the evidence within the pictures. I still feel he'd have trusted it quicker, coming from me, who'd always seen through the shamans' lies.

At the time, we'd thought the shamans of Lakeside were complicit in no more than fomenting anti-Jeska sentiment in the district. We'd followed funds from Racac's strongbox to various rumormongers in Lakeside City. Heyliannin had made a connection to the Shamans' House in Jeskaryan. It bothered me that no one had followed up on that. But what could I do? No one wanted to bait the shamans in their lair.

My schedule was packed, but I tore myself free of meetings and tearing up unworkable plans that afternoon and slipped into town to meet with my first father's old boss. Over Arnim's objections, I insisted on going alone, so it was like being a kid again, dodging past the gate guards to slip out of the fortress—except now it was my own protectors I avoided. It was necessary—nothing would shut down this particular investigation like bringing an armed force into the Shamans' House.

The doorman let me in without comment. He must have recognized me, because he let me find my way to the Master Shaman's office without an escort.

"For old time's sake." I lifted the flask of what a vendor had assured me was high-class fermented fruit. Never much on wine myself, but a guest brings gifts for the host, not himself.

Fennic, who'd been Master Shaman of Jeska since before my father signed up, broke into a fit of coughing, and his eyes skittered over me like he expected me to plunge a sword into his guts. Not that I didn't want to, but I'd left the serious armament at the fortress.

He should have felt more at ease in his own place, but then again, our last meeting had been less than comfortable for him. While he wobbled from side to side, trying to decide how to greet me, I studied the room. It seemed more crowded than I remembered, fewer shelves and more closed cupboards to hide his secrets in. I was down to analyzing the wood grain to decide if the cupboards were domestic or imports, when he finally settled on taking the seat closer to the door.

He gestured to his own usual place. "Highness. Be my guest. The cushion there will suit you better."

It didn't matter to me. I could cut his throat from either direction, and I entertained the idea while he set out cups and I worked the stopper on the flask. Arnim and I had talked over the choices here. We'd agreed it best to keep this traitor in his place, rather than letting a fresh crop grow in his stead. We had our eyes on him, that was all he needed to have carved into his heart.

This time, I led the conversation around the usual topics. How was he faring with the arthritis? Was he needing any support for collecting unpaid client debts? Had the shortage of candidates for my father's mantle been a problem?

"No, no, not at all. They'd a crop of likely youngsters down in Lakeside. We're all brothers together, like the runners. Though not like them." He laughed in the middle of a gulp, which made him choke. I got up and pounded his back for him until he felt better. Or until I felt better, it was hard to tell which.

"Well, now, there's nobody like the runners, Fennic."

That made him sit up straight. Masters don't like to be called by name. *It breaks the mystery*, that's what Papa said, but he would say it with laughter and then tell me a tale of a nonsensical landscape beyond a thin patch. Fennic sipped his wine slowly, working on how to interpret me.

I decided to poke him again. "Now then, Fennic, speaking of Lakeside, a few questions have come up in the audit."

"Oh?" His eyes flicked side to side, seeking anything he might have left out for me to use against him.

We'd toyed with the idea of shocking him by using the snake-man book to present the proofs, but I'd put a stop to the notion of letting any shaman get close to such valuable secrets. Instead, we copied out the most incriminating page. Well, had a competent scribe copy it.

I slid the bad news across the table and poured myself a fresh cup as he took up the paper and stared at it. I could get used to wine, given enough time.

He coughed and set down the page, with its columns of figures and notes. Heyliannin had made sure I knew which particular items posed problems, but said she didn't have four years to teach me why. I'd surprised her a little, being able to track from income to expenditures.

"The sequence there, last summer, now that's the worst," I said, keeping it casual. "As you see, though, it's by no means the only irregularity. Likely, there's much more to be found."

"I assure you, Highness, this is indeed concerning. We'll take this up, begin an investigation right away. Whoever has been taking liberties must not be allowed to continue in our company." He reminded me so much of Racac, the Lakeside Master Shaman, with his false promises of a thorough 'investigation.'

"Indeed." I formed a nice, fake smile. I needed him fearing that we had more incriminating information, such as notes he'd signed in his own hand. Which we did. I left nothing in my expression to reveal it. Probably not all of the evidence there might be, but enough to add him to the pyre. Worry and hope combined can drive a traitor to betray himself.

He spread his fingers on the table, reminding me of that other time we sat together, places reversed, and he ran those fingers over my father's mantle. "I'll tell you, Corren, it's not so much a shock to me, given your stance against the brotherhood."

"My what?" The elder's voice, accusing me of slander, my automatic response, flashed through my mind. I let it go, that he'd used my name.

"It's well known you don't respect our calling."

"Oh, so that's where it comes from? I refuse your offer to take up the mantle—because I have my own calling—and that makes me your enemy?" I drained my cup and set it down. A bead of red rolled down the outside, to pool on the table. I ran my finger over it. Red, like blood, but not so thick.

"You're not a believer. I hear my subordinates grumbling about it."

I sighed and wished I'd left my knife at home, so I wouldn't be so tempted to draw it right now. "My beliefs are my own. I'm not forcing them on anybody."

"Do you not see you could have been both? That you could unite Jeska as both shaman and king?" Did he still think he could draw me in?

I thumped my fist on the table. It let out some of my anger, bled off a few drops of the hate that boiled inside me since our visit to Frogtown. Who did he imagine controlled this country? "You're crazy. The elders would never stand for it."

"We could have persuaded them. The brotherhood and the sisters of Jeska are closer than you might think. We all want to preserve this country, to make it strong and safe."

It felt like he was mocking my position. Did he suspect I knew about the collusion between the elders of Lakeside and the shamans there? Was he fishing for turtles while I fished for frogs?

I considered my chances and threw out one more line. "You'll be pleased then to know my brother's gone for an apprentice."

He said nothing, but watched my face intently. I half-expected him to wriggle his fingers in a fake magical gesture. He did snug his cape a little tighter, despite the warmth of the day.

I went on with the yarn. "Yes, he said he'd tired of running up and down the valley. He cashed out his retirement savings and joined the training program. Down in Lakeside, of course, since that's where Yutek had me assigned. Do you think, next year, when he qualifies, you could see if he might be posted north?"

The smile that story generated gave me pause. It wasn't that Fennic was pleased to find me so at ease about my brother deciding to become a fraud like my first father. Nor was he putting on a big fake happy grin designed to throw me off. The thin, satisfied curl of his lip was genuine, unforced, full of wicked, scheming anticipation. I remembered stories I'd heard, of apprentices who'd never become shamans, but never returned home, either. Was Tymon a hostage, then? Had I played out a card they'd been holding, ready to control me with the knowledge they had him in their grasp?

One thing for certain: the Master Shaman wouldn't be explaining himself.

I'd thrown all the bait I had in stock. "You can keep that copy," I told him. "Clear out the corruption in your House, Fennic." I got my legs untangled and pushed myself back to standing, so I could look down on him, like the scum he was. "If you don't, we'll do it for you."

The edge of his cloak brushed my leg as I walked past, as if it might try to grab hold of me. I'd never told anyone else what I suspected, that the capes were alive. It seemed too strange, more unbelievable than the usual shaman crap. I didn't feel safe until I was halfway up the street.

54

I CAME TO A STOP in the center of the market road, busy people passing by in both directions, no one paying me any notice. The friendly banter of buyers and sellers wove through the sounds of buskers wheedling at the generous. Smells of roasting meat and frying bread drifted on the wind. I took a couple of steps towards the nearest stall, and reached for my purse. Then I recognized where I'd stopped.

That lane, there, led to our house. Eldennian's house.

I abandoned the prospects for an edible meal and followed my instincts down that twisting alley.

It was too much like the day she'd refused me. She stood in the kitchen, stirring up bannock, with Deliasin slung tight to her back, facing the door.

She was huge—our daughter, that is. So much had changed in a few short months, but she had changed more than I imagined. She sang out syllables as her mother worked, "Ba-da-ba-da-ba!" When she left off studying her own stubby fingers, she saw me there in the doorway and shrieked like a hawk diving on a jackrabbit. Eldennian jumped at the noise, and the pan clanked on the table.

"It's just me," I said, by way of announcing myself.

Deliasin's excited eyes whirled out of sight as Eldennian turned to me. The strangest sensations rushed through my body. I thought I might be having one of those attack hearts Heyliannin joked about. No, that wasn't it. I struggled to understand. Was this what my wife had felt, when Tymon turned up and I was gone and the midwife's notes shouted *Likely day, likely day*?

"What are you doing here?" my non-wife demanded. Her words were harsh, but her voice had no anger in it.

I'd come because I'd paused on my way back from a fight and seen a familiar road. It could be old habit had taken over, nothing more.

"Well?" From the weariness and suspicion on her face, I needed a reason, not an excuse.

I had a reason to offer. A good one. "There's a war coming. I think it will come clear to Jeskaryan. You should go north. As far as Koresh, if you can. If we lose this war, you need to be as far from here as you can get. They won't bother with Koresh."

"You're trying to frighten me. You know I protect my own."

What, now? Her life wasn't as important as a pile of lumber and plaster? "I'll have someone mind the house. If I'm wrong, it'll be here when you come back."

She untwisted the wrap that held the baby in her perch and parked Deliasin on her hip. Then she came up close to me and studied my face like it was a map, or a legal document. I wished she'd reach over and pinch my ear like she used to do. Heyliannin never did that. It's funny, the things you miss.

At last, she returned to the table and settled on the bench, propping our girl on her lap. "You're serious."

She was Yutek, on his tall chair, and I was a runner with unwanted news. "I am serious. It's bad, Eldennian, very bad. Take your mother, and your brother, and his wife if he's got one now, and go north. Today, if you can. Tomorrow, no later."

"Today?" Her eyes danced over objects in the room, calculating.

"Hire a cart, so you can carry what you need, more than the clothes on your back, Eldennian, more than a few baby-things." I freed my purse and set it on the table. "I don't have much, but this will cover the hire, and I can send a boy with more, while you pack."

Her lip curled, but her hand went out and retrieved the purse. She weighed it without needing to unlace the fastenings. "King Corren's short of cash, is he?"

I wondered how she'd have advised me on the choice I'd had to make. "I won't have the position long. I promised to set it aside when the war is over." Why I had to tell her, I still can't explain, except that Eldennian was the one person I could never lie to.

She was also the one person I could trust to not push me on a thing like that, a choice that went against expectations. She took me as I was, from the first time she led me to her little room at the top of those rickety stairs, to this last meeting.

"Thank you, Corren." She set the purse down and came to me, with Deliasin in her arms. "Here, Delia, say bye-bye to Papa." She held her out to me, and those chubby mud-brown arms went around my neck and the spit-sticky face rubbed across my cheek, and a flowery sent filled my nose, the soap Eldennian used on that soft hair. She weighed so much. I couldn't believe a creature could grow so fast on nothing but milk.

"Such a big girl, you are, Delia," I rambled, not having any idea what I was saying. "You be a good girl for Mama, now."

"Ba-ba-da-ba," she told me, pulling out some of my hair. My parting gift.

Then she started to kick and squirm. It felt like I had an armful of puppies. I made noises in my throat. Maybe it was laughter. The weight lifted off me, and she was back in Eldennian's grasp, still a squirming mass of energy. "We'll do as you say, Corren."

"Yes. Well." Her face was blurry. I couldn't breathe, so I coughed. I wanted to tell her, that she'd been right, that she'd done the right thing—refusing me, keeping herself separate. But I couldn't speak. She had to know, didn't she? She didn't need me to tell her what she already knew.

She spared me, turned away first, and vanished into the room that had been ours.

My vision cleared, bit by bit, as I made my way back up the long, long road.

55

I DIDN'T FORGET TO SEND a well-loaded purse down to Eldennian before sundown—though I sent it with Radeo, not some unarmed boy. You never knew what might happen to a kid with a pile of money, running through the marketplace at twilight. He took his own time getting back. I was about ready to send Harad after him when he dragged in. I was alone, sitting on the edge of the dais in the council chamber, trying to cram high-class food past my unwilling tongue.

"Sorry, Cousin." Radeo had that wry curve to his lips I'd come to recognize, from all the times we'd made him cook for us on the road. "I mentioned we'd been out camping a while, and she put me to getting a traveling larder together for their journey." He cast his critical eye over the plate I was struggling over.

"What?" I demanded.

"Want I should stop by the kitchen and get proper chow sent up? No reason to put up with stuff ya can't stomach."

"This is fine." I stuffed my mouth with a slice of unidentifiable meat covered in a slimy sauce.

Once he'd done pounding my back to get rid of the choke, he took up the plate. "It'll be a few minutes, *Your Majesty*."

"Strategy meeting in a half-hour!" I told his departing back.

He waved his free hand in an imitation of a salute.

I wiped my mouth and tossed back the wine the cooks had sent up with that inedible meal. At least the alcohol cleaned the fungus taste out of my mouth. When I stood up, the stuff hit my head and I wobbled some as I walked over to the windows. *If the Six were here, they'd have made sure that was water.* It wouldn't last long, I knew, but I couldn't afford to be unbalanced now.

I didn't get time to recover from the unexpected drink, as the council-room doors banged open and a pair of haggard runners staggered in.

So far, four of Magaran's runners had made their way back, arriving before I did. He'd had the good sense to give them each a commission to gather what information they could and head back promptly should they fail to find our company. I suspected I owed the elders' suspicions to the news brought back by those four, infected by the rumors running rampant in Lakeside. I'd interviewed them myself, and one man appeared to believe what he'd heard. The one woman had leaned towards accepting the lies, too, until I told her Calestinise's story. She shut up then. Both of those had done their trips on the west side of the lake, though. The ones who'd searched on the east shore seemed more inclined to tag the rumors as gossip, not fact.

I had to conclude that things were even worse in the west half of Lakeside. Good thing we'd sent Case's "family" that way, with their "matriarch" being a proper Lakesider herself.

These runners had traveled separately, but met up on their journeys back north. They'd each made it about halfway from Lakeside City to South Point before following their orders to turn back. Before they said much, I sent one guard to fetch Magaran, who was readying the strategy room for that other meeting. He brought Harad and Arnim and a couple of the senior captains. In the meantime, the other guard had been dispatched for water and a little food for our travelers. Looked like they hadn't stopped much since they'd headed out.

"Lakeside's a rat-hole," said the one who'd gone west, a wiry, tight-sprung man who wouldn't have reached Tymon's shoulder but could probably have outrun him on a straight dash. "There's more stories about all the horrible things Governor Corren's— excuse me, sir—"

"Don't let it bother you. I've heard most of them myself." I waved him on.

"Well, as I said, there's more evil deeds being put to yourself than any man could do in a whole lifetime."

The other one put up her hand for attention. "It's more than that, sir. The stories are meant to rile people up. A lot of what ya hear is 'No taxes for the untrue,' whatever that's supposed to mean."

Harad leaned in. "You ever hear this one: 'Honor Truth'?"

She nodded, her eyes wide. "Has that shit—sorry, Your Majesty—"

"Never mind," I told her. "Speak plain."

"Sorry. I didn't expect to hear that here. Heard it repeated a lot in the marketplace in a little town in East. Sorry. Can't remember the name of the town." She went red.

Magaran spoke up. "Don't worry about it, Runner. We're glad you can share anything. Didn't mean to turn you into spies, but it seems we've got a war coming, now." His sharp eyes went to me. "You say you've heard these tales yourself, sir?"

"Ya. They come thick and fast in the pubs. I had Kul listening in most every evening we stopped in a town, and then Heyliannin and Calestinise would go shopping for rumors in the marketplace. Apparently, I'm the evilest man that ever lived."

"That so?"

"But my boy Calestinise says I ain't evil, so I'm sticking to that." I laughed.

"Your boy?" Magaran's eyebrows shifted higher than I'd seen them go.

"Well, the elders want me out of the job, so maybe it won't matter, but we figured on fostering in Calestinise and the two lads you sent down with us. The wife may be pregnant, but you never know, do you?"

Magaran coughed like he'd swallowed some of that slime stew. Served him right for thinking strange thoughts about my girl-looking son.

Radeo walked in, a tray in his hand and surprise on his face. "Have we moved the meeting?"

Suddenly, I felt hungry. Plans were coming together in my head, calculations of travel times from here to Lakeside, and back, marching speeds of armed troops, ways to leverage the new organization we'd assembled over the past year. We might still be outmatched, but we weren't the arrogant ignoramuses who marched onto the field at NeverSnows.

I collected my prize from Radeo—a real meal, assembled by a man who knew what a soldier needs to keep his mind on his job. "We'll head down there shortly. These runners had good intel for us. Magaran—"

"Yessir?"

"Can we scrounge up bonuses for them? I know the budget's in the red, but this is important."

"Yes, sir. I'll do what I can."

I went back to my spot in front of Yutek's chair and settled the tray across my knees. Then I gave them my regal wave. "Good job, runners. Thanks, all. See you a little while."

Magaran gave me the eye, the look he used to give me back when he was deciding what level of training I needed to move up to the next grade in rank. Then he cleared the room, leaving me alone with my three overqualified bodyguards.

I ate slowly, under Radeo's watchful eye. When I was done, I sent him off with the empty tray and ordered Arnim and Harad to wait outside the doors. It was my last day as myself, my last night as Corren alone. Tomorrow, the elders would make me king, and everything would be different. The world would keep changing until this war had done carving fresh scars on the body of my country.

I waited at the window for a long time. At last, an eerie silver glow grew steadily over the mountains far to the east, lighting up the bands of cloud that form over those peaks even when the valley is parched. The first flash of moonlight stole free of the horizon, flinging its clean light across the city, spreading over the roofs and walls. The torches that marked the fortress gate seemed to flare silver, instead of gold.

Everything came together here, in Jeskaryan, my heart's home.

The long years of patrolling my country, learning to serve.

The long nights at Yutek's feet, learning to govern.

The contentious hours with my commanders, arguing for change.

The connections gleamed bright in my mind, like moonlight on the distant peaks. Our enemies were on the march, but we were better prepared than they knew. I didn't have all my troop here, my closest friends, but they would come, to stand with me in this moment.

We'd sworn to protect, defend, and preserve this land, and for a sliver of an instant of time, I could see the way, clear as silver, plain as night.

•　　　•　　　•

TO BE CONCLUDED IN

FLAMES OF ATTRITION

BOOK TWO OF "THE UNREMEMBERED KING"

RANKS AND UNITS:
THE KING'S GUARD ⊙F JESKA

The King's Guard, colloquially called the Jeskan Guard, is an all-purpose military organization, created to provide a common defense against raiding parties and evolved to continue as a border-patrol service, domestic law-enforcement agency, and, when called upon, a unified battle force. While directed by the king, as for all major social structures within Jeska, the Guard ultimately exists under the authority of the matriarchy, just as the king is an instrument of the Council of Elders. Service is limited by gender (as is typical in Jeska) and age. Only men and women-looking men of regulation age (16) are recruited. Annually, each District is required to supply a certain number (which varies by population) of recruits for basic training. Of these, most are released from duty after no more than a year of service.

Other individuals may volunteer at will. Investigation of claims of gender and age are spotty. That is, underage personnel are not unheard-of (although it is also not unheard-of for underage volunteers to be dragged home in humiliation by furious mothers). Women serve at will on the principle of 'don't ask.' (The advantage women have in this circumstance is that, broadly speaking, in Jeskan society men do not question women or tell them what to do. If women want to enter the military and are willing to take orders and be referred to as 'men', there are no consequences.)

A **troop** is a basic fighting unit, originally a fixed group of eight men. Members of a troop are commonly called **troopers**, though formally they are **guardsmen**. Within a troop, there may or may not be some hierarchy set by the men themselves or by their lieutenant in charge. For payroll purposes, guardsmen are ranked first, second, and third degree, by increasing seniority. Most never advance beyond third degree. Troops are typically long-term relationships, such that when mustered-down to reserve status, that is done by troop, not on an individual basis. Men promoted to higher ranks will continue to call their original troop-companions 'my troop.'

Organizational changes enacted during the career of Corren, son of Yutek, altered the Guard's broad approach to strategy and tactics, such that troops might consist of as few as four or as many as twenty men, depending on their particular mix of skills and capabilities. After the reorganization, troops were intended to act more or less autonomously on the battlefield, obviating the need for in-battle communications. The up-front training required to implement this change was challenging, and generated higher turnover during the transition, but improved morale, soldiers' perceptions of self-worth, and overall effectiveness.

For comparison, if you are familiar with the country *United States,* a troop's function is similar to that of a platoon. Indeed, in that world, many armies use the term troop for this basic operational unit; however, past conflicts between *United States* and some of those other countries, such as *Great Britain*, mean they often choose different terminology, whether military or otherwise. Because the *United States Army* is an extremely large organization that engages in battles beyond the scale of anything experienced by the Jeskan Guard, it further subdivides its basic units, to obtain a close-band unit similar to a Jeskan troop, that they call a squad. In that world, a squad also describes a group of like-minded young people who enjoy relaxing and having fun together, which is an interesting dichotomy to imagine.

A **lieutenant** either commands a troop or performs general-service tasks for a higher-ranking officer, most likely a captain. Lieutenants are ranked first, second, and third degree, although on occasion a lieutenant may proceed directly from second-degree status to first-degree Captain. Lieutenants are drawn from the general population of guardsmen. There is little advantage for upper-class citizens in obtaining officer status. Indeed, there is not in fact a classist "officer" vs "non-officer" division in the Guard.

A **company** is a battlefield unit, originally one hundred and eight men (i.e., twelve troops, plus their lieutenants); post-reorganization, a company may be formed of any number of troops totaling approximately a hundred guardsmen. A company may be deployed singly, in a skirmish-level operation, or with other companies. Technically, a company is commanded by a captain, though post-reorganization, lieutenants in charge of their troops have as much information on the battle plan as their captain and may override plans as events unfold on the field. That is, the captain is responsible for devising (if a skirmish) and communicating (in small and large conflicts) strategies and tactics, selecting troops from those available for a given operation, and organizing materiel and supply chains for that company. The captain does not generally engage personally on the field, being responsible for reporting results, redirecting supply, initiating deployments and redeployments during an engagement, and advising lieutenants as necessary.

A **captain** may command a company (in wartime) or otherwise perform general services under a commander. Captains are ranked first, second, and third degree. In peacetime, a captain may be dispatched to perform any number of policing, border-patrol, or other government-security tasks. In practice, a captain may keep on-hand the troop they originally commanded while a lieutenant, much as troops themselves retain cohesion so do troop leaders maintain connection to their teams. This is not always the case, but has proven to foster necessary camaraderie, trust, and commitment to the mission of the Guard.

The Guard does not formally structure operational units larger than a company. This may convey somewhat of the scale of this organization. However, in common usage, one might speak of an **army** as consisting of about one thousand guardsmen or a hundred-plus troops. As such, an army would be directed by a commander; that is, where multiple companies are deployed, the overall operation requires an officer of commander rank.

A **commander** may lead an 'army' (multiple companies, in wartime) or otherwise take part in high-level command-and-control operations. In consultation with one another, commanders decide strategy, devise tactics, direct operations (at all levels), and formulate long-term plans for the Guard, including recruitment, retention, and advocacy for salary and benefits for all guardsmen. There are no formal ranks once one reaches this level, although, informally, highly-respected commanders, regardless of their time in the position, are often addressed as **Senior Commander**

Commanders report directly to the king, as **Commander in Chief**, although there is also a designated **Master Commander**, analogous to a guild-leader position. As all guild leaders must, the Master Commander reports to the matriarchy, headed by the Council of Elders. These ultimate leaders may override any decisions made by the king (ergo, 'Commander in Chief' is somewhat of a misnomer), although this is a rare necessity. However, the Council of Elders has been known to remove kings, and their instrument of action in that eventuality is the Guard, directed by the Master Commander.

ABOUT THE AUTHOR

Vanessa MacLaren-Wray writes science fiction and fantasy exploring the challenges of communication and attachment in a diverse, complex universe. She's the author of the Patchwork Universe series, including *All That Was Asked,* "The True Son", and "The Unremembered King". She's a member of the Truck Stop at the Center of the Galaxy consortium, with "Coke Machine" and *The Smugglers*. Her short fiction has appeared with Dragon Gems and in the award-winning anthology *Fault Zone: Reverse*. She hosts regular online open mics for the California Writers Club and acts as a guest host for the podcast Small Publishing in a Big Universe. She is also an active member of the Science Fiction and Fantasy Writers of America (SFWA).

As an energy systems engineer, she has analyzed electric power systems, studied climate-safe technology, and written extensively on energy issues. The oddball robots she builds out of kids' toys and stray parts do not seek to destroy humans—instead, they brew tea and play music. Vanessa lives in farm country, where fields of strawberries and artichokes hold the developers at bay. When not arguing with her cats, she works on new stories, her email journal *Messages from the Oort Cloud*, and her website, *Cometary Tales (cometarytales.com)*. Find all her connections at *linktr.ee/Vanessa_MacLarenWray*.

ALSO THIS SERIES

FLAMES OF ATTRITION
BOOK TWO OF THE UNREMEMBERED KING

The nation of Jeska stands at a crossroads. As the newly-appointed king, Corren must contend with civilian distrust, an imminent invasion, and his fractured family.

THE TRUE SON
A STORY OF THE UNREMEMBERED KING

As foster-son to the king, Corren is technically a candidate for the kingship, a position filled only at the discretion of the matriarchs of Jeska, but he doesn't want the job.

ALL THAT WAS ASKED
A PATCHWORK UNIVERSE NOVEL

Varayla Ansegwe—perpetual student, aspiring poet, and scion of the (allegedly) criminal Syndicate—didn't volunteer for this alternate-world exploration mission, and the rest of the crew have had it up to here with this pampered noof.

Available from Water Dragon Publishing in
hardcover, trade paperback, and digital editions
waterdragonpublishing.com

ALSO BY THE AUTHOR

COKE MACHINE

FROM THE "TRUCK STOP AT THE CENTER OF THE GALAXY"

Every truck stop needs a coke machine.

PARRISH BLUE

Sallie never expected to discover a world she'd forgotten how to imagine.

THE SMUGGLERS

FROM THE "TRUCK STOP AT THE CENTER OF THE GALAXY"

Attachment is everything.

Available from Water Dragon Publishing in
hardcover, trade paperback, and digital editions
waterdragonpublishing.com

YOU MIGHT ALSO ENJOY

THE DRAGON EATER
BOOK ONE OF THE "THRASSAS CYCLE"

by J. Scott Coatsworth

Raven's a thief who just swallowed a dragon.

BLOOD BENEATH THE SAND

by Evan Davies

Devlin Narre is a wizard, a sleuth, and a killer for hire — all to varying degrees of competence and consent.

JUST A BIT OF MAGIC

by Barb Bissonette

Every morning, Jenny Smith stares into her magic mirror, searching for glimpses of two girls. Today, she is joyful with anticipation, knowing that this is the day they will materialize in her village.

Available from Water Dragon Publishing in
hardcover, trade paperback, and digital editions
waterdragonpublishing.com

9 781959 804710